Taming the Playboy

Will these irresistible bachelors say *I do*?

Taming the Playboy

REASONS OF THE HEART
by
Susan Napier

SEASCAPE
by
Anne Weale

REFORM OF THE RAKE
by
Catherine George

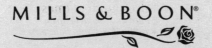

MILLS & BOON®

MILLS & BOON and MILLS & BOON with the Rose Device are registered trademarks of the publisher.
Harlequin Mills & Boon Limited,
Eton House, 18-24 Paradise Road, Richmond, Surrey, TW9 1SR

TAMING THE PLAYBOY
© by Harlequin Enterprises II B.V., 2001

Reasons of the Heart, Seascape and *Reform of the Rake*
were first published in Great Britain by Harlequin Mills & Boon Limited
in separate, single volumes.

Reasons of the Heart © Susan Napier 1988
Seascape © Anne Weale 1995
Reform of the Rake © Catherine George 1994

ISBN 0 263 82778 X

05-1001

*Printed and bound in Spain
by Litografia Rosés S.A., Barcelona*

Susan Napier was born on St Valentine's Day, so it's not surprising she has developed an enduring love of romantic stories. She started her writing career as a journalist in Auckland, New Zealand, trying her hand at romantic fiction only after she had married her handsome boss! Numerous books later she still lives with her most enduring hero, two future heroes – her sons – two cats and a computer. When she's not writing she likes to read and cook, often simultaneously!

Look out for
MISTRESS FOR A WEEKEND by Susan Napier
In Modern Romance™, Spring 2002.

REASONS OF
THE HEART

by

Susan Napier

For my husband Tony

The heart has its reasons which reason
does not know
–Pascal

CHAPTER ONE

ROSS TARRANT!

It had been over a decade since Francesca Lewis had laid eyes upon him, but she recognised him instantly. He had barely changed. He was still big and fantastically handsome, the maturity of years adding to, rather than diminishing his attractiveness.

Francesca blamed her dizziness on the shock of his sudden appearance, but the plunge of her heart and the tingle shooting up her spine were old, annoyingly familiar signs. She had always felt breathless and light-headed in his presence…even a glimpse of him used to be enough to set her off.

Ross Tarrant. Where had he been all these years? With his great athletic prowess, everyone had expected him to win fame for himself and his country in the international sports arena, but in the years since she had left Whaler's Bay Fran had heard nothing of him. Secretly she had been relatively unsurprised. It was just as she had predicted. He didn't have the drive to succeed. Everything had always been too easy for him. He had no need to stretch himself because everything he had ever wanted had always fallen straight into his lap.

Her eyes travelled up over the booted feet, up the tight, faded denims that hugged his thighs and strained across the strong hips, and over the wide expanse of rumpled fisherman's-rib sweater. God, he might have grown a bit with the years, but she could swear he was wearing the same clothes he had worn when he was seventeen!

7

By the time she looked up into his face she was braced against its devastating effect. His hair was darker than the teenage Tarrant's had been. It was a thick, glossy chestnut now instead of sun-bleached fair, and cut unfashionably long to brush the rolled neckline of his sweater. The nose which had once been broken in a game of rugby was, to her surprise, perfectly straight. Plastic surgery hardly fitted in with the swaggering macho image he had cultivated as the local, lovable 'bad boy'. The square jaw still did, and the eyes…those fathomless blue eyes, drooping slightly at the outer corners to give him the lazily sensual look that had plunged numerous schoolgirls into fits of delight. Francesca, too, at one time.

The memory brought her up short. 'Don't you know that it's dangerous to point guns at people?' she snapped belatedly, hoping that he wouldn't realise it wasn't the sight of the double-barrelled shotgun aimed in her direction that had frozen her with shock, but the man behind it.

His wide-spread stance relaxed, the shotgun drooping against the hand that supported the barrel, the stock resting securely in his crooked elbow. Now he smiled, the lop-sided smile that had been famous over three counties. Fran found it as endearing as a crocodile's grin.

'Not half as dangerous as what you're pointing at me,' he drawled.

Horrified, Fran realised that the underwater light, which she had switched on when she got into the spa, was still on. Ross Tarrant, standing above her, could see all…her breasts bobbing freely just beneath the surface of the steamy pool, the ribs lacing her new slimness down to the curving spread of her hips with their dark, shadowed centre. With an angry gasp she reached up and hit the light switch on the tiled edge of the sunken pool, then the bubble button for good measure, sinking deep into the water as the concealing froth drew an opaque screen over her nakedness. Oh, why hadn't she stopped to put on her bathing suit? She had been stiff and tired after the three-hour drive from Auckland and had merely dumped her luggage inside the cabin before seeking out the screened-off spa on the deck, too grateful for the luxury to question why it was switched on when no one had been expecting her arrival. She had thought the lateness of the hour and the cabin's isolation guarantee enough of her privacy.

'How dare you walk in here and threaten me?' Francesca blustered in the voice which she used to keep junior nurses jumping on the ware. 'You can just turn around and walk straight out again!'

'Uh-uh.' He shook his head, grinning, gun now pointed at the deck as he looped his thumbs into the front of his jeans. 'How do I know you won't plug me in the back?' He dropped into a grating Bogart impersonation, 'Stand up, sweetheart, and reach for the sky. I want to make sure you're not packing any concealed weapons, other than that lethally gorgeous body of yours…'

'Am I supposed to be amused by your cuteness?' she demanded stiffly. There was a time when she would have paid in blood to receive a compliment from Ross Tarrant. Thank God she had grown up! 'Is that thing loaded?' she demanded quellingly.

'Do I look stupid?' He shifted his weight, confidently inviting the negative.

'Frankly, yes!' Fran snapped, though it was far from true. As well as being a star sportsman, Ross had been highly intelligent at school, but too lazy to take advantage of it, content to coast through his lessons with minimum effort. 'Too stupid, obviously, to know that you shouldn't point a gun—even an unloaded one—at people.'

'I was out hunting possums when I saw the light on.' He looked amused at her little lecture. 'There have been quite a few thefts lately from holiday homes—with fire-arms among the stolen goods. It doesn't pay to be too trusting these days, especially in an isolated place like this.'

'My sentiments exactly, Ross Tarrant. Now would you mind going and waving *your* lethal weapon at some other innocent citizen and leaving *me* alone.'

His eyes narrowed at her use of his name. 'Do we know each other?'

'Unfortunately, yes.' Now that was *real* flattery, his not connecting her twenty-eight-year-old self with the shy, pudgy teenager who had proved so embarrassingly easy to humiliate. Not that he had much to go on. Her long, dead-straight hair was now permed into shoulder-length brown curls, and her recent illness had given her cheekbones for the first time in her life. The blue-grey colour of her eyes was too uncertain to be memorable and, in any case, Ross Tarrant had good reason *not* to want to remember Francesca Lewis. It gave her pleasure now, to remind him.

'I'm Francesca, Francesca Lewis. I've come up from Auckland to settle Grandfather's estate.'

'Francesca?' His thick brows shot up and then snapped down again as his humour quickly died. The blue eyes were filled with a speculative contempt that made Fran-cesca bristle. Did he still bear a grudge after all these years? He had, after all, only got what had been coming to him…

'Well, well, well…' The brown-sugar voice burned acrid with mockery. 'Princess Lewis in the flesh. Should I genuflect?'

The nickname had never been an affectionate one, and Fran was dismayed at the defensive prickle it evoked. Suddenly she could feel the steam heating the sweat beading her damp face and knew that it was time to get out of the water. But she couldn't, not while he was standing there looking down at her with such bold scorn.

'I don't care what you do, as long as you don't do it here,' she said hollowly, blinking to try and dispel a sudden wave of dizziness that she knew, this time, had nothing to do with his disruptive presence. 'Would you mind going away while I get out?'

For a moment he didn't move, his eyes on her steam-wreathed head, then he squatted down, putting the gun carefully aside and frowning into her flushed face.

'Are you all right?'

'No, I'm not all right, I want to get out.'

'Feeling dizzy?'

'A bit.' She hazily resented his demand.

'Is this your robe?' He lifted the towelling wrap off the railing that ran around the wooden deck and stood up again, shaking it open for her. 'Come on. Unless you want me to come in there and give you mouth to mouth. If you faint, you'll go under.'

'Just leave it there and I'll get out when you go,' she said weakly.

He made a rude noise. 'Princess, I'm a full-grown man. I've seen more naked women than you could shake a stick at.'

'I'll bet you have!' Annoyance momentarily cleared her head. She wished now that she hadn't turned on the deck light. It was directly above his head and made it look as though he was wearing a halo of light. Ross Tarrant, angelic? Preposterous! 'I don't suppose you've changed much in that respect. The boy most likely to score, weren't you, both on and off the field?'

'And you were the girl most likely to stay on the shelf,' he reminded her brutally, his eyes flickering briefly to the ringless left hand that clutched the tiles. 'Prediction right, I take it?'

She glared at him. 'I have better things to do with my life than be some man's domestic slave.'

'Ah, yes, the selfless career…'

'At least I have one. What do *you* do for a living?'

'At the moment, nothing.'

'Huh!' She would have said more, but suddenly his face was all hazy again.

'We can't all be model citizens, Princess, and in my experience it's often the model citizens who are the worst hypocrites—'

Fran had been unaware of her head, like her thoughts, drifting downwards, until she suddenly felt cold, hard hands grasp her upper arms, completely encircling the overheated flesh and hauling her unceremoniously out of the water. His left hand slipped as he lifted her out on to the decking and they staggered for a moment in an ungainly dance, almost falling. Fran didn't have time to be embarrassed about her glistening nudity, for Ross Tarrant stooped and picked up her thick robe, wrapping her up in it without glancing at her body and plucking a towel from the deckchair for her hair.

'You're hurting,' she complained as he briskly rubbed the sodden mass.

'At least you're alive to feel. You've been ill, haven't you?' She nodded reluctantly. 'Don't you know better than to lie around in hot water when you're not up to par? And you a nurse!'

He leant over, keeping a supporting hand on her shaky frame, and twitched the pool cover back into place. Then he pushed her across the deck and through the sliding glass doors into the warmth of the cabin.

'Get into your night things and wrap up warm.' He gave her a little shove. 'I'll put my gun away and stoke up the fire.'

Fran went unsteadily into the small bedroom to find her long, practical nightgown and thick blue robe. It was a measure of her state of mind that she hadn't even noticed the new pot-belly in the corner of the living-room when she had arrived. She looked at herself in the mirror. How had Ross known that she was ill…because of her slimness? A militant sparkle entered her eyes. Francesca had battled plumpness for most of her life and she was proud of her current lack of weight, even though she was resigned to it being only temporary. As soon as she was fully recovered her natural metabolism would reassert itself and repad her five-foot-seven frame with its over-generous curves.

Now, you go out there and get rid of him, she told herself sternly. Be gracious and polite, but firm. The trouble was that her darkened eyes and nervous mouth gave the lie to her confidence. Ross Tarrant was an uncomfortable reminder of an embarrassing naïveté and, what was more, she sensed he knew it.

She sighed with relief when she finally ventured out to find the cabin empty. Calling it a log cabin was a bit of a misnomer, she thought, as she crossed to warm her hands over the pot-belly. Although the exterior was constructed of split-logs, inside it was more like a luxury apartment, completely panelled in native timber, thick scatter-rugs softening the gleam of polished-wood floors. With twin beds in the bedroom and two lounge-settees in the open-plan living area it could comfortably sleep six. The kitchen was spacious and well equipped, opening out on to a small, covered deck at the back and the separate bathroom and laundry, which meant that summer residents didn't have to track sand through the house when they wanted to shower off after a swim. It was usually only in summer that the cabin was rented out. In the winter it was closed up, for Ian Lewis had been determined to preserve the unspoiled nature of the few acres he had retained when he retired from farming.

Intent on some melancholy memories, Fran was almost startled out of her skin by a movement behind her.

'It's only me.' Ross Tarrant closed the back door and hefted a cleaned fish on to the tiled kitchen bench which jutted out to form a breakfast bar. Using a wicked-looking curved knife he began to expertly fillet the fish.

'I thought you'd gone.'

'You mean, you hoped I had,' he informed her with annoying perception, and she tightened the cord of her robe nervously as she noticed the frying pan heating on an element on the stove, and the flour and butter and seasonings standing ready on the bench.

'What do you think you're doing?' she demanded sternly.

'Fixing dinner.'

'Dinner!' Her voice was thin with dismay. She should have known that Ross Tarrant would delight in upsetting her.

'That meal you have in the evenings,' he added helpfully, intent on the flashing knife. 'I caught this off the beach earlier. You haven't eaten yet, have you?'

'Now, look here—' She stopped, suddenly thinking that he seemed very familiar with the layout of the place, and very cool for a man who had been ordered off the premises. 'Did you have some sort of an arrangement with my grandfather about using the facilities here?'

'Some sort,' he conceded unrevealingly, and her frowning eyes drifted from his handsome face to his busy hands. Odd that such square, solid hands could wield a knife so delicately. She had seen surgeons at work who were clumsier, men whose hands were pampered and cared for, not brown and weathered like Ross's.

'Well, you must realise that things have changed since he died,' she said with what she thought was patient reason. 'I'm going to be staying here for a week or so while I settle things with his lawyer, so you won't be able to come and go as you like, though of course you can still use the beach...'

'Why, thank you, ma'am,' he drawled, with an excessive humility that made her flush. She hadn't meant to sound condescending, only to make it quite clear that she wanted her privacy. Her grandfather hadn't actually owned the little curve of black sand just below the steps of the front deck, but he did own all the land which surrounded the beach. Locals, of course, took for granted their right-of-way. Did that mean that Ross still lived here, Ross of the itchy feet and the big plans to travel? It was his younger brother, Jason, who had wanted to stay in Whaler's Bay and take over the family crop-dusting business when his father retired.

'Why don't you take your catch home and eat it there?' she suggested, assuming that the Tarrants still lived a few kilometres down the road. Nothing much changed in Whaler's Bay. But Ross didn't satisfy her veiled curiosity.

'And if I don't?' he asked, dipping a thick fillet in flour and shaking it.

'I'll—' What? Even arguing with him made her feel

exhausted, and the idea of using physical force was ludi-
crous. The black wool of his sweater rolled over impres-
sively powerful shoulders and tapered down to a hard-
looking waist. His sleeves were pushed up to his elbows,
displaying muscled forearms covered with dark brown
hair.

'I'll…I'll call the police and have them remove you,'
she said foolishly, suddenly noticing another new addition…a telephone on a low table in the corner.

'If you mean Jack Trent, go ahead, then we'll see
which one of us gets kicked out.' Jack Trent had been
the sole police presence in Whaler's Bay for at least
twenty years, and Fran wasn't surprised to discover he
was still on the job. She was surprised, though, by Ross's
unconcern.

'Why should *I* get kicked out?'

'Because, Princess, you're not the ruler of this castle.'

'Not—? But…this is Grandpa's cabin. Of course it's
going to be mine!' she stated starkly.

'Is it? Or did you just assume it would be? Actually,
your grandfather said he was leaving the place to me
when he died.' Ross calmly put the prepared fillets into
sizzling butter and pushed them around the pan.

Outrage blazed in Fran's eyes. 'To *you*? I don't believe
it.' He had to be lying, she was *counting* on being heir,
had committed herself on the strength of it… 'If you
think you can just come along and appropriate *my* inheritance you've got another think coming!'

'I didn't just "come along",' he interrupted her curtly.
'I've been living in this cabin for months—leasing it. Ian
and I got to know each other rather well during that time,
and when I said that I'd be interested if he wanted to
sell, he said that he wanted to hang on to the cabin but

that I could have it when he died. He promised, in fact…in front of a witness, too.'

'Grandpa wouldn't do that!' Fran retorted fiercely, ignoring her own uncertainty, seeing her lovingly planned future dissipating like smoke around her ears.

'Cut out his own grandchild? Why not? You certainly did your best to cut him out of your life. It didn't seem to occur to you that Ian was a lonely old man after Agatha died.' He gave her a look of contempt. 'You're something else, you know that, Princess? You take on a caring profession like nursing, but you don't seem capable of caring on a personal basis. I guess you thought the old man didn't deserve your attention because he wasn't sick. Well, I have news for you, Sister Lewis! Ian said he was diagnosed as having a heart condition years ago, and was having angina attacks even before your grandmother died.'

'I never knew, they never told me,' said Fran, stiff with guilt and resentment, familiar companions both. The estrangement hadn't been totally one-sided, but she didn't see why she should have to explain the painful details of her life to Ross Tarrant.

'You never gave them a chance to tell you. You always were a stuck-up bitch, too good for the rest of humanity.'

Stung by the reminder of the extreme shyness that had been misinterpreted by her fellow pupils, Fran drew hersef up to launch a volley of her own. 'And what made you suddenly so all-fired interest in my lonely grandfather's welfare? You were never loaded down with much responsibility yourself, as I recall. Could it be that you thought you might get something out of it…like this cabin?'

She froze at the stillness of his expression, remembering the teenager's hot temper, but when he spoke it was with a coldness that matched the ice-storm in his eyes. 'Be careful when you start casting stones, Francesca. Your own motives don't seem to be too pristine. You didn't even bother to come up for the funeral, but you're pretty quick off the mark when it comes to settling the estate.'

'I've been ill,' she snapped, angry at having the tables turned.

'Too ill even to send a wreath?' The blue eyes were deeply sceptical.

'As a matter of fact, yes!' It gave her satisfaction to tell him. 'Just after I got the telegram about Grandpa's death I collapsed. I've had pneumonia and complications…'

'All the more stupid of you to lie around in an outside spa in the middle of winter,' he stunned her by saying, completely undercutting her anger with his apparent concern. 'Were you hospitalised? Are you still on medication?'

'Yes…and none of your business,' she snapped, even more disturbed by his concern than by his contempt. 'And as for the property, when I spoke to Simpson, Grandpa's lawyer, he said that there was no will. That means that everything will automatically come to me as the only relative.'

'Not necessarily,' he punctured her smugness. 'Simpson seemed to think that the verbal promise would probably stand up in court if it came to that.'

'You've *spoken* to him?' Francesca frowned, wishing now that she had stopped off in Whangarei to appraise the lawyer of her unexpected visit. But his letter informing her of the lack of a will hadn't mentioned any possible problems and, as it had been nearing dusk by the time she'd reached the city, she had decided to press on through the last half-hour of winding roads to Whaler's Bay. She still had the key to the beach cabin, and had naturally assumed that it would be empty at this time of the year. There had been no question of staying at the old farmhouse on the hill which had been her grandfather's home, since the lawyer had told her it had been almost completely destroyed by the fire which had coincided with the old man's death. 'He can't be your lawyer, too,' she objected. 'That would be a conflict of interest.'

'We were both at the funeral, so naturally we talked. In case you don't already know, I was the one who called the fire brigade that night. I was out here on the deck when I saw the smoky glow over the hill. Thank God I'd got Ian to put in a telephone here. I made the call and raced up across the fields, but although I got there before the volunteers, it was too late. The old place had gone up like tinder and there wasn't a hope in hell of getting to Ian.'

'I'll bet there wasn't…' Guilt and resentment uttered the sly sneer and Francesca closed her eyes briefly in horror and self-digust. She wasn't really surprised to feel Ross grab her wrist and drag her against the hard edge of the bench. She opened reluctant eyes. His were glittering slits, the ridge of his cheekbone dark with angry blood. A rasp of whiskers coated the rigid jawline, emphasising his tough masculinity, and Fran felt a frisson of fear.

'If you intend to sling mud like that you can do it in a court of law, and back it up with more proof than just your avaricious insinuations,' he grated rawly. 'You know damned well that the coroner's report stated that your grandfather died of a heart attack before that electrical fire ever started. Or are you going to suggest that *he* was in on a conspiracy to murder?'

'I…I…' Francesca licked her lips, knowing he was due an abject apology for her unwarranted bitchiness, but choking over the words. She strained against the iron fingers, breaking the grip only when he let her.

'If I had doubts about keeping this place, you've banished them,' he told her grimly. 'Ian said that you never pretended to like coming back, and that you were bound to sell out to the highest bidder. Have you thought what that'll mean to the people who live here? No? He shrugged contemptuously at her flush. 'I thought not. Well, I can't stop you turning over the top twenty acres to some greedy, get-rich-quick developer, but I can sure as hell stop you getting your hands on this beach.'

'We'll see about that!' Fran turned on her heel and marched unsteadily towards the bedroom. She wanted a fair price for her land, but she wasn't out to rape the enviroment, for goodness' sake!

'Where are you going? This fish is nearly done.'

Jolted, Fran turned and stared. Did he really expect her to sit down and share a meal with him, after what they'd just said to each other? 'I'm going to get dressed. If you won't leave, *I* will. I'll get a room at the Bay Hotel until I can get an eviction notice.'

'My lease isn't up yet, Princess, and you're not going anywhere at this time of night, in your frame of mind, with a storm settling in. That's a treacherous road back down the cliffs. You'd be over the side in no time.'

'You can't stop me!' Fran's anger overrode her normally strong common sense.

'Can't I?' There was a chink as he dangled her car keys from his hand. He must have picked them up from the top of the fridge where she had tossed them when she had arrived.

'Give them to me, please,' she said firmly, resisting the urge to dash over and wrest them physically from his taunting fingers.

'In the morning, when you've calmed down.' He grinned at her fury and pushed the keys into his jeans pocket, sucking in a breath to get them past the straining denim hip. 'Of course, if you're determined to get them...' He trailed off suggestively, and Fran swallowed her rage as she toyed with the idea of accepting the challenge.

But, eyeing the outline of her keys so close to the zippered fly of his jeans, she knew she didn't dare. She imagined having to thrust her hand into the tight pocket and wriggle it down the angle of his groin to reach the keys. Oh, he would love that! And it would remind her of that other time she had struggled with his tight jeans, of his groans of delight and her illicit sense of power. Oh, *damn* this weakness! She could feel her limbs trembling with fatigue and it galled her to admit that he was right, it would be foolish to try and leave now.

'I'm not eating with you,' she said flatly, as a feeble attempt to reassert her authority, and his grin widened. He shrugged and thick, mahogany lashes screened the blue eyes as he slid the crisp, golden fillets of fish from the pan on to a platter garnished with lemon slices and bread and butter. Fran felt her mouth water treacherously and her nostrils twitch at the tempting aroma as he carried the platter over to the kauri slab table that dominated one half of the living-room. She noticed that his movements didn't have quite the old fluid grace. He must be just over thirty now, perhaps he was beginning to pay for the many follies of his youth…and probably his adulthood, too!

He sat and began to eat hungrily, ignoring her hovering figure until he had finished his first two pieces of fish. It flaked gently as he ate, lemon juice glistening on the crusty surface.

'Come on, Princess,' he jeered softly, when her hunger became embarrassingly obvious. 'Come down off that high horse and eat.'

She could have gone out and got her own carton of food supplies from the boot of her car, but Francesca found herself sitting down opposite Ross and allowing him to dish up a second plate.

The fish was juicy and tender and meltingly good, but although Fran ate hungrily she was too furtively aware of her companion to enjoy it. Just being in the same room with him made her feel like a gauche fifteen-year-old again, and that led her on to remember the last time they had been alone together, in the cramped back seat of a car…

'No!' Fran clenched her teeth in an effort to keep the heat from her face as she realised that she had yelped the denial aloud. She stood up hastily and carried her plate to the kitchen, avoiding his gaze as she cleared her throat. 'I…I'm tired…I think I'll go to bed now.' She was too nervous to care about being rude. Let Ross do the dishes—he had been the one to insist on making the mess!

He studied her agitation curiously for a moment then shrugged. 'Suit yourself.' He began to swab up the juices from his plate with a folded piece of bread.

'I've been using the bed by the window,' he added as she crossed the room with jerky steps, 'so I'll keep it if you don't mind.'

Sleep in the same room? Fran felt her stomach knot. She opened the bedroom door and paused as she noted the sturdy lock on the inside. She turned, and gave Ross a primly triumphant smile. 'As a matter of fact, I do. Since *you're* the temporary guest, you can sleep out here.'

She leant against the locked door and grinned at the memory of his disgusted expression. The wisdom of years might have dictated that she forgive Ross Tarrant for the adolescent humiliation she had suffered, but that didn't mean that she had ever forgotten it!

She froze as the doorhandle twisted experimentally against her back. 'It's locked,' she said unnecessarily, her voice high-pitched with apprehension. What did she really know about the man out there?

An exaggerated sigh buffeted the door. 'Well, at least pass out some blankets for me. It's going to get a lot colder out here before the night's through, and we've only got a limited amount of firewood left.'

Fran chewed her lip as a distant roll of thunder backed his claim. He *sounded* resigned, but...

'Promise you won't come in if I open the door?'

'Francesca—' He sounded more impatient than annoyed, and Fran decided to risk it. She opened one of the divan drawers and took out three thick blankets, then added the pillow from the window bed to the pile. She unlocked the door and thrust the blankets at Ross. His sudden move to take them made her shy nervously. The blankets fell between them, pushing the door open.

'What in the hell did you think I was going to do?' he growled irritably, and Fran flushed. His face took on a sudden, mocking derision. 'Surely you don't imagine that I'm so hard up for a woman that I'll leap on anything remotely female?' He grinned at her reaction to his subtle insult. 'Look, Princess, I may have been a bit raw in the old days, but I've acquired a bit of polish since then. In fact, to set the record straight, my life is overcrowded with willing women.' His grin widened and Fran had the inescapable feeling that she had overlooked some vital point. Why did he look so thoroughly amused? 'Women are always ringing me up at all times of the day and night, begging me for attention, taking off their clothes for me at the slightest suggestion. It's one of the reasons I came back to Whaler's Bay, to get away from the insatiable women in my life…'

He was exaggerating purely for effect, but the trouble was that Fran's overheated imagination could well believe it. He was too handsome for his own good…and for hers. He shifted his weight in preparation to pick up the blankets at their feet and Fran jumped. He sighed.

'I can see, Princess, that you're not going to rest until I've made the obligatory attack on your virtue, so…' He reached over and swept her across the jumbled pile and into his arms.

His mouth was a shock of warmth against hers, his large hands spreading across her shoulderblades to ensure that any resistance on her part merely rubbed their bodies suggestively together.

Thinking that it would be fruitless and undignified to struggle against his superior strength, Fran suffered the tiny, stinging burn of his tongue against the corner of her clamped mouth. His hands moved with a slow, sliding pressure all the way down her long, slender back to ride the upper curve of her buttocks, his thumbs curling around to press against her hipbones. As she tried to protest at the liberty, his tongue plunged into her mouth, filling it, whipping back and forth, stroking the sensitive upper palate, burrowing into the slick moistness under her tongue, smothering her senses with male taste and smell.

Fran felt as if she had inadvertantly touched an electric fence. A warning hum vibrated through her body, setting up a sharp tingling in her breasts and shivering up the insides of her thighs until she dug her fingers into his shoulders and tried to arch away from the treacherous current.

He took the opportunity to test the resilience of her hips with his own, his hands beginning to circle in slow, kneading motions as they sank to cup her closer to the centre of his heated hardness. The scrape of his whiskers against her tender chin provided an erotic sensual contrast to the soft, moist pulse of his tongue in her mouth and Fran suddenly found herself clinging where she had pushed. The man could kiss up a storm!

When he took his mouth away, Fran found that breathing required a voluntary command from her stunned brain.

'Satisfied?' he murmured huskily, his hands moving back to the neutral territory at her waist, blue eyes alight with a surprised speculation that flustered her. 'I hope I've managed to prove that I don't necessarily take up every invitation I'm issued.'

'I wasn't issuing any invitations!' Fran shook herself free, finding it hard to articulate with a tongue that felt twice its size after the sensual battering it had received.

'No?' He cocked his head with a wicked smile as he touched a finger to the smooth skin just behind her ear. 'You're flushed...' His finger ran down to the pulse in the shoft hollow of her throat. '...Your skin is damp, your temperature and pulse rate have increased... An invitation doesn't have to be verbal to be explicit.' His lids drooped, masking the intention in his eyes. 'And if you're so hot…' he pulled the front of her robe apart with a single, swift movement, his hands crowding in to capture her breasts, encircling the little, stiff peaks that thrust against the soft bodice of her modest nightdress '…why aren't these still sweetly soft?'

He bent his head and kissed the objects of his taunt with maddening precision before scooping up his blankets and backing out the door with a final salute of laughter at her furious confusion.

'Night-night, Princess. Safe dreams…'

CHAPTER TWO

'As you can see, Miss Lewis, the lease agreement is pretty watertight and still has several weeks to run. The death of your grandfather doesn't invalidate the document; the lease will merely be paid to his estate until such time as it is settled.'

Frustration seethed in Fran's breast as she listened to the dry, precise, ponderous tones of the elderly lawyer.

Damn! She had bounced out of bed this morning, refreshed by her first solid sleep in weeks. She was a woman with a purpose, and to achieve that purpose she was willing to talk things over in a calm and reasonable manner. She was even willing to overlook Ross's arrogant, macho attempt at intimidating her last night.

She had marched confidently out to battle, only to find her opponent missing. A note was taped to the fridge, an almost incomprehensible scrawl. Typical! she thought as she squinted at the message: 'Gone fishing. PS What's with the jungle on the porch?'

Fran had shrieked and run outside. Her precious plants, how could she have let herself forget them? Fortunately the porch was fairly sheltered and none of them seemed to have suffered from their night out on the tiles, but her carelessness was most unnerving. She couldn't afford to forget such things, not *now*…

'What about this option to buy?' Fran jabbed her finger at the offending clause.

'It is only an option, Miss Lewis,' the lawyer said cautiously, seeing something of the old man in the stubborn set of her jaw. A most…determined lady. It was evident that she and Ross Tarrant had already clashed over the matter, and out of duty to his late client he felt obliged to try and smooth things over. 'All it means is that if your grandfather decided to sell within the next year, Tarrant would have first refusal.'

'It gives strength to his claim about the cabin, too, doesn't it?' Fran said gloomily. 'Here it is in writing that Grandfather approved of him as a buyer. So even if I do get the entire estate, if I want to sell straight away I have to offer that part of the property to him first.' Why it disturbed her to think of Ross living in that cabin she couldn't quite fathom. But it did.

'True, but his offer would have to be acceptable to you,' Simpson pointed out.

'You mean I could ask some outrageous price that he couldn't afford?' said Fran thoughtfully. Actually, she doubted that there was much he *could* afford, if he wasn't working. But perhaps he was banking on the generosity of his family?

'If he could prove that you were demanding more than the market price simply as a device to deny him purchase he could take you to court.' Simpson didn't try to hide his disapproval.

Francesca sighed. 'So there's no way I can get him out?'

'Not until the lease expires.'

'And what about the claim of his that Grandfather left him the cabin?' Fran abandoned the hopeless for the merely hopeful. 'How much legal weight does that carry?'

'He does have a case, although as sole surviving blood relative you have a stronger one,' Simpson hastened to add as he saw the grey eyes simmer. 'However, there is the question of estrangement. It's fairly common knowledge locally that Tarrant and your grandfather were fairly good friends, whereas you and he...' He shifted uncomfortably in his swivel chair under her cool regard, as if the spare, roomy office was suddenly too small for him '...well, it had been some time since you saw each other. And, of course, Tarrant is the sitting tenant...'

'Possession being nine tenths of the law, I suppose,' Fran said, drily, conscious that she was sinking rapidly in the lawyer's estimation.

'It could be one of the considerations in this case. Your grandfather's intent could be implied by that lease agreement. Why don't you leave it with me, Miss Lewis? I'll register your claim against the estate and have the matter investigated for you.'

In other words, go home and let the professionals handle it. Fran's fingers tightened on the document in her hand. She had the sinking feeling that if she wasn't there to keep an eye on things, Ross would have everything his own way. In retrospect it had been foolish to resign before she had the money in hand, but for once in her life Fran had been guided by impulse, eager to get all the paperwork and planning out of the way by the time she was well enough to tackle the physical labour involved. She had come this far, she had no choice now but to fight for her rights, but she had better go back to taking things one step at a time. Up until now her whole life had been closely structured, from the rigidly old-fashioned discipline of her grandparents' home, through the narrowness of life in a Catholic girls' boarding school, to the methodical order of nursing. Now that she was breaking free of the mould she must be careful not to go overboard in her enthusiasm.

She sighed, and gave the startled lawyer one of her

sudden, unexpectedly warm smiles. 'I'm sorry if I seem
to be a bit like a bull at a gate, it's just that…well…I've
been saving for years towards a dream of mine, and this
puts it all within my grasp. I never expected…I mean, I
never imagined Grandpa dying. I know he was old, but
he's always been so *enduring*…' She gestured helplessly.
It was still hard to believe that he was dead, so fixed was
the image in her mind of him hovering: the gruff, critical
arbiter of her childhood.

Arthur Simpson found himself smiling reassuringly
back. He was changing his mind about his late client's
granddaughter. She wasn't quite as tough and unfeeling
as she tried to appear. And, as she talked about her future
plans, animation chased the shadows from her eyes and
the wan hollows from her cheeks. Why, she was rather
pretty…very pretty, in fact, when she smiled like that,
with a slightly shy diffidence that was surprising in a
woman who had earlier projected such an aura of self-
confidence.

'I'll do what I can to speed things along,' he promised
as he ushered her out. A thoroughly nice young woman,
was his final decision, if a little confused and guilty about
the source of her current good fortune.

If he had known what the 'thoroughly nice woman'
was thinking about on the drive back to the Bay he might
have had third thoughts about his new client's character.
She wasn't feeling 'nice' at all. She was brooding darkly
on ways and means.

She could sink her pride and pour her heart out to Ross
in the hope of gaining his understanding, or she could
beat him at his own game. Fran knew which appealed
more. Beating him, preferably senseless. It went against
the grain to repeat an error of the past. Trust Ross Tarrant
as a repository with her precious dreams? Look at what

had happened last time! She frowned at the unwinding ribbon of road ahead as the years peeled inexorably back…

At fifteen she had been as innocent as a babe in arms, released by her grandparents' financial reverses from a decade at a convent boarding school to the unimagined freedoms of the local high school. Unfortunately the transition wasn't as simple as she had expected. Plump, aware of being achingly plain, Fran tried to hide her intense shyness behind a cool façade that rapidly acquired her the reputation of being 'stuck up'. The teasing and physical jostling between the sexes was also a shock. In time Fran made a few friends, but they weren't the kind she really wanted, the bright, fun kind, the kind who flocked around Ross Tarrant and his cronies. Like every other girl in school Fran had endless fantasies about Ross. At seventeen he was almost a full grown man, his reputation as the local 'golden boy' of sport allowing him to coast through his last year of school with little academic effort. His easy-going charm meant that he was forgiven his streak of wildness, and when people shook their heads over his latest escapade they did it with a smile on their lips.

Fran longed to catch his eye, but not as part of the giggling, blushing crowd of girls who hung around him. She wanted to be somebody special, to be singled out. She wanted the impossible, to shed her pudgy, spot-prone skin and tongue-tied shyness and be transformed into the kind of sleek, bubbling, pretty blonde that Ross seemed to favour.

The day that Ross Tarrant asked Francesca Lewis to the local Saturday night dance would live, reluctantly, in her memory for ever. She accepted his casual invitation with a dazed aplomb that masked her utter stupefaction.

For the rest of that week she felt like a mini-celebrity, basking in the glow of acceptance generated by the knowledge that *she* was Ross Tarrant's chosen date. By Saturday evening she was almost mindless with agonised nervousness and bliss. She had never been to a dance before, or even on a date. Her grandparents had an unswervingly strict moral code that had further set her apart from her fellow pupils, most of whom had grown up together, but evidently even they weren't immune to the Tarrant charm. Of course, the Tarrants were regular church-goers, and the dance was being run by the church social committee and her grandfather was going to take her to the dance and pick her up afterwards, so Francesca knew that this wasn't exactly a gesture of unreserved trust, but it was a start! Her first step towards adulthood.

The dance was a revelation to a girl starved of frivolous gaiety. Ross was stunningly handsome in his blue open-necked shirt and dark trousers and, although Fran briefly mourned the fact that her dress was so much plainer than those of the other girls, she was soon enjoying herself too much to worry about it. Ross made mixing in easy, he was so relaxed and natural that Fran blossomed under his attention, surprising even herself by the way that she laughed and joked and joined in conversations with shy wit. There was no alcohol, of course, but Fran felt light-headed just drinking in the atmosphere and revelling in the feeling of belonging. Ross never once strayed from her side to dance with anyone else, and sent warning glances to any of his friends who showed signs of lingering around Fran. Only later did she realise why he hadn't wanted them around. At the time she thought he was kindly buffering her, had fantasised that perhaps he was jealous. What a gullible little idiot she had been!

In her ignorance she had been flushed and happy, letting her feelings show in the way that she danced, her silky hair flying out around her. For Ross she dropped the barriers and was delighted by the sparks of interest that she thought she saw in his eyes.

As her curfew time of ten o'clock neared she almost suffocated with joy when he leaned over his Coke and said in a deep voice, his eyes teasingly warm, 'How about we go out for a little walk? It's a really nice night out there…'

Excitement knotted in her stomach as she agreed. He wanted to be alone with her for a little while! He didn't want the evening to end either! They sneaked out separately when the parent-chaperons weren't looking, but they didn't walk very far. A car was parked under the trees behind the hall and Ross took some keys out of his pocket.

'Neville said we could sit in his car, if we liked. Do you want to?'

Fran would have jumped over the moon if he had asked her to. He unlocked the door and helped her into the back seat. She sat, tense with excitement, trying to think of something to say that would help spin out the moments before she bumped back down to reality. Ross had been so warm and protective all night, quite unlike the arrogant, brash boy he was at school. Perhaps he was showing her a side of himself that he reserved for special friends…

'You know, you're looking pretty tonight,' he told her, his voice soft in the darkness of the car.

'Thank you.' She blushed. She had dieted madly all week, to not much avail, but at least her skin had stayed miraculously free of spots and she knew she had a nice smile. People always looked a bit surprised when she smiled.

'You should always wear your hair down like that. It's the colour of milk chocolate.'

'Grannie says it's untidy and I guess it does rather get in the way. But I like long hair…that's one reason why I could never be a nun,' she said shyly.

'You were thinking about being a nun?'

She laughed at the horror in his voice. 'I wasn't. But I think the school wanted to steer me in that direction, and I think that Grannie feels there are only two worthwhile careers for a woman: nun or wife and mother.'

'Francesca—' His voice was slow and doubtful, and ever after Fran wondered whether he had actually intended to kiss her or just wanted to talk some more. She liked to think, for the sake of her wounded spirit, that he was going to confess the truth and ask her forgiveness but that her eager response deflected him. He was at an age when his sexual urges were strong and easily aroused, and the chemistry between them took them both by surprise.

She turned towards him in the moonlit darkness and somehow their lips met. With her eyes wide Fran had her first taste of man, and liked it.

'Put your arms around me.' He muttered the soft order and Fran obediently complied. Her fingers felt his shifting muscles as he pushed her against the upright seat, his hands on her shoulders burning through the thin sleeves of her white dress. He lifted his mouth from hers and this time she saw impatience written on his darkened face and felt a flutter of desperation. He was annoyed by her ineptness…

'What's the matter? Don't you like to french kiss?' he asked huskily, and she stared at him in ignorant dismay.

She opened her mouth to ask what he meant and found out. She was stunned by the intimacy of it. He was putting his tongue into her mouth and moving it around, creating a moist friction which sent a hard jolt through her body.

Her hands clenched against his back as a strange, sweet ache began to seep into her muscles, investing them with a delicious, straining tightness. She pushed her tongue experimentally against his and felt a shocking delight as he abruptly withdrew, enticing her to follow into the spicy warmth of his open mouth. She did so, eagerly, trying to do to him what he had done to her. Was he feeling the way she was…all buttery and melting inside?

He broke the kiss and they stared into each other's eyes. There was a gleam of male recognition in his that stopped her breath. Then his hands were cupping her face and his mouth fastened over hers again, gentle, teasing, yet deep and satisfying too. When she trembled, his mouth tensed and hardened, gathering her in even further, stunning her with the tremors she felt in his own body, as if it was part of hers.

'You taste good, Frankie,' he murmured in thick amazement, his trembling fingers finding and stroking her breasts in a way that made her kiss him back with untutored enthusiasm. He groaned.

'Touch me, Frankie, the way I'm touching you.' He pulled her hand to his chest, thrusting it inside his shirt. Soon both hands were roving across his skin, admiring the compact strength so different from her softness, the hot silkiness that almost burnt her fingertips. The only sound in the car was their gasping breath and the soft murmurs and groans as Fran innocently poured more fuel on the fire. Her exploring hands moved down the flat stomach to where the waistband of his trousers formed a barrier, and he stiffened with a jerk that made her freeze, afraid she was hurting him in some way. His fingers were doing things to her taut young breasts that made her feel that she was going to explode. It was so sweet, so good, that when she felt him unzip her dress and pull it off her shoulders she couldn't believe that what they were doing was wrong.

'I won't hurt you,' Ross said huskily as he sensed her momentary doubt. 'I promise…I just want to see you…'

'If…if I can look at you, too,' she whispered, half-frightened, half-excited by the shaking plea in his voice. She trembled on the verge of a new and terrible knowledge.

He tore off his shirt and she saw the moonlight ripple over bone and muscle, and caught her breath at his sheer male beauty.

'You're beautiful,' she said helplessly and he laughed uncertainly.

'You're not supposed to say that kind of thing to guys.'

'But you are.' She hardly noticed his hands returning to her bodice, easing it down further until he could reach around to the clasp of her demure cotton bra.

'Oh, no—'

'Only to look, Frankie…' His mouth opened over hers and this time it had less gentleness and more passion. It was an adult kiss and it drew an adult response from her body. She felt her breasts tighten painfully against the crisp cotton, the straps bite into her soft flesh, and moaned.

'I'm not beautiful…I'm fat…' Afraid that he would agree.

'No, you're not…you're soft and curving, the way a girl should be…' He drew a sharp breath as he released her aching breasts into the cool night air and saw the tight, dark discs that crested the plump white roundness.

'I…don't think we should do this…' Fran quivered at

his look, torn by the racking desire to push herself against him and the innate maidenly modesty that cried at her to cover her nakedness. But this was Ross looking at her with such an expression of longing. Ross, whom she loved with every beat of her tender young heart…

'Oh, Frankie…' His eyes rose to her face and they were black and hot and sweet. 'Can I touch you?'

His asking made it all right. He wouldn't hurt her, not Ross. She felt the pound of his heart against the dampness of his chest and nodded dumbly.

His hands traced over her fullness very lightly, then cupped her, rounding her towards him. His palms shifted to support her, scraping across her rigid nipples, causing her to arch her spine involuntarily. Her eyes fluttered closed, her head sinking against the seat as he fondled her for long, agonising minutes. Francesca felt a wild and restless growth inside her that she didn't know how to satisfy. Her hands slipped on his slick skin and fell into his lap. He gave a loud groan that startled her into pushing against the rough cloth. He groaned again and fell across her, pushing her into a lying position. Suddenly his mouth had replaced his hands on her breasts, and he was kissing and licking at her with a roughness that set off nerve-blistering explosions throughout her body. Her hands were trapped beneath his writhing hips, pressing against a growing hardness that frightened her. His body jerking against her and his mouth tugging at her breasts made her feel sick and excited at the same time. She gave a choking gasp as she felt his hand on her thigh, under her crumpled dress. She clenched her thighs together and felt a surging heat there that built with each nip and suckle of his mouth. Then, shockingly, his hand was nestling at the apex of her thighs, touching her through the thin panties. Even she never touched herself *there*. The nun's dire warnings about the consequences of letting a boy take 'liberties' rose up to terrify her even more, and yet she still felt the terrible thrill. She gave a half-sob of shame.

Looking back it was amazing that the young, sexual animal that Ross Tarrant had been had even heard that pitifully weak protest, let alone been able to control himself sufficiently to pull away, taking huge, deep, shuddering breaths as he rested his head against the cold glass of the side window. But he had, and when he had calmed down he had even helped her readjust her clothing and told her that it was all right, they hadn't done anything wrong, that they had stopped in time. Not wanting to reveal the profundity of her ignorance she had allowed the moment to pass, conscious of his strained expression and feeling somehow to blame for being so inexperienced. As they got out of the car and she saw the anger on his face she touched him tentatively.

'Ross?'

He pulled sharply away, then groaned at her expression of hurt. 'Hell, Frankie, I'm sorry…'

'I'm not.' She smiled a brave, if shaky, smile. In spite of her earlier fear it was true, but the soft glow in her eyes just seemed to make him feel worse.

'Then, damn it, you should be. Frankie, you're not even sixteen yet!' He shuddered, and suddenly fixed her with an earnest look. 'I'll tell you what, Frankie, let's forget about tonight, OK?'

'Forget?' Forget the best night of her life! How could he even ask?

'I mean, let's start all over again and take it slow. As friends.'

'Oh, yes!' She blossomed anew with a painful sweetness that made the young man fighting his own inner battle wince. Her heart was in her eyes and he felt like the lowest swine, but perhaps it wasn't too late to redeem himself.

'And look, don't tell anyone else about tonight... I...we need to talk first, OK?' He took her hand and squeezed it, and thus it was they walked out of the darkness straight into her grandfather, waiting at the door of the dance-hall with a thunderous expression on his deeply seamed face. Fran was hauled off home in disgrace and delivered of a searing condemnation of her wicked, ungrateful behaviour. She had listened to the stern lecture with eyes downcast to hide her rebellious indifference. She didn't care if she was grounded for ever! She would still see Ross at school and they were going to be *friends*. Friendship with Ross was worth suffering chilly disapproval at home...she would be a martyr to love!

A martyr to a bunch of male chauvinist piglets more like! Francesca poured mature scorn on the disturbingly vivid images of a long-dormant memory, shocked by their erotic intensity. As she bumped down the track to the cabin she told herself sternly that she wasn't going to think about the traumatic aftermath of her first date. She had long got over her girlish disillusionment, aided by the knowledge that she had got a sweet form of revenge at the time. Besides, Ross's cruelty had actually done her a favour. It had taught her that one couldn't build one's life around someone else's. Rosy dreams were all very well, but if she was to make her way in the world, to gain acceptance from her peers, she had to earn it for herself.

And she had. She had gained top marks in School Certificate that year for the entire Northland region, and devoted her restricted spare time to convincing Agatha

Lewis that nursing was almost as worthy a career as taking religious orders. The beginning of the new school year had found Francesca starting on a pre-nursing course at Auckland Technical Institute, living under close supervision in a girls' hostel.

Ross had also taught her another valuable lesson. By the time that Francesca, a nervous first-year nurse, encountered her first raft of medical students, she was well armoured against charming young men who thought that plain-looking girls should be grateful for their indiscriminate attentions.

In a way, I suppose, I should be thanking the snake instead of resenting him, Fran thought with a wry grin. Her grin faded as she came into sight of the cabin and saw Ross rummaging around in the boot of a green convertible. In front of it was parked a battered-looking pick-up truck. Neither vehicle had been there when she'd left. She swung her car in beside the convertible and got out.

'Hel-lo, pretty lady.'

She thought he was being sarcastic and frowned at the white smile, then blinked, wondering if she was going mad.

'It *is* Francesca, isn't it?' he said, his smile widening, and the reason for her momentary disorientation clicked.

'Hello, Jason.' How could she have thought he was Ross, even from the back? Jason was leaner, his hair the same shade as his brother's, but cut shorter. 'My, haven't you grown!' She imitated the teasing once-over he had given her. 'I thought you were Ross for a minute.'

He laughed. 'Give me a break, I've got a few years yet before I hit the big three-O. Come and say hello to Neville and Tess. You remember Neville Wilkins, don't you?'

'How could I forget?' Fran murmured. It had been Neville's car they had used that night. 'What is he up to these days? Is Tess his wife?'

'Tess is nobody's wife...yet. But she has a Tarrant dead in her sights.' Jason grinned as they went into the cabin and Fran struggled with a ridiculous sense of betrayal. She must be some woman if she thought she could domesticate Ross. 'As for Neville, would you believe it—he's a cop, stationed in Whangarei!'

Fran burst out laughing. Neville had been the terror of the countryside in his souped-up old Zephyr, his delinquency verging on the criminal with ominous frequency. Neville, a policeman! That was almost as funny as Ross a married man...

She was still smiling when she stepped out on to the sunlit deck to greet the three people lounging in deckchairs. Ross didn't bother to get up, but Neville did, with appreciative speed as he returned her greeting.

'Hi, Francesca. Wow! Ross didn't tell me how much you'd changed. 'His hand froze in mid-handshake as he realised how unflattering that sounded. 'I mean—er—you're looking terrific.' A slight tinge of pink entered the broad face at the compounding of his gaffe and Francesca enjoyed his momentary confusion.

'Thank you, Neville,' she said sweetly. 'But I've been ill. Give me a few weeks and I'll be as chubby as ever.' She grinned to show she wasn't offended. Nursing had taught her to take insults and compliments with equal aplomb. It was only when you really cared about someone that their poor opinion could hurt.

'I find that very hard to believe.' Neville recovered his cool at her relaxed good humour. As they smiled at each other Francesca noticed Ross lean back in his canvas chair. What was he looking so suspicious about? Then it came to her—he was wondering what had put her in such good spirit. He had expected her to come back from the lawyer covered in gloom and despondency. Fran stretched her smile wider.

Neville's brawny body moved out of her sightline as he dragged up a chair for Francesca to sit on, and she got her first look at the woman sitting beside Ross. She was tall and slender, with cropped brunette hair, lovely skin and warm brown eyes. Trust Ross to have a beautiful girlfriend, thought Fran, feeling suddenly frumpy. Her eyes fell on the unmistakable diamond ring on the slim left hand and she stared in disbelief, her heartbeat flickering. So Ross had her dead in *his* sights, too!

Jason handed Fran a cup of coffee, then circled round to stand behind the brunette. 'You don't know Tess, she only came to Whaler's Bay a couple of years ago to help her uncle at the hotel. This is my fiancée, Tessa Armstrong…Francesca Lewis.'

Fran could feel herself blush faintly as she nodded hello. Why had she automatically assumed that it was Ross, not Jason, that Tessa was attracted to? She didn't even want to know the answer to that one.

'Ross has told us the reason for your visit. I'm sorry about the circumstances,' Tess said with friendly sympathy. 'It must have been a shock for you to arrive and find somebody already in residence.'

'I think it was the gun, rather than the resident that shocked me,' Fran lied with a rueful smile.

'Gun? What gun?' Jason looked at his brother with sharp enquiry.

So he hadn't told them. Why? She would have expected him to make a meal of the story. She met the brooding blue eyes. Surely he hadn't been trying to save her embarrassment. No, he must have an ulterior motive.

'Didn't he tell you?' She decided to torpedo it, whatever it was. 'Ross arrived home to catch me skinny-dipping in the spa and tried to run me off with his shotgun. Maybe I should report him to the police for careless use of a firearm,' she said to Neville, catching him out in a flatteringly lecherous survey of her body.

'Maybe I should report you for indecent exposure!' Ross fired a return volley with deadly accuracy. 'I had to haul her out and rub her down,' he told their amused audience, while Fran tried to grapple with the turning of the tables. 'Not to mention cook her dinner and tuck her in for the night.'

'This obviously calls for a lengthy investigation,' Neville grinned. 'Are you staying on for a few days, Fran? Perhaps I could question you over dinner one night?'

'I think you'll find that Francesca will be wanting to get back to Auckland,' Ross said smugly, and a flare of indignation banished any thoughts of conciliation from Francesca's mind.

'On the contrary,' she said sweetly. 'I did only plan to stay a couple of days, but Mr Simpson changed my mind.' She felt a delicious fillip of satisfaction as the taunting blue eyes narrowed, revealing a distinct wariness.

'What did Simpson tell you about me?' he demanded.

'Exactly what you expected. That you could possibly make a claim against the estate.'

'That's all?'

'You weren't the prime topic of conversation, Ross,' she said crushingly. 'We did talk about more interesting things, like the weather, and the price of fish.' He raised his eyebrows and for some reason she thought that he was amused rather than annoyed by her put-down, though his face was deadpan.

'Are you going to stay at the hotel?' Neville asked.
'They do a very nice meal these days.'

'Oh no, I'll be staying here,' Fran said, driven by a
reckless impulse to find out what was under that deadpan
mask. The impulse was rewarded handsomely.

'The hell you are!' Ross growled as he shot to his feet.
'I have a tenancy agreement, as you bloody well know.
Surely you two discussed *that*?'

'Language, language,' Fran tut-tutted with an irritating
smile. 'Tenancy, yes, but not *sole* tenancy. That wasn't
specified.' It was her turn to be smug. My, he was steaming! How lucky that she had read over the agreement so
carefully, looking for non-existent loopholes. 'As of last
night I'm afraid that you have gained yourself a co-
tenant. Me.' Three surprised faces and a furious one
egged her on. 'You wouldn't turn out the grandchild of
such a *dear* friend, would you, Ross? Especially in such
sad circumstances? How would such callousness look to
a judge? Sole relative, weak and helpless from a serious
illness, and instead of compassion you threaten her with
a gun, molest her and then throw her out into the cold...'

'You're about as weak and helpless as a piranha!' Ross
snarled. 'What about your pristine reputation, Princess?
Aren't you afraid of besmirching it by cohabiting with a
commoner?'

His sneer was a mistake. Up until then, Francesca had
merely been trying to annoy him, but at his use of the
hated nickname her humour took a sharp turn for the
worse. If her reputation was pristine among their listeners
she would be very much surprised, considering how
much effort he had put into besmirching it himself thirteen years ago. She stood up and returned him glare for
glare. If he was going to fight dirty, so was she!

'Since I slept here last night, I'm afraid the damage is

already done,' she pointed out acidly. 'If I'm going to acquire a reputation, I'd rather it was for something a little more flattering than a cheap one-night stand.'

They stood, bristling, scowl to scowl until Jason broke the tension with a laugh. 'Hey, you two, break it up! I don't think you'll have to worry too much about local gossip. People will only have to take one look at you together and they'll know there's nothing going on. I swear you look like a couple of gunfighters squaring off at the OK corral!' He looked at his watch and pulled a wide-eyed Tess up from her seat. 'Much as we'd like to stick around for the draw, we're due at Neville's sister's for lunch. Nev?'

'Huh?' The other man had been studying the protagonists and made his decision. 'Oh, sure. Look, Fran, since you *are* staying, how about that dinner? How about to-night?'

'You don't waste any time, do you?' Fran turned to meet the balm of Neville's soothing admiration. 'But yes, I'd love to,' she added hurriedly, sensing Ross's impotent anger behind her and thinking that he couldn't very well murder her if she had a date with a policeman to keep. Besides, it would be a good opportunity to find out a bit more about Ross, and forearm herself against further nasty surprises.

'Nice to meet you, Francesca,' said Tess as they left, and she seemed to mean it.

'Thanks for returning the pick-up, Jason,' said Ross impatiently, obviously eager for them to be gone so that he could rip into Francesca.

'Oh, I was also supposed to pass on a message from Mum. She wants to see you at Sunday lunch, *without fail*. And, hey, Francesca, if you're still here why don't you come, too? Mum loves company.'

'Jason—' Ross's protest came through clenched teeth and his brother's mischievous expression intensified.

'No sour grapes, now, Ross. You said you and Francesca were going to settle it all amicably.' He grinned at the flash of lightning in the stormy grey eyes and the frustrated resignation in the blue. 'And you know Mum, she's certain to want to meet the girl her son is living with!'

CHAPTER THREE

SHE wasn't running away, Fran told herself, as she nego-
tiated her city-slick shoes over the slippery, weed-
covered rocks leading around the point, hitching up her
skirt to jump the small gaps. It was just a strategic retreat.
Before she moved out of sight she looked back over her
shoulder and saw the distant figure on the deck of the
cabin. Ross had been furious and she was nervously
aware that in baiting him she had rather painted herself
into a corner. How was she to get out of it without looking like more of a fool than she did already?

The sea, modest in its demands on the beach, was more
aggressive against the rocks, throwing up small swells
that broke and spattered her lightly with spray. It was
further than she had thought around to the next bay and
she was panting as she rounded yet another curve to yet
another tiny inlet. And stopped dead.

There, sitting on a small rock, his arms folded, was
the very man she had been fleeing from. And he wasn't
even breathing hard!

Francesca wobbled indignantly on her rocky perch.
'How did you get here?'

'I know a short-cut,' he said, and she scowled at this
subtle reminder that he knew more about her inheritance
than she did. He met her glare with a lift of thick brown
brows and stood, holding up his hand to help her down
on to the sand.

'You're limping,' she noticed automatically from his

47

few steps. 'Maybe you're getting too old to take short-cuts.'

She had thought he would laugh it off with a taunt in reply, he was obviously such a prime specimen of manhood, but instead he gave her a look of such dislike that she recoiled and slipped on the hard, wet surface. As she teetered he reached up and grabbed a fistful of her tailored skirt, jerking her forward into his arms. Angry at his ability to unbalance her both physically and mentally, she pushed at him.

'Let me go, damn you! I want to go back.'

'We can never go back, Francesca,' he said, giving her words a deeper meaning, but he let her go. 'Is it really just the money, Princess? Or is it specifically *me* that you object to sharing with?'

He had hit the nail on the head, driving it clean through the fleeting satisfaction she had felt that he was now doubting that she had acted from purely mercenary instincts.

'I... *Why* did he say he would leave it to you?' She struggled to whip up her anger in the face of his cool control. 'Grandpa always believed in the work ethic. Rewards have to be earned with sweated labour. He believed quite literally in the parable of the talents. I...why *you*?' She wanted him to justify himself, to give her a reason she could logically understand.

'What makes you think that I buried mine?' he asked tautly, refusing the opportunity. 'Because I don't wear designer jeans and drive an imported status symbol? Is that how you measure success, Francesca? If so, I'm sorry for you. One can have all the material trappings of success and yet still be a failure as a human being.'

'Is that what you think I am?' she was goaded into asking, as if she cared what he thought of her.

'That's not for me to judge. Unlike you, Princess, I don't estimate a person's worth on appearance.' A faint smile touched the sensuous mouth as he allowed his eyes to peruse her stiffened figure. 'If I did I would be thoroughly confused by now, wouldn't I? Are you the satin-skinned sensualist who likes skinny-dipping and french kissing? Or the neatly tailored spinster who doesn't approve of anything or anyone that deviates from her prim conception of the norm?'

His reference to french kissing was unnerving. Had it been a deliberate reminder of her youthful indiscretion, or was she reading things into his words that didn't exist? *Satin-skinned sensualist?* Absurd!

'If you really want to live at Whaler's Bay, why don't you go and live with your family…or don't *they* want you around, either?'

He merely grinned at her abrupt change of subject. 'Quite the contrary. Mum would love to have me back in the nest but I'm way past the stage, in age and experience, where I'd be comfortable there for any length of time. They're a great crowd, but they're just that, a crowd. Tess is living there until the wedding, Dave has started a rock band who seem to have taken up permanent residence in the barn and little Beth has blossomed into a seventeen-year-old beauty trailing clouds of mooning youths who clutter up the passageways. Add to that a mother who longs to have me safely married off, and a father who cons any hands idle for more than a few seconds into helping on his interminable home-improvement projects and you have some idea why I appreciate the peace of my own establishment.'

'*My* establishment,' Fran corrected firmly, 'and since when did *you* ever seek the peaceful life?'

'Ever?' he repeated mockingly. 'We were only acquainted for a shortish while, Frankie, so you can't claim that sort of knowledge. Any at all in fact—you didn't want to contaminate that dainty, narrow mind of yours by mixing with a crude lout like me, remember? Crude or not, I've lived and learned a lot since then.'

'Oh, really, learned what?' she snapped, stiffening her spine against that silky *Frankie*. Ross had been the only man to call her that. And the crack about louts came dangerously close to an open reference to that awful Monday she had tried so hard to forget. 'Learned how to con old men? Is that how you scratch a living?' She had to insult him. He wasn't going to slip past her guard by making her curious about what he had been up to in the meantime. She didn't care, except so far as it affected *her*.

His nostrils flared slightly, but there was no other outward sign of temper. Instead he squared his stance and cocked his head and said, very, very blandly, 'Women.'

'What?'

'I make a living from women.' He enjoyed her startled suspicion. 'They pay to visit me, or sometimes they ring me and I visit them. We exchange…er…intimate information and part with satisfaction on both sides. I have a lot of *very* satisfied clients.'

'You're…a…a *gigolo*?' Fran's shock and suspicion melted into distaste. She had expected something disreputable, but this…!

He gave her a smouldering smile. 'That term is a bit outdated, not to say obvious. I prefer to think of myself as serving mankind…or, in my case, womankind.'

'I…that's disgusting!' Fran spluttered.

'Is satisfying human need disgusting?' he said, feigning surprise. 'You should be the first to congratulate me,

Princess. You were the one who told me I was wasting my potential.'

'I didn't mean your sexual potential!' she hissed, flushing furiously when she realised where the conversation had led her.

'As I recall, you didn't specify, but perhaps your memory is more vivid than mine,' he goaded her softly. 'No? Then let me see if I can refresh it. You told me, after making sure that half the school was listening, of course, that I was quite fun on a date, but a little too crude and clumsy for your taste. That the boys you used to sneak out on dates with when you went to that snooty girls' school of yours had much more class. Who wants to be friends with a guy on the fast-track to nowhere? you said. I was spoiled and lazy and I would never realise my potential because whatever natural talent I had would always be stifled by my even greater talent for taking the easy option...'

'I'm flattered you bothered to remember what I said,' Fran murmured stiffly, unnerved by the thought that his memories might be just as vivid as hers. 'What a pity you obviously didn't take it to heart.'

'What makes you think that?'

'Well,' she floundered, trying to come up with a reason for her reasonless conviction. 'You were just as much a hell-raiser as ever when I left, and I didn't see your name listed in the Bursary examination results...'

'Keeping tabs on me, Princess?' he needled softly.

'Nothing of the kind,' she denied, pink-faced. 'I just happened to notice.'

'I got by without.' Surprisingly he didn't pursue the blush, but he didn't hide his humorous satisfaction either. 'I decided to exploit my natural talent with women...and guided by your advice I decided not to stifle my skills by restricting myself to only *one*…'

'No wonder you don't dare live at home!' She drew in her mouth primly, unable to help responding to the provocation, even though she knew it was deliberate. Her antagonism towards the man seemed inbuilt, and drove her into uncharacteristic over-reaction. 'If you think I'm going to let you use my cabin to—'

'Rest—I told you I was after some peace. Even gigolos need holidays.' His mouth quirked as she bridled. 'Don't worry, Princess, I won't ask you for money. I doubt that, even with your inheritance, you could afford my rates!'

He was that good? Fran found herself thinking wryly, then was horrified at herself. Ross was grinning openly at her now and she didn't know whether to believe him or not. He was so damned sexy it was easy to believe that he could flatter women into paying for the privilege of his company.

'I'm not as gullible as all that, Ross,' she said, to convince herself. 'You're not going to scare me off with those tactics. I don't care what kind of low-life you are, I'm not backing down. Were you ever this ''honest'' with Grandpa?'

'I respected the old man too much to upset him by flaunting the differences in our philosophies in his face, but I never lied to him. At least I was there for him to talk to. He was pretty stubborn and opinionated, and set in his ways, but interesting for all that. A pity you never showed any interest. Not very dutiful of you, Fran…'

Duty. How that word stung. 'I wrote—'

His sound of disgust cut her off. She wanted to shout at him to leave her alone, and yet she knew she couldn't just walk away from his accusations. Something about him compelled her to stand up to him. She had the feeling that if she let him have any kind of victory over her, no matter how small, he might glimpse how really vulnerable and uncertain she was. Her life was already in the midst of a state of flux and she didn't know if she could handle any more complications right now.

'A few letters may have salved your conscience, but what that old man needed was *you*. You never came much, apparently, even when Agatha was alive. Were you ashamed of them? Too good for the people who took you into their home and brought you up? God, the way Ian talked it was as though you were some sort of saint! He was so proud of you...of how well you were doing and how busy you were, even if it meant you were too damned busy to take an occasional weekend off to visit an old man.'

'He didn't want my company. He never did!' Fran defended herself fiercely. 'Maybe, towards the end, he did need it, maybe I should have come, but for what? He never talked to me and I didn't know how to talk to him. I don't even know if I liked him. He certainly never tried to like me.' When she saw the protest form in the blue eyes she went on, doggedly, 'Oh yes, he and Agatha were *proud*, but not of me, personally. They didn't know what kind of person I was, they never wanted to know, they just wanted a shiny image to show the world. As long as I did what I was told and didn't disgrace myself, as long as I was *dutiful*, they never asked for more. Do you wonder I didn't like coming back here? This was never really home to me. Home is where the heart is, and there was no heart in my relationship with my grandparents, only duty.' She laughed bitterly into his suddenly still face. So he thought he knew it all! 'They were such pillars of the community. Everyone thought they were so wonderful for taking in their illegitimate granddaughter and bringing her up, but their pride gave them no choice. They *had* to take me in. And I was a constant reminder of how they had failed in bringing up their own child. I suppose they decided they had been too lenient with my mother, because they obviously couldn't trust themselves to control the taint in *my* veins. They handed me over to strangers to bring up through my formative years. I was six when they packed me off to that school. Six! The nuns were kind, of course, but they had their vows. Their love was detached, it couldn't be squandered on individuals...

Her voice hoarsened in an echo of the lost bewilderment she had felt in those early years. 'It didn't take me long to realise that my grandparents were proudest of me when I wasn't there. They even encouraged me to take my holidays with schoolfriends, rather than come back home. I'd be lonely, they said.' She laughed again, but this time it was ironic. 'Maybe they were afraid I'd contaminate *you*, rather than the other way around.'

'They were victims of their own upbringing, too.' Ross's voice was deep and slow, and full of a compassionate understanding that she didn't want to believe he was capable of. 'It can't have been easy when your mother was killed and they suddenly found themselves with a baby on their hands, just when they were looking forward to their retirement years. They did their best...'

'Best for whom?' Fran asked wearily. 'I could have been adopted by a couple who *did* want me, been able to feel part of a family instead of never being able to shake off the feeling I was here on sufferance.' She threw her head back and challenged him. 'I happen to think that they owed me more than duty, they owed me *love*. More than that, they owed it to me to accept *my* love, but shows of affection were very much discouraged.

They expected the worst of me, even when I gave them the best. They never trusted me, and as a consequence I never really trusted them. I'm sorry Grandpa's dead, but I can't say I shed many tears, except for what might have been. I am what they taught me to be.' She faced him proudly, showing him that although she had explained, she wasn't apologising.

Ross shifted his uncomfortably intent gaze to the sea and the silence began to stretch. Fran felt her nerves stretch with it. She had probably sounded like a self-pitying idiot, throwing all those old resentments at him. She had never opened up like that with anyone before, not even in a temper, so why now, to *him*?

'If I offered to withdraw any claim to the cabin, would you move out and let me stay out my lease?'

Fran's eyes snapped to his face. It was totally without expression, as if he was carefully repressing his thoughts. He hadn't shaved this morning and the rough stubble along the hard jaw and untidy hair gave him a heightened air of masculinity. Fran was appalled at her sudden desire to trust him, to give in to his strength.

'No,' she said flatly, daring him to try and talk her into it.

'Surely we can reach some sort of compromise—'

'No!' Fran had been compromising her needs and emotions all her life. She was tired of deferring to other people, of doing what *they* wanted her to do. She was putting her foot down, now. 'You started this, Ross Tarrant, but I'm going to finish it. If anyone compromises, it'll be you. *I'm* staying in *my* cabin!'

'For God's sake, I don't want the damned thing…I never did!' he exploded at her.

Fran went rigid with disbelief. 'You're lying…you just want me out of the way so that you can—'

'Look, Francesca—' his voice was gritty with constraint '—*yes*, your grandfather said I could have the place when he died, and *yes*, I'm interested in buying. But I had no intention of contesting any claim until you walked in with your lady-of-the-manor act. All I knew was that you let the old man down when he needed you, and now you were strolling in to rake up the goodies. I still don't like the idea of your selling to anyone but a local, but what the hell—' he shrugged impatiently '—I'm not a local any more myself. So why don't you go back to wherever you came from and let Simpson expedite the estate for you, and just leave me in peace?'

Instead of soothing her, his curt explanation infuriated Fran even more. In the midst of a strenuous battle with the enemy she found herself punching air. How dared he think he could upset her like he had and then shrug off his deliberate obstruction as a misunderstanding! And he was actually putting some of the blame on *her*!

'You should have thought about the consequences before you started slinging threats around,' she took pleasure in telling him. 'But then you never worried overmuch about the future, did you, Ross? Only about the pleasures of the moment. Well…tough. For once you're going to have to live with the consequences: namely— me!'

She felt good as she began to scramble back over the rocks. Ross Tarrant was a symbol of the negative aspects of her life, the things she could never have, could never be. Now for the first time she felt that she was dealing with the sense of inadequacy he raised, and which she tried to hide by professing to despise everything about him, on an adult level. She wanted to hold on to this heady feeling of triumph for as long as she could.

Her confidence in having the upper hand was reinforced by having him trail, muttering, after her. When they reached the smooth sand again she noticed from a brief flick of her head that he was still limping. The nurse in her rose up.

'You'd better let me take a look at that leg of yours when we get back. You might have pulled a muscle or something.'

His rude rejoinder didn't put her off.

'Don't be silly, a person who's perfectly fit doesn't limp for no reason.'

'I fell coming down the cliff,' he snarled sullenly at her, bringing her to a dead stop, her hands automatically settling on her waist.

'The cliff? The short-cut was down that cliff?' Her eyes flickered closed as she visualised for an instant that apparently smooth clay face. 'You must be mad!'

His glare was pronounced, his face stiff with what she recognised was offended male pride. He had always had too much of it. 'I haven't got one foot in the grave yet, Princess. I've been rock-climbing half my life…and jogging, and scuba-diving, and sky-diving. I'm not one of your city-soft coronary-candidates sliding into middle age. I can take care of my body myself, thank you.'

'No wonder you don't work, you're too busy working out. Once a jock, always a jock, huh, Ross?' she mocked. 'And I suppose it isn't macho to admit that enough is enough. People who *over*-exercise have coronaries, too, you know.'

This time it was Fran who trotted behind while Ross strode on, and she took the time to professionally study the swing of his leg. By the look of him it was his left hip as well as his ankle that was bothering him.

'I don't "exercise",' he threw over his shoulder. 'I set myself physical challenges.'

'You call plunging down a cliff a challenge? I would say it was stupidity.'

'Yes, I suppose you would. You don't trust yourself any more than you trust other people, do you? You like things to be nice and safe. You wouldn't understand how much pleasure the element of risk adds to an activity. I don't suppose you ever took a risk on anything in your life.'

Francesca began to laugh, and Ross stopped and stared at her. She was genuinely amused, grey eyes dancing with slivers of blue light, her thick caramel curls flowing over her shoulders as she tilted her face to the sky. A month ago his words might have been true, but at the moment her entire life was one big risk. Was it a pleasurable one? No, but she couldn't honestly say that she wasn't enjoying *parts* of it. Parts that didn't include Ross, of course, she told herself, biting off her laughter as she caught the lancing puzzlement of his gaze.

'What's so funny?' he asked, with the slightly sulky tones of someone who hasn't understood a joke that everyone else finds hilarious.

Fran had no intention of telling him. It gave her a much-needed sense of security, knowing that he couldn't read her half as well as he thought he could.

'Are you going to "risk" showing me that leg?' She grinned smugly at him.

A tiny flame flickered in the deep blue eyes. 'I'll let you play nurse if you let me play doctor,' he said slyly, his grin replacing hers.

Smugness and compassion died a rapid death. Let him suffer then! She sniffed and stalked into the cabin. He would have to *beg* before she'd lift a finger to help him!

They lunched separately, Fran reading a gardening manual at the table, Ross taking a repulsively large sandwich out on to the deck. He propped his leg up on a stool, she noticed, steaming lightly at the bull-headedness of *some people*. After she had eaten her dainty triangles she soothed herself by spending the afternoon emphasising her presence: arranging her plants around the cabin, finding the best position for each, and watering and chatting encouragingly to them.

'If you're so hard up for company, Princess, why don't you come out here? I guess I can endure some conversation. I'm certainly not getting any peace with you burbling about in the background.' Ross lowered his book to watch her admonish a Boston fern for being reluctant to grow.

'You can always leave,' she said loftily, brushing a curl away from the corner of her mouth and casting a brief look of scorn at the lurid cover of his paperback. 'I think the conversation I get in here is much more intelligent than any I might get from you.'

'Still the intellectual snob?' He was irritatingly uncrushed. 'Look, Frankie, living with someone who's a friend, or family, is hard enough. Living with an enemy would be hell on wheels. Pull in your horns, Sister Lewis, I'm through arguing with you for today.'

He took his book and went out and lay in the tall, yellowing grass that waved on the little hillocks that presaged the hills behind the cabin, his head resting against the upturned, aluminium-hulled dinghy that Ian Lewis had hardly ever used, preferring to fish from the rocks.

Time hung heavily on Fran's hands. She wasn't used to having any spare time, and the quietness was almost too intense. The sea, like rippling grass, barely whispered on the shore and the only other sounds were from the gulls and shags and terns that shared nesting places in the clifftop trees.

She took her leisure getting ready for her dinner with Neville, lingering in the shower and making-up with slow precision. It was a long time since she had gone out with a man she didn't know...a long time since she had gone out with anyone other than Brian. The hand applying eyeshadow paused as she thought of the horrendous row they'd had before she had left for Whaler's Bay. They had said bitter things to each other, but in Fran's case it had been a bitterness tinged with relief. Brian had been part of the life that had been closing in on her, and an indivisible part, judging from the comments he had made about her resignation. He didn't approve, had even accused her of going through an early mid-life crisis, and Fran had discovered that she really didn't care what he thought. Scarcely the basis of a good relationship!

She finger-dried her hair, glad to see some of the highlights returning after the lank lifelessness of the last few weeks, and fluffed out the perm to give her a carefully tousled look. The mouth that she had always thought was too narrow looked wider and fuller in the fined-down version of her normally rounded face, and the plum-coloured lipstick emphasised the difference.

She was wearing the one 'good' dress she had packed for unexpected eventualities just like this: a blue wool crêpe with a modestly plunging neckline and a skirt that warmly followed the contours of her hips and thighs. It was slightly loose on her, but Fran hadn't wanted to invest in a whole new wardrobe when she knew that she would soon be back to her old size. She looked at herself in the mirror screwed to the bedroom wall and was pleased. This would show Ross that she wasn't a starchy Sister, or a snobby Princess. She was a woman, too, and even though she wasn't beautiful, at least she didn't have to *pay* a man to go out with her!

Ross had opened a can of tomato soup for his dinner and was drinking it out of a thick mug when she walked into the lounge. He set the mug on the table, thoughtfully dunking a slice of toast into the wide mouth and chewing on it unhurriedly as he looked her over.

'All this for Neville?' he murmured at last, hiding the gleam in his eyes under lazy lids. 'Go easy on him, won't you, Princess? He's only a country boy like me; he might not know the right protocol to follow.'

Against her will Fran felt herself flush with pleasure at the oblique compliment and tore her eyes away from his handsome face to stare at the hand which held the toast. The back was covered with dark hair which ran up under the folded cuff of his sweater. She guessed that his arms and legs, like his chest, would be thickly furred. She blinked as her eyes settled on his expensive-looking watch. A 'gift' from one of his 'clients'?

'For goodness' sake, he's a grown man! He doesn't need you to run interference for him,' she said tartly.

'Even grown men have trouble figuring out women sometimes. Why are you going out with him, anyway? I wouldn't have thought he was your type.'

'And what is my type?' she was unable to resist asking.

His eyebrows rose mockingly. 'Don't you know? Dear me, Frankie, it sounds as if your love-life to date has been sadly lacking.'

'My love-life has been entirely satisfactory,' she fibbed.

'Damned with faint praise, huh?' he grinned tauntingly. 'Seems us country boys might be able to teach your sophisticated city slickers a thing or two, after all.'

'You can cut out the ''down home'' accent, Ross.' Her eyes sparkled with temper. 'You said you didn't live around here any more, and I scarcely think that there'd be much call for *your* kind of services in quiet rural backwaters!'

'You can take the boy out of the country, Princess…' he said mirthfully, and again she had the uncomfortable feeling that he was laughing at more than just the present conversation. 'But you're right, the pickings are richer in the cities…more women to the square metre.' He took another swig of his soup and eyed her provocatively. 'But you're very cleverly evading my question. Never mind, we both know the *real* reason you agreed to go out with Neville…'

Fran gave him a haughty look. She wasn't going to touch that one with a barge-pole. Besides, she knew he intended to enlighten her anyway. And so he did.

'Actually there are two. The first is that you don't trust yourself alone with me…and the second is that you're dying to pump poor old Nev for information, or should I say ammunition, you can use against me.'

'You arrogant hulk!' Fran snapped, furious that he had caught her out in the latter, and insulted her by the former. 'It's *you* I don't trust.' She thought of adding that he left her cold, but the words suddenly stuck in her throat. Also, his gross male ego might take it as a challenge. 'I happen to think that Neville is an extremely attractive man.'

Her dignity cut little ice. 'Oh, sure, and you have no intention of even *mentioning* me during your hot date.'

'Why should I spoil a nice evening?' Fran flared. 'But maybe I ought to warn him about how you make a living, if he doesn't already know. The police might want to issue a warning to people to lock up their daughters.'

'And wives,' he told her with outrageous cheerfulness.

'And mothers and grandmothers. No woman is turned from my door.'

'Except those who can't afford your fees,' she said, certain that he was exaggerating just to rattle her. With his looks, Ross could probably pick and choose his 'clients' very carefully.

'Oh, I do a certain amount of charity work,' he laughed. 'Ask Neville. I bet you won't be able to resist. Admit it, you're as curious as a cat about me. Why don't you just forget about going out with Neville and stay home with me? That way you cut out the middle man.'

A flash of headlights shone through the kitchen window and rescued Fran from a fast degenerating situation. 'That's him now,' she said with visible relief, taking the cabin key from the top of the fridge and putting it in her slim clutch bag. 'We might be late, so don't bother to wait up for me.'

'Don't do anything I wouldn't do,' he chuckled, toasting her with his mug.

'That *really* narrows the field down, doesn't it? Sarcasm dripped from every syllable as she threw open the kitchen door and stepped outside, pursued by his laughter.

'Ten bucks says you won't get through the night without giving in to your insatiable desire to know me better, Princess!'

The throaty challenge rang in her ears as she greeted Neville's appreciative hello. Unfortunately he had heard Ross's laughter, if not his comment, and, as she got into the car, asked her what the joke had been. The date was only five seconds old and already the subject was that wretched man. Well, she would eat poison before she would let him be proved right! She would forget all about her insufferable house-guest and just enjoy her night out.

It wasn't easy. The consciousness that she wasn't going to mention his name kept in the forefront of her mind, an invisible third person at the dinner table, monitoring her conversation. In spite of that, the evening was pleasant. In a way, Neville reminded her of Brian; they both had the same, rather complacent view of their lives stretching ahead of them, from point A to point B, like a neatly kerbed and well sealed highway. Fran, who had just taken an abrupt turn on to a sharply rutted side-road, felt the faint stirrings of impatience even as she enjoyed the comfortable tenor of Neville's unthreatening flattery. He was obviously interested in seeing her again, but Fran was politely non-committal. She had just escaped one dead-end relationship; she didn't want to embark, even briefly, on another. She needed to reserve her energy for more important things...

'...coincidence that you're both up here from Auckland convalescing at the same time. Did you ever run into each other in the big city?'

Francesca suddenly registered what he was saying, and her firm resolve vanished on the instant. 'Has Ross been ill?' she enquired sharply.

'Didn't he tell you?' He looked surprised, then grinned. 'I suppose he's fed up with all the sympathy— he was always so savagely healthy, I guess being laid up has been driving him crazy. Remember that time he broke his nose? The coach had to practically manhandle him off the football field. Never say die, that's Ross's motto.'

'How—?' Fran took a sip of wine to stop herself forming the question. If Neville chose to tell her she would listen, but she would not *ask*.

'Sky-diving,' he obliged genially. 'His 'chute tangled and wouldn't detach, and so did his emergency. Smashed himself up pretty badly…oh, about four months ago, I think it was.'

'He was lucky even to survive,' said Fran, tight-lipped, her surge of horror overtaken by anger. If he was convalescing, what was he doing sliding down cliffs? Not that his pig-headedness was anything she could control. She felt thoroughly sorry for the doctors and nurses who had looked after him; he had probably made their lives hell. Or, in the case of the nurses, heaven—the traitorous thought sneaked into her mind.

Determinedly she managed to get through the rest of the evening with her curiosity under tight rein. In a complete volte-face she decided that she didn't need to know anything personal about Ross Tarrant—she didn't *want* to know anything. She would just hang on grimly to her hopes and soon he would be back firmly where he belonged…in her past.

CHAPTER FOUR

ROSS TARRANT lowered his book and stared broodingly towards the clatter in the kitchen which had penetrated his concentration. Francesca was attacking the evening dishes as though to leave them a second longer would herald the death of the civilised world. His eyes moved from the set of her shoulders to the long line of her back. Apart from its uncomfortable stiffness it was rather a sexy back.

His connoisseur's eye slid to the swerve of her hips, recalling how she had looked nude and steamy, flushed and feminine in her weakness.

He frowned. Three days ago it had seemed such a simple, foolproof plan: drive out the irritatingly neat Sister Lewis by driving her up the wall. But the foolproof plan had backfired. He was the one quietly going up the wall!

How could one woman be so infuriatingly obstinate and yet so easy to manipulate? He lifted his book again to hide a slow grin. It might be childish of him, but he enjoyed fuelling her misconceptions about him. She was so deliciously easy to provoke into a passion that belied that prim exterior.

His grin faded. There was the rub. He was curious about her. Before she had turned up, the peace and quiet had begun to pall and yet he had known he wasn't ready, physically or psychologically, to ease back into the swing of his life. Thwarting Francesca had been in the nature of a diversion that, once his initial temper had cooled, amused his restless mind. He had not felt in the least guilty. Francesca had proved that she could look after herself, and at least she came alive at his taunts. Flaring back at him she didn't look quite so much like a wind-up doll marching stiffly towards some predetermined fate. He was doing her a favour, loosening her up.

Liar! he told himself disgustedly. His motives were entirely selfish. He never could resist a challenge and Francesca was the most flagrant one he had come across in a long time. What marvellous irony to be penned up with one of the few women who had ever rejected him outright! Actually, Francesca had the distinction of being the first, and as such had earned herself a special place in his memory. For another reason too, one that she would no doubt be astonished to hear, but he intended to save the telling until the right moment. She had earned the embarrassment. It might teach her a little humility to realise how gullible her rigid thinking made her. And in the meantime he wanted to explore the fascinating perversities of human biology.

To his amused chagrin Ross had realised that the old chemistry still existed and that, if he was any judge of body language, it wasn't only one-sided. Fran was giving out unmistakable signals to a man who had built part of his professional reputation on his ability to read and interpret the nuances of female expression. She resented the undercurrent of attraction, that much was obvious, and he shared her reluctance. Francesca was not the sort of woman he sought out for male/female games. He liked women who were frank and open about their desires and emotions, women who preferred lovemaking to fighting, who were fun to be with and didn't tax his patience by demanding too much of his valuable time. Francesca was the total opposite. She was rather like a locked room...perhaps the female equivalent of Blackbeard's lair, he speculated mischievously, littered with the bodies of past unfortunates who had been chewed up and spat out by that discreetly sexual, but tightly controlled personality. What was the key to Francesca? he wondered. What might he release if he found it? He had the time, but did he have the inclination—or the courage?

Francesca was aware of the strange vibrations from across the room. What was he thinking about? New ways to drive her up the wall? Surprisingly he hadn't even mentioned her date with Neville. Instead of baiting her mercilessly about his bet he had greeted her the next morning with a slightly expectant silence. She had ignored him until driven to point out that he hadn't even bothered to wash his few dishes from last night's dinner, adding snidely that perhaps he might find work as a dishwasher if nothing else. That had restored his acid humour and it hadn't faltered since.

Francesca had to concede that she had overestimated her ability to outstay him. As a nurse she had frequently lived in shared accommodation, but fellow nurses were quite different from a *man*. A man, moreover, who didn't want you there, who had no sense of organisation, who was sullen and uncooperative and didn't seem to know one end of a broom from the other. The only other man that Francesca had lived with had been her grandfather, and he had been a rigidly correct man who never came to a meal unless he was fully dressed, and liked everything to be in its rightful place.

Ross Tarrant was a creature of impulse. He slept when he was sleepy, ate when he was hungry and had a disconcerting habit of walking around half-naked. He was untidy and inconsiderate and refused to share the chores.

Francesca had caught on very early. He was doing it

deliberately. No one could be that slovenly and not have died of some certifiable disease years ago!

She extracted her revenge by carrying her desire for neatness to obsession point. The fact that her constant nagging of him to tidy up got on her own nerves as well as his was beside the point, although sometimes she forgot entirely what the point was supposed to be!

Francesca was drying the last dish when the telephone rang. She turned automatically. Although Ross was well within reach of the phone it would be just like him to let it ring and ring until she was forced to answer it. But this time she had misjudged him.

'Tarrant.' He listened for a moment. His eyes shot to Fran and a devilish grin lit out across his lips. 'Yes, you have, and she is here, but she's just...er...got other things on her mind at the moment, if you know what I mean...'

Propelled by that leering innuendo Fran scooted across the room and grabbed at the receiver. Ross fended her off from his chair with mocking ease.

'Who am I? Her live-in boyfriend. Who are you?'

'Stop it! Give that phone to me!' Francesca hissed furiously, rushing in under his guard and wrenching the phone away from him. 'Hello?'

'Hi, Fran. Who's the hunk?'

'Oh, hello, Christina.' She had rung her friend from the lawyer's office to let her know of the hiccup in their plans. Christina had been less upset than Fran, pointing out that they couldn't do anything anyway until the Council had made up its mind about the Change of Land Use application, and the bank had officially notified them of their loan approval. 'No panic, just relax for a few days. You need it,' had been her cheerful advice.

'Look, I can call back if you and the hunk are—'

'We're certainly not!' snapped Fran, giving her tormentor a killing look. 'That was his idea of a sick joke. He's just a co-tenant, that's all.'

'Pity, he sounds nice.' Like a true friend Christina took the hint in Francesca's terse reply and dropped the subject. 'I just called to let you know that the Council came up trumps. Now we only have the loan to worry about.'

'That's great!' Fran's face lit up, her whole body expressing delighted relief to her interested audience. She listened while Christina brought her up to date with the rest of her activities, feeling buoyant again after the frustration of the past few days.

'Doug and I had a spat, and Brian phoned, full of remorse, wanting to know where he could reach you. I told him, politely of course, to bug off.'

'Thanks.' Christina had never really taken to Brian, although she had always been pleasant to him.

'Perhaps I should tell him you're living with someone up there. That should ram home the message.'

'No, thanks,' Fran shuddered. Things were complicated enough. She looked at Ross, unashamedly listening, and buoyancy made her rash. 'I don't think he'd be very impressive, he's the immature pretty-boy type.' Ross's eyes narrowed as he realised who she was describing. 'He fancies himself as a lady-killer,' said Fran gleefully, 'but he's handicapped at the moment…smashed himself up in a sky-diving accident. He's pretty seedy all round, but I guess when he's not sulking or flexing his beach-boy muscles he has a certain frayed charm.'

She hung up on Christina's laughter, suddenly nervous at the smug look that Ross was directing her way. He didn't look at all disturbed by her insults.

'Who told you about my accident?'

Dammit, she had forgotten she wasn't supposed to know! She flushed guiltily, turning on her heel and fleeing back to the kitchen. Ross followed her crowing with triumph.

'You owe me ten bucks!'

'Oh, no, I don't.' Fran grabbed the dishcloth and began wiping the bench diligently. 'I never bet. *You're* the gambler around here.' She'd been waiting thirteen years to make that taunt, but of course it sailed right over his thick head.

'And what other titbits of information about me did you wheedle out of my unsuspecting chum?'

'I didn't *wheedle*. He mentioned it, that's all.' She crossed her fingers in the folds of her skirt. 'That's the only time I even thought of you all night.'

He grinned so jauntily she wanted to hit him. Instead she poked a stick into his weak spot. She had noticed how impatient he was for total recovery, it showed in the way he pushed himself and stubbornly refused to make concessions to his injuries or admit to feeling pain, snarling at her if she dared comment.

'How long do you think you'll have to take it easy? What will you do when you're completely recovered?'

'I'm practically recovered now,' he was quick to answer, scowling at her.

'Maybe you'd better think about finding yourself a proper job, then,' she said scathingly. 'Your old one might not support you in the style to which you're accustomed. You might find that women baulk at paying top price for damaged goods.'

She saw his mouth tauten on a quick intake of breath. 'Bitch,' he said softly. 'That was below the belt.'

Francesca was suddenly ashamed. How could she, a nurse, an *ex*-nurse, mock someone's affliction? It went against every principle of her training, as well as viol-

ating common human decency. It was just that he made
her so mad!

'I'm sorry,' she said gruffly, avoiding the sudden darkness of his eyes. 'Er…what *were* your injuries, anyway?'

He continued to look at her for a moment in silence,
as if to judge her sincerity, then leaned on the breakfast
bar and told her, with an almost clinical detachment that
both fascinated and repulsed her. He was talking about
himself, not some nameless textbook case.

'I was lucky that I landed in bushy scrub which
cushioned my fall; I was lucky, in fact, that most of the
breaks were clean. I had a compressed fracture of the
vertebrae but there were no complications. It's my left
arm that's the problem, a vertical fracture of the humerus
is pretty difficult to deal with.'

Fran wasn't interested in technical details, she was trying to cope with a rush of complex emotions—fear, relief, a bewildering empathy with his pain. 'You're lucky
to be alive at all, let alone walking around,' she said
shakily.

'I know,' he said gently, sunning himself in the brief
warmth of her compassion. 'It's going to make the next
jump that much more difficult.'

'You're going back up, after what happened?' Fran
was milk-pale in disbelief. How could he risk putting
himself, his friends and family, through that all over
again?

'I have to.' He smiled wryly at her blank incomprehen-
sion.

'Weren't you warned?' she asked feverishly. 'Didn't
the doctors tell you that there'll probably always be a
slight weakness on that side—'

'What thoroughly boring, predictable lives we'd all
lead if we allowed ourselves to be governed by *proba-

bly,' he replied calmly. 'You wear blinkers, Princess, if you think you can make life safe by sticking to the straight and narrow. Hasn't your profession taught you that one can never be completely safe, that death, disease and accidents are appallingly random?'

'It's taught me a certain amount of fatalism,' she said, not entirely truthfully. When you're busy carving your own fate, fatalism doesn't have quite the same meaning.

He sighed and shook his head. 'Princess, you need drastic loosening up. You need to relax, or you're going to turn into one of those arid, iron-skinned, sour-tongued martinets that nurses and patients alike love to hate.'

What would he know? Francesca gave him a sharp look. Perhaps he had had one on the ward he had been in? It was on the tip of her tongue to tell him that officially she was no longer a nurse, but he would probably give her that wretchedly smug grin and make jokes about abdication. And then he would ask what she was going to do and be even *more* impossibly smug that she was doing exactly as he told her she should.

She couldn't quite put her finger on it, but that conversation seemed to mark a turning point in her relationship with Ross. His teasing became lighter, lacking the sullen, threatening undertones it had had since she had announced her decision to stay. However, instead of making her relax it made her more suspicious of him than ever, convinced it was merely a ruse to lull her into thinking he no longer cared whether she stayed or went.

Impossible as it seemed, Ross became even more casual around the cabin, until every crevice appeared to harbour evidence of his inhabitance: a discarded sock under the table, *Sports Digest* magazines migrating from room to room, shaving foam on the mirror, and food— he always seemed to be eating—which he would put down somewhere and then forget about. He was always mildly apologetic when Fran pointed these things out to him, but he never changed one iota until at last she gave up nagging and resigned herself to cleaning up after the worst of his untidiness and resolutely ignoring the lesser irritations.

It seemed silly to prepare food separately, so they worked out a tacit arrangement whereby Fran provided breakfast, they got their own lunches, and Ross cooked the dinner. He was a far more imaginative chef than she was, not to mention a better cook, and Fran found herself thinking that if they lived together much longer she would have to start worrying about dieting again. She had no scales to weigh herself on, but just by looking at herself in the bathroom mirror she could see her ribs filling out.

Sometimes Ross would bring back his fishing catch for a meal and every now and then he would disappear in his rackety pick-up and return from a tour of the local roadside produce stalls laden with garden-fresh vegetables. Fran made sure that the expense of their bought food was strictly shared. She had no idea what the state of his finances were; perhaps he was slipping into Whangarei on his outings to collect his unemployment benefit cheque, or perhaps he was still on Accident Compensation? Anyhow, once or twice he visited his parents and came back with a pie or a casserole, so perhaps his family were helping make ends meet. How awful, to be thirty and still living such an apparently meagre existence, she thought with a shudder. At least she would always have her training to fall back on. She might lose her savings in this new venture, but she need never be destitute.

The weather over the next few days continued warm and sunny, unseasonably so, and Ross had taken to strip-

ping down accordingly. The first time Fran walked in and
saw him standing there, dressed only in tight, cut-off
denim shorts, she almost had cardiac arrest. He was behind the kitchen bench, the shorts slung so low on his
hips that at first she had thought he was naked. There
were a few scars and still some signs of deep tissue bruising, but even so he had a beautiful body! Fran could only
see slight signs of softening from his months of curtailed
activity.

'Does my body embarrass you?' He had raised innocent eyebrows at her dropped jaw, forcing her to reach
for nonchalance.

'Of course not, I've seen better.' A valiant lie. 'You've
got a bit of weight settling in, haven't you?'

To her delight he scowled. 'I'm working on it.'

He got his revenge that evening as she sat by the fire,
reading one of his awful paperbacks with a frown on her
face and a certain guilty fascination with the machi-
nations of the rich and promiscuous characters. Ross usually took a long, relaxing spa after dinner, and tonight he
wandered through with only a towel hitched around his
hips, apparently to fetch a magazine.

As he bent to flick through the stack on the coffee
table, Fran couldn't help seeing the towel part where the
edges were rolled over at the hip, revealing the solid
thigh flowing into his flank, the pale flesh there smooth
and hairless in contrast to the thick dark coating on the
strong legs and wide chest. He straightened and turned
so that she was now staring at the front of his body, at
the dangerous dip across his belly which showed the triangle of hair which faded to his navel, thickening out
again below it. He sauntered casually over to stand boldly
in front of her, magazines tucked under his arm.

'You don't seem very interested in that book. Want to come and join me?'

'No, thank you,' she said quickly, too quickly, mind tensing from the impact of all that bare male flesh.

'Come on, Frankie,' he wheedled. 'Don't be shy. You told me that nurses were blasé about nakedness. Or is it *your* body that embarrasses you?' His voice became infuriatingly earnest. 'I know you're pretty skinny at the moment, but from the glimpse I got the other night you still have lovely breasts. Not as big as they used to be, but still nicely shaped. That's one of the things I remembered best about you, your—'

'Will you shut up?' Francesca threw the book aside, her face red with embarrassment and temper. 'We both know that I was fat. Fat and plain. I admit it, OK? You've got back at me for this morning, so let's just forget it now, shall we?'

The tormenting mockery left his face, but Fran was too busy staring hard at her feet to notice. 'You weren't fat, you were plump and the plumpness was in all the right places. I know that thinness is fashionable, but it flies in the face of human physiology. Women are *supposed* to carry extra pads of fat, their bodies are designed to have curves. I personally prefer a woman to look as nature intended her to, rather than to force herself into a fashionable strait-jacket of skin by excessive dieting or the offices of some quack plastic surgeon.'

Fran's eyes flew to his face, and away again, a warmth spreading through her body as she realised he was utterly sincere. It was all the more believable because he hadn't disputed her claim to have been plain. They both knew that she had been.

'Who are you to call plastic surgeons quacks?' she said

teasingly, to hide the embarrassed pleasure she felt. 'Or am I mistaken that you've had your nose fixed?'

To her amusement Ross's hand flew to his nose and he actually flushed, forgetting he was supposed to be menacing her with his gorgeousness. 'Well, yes, but it wasn't my idea. The guy who did it got me to sign the form while I was still bleary with drugs after my first operation. He did the nose job before I realised what was going on.'

Fran was horrified. 'That sounds like a serious breach of ethics. Who was it?'

'Er…a personal friend,' Ross seemed uncomfortable. 'He'd been nagging me for years to get it done.'

'He should have left it the way it was,' said Fran tartly, when it seemed he wasn't going to enlarge on the statement.

He raised his eyebrow with a return of humour. 'To stop me from being stuck with the 'pretty boy' label? Do you think I'm *too* handsome, Princess? I assure you, I may be pretty, but I'm all man…'

The low, masculine purr made the hairs on the back of Francesca's neck rise as she watched, dry-mouthed, as he ran a caressing hand across the rippling muscles of his chest, down over the hard, slightly concave belly to the tuck of his towel. She jerked out of her chair and backed away from that awesome body.

'Oh, go and have your damned spa!' The warmth of his laughter followed her into the bedroom where she slammed the door and stood trying to control her breathing. Involuntarily her hand moved to cup her breast, and she flushed as she remembered his admiration. At fifteen she had been shocked as well as excited to discover how sensitive she was there. Her next sexual encounter, several years later, had reinforced that discovery, disappointing as the affair had been in almost all other respects, including her ultimate satisfaction. In fact, that short flirtation with modern sexual mores had persuaded her that she was one of those women who didn't have a particularly strong sex drive...or so she had thought until now! But then, she had never met a man who exuded blatant sexuality the way that Ross did. She must try and conquer this silly habit of getting hot and flustered by his suggestive teasing, that was what he *wanted*...

The next morning she ignored his insufferable good humour at the breakfast table and took herself off for a leisurely walk, hunting for interesting pebbles on the beach. Idly she thought how nice it would be to spend a little time every now and then in such peaceful surroundings. Was there some way that she could perhaps keep the cabin and...

She stopped short, dropping all her carefully collected pebbles with a faint sound of dismay. Perhaps there was a way, but it would mean even more juggling of finances, and negotiating with the bank and perhaps trimming back on her capital investment. No, better to sell. A holiday home was hardly on the list of her priorities...it might be years before she had the time, or the spare cash, to take enough holidays to warrant one. Besides, a naughty voice whispered, without Ross around, the peaceful life would pall pretty quickly...

'What are you doing? Put that down!' she ordered tightly when she got back to the cabin and found Ross had taken it upon himself to shift around some of her plants. It seemed symptomatic of their relationship, Ross acting and she reacting.

'What does it look like I'm doing?' said Ross mildly, holding the maidenhair fern from the coffee table out of her reach. At least he was wearing a shirt this morning, even if it did have some interesting holes in it, matching his tattered jeans. 'I'm putting some of this greenery out. It's shedding into my coffee. If you were only coming up for a few days, what did you want to lug all these things up here for?'

'I couldn't ask my neighbours to look after *every*thing. Anyway, the ones I brought were special. Some of them are quite rare and others need specialised care.'

'This isn't rare. Even I know what this one is, it's as common as grass.'

'It happens to be going through a rough patch,' said Fran, managing to snatch the offending, offended plant and set it gently back down on the table. 'Plants don't just need food and water, you know, they need company, too…'

'You can't really believe that!' He was laughing at her, as usual.

'I happen to *know* it,' she said haughtily. 'I've done experiments on my horticultural course to prove it. This little fern was ailing until I began to chat to her every day. Now she's starting to perk up.'

'She?' He looked from plant to Fran, his face a study of disbelief. 'You divide your plants into *sexes*?'

Ross would bring sex into a discussion about rocks! 'A lot of plants put out male and female flowers on different bushes. If you want to cross-fertilise you need to know which is which.'

'And this is female?'

She flushed at being caught out. 'Well, I could hardly call a *maiden*hair ''he'', could I?' She was unaware she'd put her hands on her hips and thrust her chin out challengingly. So she talked to her plants and invested them with personalities, so what? It was a harmless eccentricity. If he thought her crazy for talking to her plants, imagine what he would think if he knew that she was about to devote her life to them? He would be rolling on the floor. Sister Lewis, nursing plants rather than patients…he would tell her that it was because plants were no threat to her—they couldn't answer back.

She built an effective case against herself that was abruptly demolished when he said mildly, 'No, I guess not. Did you propagate all these yourself, or do you haunt the garden centres?'

Yes to both questions, she was tempted to reply, one garden centre in particular, but she contented herself with, 'I like to grow things from scratch, there's more satisfaction that way.'

'Only pot plants, or do you have a garden?'

'Sort of.' She hesitated but, seeing only interest in the blue eyes she continued, 'It's not really mine, it belongs to the whole block where my flat is, but it's enormous and nobody else takes much of an interest so…'

'So it's yours.'

She smiled a little sheepishly, grey eyes shifted to a deeper, warmer shade, her mouth curving to soften the pale contours of her face as she told him how she had slaved over that piece of land, planned and plotted and landscaped to her heart's content, until it had won a local Garden Beautiful contest. The landlord had been blasé, until he discovered that the improved environment could entitle him to put the rent up when new tenants moved in. Pointing out to him that he had outlaid nothing, therefore couldn't claim increased costs to the Rent Commission, Fran had bullied him into a business arrangement.

'It sounds as if you have green fingers. Must be a good way to work off the stress of your job.'

Her eyes took on an intriguingly secretive glint of

amusement which made him probe gently, watching as she blossomed with enthusiasm, her gestures wide and sweeping, her body held confidently, her mouth mobile with pleasure. This was how he liked her to look.

'You really are a nature baby, aren't you?' he teased gently when she ran down and began to look abashed at her childish enthusiasm.

'I suppose so,' she murmured, wondering what she had said to put that curious expression on his face. It was almost...tender. Her eyes dropped to see his hand stroking through the maidenhair.

'Don't do that,' she said involuntarily, disturbed by the sexual symbolism of the gesture. Would he run his fingers through a lover's hair like that?

'Why?' A forefinger lifted a tiny, delicate leaf so that it lay submissively on the tip. He leaned forward to inspect it, his breath stirring the other leaves, his other hand cupping a trembling frond on the far side with a gentleness that, absurdly and totally illogically, seemed highly erotic. He looked up at her silence, the hazy blue eyes fusing with hers. 'Jealous?' he asked softly, as if he could read her mind. 'Of a *plant*, Frankie?'

'Maidenhairs bruise easily,' she said huskily, thinking that she should summon anger at the arrogance of the taunt, but drawn instead by the silent message in his eyes.

'So do people, Princess,' he said, confirming the message. 'Shall we agree not to bruise each other?'

Francesca didn't answer. She couldn't. She had the frightening feeling that it might be already too late to escape her reacquaintance with Ross Tarrant totally unscathed...

CHAPTER FIVE

'COME on, Francesca, jump! I'm not going to wait around here all day.' Ross sounded thoroughly fed up.

'I can't, it's too far.' Fran hated the slight whine in her voice. She was fed up with him, too. It wasn't enough for him that they were out in the fresh air. Oh, no, Ross always had to go that extra distance, round the next point or over the next ridge. Looking down at the sea boiling into the crevasse below her, and Ross impatiently waiting on the rocks on the other side, she decided that enough was enough.

'I can't do it.'

'There you go again. Every time I ask you to make a little extra effort it's the same: I can't! Until I *make* you.'

'Little?' Fran exploded at him, trying to force the tangle of curls out of her eyes as the wind whipped them to a froth. 'I don't call this *little*. ''Let's go around the rocks,'' you said. You didn't say you were taking me mountaineering!'

'Don't exaggerate, Fran,' he drawled, with a grin at her flushed face and heaving breasts.

'This kind of thing may turn you on, Ross Tarrant,' she said bitingly, unreasonably annoyed by that masculine gleam. 'But I don't find it at all exciting.'

'What kind of thing?' He leaned his shoulder against the rock, as if there was a square kilometre of solid ground beneath his feet instead of a narrow ledge above a three-metre drop to some treacherous seas.

'Danger,' Fran gritted at his handsome, dangerous face.

'It's not really dangerous, if you know what you're doing.'

'But I *don't* know what I'm doing!' she wailed with a shiver. Down on the beach it had been warm, the sun high in the sky, but up here the wind cut through her sweater and chilled her skin.

'I do, and that's all you have to worry about,' he said complacently. 'Now jump, sweetie, and I'll catch you.' He held his arms wide, bracing himself with one hip and knee against the rockface.

'What if I fall?'

'I won't let you fall.'

'What if you can't help it?' she persisted. 'You know your shoulder's still weak. What if your arm gives way?'

'It won't give way.' Some of his impatient humour died and she regretted reminding him of his weakness. It had been fear finding an outlet but, from his brooding expression, he thought she had done it deliberately. 'Are you going to jump? Because if you're not, you can damned well stay there.'

'You wouldn't leave me!' Fran exclaimed accusingly, looking behind her and remembering all the encouragement she had required to get *this* far.

'Wouldn't I?' he smiled grimly. 'A no-good layabout like me? If you fell, there'd be no one standing between me and the cabin, would there?'

'Oh, don't be ridiculous,' she snapped, fingers digging into rock as she looked nervously down. Neither of them had mentioned their dispute for days and he had to bring it up now!

'My, my, Princess, we have progressed. At one time

you intimated that I had murdered your grandfather for his property. Have you changed your mind?'

'I...I was angry, I didn't mean it,' she said sulkily, adding, with immense reluctance, 'I'm sorry. *Now* can we go back?'

'A handsome apology,' he said softly and her flush deepened.

'I *am* sorry...I...you make me so angry sometimes I forget myself...'

'Or, sometimes *remember*...mmm?' he said with unnerving accuracy. His voice became coaxing instead of challenging. 'I would never have brought you round this way if I really thought you couldn't do it, Fran.'

She wavered, knowing she was being silly, but unable to make the move. How did he know what she could or couldn't manage, when she wasn't sure herself? 'I'm going back,' she decided firmly.

'You can't. The tide will have covered all those convenient stepping-stones we hopped across on our way around the point. You have to come this way, you haven't got any choice.'

'You didn't tell me this was a one-way trip!' Fran screeched at him. 'How do we get back? Swim?'

'A little further round there's a reserve that comes right down to sea-level. It's a gentle stroll up the hill and across the fields to home from there.' He was unmoved by her spluttering fury. 'I didn't tell you because I knew you wouldn't come if there wasn't a comfortable option for you. Now, are you going to jump or do I go on without you?'

'You wouldn't dare!' The unwise words were out before she could stop them. There was an infinitesimal silence, then he smiled, a predatory-shark smile.

Fran stared furiously at the place where he had been.

She waited apprehensively for him to reappear around the corner after he had considered he had taught her a lesson. He did not return.

Apprehension turned to fear, then to anger. If she fell and broke her neck it would be entirely his fault! How dared he take risks with her life the way he did with his own?

Anger is a great motivator. When Fran jumped it was with a full head of boiling steam. Clutching frantically on to the rock face as her feet steadied on the ledge Fran felt a furious sense of triumph. When she looked back, she was chastened to discover that during her leap the chasm had shrunk…it wasn't *that* wide or high. Achievement had reduced what fear had magnified. Still, he had no right to make her do it!

She was even more annoyed when she edged around the corner and discovered that Ross wasn't smugly waiting there, just out of sight, ready to fly to her resuce if need be. He really had gone on! Breathing heavily, she struggled on around the rocky spur for what seemed like an age.

She came upon Ross eventually, sunning himself like a seal on a flat rock in a sandy inlet riddled with caves. He had stripped off his shirt and draped it over his face, his jean-clad legs stretched out so that the grubby sneakers hung over the edge of the rock, the soles lapped by the tide. At shore level the wind was no more than a gentle breeze, and Fran could feel the sweat trickling down the neck of her wool sweater.

'You pig!' she attacked his peaceful indifference. 'I could have fallen back there!'

A lazy hand lifted the shirt from his face, the muscles in his arms flexing under a light sheen of sweat as he propped himself up on an elbow, eyes slitted against the sun. 'I knew you wouldn't let yourself fall, Princess. You were too anxious to give me the sharp edge of your tongue to worry about mundane things like falling.'

'Well, you had more confidence in me than I did.' She suddenly felt weak and wobbly, and didn't know whether it was from delayed fright or the sight of that crisp pelt of red-brown hair catching the sunlight and playing it over his well developed chest. His jeans, as usual, rode low on the lean hips.

'I think that's your problem, Princess. Your self-confidence has gaping holes in it…it makes you prickly and defensive.'

'I don't need any of your rockside psychiatry, thank you, Dr Tarrant,' she said sarcastically, but he only chuckled indulgently.

'Admit it, Princess, you got a big thrill out of besting me and that damned crevasse.'

'I hate you, Ross Tarrant—' she began heatedly, wondering why, considering the lengths he had driven her to over the past week, she was still on speaking terms with him.

'No, you don't, you just hate it when I'm right,' he said with lazy perception, lying down again. 'Take off your sweater and get some sun. You could do with some extra Vitamin D, and you're far too pale.'

'Fear tends to do that to me,' she muttered blackly, but she did what he suggested, lying beside him on the rock after first making sure there was ample space between them. The hard warmth at her back, and the soft caress of sun on her exposed skin soon melted away her ill-temper. Perhaps she did need to be prodded out of her native caution once in a while…but not too far and not too often! As if he sensed her softening, Ross began to talk about some of the places he had travelled to during his apparently peripatetic life…places that Fran had only dreamed of seeing. He didn't satisfy her curiosity as to how he had afforded his travels, and she didn't ask.

'It sounds as if you've been just about everywhere,' she said wistfully, not opening her eyes. 'I've barely travelled around *this* country.'

'You have to take your chances when they come…or make your own. Nurses are always in demand overseas. Or why don't you use some of your inheritance and take a trip?'

'I already have plans for that.'

'Oh, what?' She heard his head turn, felt his gaze on her sun-warmed face, and took pleasure in denying the curiosity she heard in his voice.

'None of your business.' She smiled, the movement making jagged red patterns on the inside of her eyelids. To the man who had propped himself up beside her that secretive smile was an alluring challenge. He had a sudden desire to burrow inside that mysterious contentment of hers and lay her bare to his senses. To strip away the defensive barriers of her mind, as well as her clothes, and satisfy both curiosity and libido at the same time.

When there was no comeback to her provocative remark Fran opened her eyes. Ross's long, half-naked body was suffocatingly close, the expression on his face as unidentifiable as it was disturbing. She sat up, tucking her legs protectively against her chest and clasping her arms around her blue corduroy-covered knees.

'I suppose, on these great travels of yours, you pursued your usual obsession for danger. Did you conquer the world's natural wonders? Ski the Alps, swim the Rhine, climb the Eiger…?'

His face relaxed into teasing lines. 'Dave is the mountaineer of the family, not me…he's planning a Himalayas trip next year…and most of the Rhine is too polluted to swim, but I definitely skied. Nearly got caught in an avalanche once, as a matter of fact.'

'You would,' Fran grumbled. If he wasn't looking for danger it was obviously seeking him. 'What is so attractive about dangerous sports?'

'It's not the danger *per se*, although as you just discovered that does generate a certain exhilaration in the bloodstream. It's the challenge of testing oneself, of discovering just how far one can push one's limitations.'

'But…to risk life so *casually*—' She struggled to understand.

'I'm far from casual,' he said, sitting fully upright so that his hip brushed hers. She edged away from the scalding contact. 'I use all the necessary safety precautions and I never tackle impossible odds.'

'Is it your courage you're trying to prove? Your fearlessness?'

'I don't believe that courage *is* fearlessness,' he said, tilting his proud head to the sun. 'I think that courage is far more than just an absence of fear, or a reaction to danger. I think courage is *resisting* fear, acknowledging and mastering it instead of letting it master you.'

His philosophy was unsettling to Fran, who thought fears were far better tucked away out of sight and, if possible, forgotten altogether. The man himself was a challenge to everything she thought and felt. More than a challenge—a threat. He seemed to have the ability to persuade her to do things that she really didn't want to do, undermining her initial refusals with a mixture of logic and teasing that never failed to ignite her normally controlled temperament. In fact, she realised with horror as she trailed him back to the cabin, he had her seeking his approval, acting like a lovestruck child instead of a mature woman who needed no one's approval but her own!

Francesca looked about her with fresh eyes when they got back to the cabin at last, and she was aghast at the evidence of Ross's influence over her better nature. The clutter was verging on mess...and she had even allowed herself to fall into his habit of leaving the dinner dishes until the following morning, and even then to merely wash and leave them draining on the bench!

Alarmed at how quickly her natural discipline had been undermined, Francesca punished herself with an orgy of cleaning that, over the next twenty-four hours, sent Ross into spasms of mocking abuse which culminated, the next afternoon, in a trivial but fiercely escalating row that sent him storming out of the cabin, declaring her to be a neurotically obsessed personality with delusions of sainthood.

'Better than having delusions of godhead!' she flung after him, pleased at having pierced his easy-going skin. 'Only gods are invulnerable, Ross Tarrant, but you'd rather kill yourself than admit it!'

When the cabin was aggressively sparkling Fran stomped out of it herself, finding the pleasure in his absence was short-lived. She had thought of some magnificent put-downs to his insults and he wasn't there to hear them. He was always going on and on to her about accepting people the way they were and not imposing *her* expectations on them. What about him? Wasn't *he* trying to change *her*, imposing expectations of his own?

She glared at the sight of Ross in the dinghy, rowing vigorously across the bay. He could row to China for all she cared! She tried skipping a few stones, failing miserably. Another lesson of Ross's that hadn't taken.

When she looked up again Ross had stopped rowing

and was leaning back in the dinghy, letting it drift. He was several hundred metres off the beach now, slowly moving towards the point. The sun, which had promised another jewel-like day, had reneged and slid behind a flowering cloud which was turning the sea grey-green.

Ross began to row again but this time, instead of moving smoothly, the dinghy began to spin in circles. Fran frowned. What was he doing now? He was acting like a complete amateur. The drift seawards continued and her scathing thoughts disappeared in a puff of smoke as she suddenly realised that he wasn't kidding around. Something was wrong.

If he drifted out past the point into the channel, the current would take him God knew where…and he hadn't a hope of making it to the rocks unless he got control of the dinghy. His arm! Of course…typical Ross, so convinced of his physical prowess that it never occurred to him that his arm might not be up to rowing a heavy dinghy.

Fran tried to shout out, but the breeze which had sprung up took away her breath, the same breeze that was creating tiny white-caps on the choppy water. She felt an instant's panic as she wondered what to do. Should she run in and telephone for help? What if the weather suddenly changed for the worse in the meantime and Ross got swamped? What if he wasn't in trouble at all? He would be furious if she humiliated him by calling out the coastguard for nothing.

Her eyes measured the distance. Three hundred metres? Easily within reach. Without a second thought she stripped off her slacks and jumper, carefully placed her watch on top, and ran down into the water, not even flinching as the frigid waters closed around her, her eyes fixed on Ross, still going around in circles, still drifting. The fool! The blind idiot! She would tear him into strips!

It wasn't until she was half-way out that she began to feel the cold. She stopped, treading water for a moment, noticing with a leap of fear that the distance between them seemed to have widened rather than narrowed. What if she got cramp? Ross wouldn't be able to help her. What if he kept drifting, just out of reach?

She refused to go back. She gritted her teeth and put her head down and swam. She alternated strokes as she felt herself tire, trying not to think about cramps or sharks…it was too cold for sharks, wasn't it? So intent was she on not dwelling on the awful possibilities that she almost swam into the side of the dinghy, banging her hand painfully on the hull, only to have it grabbed even more painfully.

'What the *hell* do you think you were doing?' Ross yelled at her as he hauled her roughly into the bottom of the boat. Gasping for breath Fran stared up at the pale, thunderous face. 'What a bloody stupid thing to do! That water is like ice. Are you trying to extend your sick leave by getting another bout of pneumonia?'

Fran was shaking, but it was with combined shock and rage rather than cold. 'You were floating out to sea!' she yelled back at him as she sat up. 'Talk about being bloody stupid! What did you take the boat out for in the first place? You *know* your arm isn't up to sustained activity like rowing. I thought you never tackled impossible odds.' She snatched the oars and began to row furiously.

'I could have managed,' he said tightly, trying to take one oar. 'You didn't have to risk your fool neck—'

'Shut up, Ross Tarrant. Just sit there and shut up!' She spurned his effort to help furiously. She didn't feel the wind chilling her skin, she didn't feel the rivulets from her hair streaming down her shoulders, she wasn't aware of the wet transparency of her bra and panties. She was sustained by sheer temper.

The silence was a solid wall until they reached the beach and hauled the dinghy up on the sand above the high-water line. Ross's face was stiff and pale, his eyes shuttered as he watched her bundle up her clothes and start jerkily towards the cabin. Then she stopped and turned on him, unable to help herself.

'What is it with you, Ross? Was this another test to put yourself through? Do you have a death-wish or something? You weren't even wearing a *life-jacket*—'

'Why don't we continue this discussion *after* we've dried off?' Ross interrupted her tersely, plucking at his spray-damp shirt as he took in her huge eyes in a frozen face, the thick lashes meshed with salt. 'You need a shower, and a session in the spa to warm up.'

Suddenly feeling too exhausted to argue, Fran stumbled away. The shower felt like hot needles piercing her skin and yet not warming her. It was with a shudder of gratitude that she sank into the spa and felt its comforting heat seep into her aching bones.

Ross appeared on the deck wearing a towelling robe that skimmed the tops of his thighs. He was carrying a tray which he set down on the tiled edge of the pool.

'What's that?' She looked suspiciously at the bottle and two glasses.

'Brandy. For shock.'

'I'm not *in* shock.' A moment later she was, as he shrugged off his robe and stepped down into the water. Confronted with a naked Ross Tarrant, sculptured muscle from head to foot and supremely unself-conscious of his undeniable maleness, Fran's brain went into overdrive. She gaped, blushed, paled and closed her eyes. When a glass was thrust into her trembling hands she gulped it indiscriminately. It was like swallowing molten metal. Her eyes flew open and stung with tears, blurring the image of him sitting calmly across from her, waves lapping at the solid slope of his shoulders as he sipped his own brandy.

'You're suppose to sip it,' he told her gravely.

'Don't you tell me what to do! Don't you *ever* tell me what to do, not after—' She clenched her teeth and stared at him with fierce eyes. Defiantly she tossed back the rest of the brandy, trying to ignore the way it peeled the lining from her throat, and held up her glass. He poured and she drank that too, to make her point. Ross was no longer pale, but there was still tension around his mouth and a kind of quiet resignation in his eyes that made her feel very odd. Or was it the brandy?

'Why?' She whispered suddenly and he sighed as if he had been braced for the question and actually welcomed it.

'I'm sorry, Princess. I was in a temper and out to kick the world in the teeth. It was a very dumb thing to do and it put you in danger. Forgive me?' He was very, very quiet and Fran gulped, taking a grip on her anger. It was the only thing holding back the tears.

'Even a child would have had more sense.'

'I agree.'

'You could have floated out to sea and drowned.'

'I know.'

'And *I* would have felt responsible.'

'I'm sorry.'

'And will you stop being so humble?' she shouted at him. 'It doesn't suit you at all.' She slopped some more brandy into her glass, frowning when it brimmed over into the steamy water. Suddenly she wasn't angry any more, she was sad...so sad. Tears welled up and she didn't have the strength to stop them. She sniffed. 'I was so scared...'

She heard a vague clink as he put his glass down. 'Oh, Frankie, so was I...I knew that I wouldn't be much use to you if you got into trouble...I couldn't even help my-self...this damned arm!' His voice relaxed again as he took her glass away and cuddled her close to his side. 'Don't cry, darling, we're both safe...safe and warm again.' He nuzzled her mouth reassuringly, his broad arms scooping around her back so he could stroke her gently. Fran forgot her sadness as her breasts were crushed against the silky-wet hair of his chest. She wriggled closer, blissfully revelling in the movement of skin on skin, and he gave a wry half-groan against her cheek before his mouth found hers. The kiss was long and deep and slow, and it made Fran's brandy-muddled head rock. In fact, the whole world was rocking.

'I think I feel seasick,' she murmured languorously, not at all dismayed. 'Do you think I should have some more brandy?'

'Definitely not.' He closed her eyes with kisses and when she opened them again after another pleasant sea journey she found herself back in the cabin, swathed in towels, on a rug on the floor in front of the fire. Ross was beside her, back in his bathrobe, with her nightgown and robe slung over his arm.

'It's too early to go to bed,' Fran protested dreamily.

'You don't have to go to bed, but you're not going out again. The weather's closing in, so you may as well put these on.'

'I can't, I'm too weak,' she slurred smugly. Lead weights on her hands and feet prevented her from moving.

'Are you asking me to put them on for you?' His face held mingled amusement and wariness, confronted with a wide-eyed, kittenish woman who aroused his protective instincts as well as making him aware of baser ones. It was a Francesca at once strange and disarming.

Emboldened by brandy, she gave him a slow up-and-under smile that he couldn't fail to mistake.

'Sit up.'

She sat up obediently and watched with interest as he slowly unwrapped the towels. There was silence as they both looked down at her body. Ross drew a long, unsteady breath as he unfolded her nightgown.

'Do you think I'm pretty?' Fran demanded, offended at his lack of reaction.

'I think,' he said firmly, 'that you're drunk.'

'You don't think I'm pretty,' she mourned, blinking at him. 'I'm too thin, aren't I? First I was too fat and now I'm too thin.'

'I'm beside myself with lust,' he said drily, not entirely untruthfully. 'Arms up.'

She looked at him. How lovely he was! She wanted him to hold her again, to make her feel safe. He didn't usually make her feel safe, quite the opposite, but tonight he didn't seem threatening. He was soft and gentle and when he touched her he made her feel wanted, made the woman part of her fill with an aching longing.

'Francesca,' he said thickly, as he watched her eyes becoming heavy-lidded with unspoken desire, 'if you don't let me put this nightdress on you something is going to happen that we'll both regret tomorrow.'

'I won't regret it,' she said sulkily. How could she regret being loved? She put her hand out and touched him on the chest, sliding inside the damp towelling to find the powerful thud of his heart.

'You might not, but I would,' he murmured, his hand gently shackling her wrist as he removed her hand. 'I refuse to be seduced by brandy and shock.' He kissed her hand and smiled with wry self-derision. 'Perhaps if it was one or the other, but not both! Ask me again in the morning when you're in full possession of all your senses and I'll be delighted to respond.'

While she absorbed his rejection he wrestled her, with some difficulty, into her gown and robe, roughly tightening the belt as if it would provide more than a flimsy protection against their desires, should they get out of hand.

'A pity you weren't always so scr—scrup—' she hiccuped and abandoned the elusive word, '—didn't always have such scruples.'

'What do you mean?' He cupped her head with one hand while he rubbed her hair with a towel, then combed his fingers through the damp curls.

'You were quite happy to seduce an innocent—' the word tangled on her tongue, '—girl for a bet.'

His hands stilled in her hair, then slowly lowered to tilt her flushed face to his. 'You *knew* about that?'

His shock briefly penetrated her protective haze. Oops, she hadn't meant to tell him that. 'Knew about what?' she asked with what she thought was extreme cunning, unaware that her eyes were grey with guilty knowledge. Ross sighed and reached back for the half-empty brandy glass he had put on the coffee table. He held it to her lips, which she pressed together with a lop-sided frown.

'Are you trying to get me drunk?'

'You're already drunk, Princess. A little more isn't going to make much difference.' But it might loosen her unwary tongue.

It sounded supremely logical. 'I've never had a hangover before,' she confided proudly and wondered why his mouth tugged down at the corners in that funny, kind of sad way as she sipped. Tenderly he fed her the rest of the glass and between sips softly kissed and coaxed her into rambling honesty. He was behaving like an unprincipled bastard, but dammit, he *needed* to know.

When she told him, half-way between a giggle and a sob, that she had overheard the settling-up of his bet about their date that fateful Monday morning in the bike shed, he groaned and closed his eyes, tilting his lovely shaggy head back. 'Oh, God...'

When he looked at her again, nestled against his side, his eyes were deep blue with regret. 'I'm sorry, Fran, but if you heard everything, surely—'

'I didn't stay to hear *all* the gory details,' she interrupted him with a tipsy attempt at haughty dignity. She had rushed away and hidden in the girls' toilet, feeling ugly and soiled and utterly humiliated.

A few more sips and she let it all spill out...how she had been too shy to actively seek him out in the school grounds, but had hovered near the bike sheds where the boys gathered, hoping to 'accidentally' run into him and defy her grandparents' strictures by cementing the friendship that he had proposed on Saturday night.

'Did you get her blouse open? I'm not paying up on this bet until you give us the brand of her bra. I bet it was an armoured one, with a royal crest on it: Princess Pudge.' The snickering adolescent voice had hit Francesca like a blow.

'I guess you really earned your dough, huh, Ross? We should have offered you danger money on top of the bet...you could have been suffocated just *trying* to find first base, let alone touching it!'

Francesca hadn't waited for the raucous young laughter to die so that she could hear Ross besmirch the lovely memory of their hours together. Princess Pudge! The tender shoots of womanhood had shrivelled before the vision of him parading her loving vulnerability for his friends to paw over and laugh at. Later, when Ross had asked her to sit with him at lunch, she had lashed out at him with all her pain, grinding his pride into the dust as he had hers.

'Ah, Princess, if only I'd known,' Ross sighed, rocking her gently in his arms, finally solving the puzzle of how the shyly passionate girl who had touched his arrogant young heart had turned into the cool, disdainful princess his wounded ego demanded he dislike and avoid. 'No wonder you attacked me with those painful truths…you must have hated me…'

Fran twisted her head to peer up at him, wondering why he was suddenly receding like that, going furry around the edges. And he looked so serious, so regretful. She wanted to make him smile, make him feel all warm and deliciously woozy, the way she felt…

'Don' hate you, Ross…' Her tongue got tangled up as she tried to screw her eyes into focus, 'Only you…' Her words sank into a drowsy slur, '…was lies, 'nyway. No boys…' She smiled dreamily. 'Only you…'

'Francesca? What do you mean, lies? Francesca, wake up!' Ross looked in exasperation at the sleeping woman curled so trustingly in his arms. He didn't have the heart to wake her up; their unfinished business would have to be settled in the morning. His mouth curved wryly. In the morning she would be bolting for her high horse again, and he welcomed the notion of being there when she found the stable empty!

CHAPTER SIX

'FRANCESCA, wake up!'

Francesca surfaced reluctantly, a suffering husk of nauseous vibrations. She groaned as sunlight pierced her aching eyeballs. The act of lifting her head prompted an excruciating pain in her skull that screamed for relief. Her mouth tasted so vile that every time she swallowed her stomach tightened ominously. She groaned again, softly, as she became aware of someone perching on the edge of her bed, causing dangerous fluctuations in the mattress.

'Go 'way,' she slurred, wanting to be left alone in her misery.

'I've brought you some coffee, and this…' The monster of callousness waved a plate with a piece of thin, scarcely buttered toast on it, across her bleary vision.

'Oh, God—' She clapped a hand to her mouth.

Ross grinned an offensively healthy grin and put the coffee and plate down on the chair beside her bed. He hauled her protesting body up against her pillow and held her there with one large hand braced on her shoulder.

'Part of the problem is that you haven't eaten anything for nearly twenty-four hours—it's nearly eleven am, you know—and you're probably suffering a bit of dehydration as well. Come on, it's only weak, but it's liquid.'

He held up the coffee cup to her lips and tilted it so that she had to sip, or have it poured down the neck of her nightdress. It hit her stomach, warm and wet, but before she could moan again a piece of toast was inserted into her unwary mouth.

'Nibble.'

Fran chewed and swallowed cautiously. This time when Ross put the cup to her lips she removed it from his hand and drank. He watched approvingly, his blue eyes clear and sparkling with life, his skin smooth-shaven and glossy, his chestnut hair combed damply into unaccustomed style. Fran closed her eyes to shut out the vision of physical well-being, grateful and annoyed to find his simple remedy working. She felt marginally better.

'You got me drunk,' she accused.

'*You* got drunk, I only provided the bottle.'

Fran opened her eyes with a suddenness that hurt. 'I distinctly remember—' she began as aggressively as her condition would allow. Then she distinctly remembered…

'What?' Ross looked interested, his mouth a give-away straight line as he watched her face change from a sickly shade of green to a delicate rose.

'Nothing.' She buried her nose hurriedly in her cup.

'Nothing? You mean, you don't remember.'

She scowled. 'I remember what we *didn't* do.'

'Only because I was too much of a gentleman to take advantage of your kind offer,' he said smugly.

'*You*, a gentleman!' Her snicker hurt the back of her eyes and she rested her head momentarily on her shoulder, unaware that the hunching movement made her neckline dip alarmingly, enticingly.

'Darling,' came the purring answer, 'you batted your eyelashes at me, and draped and nestled and nudged like a little kitten wanting to be petted. And *I* said, ask me again in the morning. Are you going to follow through, Princess, and bless me with your royal favours?'

'Go to hell,' she snarled wretchedly, not wanting to dwell on her brandy-induced wantonness of the night before. He was taking shameless advantage of her hangover and if she weren't so weak she would make him regret it.

'I can't do that, I'm afraid, Frankie. Not until we've finished our little talk. You passed out on me last night just as things were getting interesting.'

Fran's stomach somersaulted. Her memory was fragmentary, but she had a sinking feeling she had really let it all hang out. 'Please, can't we leave it until later? I'm really feeling pretty rotten.' She nibbled forlornly on another triangle of toast, making her eyes as big and as shamelessly mournful as she could manage.

He grinned. 'No dice, Frankie.' He folded his arms across his chest, swivelling sideways on the bed so that he loomed over her shrinking figure. 'You were saying something about lying about the boys…about there being only me. Were you, by any chance, referring to those classy dates of yours that you compared me so unfavourably with?'

He waited patiently until she had finished all the toast and let her fiddle with her coffee cup for a long minute before he demonstrated his determination. 'Francesca,' he said silkily, 'shall I fetch the brandy?'

The very thought made her pale.

'You're not in the best physical condition at the moment and it wouldn't take much effort to hold you down while I pour the stuff down your throat,' he said with cruel relish. 'When you're drunk you're very suggestible, and it doesn't seem to take much to turn you on your ear. In fact, I think I like you tipsy, Princess, falling all over me, trying to pull off my clothes…'

'I didn't!'

He grinned at her, and took the cup from her nerveless fingers.

'Beast,' she protested half-heartedly as he bent to put the cup on the floor.

His grin faded. 'Frankie, it started out as a bet, but I really liked you…'

'Sure. Look, Ross, it was a long time ago, I don't see that it needs dragging up again. For God's sake, we were children!' she burst out. Humiliations, like fears, were best forgotten.

'*You* were a child. I was everything you accused me of being,' he astounded her by saying. 'An arrogant young punk without the guts to apologise for doing something that I knew was wrong.'

Was her hangover causing her brain to mistranslate what her ears were hearing? Francesca stared at his expression of wry self-derision, slightly open-mouthed, and highly suspicious of his motives.

Ross lent over and gently pushed her lower jaw closed. 'I'm telling you this because then we can wipe the slate clean of any old grievances that might be cluttering up our subconscious. If only you had thrown that bet in my face at the time, or if you had hung around the bike shed a bit longer: I paid up, Frankie.'

'You…?'

'I paid up.'

She believed him. Why did she believe him? Francesca was shaken by the tiny bud of delight in her breast. What on earth did it matter, after all this time? But it did, and she was acutely conscious of it as Ross continued his wry confession.

'I told the guys that I had lost the bet. That you'd come out with me, but that you'd refused to fool around. They gave me hell, but I thought it was worth it. I liked you.

Why do you think that no one taunted you about it? Because I'd threatened to punch the lights out of any guy who breathed a word outside the gang…they thought it was because I didn't want anyone to know how much I'd bombed out, but it was really because I didn't want it to get in the way of our friendship…not until I'd confessed to you, although I do admit there was a large chunk of ego involved, too.' He looked at her surprise-softened grey-blue eyes and his mouth pulled down. 'Then, when you gave me that haughty put-down in front of them all and I thought that you were just a clever tease who had gone slumming for a night, I wished like hell that I hadn't made the big sacrifice, but I couldn't recant without looking more of a fool than I already did. So I pretended that I didn't care.'

'I…you did a good job,' said Francesca shakily. When he had shrugged off her insults that day she had thought it merely confirmed his shallowness. In the intensity of her hurt she had never permitted him a point of view. As far as she was concerned, he hadn't deserved one.

'So did you,' he said with a pointed smile. 'On that date you were so serious to begin with, and so shy, and then you began to open up and I had flattered myself it was because of me. And when I touched you, you were so warm and soft and shyly generous that *I* was touched, macho jerk that I was. You came across as innocent and yet quietly mature, and so different from the general run of girls that I dated that I felt ashamed of what I had set out to do…see how far I could go with you just for the sake of impressing a bunch of guys. I realised that it was demeaning to both of us. I wanted to stand up to your grandfather for you, but you wouldn't let me and that made me feel even worse. And then, when Monday came around, I felt incredibly betrayed—hoist with my own petard. I couldn't stomach the thought that you were laughing up your sleeve at this crude jerk who had actually presumed that you'd want to get to know him better.'

'And I thought that you and your friends were all laughing behind my back at me,' said Fran ruefully, remembering the adolescent misery of that last term with an almost affectionate nostalgia.

'I never meant to hurt you, Frankie. I guess I got my just desserts.' He smoothed a curl back from her flushed cheek. 'I had some brutal thoughts about teaching you the dangers of putting on that act of sexy, eager innocence with guys with no claim to class. But it wasn't an act, was it, Frankie?'

'I—' She knew that his belated honesty begged honesty in return, but she was beginning to panic, wondering where all this was going to lead.

'There weren't any other boys, were there? Classier or otherwise. No sneaking out from boarding school?'

Francesca shrugged and picked at her nails to avoid his gaze, mumbling her reply into the neckline of her gown.

'What?' Ross ducked his head closer and she caught the spicy-clean male scent of him. It had almost the same effect as brandy. She jerked her head back against the pillows to try and preserve her ragged composure.

'I said no,' she muttered grudgingly.

'That was just wounded pride talking?'

'Yes.' She sighed. it was ridiculous to feel resentful after he had just delivered such a handsome apology.

'And you didn't really find me crude and clumsy, that was pride, too, mmm?' He was walking two fingers up her arm and Fran watched them approach the vulnerable scoop of her bare collarbone with bated breath.

'I…I suppose…'

'What do you suppose?' he asked, finding her warm, rapid pulse with one finger while the other stroked the fine soft skin of her throat. 'Did you mean it last night when you said there was only me? Was I the first boy to touch you? Was *I* the one who taught you how to french kiss?'

He watched the colour flow up under his fingers and his eyes deepened to a potent azure as he studied her blush. 'You're not still shy, are you, Frankie? I may have been the first, but I wasn't the last, was I?'

Her eyes flew open to deny him that arrogant satisfaction. 'Certainly not!' Though he wasn't going to force her to admit that he had been the yardstick beside which she had measured physical attraction ever since…and no one, not even the man she had eventually gone to bed with, had aroused her as strongly and easily as Ross did…*had*! 'You didn't blight my life, you know, Ross. I haven't been a languishing case of arrested virginity—'

'Waiting for Prince Charming to come along and re-awaken you,' he finished when she paused to wonder where that sentence was taking her.

'Precisely,' she said, brushing his unsettling touch away and adjusting the bedclothes primly across her breasts. 'I'm a normal, mature woman, quite comfortable with my…my…'

'Sexuality?' he supplied helpfully.

'Yes.' She glared at him and he laughed.

'Good. Then you're not going to get all uptight when I tell you that last night we slept together.'

'What?' Her shriek only made him laugh harder. Her blush deepened as she suddenly noticed the extra pillow that lay on the floor beside the bed. A vague remembrance stirred in the back of her mind, of a delicious warmth that she had clung to. Oh, God, had she actually let him...?

'When I tried to tuck you in you wouldn't let me. You kept saying that I was rocking the boat. You wouldn't quieten down until I got in beside you and anchored you in my arms.'

Francesca groaned and closed her eyes. 'We slept together?' Why couldn't she remember the details? She didn't imagine that making love with Ross Tarrant would be a forgettable experience. Perhaps he had been so fantastic that her mind was in a state of shock. Yes, that was far more likely!

'"Slept" being the operative word,' he said with a humorous gravity that jerked her eyes open. 'We were both too tired to do anything else. Besides—' his mouth indented wryly, '—the bed is a bit narrow to do much else...I like a bit of space when I exercise my desires, and my women willing, if not actually conscious...'

Fran opened her mouth to make a stinging reply, but closed it again when she realised that she had nothing to reproach him with. Whatever his motives, he *had* looked after her yesterday, in spite of their earlier row, and he hadn't taken advantage of her with anything other than words. *Worse luck*, whispered a voice from her heart which she drowned out by asking, 'How are you? Is your shoulder all right?'

He moved it experimentally. 'A little stiff. But stop trying to change the subject. I think your behaviour last night acknowledges an important truth, don't you?'

'Oh?' She looked at him warily. Was he going to accuse her of being a frustrated spinster...or a wanton?

'That it's still there.'

'W-what is?' she asked huskily, transfixed by the sapphire eyes.

'Whatever chemistry that was at work between us when we were too young to appreciate its potent rarity.'

'I…I don't know what you're talking about,' she denied hollowly.

'Frankie…' He shook his head in amused reproof, reading the feminine panic in the flickering grey eyes as an invitation to seduction. 'I considered myself pretty blasé at seventeen. I thought I knew it all…particularly where girls were concerned. You taught me differently. You taught me that sex is the greatest and most unknowable mystery of all…that it has as much to do with the mind as with the body. You can't force an attraction to someone, it's either there or it's not, and the chemistry is in the brain rather than the loins. You may see no rhyme nor reason for it, but it's there…as it is for us, as it was then, and now…'

And ever shall be the little voice echoed the prayer, *for ever and ever.*

'No…' She feebly denied the inevitable even as she lay there, watching his mouth approach, wanting yet afraid…

'Yes…' His teeth sank softly into her vulnerable lower lip, his certainty absorbed into the pores of her skin as he lowered himself on to the bed, pushing her back into the pillow, so that she accepted the weight of his chest against her tingling breasts, the fresh, clean scent of him in her nostrils, the taste of him in her mouth.

The intimate curl of his tongue inside her mouth set off a chain reaction in her body which recoiled even as it delighted in a trapped feeling of pleasure. *You can't escape*, she thought eagerly, *so you may as well enjoy it.*

As a hangover remedy it was without equal. The touch and taste of him sweetened every sense and sent a burst of adrenalin through her veins. It was like leaping that crevasse, all fear and a crazy sense of triumph at the challenge of the unkown…for, to Fran, this heated sexual urgency *was* largely unknown. It had been building inside since she had first seen Ross staring at her nakedness in the spa pool, a brooding, masculine threat…since long before that, since he had planted that dormant seed in a young girl's body, now germinating into the full flower of passion.

The kisses flowed like heady wine from mouth to mouth, and they were both breathing hard when he finally lifted his head and they stared at each other in crackling silence. He noticed with satisfaction the stormy glaze of the grey-blue eyes, the flush of arousal mantling the creamy skin of her face and throat, the provocative part of her slightly swollen mouth, while she was conscious of the full heaviness of his body as he lay on top of her, the hard, masculine pressure points imprinted on her as if he were the erotic template and she the silky bolt of cloth to be cut to fit his shape.

He kissed her again, a long, slow, thorough kiss, and then murmured against the corner of her mouth, 'If you're thinking what I'm thinking, Princess, I'm afraid we'll have to postpone. I don't think I could look my mother in the eye if she asked why we were late for lunch.'

Fran gasped. It was Sunday! She had forgotten about Jason's invitation.

'I wasn't thinking—'

He cut her off with another quick kiss. 'Yes, you were, and this time you can't blame the brandy.' He rolled off her and stood up beside the bed, looking down at her flushed confusion. 'Some time soon we're going to be lovers, Francesca, and finish what we started thirteen years ago…'

She gazed at his retreating back with a mixture of fascination and stunned anger. He made it sound so simple, like predestination. But Fran wasn't about to be seduced by fate. She tried to shake off the odd, empty ache in her body as she armoured herself in a carefully demure skirt and blouse. So what if there was a strong physical attraction between them? They weren't animals, they didn't *have* to give in to it just because it was there.

To her chagrin Ross chuckled when he saw her clothes.

'Who do you think that's going to fool, Princess? I know what sinful passions lurk beneath that starchy breast.'

'If you don't behave, I'm not coming,' she told him haughtily.

'Scout's honour.' He held up a hand, a pious look on the handsome face.

'You were never a Scout, Ross Tarrant,' she accused.

'Gigolo's honour, then.' He grinned at her disapproval.

'I don't believe that, either,' she sniffed as she marched out of the cabin.

'Took you long enough,' he said lazily as he handed her into the pick-up. 'Would you like to know what I really do for a living?'

'No.'

'Sure?' he teased knowingly, reading the frustrated curiosity in her stubborn profile. Now when she put on her prim and proper act it amused rather than annoyed him, because he knew it was only an act, that underneath she was feeling vulnerable.

'I'm not in the least interested,' she lied loftily, planning to dig the information out of his family over lunch, but casually, so he wouldn't realise what she was doing.

'Still, I think you ought to be prepared—'

'Are you going to start this thing, or do you want me to drive?'

'But, Fran—' He was laughing at her again, over some secret joke, and she had no intention of playing the straight woman to his punchline.

'Oh, go row a boat!' she snapped childishly.

'Shrew.' He clicked his tongue in tender exasperation as he started the car. 'OK, but it's your funeral, Princess. Don't get mad at me later.'

'Of course I won't.' Managing to imply that he wasn't worth getting upset over.

His hum filled the silence between them as the car wound along the inland road. Fran looked out the window to hide her smile. She didn't want to admit it to the smug man beside her, but she enjoyed bickering with him. She had never allowed herself the luxury of arguing with a man before, flexing her will against his; she had always been too shy, too uncertain of herself as a woman. If she hadn't liked or agreed with what a man said, she had simply withdrawn and naturally, she realised with hindsight, that had set limits on every relationship she had entered. Not even Brian had known what she really thought or felt, so she couldn't really blame him for his furious reaction when the cumulation of years of frustration had exploded on his head.

With Ross it was different. From the very first his boldness had made her bold. Because he had expected the worst from her, and she from him, she had felt free to let her feelings rip. And the unspoken physical attraction that had run concurrent with the surface animosity had spiced her reactions with a delicious exhilaration. But what would happen now, now that the unspoken was voiced? Where did they go from here? Where did she *want* to go?

Lunch with the Tarrants proved to be a small series of revelations, capped off by an enormously shattering one.

First surprise was the warmth with which Florence Tarrant welcomed Fran into the big, sunny kitchen of the large, rambling old house. After scolding her son for his tardiness in not bringing Francesca along before, she simply opened her arms and hugged the young woman as if she was a long-lost relative.

'You're looking as if a puff of wind would blow you away. I hope Ross is looking after you. I'm so sorry about Ian, my dear. It must make you feel very alone now.'

Fran felt a prickle of unexpected tears at the back of her throat and swallowed hastily. The casually affectionate embrace touched a deep chord within her. Such gestures had been few and far between in her past. Physical affection from her grandparents had been rationed so that she wouldn't be 'spoiled', and she had no memories of her own mother, who had rejoined her roving lover when Fran was only four months old and been killed with him in a car accident two years later.

'It does a bit,' she admitted to the slim, dark-haired older woman, surprised at the impulse to confide to an almost total stranger. 'Which is a bit hypocritical, I suppose, since we saw each other so little, and didn't get on very well when we did get together.'

'Not silly at all.' Florence Tarrant smiled in warm understanding. 'We all tend to take certain basics in our life for granted, like family ties, until suddenly they're not there any more.' The soft brown eyes began to twinkle as she looked from Fran to her son. 'You'll just have to create some blood ties of your very own to take for granted.'

It took Fran a moment to realise what she meant. When

she did she blushed to the roots of her hair and sent Ross a speaking look when he laughed at her stammering attempts to explain that there was nothing between them.

'If you say so, my dear,' Florence Tarrant said, with a placid smile that was both sympathetic and disbelieving.

'I told you she was trying to marry me off,' Ross whispered in her ear as they went into the large, wood-panelled dining-room.

'I can understand her desperation!' Fran shot back. 'Ageing playboys must have a pretty limited value on the glutted marriage market.'

Ross got his revenge for that remark when they were seated and Fran had been introduced to a bewildering array of people: Beth, a sweetly feminine version of Ross with long, straight dark hair and flashing blue eyes, and her morose-looking boyfriend, John, who seemed glumly aware he wasn't going to hold this young butterfly's attention for long; Ross's youngest brother, David, who worked with Jason in the family business and, except for his husky size, took after his mother with his dark hair and eyes, and the three, leather-jacketed and vaguely menacing members of his band, Mo, Bean and Adam; the patriarch, Mike Tarrant, as broad-shouldered as his three sons and looking amazingly fit for a man in his mid-sixties, his blue eyes alert and his gruff voice offset by the same world-embracing friendliness that his wife possessed. Jason and Tessa, to Francesca's left on the long, polished wood table, were welcome, familiar faces, but she wasn't given a chance to say more than hello before Ross made his dramatic announcement.

'Sorry we were late, folks, but you can thank Francesca that I'm sitting here at all. She saved my life yesterday.'

'Saved your life? Wow!' Beth's lovely eyes widened with awe. 'What happened?'

Stricken with embarrassment at being the centre of attention, Fran could only stare daggers at Ross, lounging cheerfully at her right elbow. She had thought he would have kept silent about his ignominious expedition, but it seemed that he was happy to court his family's disfavour for the sake of embarrassing her.

Grinning back at her, he launched into a colourful, graphic description of the previous day's rescue, drawing a clamour of admiration for the blushing heroine.

'He wasn't really in any danger—' she tried to say, but her attempted modesty was brushed aside as Ross came in for his share of derision.

'I would have tipped him out of the thing and made *him* swim back, 'David crowed cockily over his brother's ignominy. Two years younger than Jason, he obviously grabbed every opportunity he could to repay years of teasing by his two impressive elder brothers.

'I wouldn't have blamed you, Francesca, if you'd left him to the coastguard,' his mother said with amazing placidity. 'They would have given him a good talking to. I hope you have no ill effects from your heroics, my dear.'

'Only a hangover,' put in Ross wickedly, but this time Fran refused to blush. He had actually done her a favour, in an embarrassing way. He had ensured her instant acceptance by his family. Or is that what he had intended? She looked at him uncertainly, and he winked.

'He plied me with brandy afterwards,' she said, deciding to twist his mockery to her own advantage. 'So I guess the hangover is his fault too!' She shrugged with an air of injured innocence.

'Ross!' His mother's reproach was all that she could have wished for.

'Medicinal purposes only, Mum,' said Ross defensively. 'She was in shock. I think she realised what an unnecessary risk she had taken.'

'Unnecessary risk? *I* took?' Encouraged by the empathetic vibrations from around the table, Fran took umbrage. '*You're* the dumb ox who thinks that risks are only there to be taken. *You're* the one who rowed off in a childish huff just because I wouldn't lie down and let you wipe your arrogant feet all over me! *You're* the one who started the whole argument by trying to get rid of me by domestic violence.'

'He hits you?' sqawked Beth, looking at her brother with new eyes, and to Fran's surprise and amusement Ross actually blushed.

'Of course I don't hit her,' he growled. 'That's not to say she couldn't do with a damned good spanking on occasion.'

'Ross!' Florence Tarrant metaphorically rapped his knuckles.

'That's a pretty sexist remark to make. I'm surprised at you, Ross,' Tessa put in her quiet voice. Her face was serious, but when she flicked a glance at Francesca her eyes were filled with the same amusement reflected in her fiancé's. Francesca grinned back.

'I didn't mean physical violence,' she explained sweetly. 'I meant his horrific lack of willingness to lift a finger around the house. He's as domesticated as a wild boar.

'But I taught all my sons domestic chores,' Mrs Tarrant protested, 'Ross, what have you been doing to poor Francesca?'

'What indeed?' murmured Ross, humour twitching at

his mouth again as he met Francesca's demure gaze.
'Stirrer,' he muttered, for her ears only.

'I must admit that he does more than his share of the
cooking, though,' she said quickly, conscious of the
threat of the long, hard thigh suddenly pressed against
hers. She shifted her legs. He followed, tangling his feet
with hers. Above the table their eyes duelled. 'He's a
great cook, but he's useless anywhere else but the
kitchen.'

'Oh, really?' Jason gave a shout of laughter. 'Poor
Ross. Bedside manner slipping, is it, doctor?'

'Now, Jason,' his mother admonished him mildly.

'Sorry, Francesca,' Jason's apology was unabashed.
'It's just that you must be the first nurse Ross has ever
met who hasn't instantly succumbed to the great healer's
charm. Told you it was just the white coat, Ross.'

Fran's slightly bewildered smile froze on her lips. She
felt Ross's hand come down warningly on her knee.

'You should have let me explain when I wanted to,
Princess,' he breathed in a singsong manner out of the
corner of his mouth.

Her puzzlement, however, was misinterpreted by
everyone else. 'I can see by your blank expression that
you haven't worked at National Women's Hospital, Francesca,' Beth giggled. 'After the Dream Consultant has
made his rounds there they have to sweep 'em up from
the hallways…swooning nurses and patients alike!'

Consultant? Doctor? Ross was a *doctor*?

Fran's head swivelled stiffly to her right. The deep
azure eyes were filled with rueful apology, and an unholy
amusement that was almost her undoing.

He was a doctor! Ross…that lazy, teenage intellectual
sloven, had trained to be a *doctor*! When? How? She
went icy with embarrassment when she recalled some of

the things she had said to him, and then sizzled hot with fury. How he must have enjoyed watching her make an arrant fool of herself! The only redeeming feature of his wretched joke was that he didn't appear to have told anyone else of her misconception...the misconception he had deliberately fostered!

CHAPTER SEVEN

'FRANCESCA?' She came out of her fierce trance to meet Mrs Tarrant's concern. 'Are you all right? You've gone quite pale. Ross, perhaps you should have kept her in bed.'

'I tried, believe me, Mum, I tried.' Ross's smirk sent the colour flooding back into Francesca's face. She placed her hand on his under the table and dug in her nails. He jerked back in his seat with a strangled cough. Nursing his branded hand in his lap, he had the gall to send Fran a reproachful look. 'I...er...think she's recovered now. Perhaps it was a momentary swoon...'

'It takes more than just a pretty face to set Auckland Hospital nurses swooning.' Francesca gave him a sweet, murderous smile.

'No, it takes a good slug or two of brandy to do that,' Ross agreed, equally sweetly.

Francesca wanted to sink through the floor. Even the ravenous, leather-jacketed trio at the other end of the table stopped eating their way through third helpings in order to follow the intriguing conversation.

'Now, Frankie, you said you wouldn't get mad,' Ross teased, his eyes glinting with provocative triumph, knowing that she could say little without revealing what a gullible idiot she had been. Why hadn't she suspected? The way he'd talked about his injuries, the intelligent questions he had asked when she'd talked about her work—they should have given her clues. But she had been blinded by other things, not the least of which had been the instant, unwelcome attraction she had felt for him.

He was enjoying this, damn him, and she could tell from his disgustingly smug expression that he thought that just because he had now proved how utterly respectable he was that everything would go his way...that she would fall gratefully into his manly arms!

She managed a creditable laugh. 'I'm not mad. I was just thinking that whatever we do we seem to end up diametrically opposed.' She dazzled Ross with a brilliant smile that made the amused blue eyes narrow with suspicion. Brace yourself, *Doctor*, Fran thought with grim satisfaction, one good bombshell deserves another! 'Here you are, local boy made good...a doctor, no less, and here *I* am, always the goody-two-shoes at school, going sadly to the dogs, according to my friends.'

She savoured the laughing protests and enquiries, not taking her eyes off the still and silent Ross, seeing his suspicion harden into scepticism. He thought she was just coat-trailing.

'But you're a nurse. That's as good as a doctor in my book!' Beth was saying. 'Ross says that nurses are the backbone of the Health Service.'

'They are. But I'm not a nurse any more.'

Ross didn't change colour and not a muscle moved in his face, but the sheer blue shock of his eyes was worth the price of baring her life to a bunch of virtual strangers. Francesca raised her eyebrows mockingly.

'Shall I loosen your collar, Doctor? Some hot, sweet tea, perhaps?' A brief storm darkened the blue eyes and she grinned delightedly, a wicked mischief dancing across her wide mouth. And he thought that *he* had the monopoly on provocation!

'My dear.' Florence Tarrant tugged her attention away

from her helpless victim so that Francesca didn't see the storm clear as swiftly as it had come, to be replaced by a sultry gleam of admiration, and a determination which would have disturbed her greatly had she seen it. 'Surely you haven't had to give up your career permanently because of your illness? After all your training!'

'Oh, no,' Francesca told her hostess, touched by her evident sympathy, and guilty because she didn't really deserve it. 'I resigned just before I came up here, but I never actually intended nursing to be a life-long vocation when I started out. It was as much a way to escape home as a desire to help people.' Florence Tarrant smiled understandingly, without a hint of the disapproval that Fran had faced from others about 'wasting her training', and she was encouraged to expand. 'I've enjoyed myself, and learned a lot but…well…now I have a chance to do what I always wanted. I'm going into business with a friend.'

'Really? What kind of business?'

'Gardening.' Fran flushed slightly at the soft, incredulous sound from the man beside her. She kept her gaze firmly fixed on Florence Tarrant's surprised interest. 'My grandmother said it wasn't any kind of job for a well brought-up young lady, and I wasn't very assertive back in those days so I chose second-best. But I've kept up gardening as a hobby and taken several extensive courses on horticulture. Since I've become a qualified nurseryman—'

'Nursery*person*,' corrected Tessa with a grin which Fran returned in brief.

'—my friend Christina—who runs a plant shop—and I have been making plans to expand her shop into a garden centre as a base for a contract-gardening business. We were having trouble with our bank loan and probably would have had to postpone for another few years until…well…when Grandfather died I realised that our problems were solved.'

'One door closing, another opening.' Mrs Tarrant eased Francesca's fear that they would think her mercenary. 'I wish you the best of luck, Francesca, it'll be a great adventure. I'm a keen gardener, too, but I'm not terribly knowledgeable. Perhaps you'd like to give me some advice…I've got some stubborn spots where nothing seems to grow…'

· Ross settled back in his chair, turning his powerful body in Fran's direction as she ignited to his mother's interest.

So…Francesca wasn't going to invest her unexpected windfall in blue-chip stock or a nice, safe, retirement fund. She was going to risk it on the roll of a die! For, in the current economic climate, anyone starting up a small business, even one with solid financial backing, was taking a gamble.

How she had enjoyed throwing it in his face. Ross looked down at the fast-fading indentations in the back of his hand and smiled inwardly. At least her tit-for-tat revelation had defused her anger at his own. She could hardly start throwing stones in his direction now. He lifted his eyes to her animated profile, amused by her determination to ignore him, but content to study her at leisure as she chatted with his mother. Some of that bright confidence was bravado, he realised…typically Fran. She was such a mixture of fierce independence and sweet vulnerability, bravery and cowardice, that it wasn't surprising that she had confused him at times. In all probability she confused herself even more. She would never admit it, of course, but Fran was starved for praise, for approval…for love…it showed in the way that she flowered shyly under the slightest sign of interest, and the startled pleasure she took in the easy acceptance of his family. And yet a veneer of protective caution prevented her from reaching out, from trusting that she wouldn't be rebuffed. It was typical that even in making this quantum leap into an unknown future she was still following some immutable plan, her eyes fixed firmly on her goal, allowing for no deviation from her set course.

Ross intended to show her some interesting detours, only slightly concerned that he had no particular destination in mind, only a series of intriguing signposts to follow. He wasn't sure when she had stopped being merely an intellectual and sexual challenge—and he was never one to resist *that*! If the compulsion to have her had been merely physical he could have done so by now, he had that much confidence in the mutuality of the attraction, but the complex shadings of her deceptive personality had added a completely unpredictable element to his desire.

Francesca, becoming increasingly uncomfortable at the silent, heavy-lidded stare she could feel from the man next to her, was grateful for Mrs Tarrant's suggestion of a tour of her gardens. But she couldn't escape Ross for long. He came out to tell his mother that she was wanted on the telephone, then stood, barring Francesca's way through a vine-covered arch between the barn and double garage.

'Are we quits, Frankie?' he asked softly, tilting his head to one side so that the sun gilded his hair and the smooth, hard line of his jaw.

Fran stiffened her shoulders. 'I suppose you thought it great fun to pretend to be some out-of-work hobo. You must have really laughed when I worried about your health!'

'Actually, it annoyed the hell out of me,' he said

wryly. 'I'm afraid I was too busy trying to strut my macho stuff to thank you at the time. Thanks for caring, Fran.'

'I didn't care,' she denied with a sniff. 'I would have been the same whoever you were. It was nothing personal.'

'Does your impersonal concern always lead to your seducing your patients?' he enquired with interest, and to her fury she blushed.

'You…you…you…' She sought for an adequate description.

'*Doctor!*' spat out Ross in such tones of loathing that Fran felt a traitorous frisson of laughter shiver up her spine. 'Somehow it doesn't sound as insulting as gigolo, does it?' he asked coaxingly.

'Ross—' Her voice trembled on the edge of a laugh. How dared he make her laugh when she wanted to be furious with him!

'Ah, Fran, stop trying to pretend that you're a prig. I think we've disproved that one entirely, haven't we? No woman with such passionate responses as yours could be a prig. I think your affinity with plants and nature is your basic earthiness seeking an outlet…'

Passionate? Earthy? Fran stared at him blankly. Neither she nor anyone else thought of her in those terms. Practical, disciplined, *com*passionate, yes…except in Ross's presence—then all those neatly dove-tailing pieces of her personality tended to break apart and float dizzily away. Each time she had more and more difficulty fitting them back together again. While she pondered the disquieting mental image, Ross moved closer until she became aware of the sun reflecting off his soft white linen shirt, warming the skin of her face. His blue eyes, like twin seas, beckoned her into deep waters.

'Let's face it, Frankie,' he said softly. 'It was you, not me, who was so anxious to preserve your misconceptions...I just went along for the ride. I'll admit that, at first, I thought you deserved the come-uppance, but that was before I realised *why* it was so important for you to think that I was an uncouth, muscle-bound, immoral reptile. It was both a defence and a weapon. You were afraid of your feelings for me. You were attracted to me, but you didn't want to commit yourself to that attraction. You felt safe wrapped in your moral outrage, because it meant that you could experience the vicarious sexual thrill of being with me without risking the emotional involvement that intimacy inevitably brings. In short, Princess, you were running scared.'

'Why, you conceited moron!' Fran was appalled at the accuracy of his guess. For the first time she wondered what kind of doctor he was. Was he, God forbid, a psychiatrist? Used to probing for motives and meanings? 'Is that a pompous way of accusing me of being a tease?'

She was horrified the moment the words popped out. She hadn't meant to say that. Hurriedly, she tried to recover. 'I mean, do you assume that every woman you meet is wildly attracted to you? That's one way of turning a rejection into an ego booster, I suppose.'

He ignored her jeer, choosing to answer the involuntary cry that she had revealingly blurted out. 'A tease is a woman who deliberately arouses a man just for the pleasure of slapping him down.' He moved suddenly and Fran flinched, but he was only stretching out his arms to lace his fingers through the woven wire of the archway in an attitude of unthreatening openness. Fran's restless desire to escape this disturbing discussion evaporated. As long as he didn't touch her she could handle the situation. Of course, there were other ways of touching. Having

Ross's tapering masculinity spreadeagled in front of her was like a caress to the senses. It presented a tempting illusion that Ross was offering himself to her, making himself vulnerable, the male as victim.

'I think that for the most part you don't realise what the hell you're doing, it's just pure instinct. But, Fran, sometimes you make me ache...'

'Then why didn't you—?' She bit her lip, but it was too late, the question was asked.

'Last night?' He understood her so well, too well... 'Because that's not the way I want it. I don't want to just relieve an ache in my groin, Frankie. I think that's what makes you so scared, mmm?'

She looked away from the warm blue invitation. 'I think *you're* the tease, Ross Tarrant...' she said shakily.

'I would never slap you down, honey, don't ever be afraid of that. Ever since I was seventeen I've had intermittent dreams about you, sometimes so vivid that it was as if I was actually touching and tasting you, the sweet, wild scent of you perfuming my lonely sheets...'

'Lonely!' Fran had to stop that erotic imagery. 'I doubt your bed is ever empty, let alone lonely. You know too much about women for your own good.'

He laughed. 'That's your fault, Princess.'

'Mine?'

'I have you to thank for what I am today.' His laughter faded into a wry seriousness at her puzzlement. 'What you said to that arrogant young punk took, Frankie. Initially it was my pride that drove me to try and prove you wrong about me, to take the hardest option there was. I didn't have bursary, but I went to university the next year. I was going for Bachelor of Science, but I did so well the first year that I switched to Medicine. It *wasn't* easy. As you so succinctly told me, I'd been lazy; I had to learn to discipline myself all over again—' he grinned at the memory. 'I didn't even have time to play sport. And then, when it came to specialising, I again used you for inspiration.'

'Oh?' Fran could tell by the glint in his eye that she needed to brace herself.

'Mmm…my natural talent, remember? My skill with women? I didn't lie to you about that, Frankie, they do pay to come and see me. I'm in great demand…as an obstetrician. Do you know, darling, that you look like a fish?'

Fran snapped her mouth shut. Suddenly it all made sense…the wicked way he had misled her by telling her *almost* the truth. She closed her eyes against that teasing grin. 'You…*wretch*!' Against her will she was laughing, and he was watching with a peculiar smile of satisfaction.

'I must say I was slightly miffed that you hadn't known, perhaps that's why I let you wander so far up the garden path,' he admitted when her laughter faded to adorable giggles that made her look like that shy teenager again. 'I had flattered myself that I was fairly well known in the medical fraternity…I'm in private practice, but I'm a consultant at National Women's, too.'

'Well, hospitals do tend to be rather insular,' Fran offered with a trace of apology. 'We get absorbed in our own little microcosm of wards and shifts, and I haven't been on an obstetric ward for years. I…can't believe it…' She stared at him and he could see from her face that she was threatening to go off into giggles again.

'Don't apologise, Fran,' he said drily. 'You don't want to break your record of consistently deflating my ego…although, thank God, there's one area in which you never fail to respond but flatteringly.'

The giggle froze in her throat, as he had meant it to.

They stared at each other. Vine shadows laced the handsome face, sending ripples of darkness across the unruffled blue calm of his eyes. He hadn't moved, arms still outstretched, only the white tension-lines where his fingers gripped the wire revealing the control he was exercising. It would have been easy to take her into his arms and convince her that what he wanted she wanted also…but with Fran the easy option wasn't an option at all. Her submission had to be voluntary or it was valueless to both of them. The tightly wrapped petals protecting the feminine core of her personality couldn't be forced open…they would respond only to warmth and light and the promise of life-giving nourishment. Surely the Fran that he had learned about this afternoon could be coaxed to take the inevitable gamble that was involved in any human relationship…

'Why didn't you tell me what you wanted to do with the money, Fran?' He chose to take the oblique route.

The soft lilt in his voice as much as the abrupt change of subject disconcerted her. 'I…it was none of your business,' she said huskily.

'And now it is?' He deftly manipulated her answer. 'Have you decided that you don't need excuses any more?'

'Excuses?'

'To stay. You can't still believe that I'm after your inheritance any more…I never put in a formal claim anyway. So if you stay now, it's for one reason. You want to.'

Predictably, when cornered, Francesca panicked, looking for the exits. 'You think, just because I know you're a doctor and not some…layabout—'

'Oh, no, we've already dealt with that one, Princess,' he told her with quiet, inexorable reason. 'The attraction we share has nothing to do with what we *are*. Your status or mine has nothing to do with it. And don't make the mistake of thinking that just because I'm a professional that I'm suddenly invested with emotional respectability. Part of me will always be a hell-raiser, always open to a challenge…I've learned to reconcile the conflictions of my character…I think you're just starting to. You can be a woman *and* run a business, Francesca. They aren't mutually exclusive.'

'I don't know yet that I can run a business.' Under stress she admitted something that previously she would never have dreamed of admitting. 'I…I'll need all my time and energy to find out. I'm so close now, I can't afford—'

'Other commitments? Spending a few more days with me isn't a commitment, Fran. Hell, I have enough responsibilities in my own professional life to ensure that I evade them as much as I can in my private life.'

A more straightforward proposal of dishonourable intentions Fran couldn't imagine and she felt strangely reassured. In effect it was a promise to let her dictate the terms of their relationship which, combined with the powerful feeling of inevitability which he had engendered this morning, proved unbearably tempting. But there were cross-currents between them that tugged dangerously at her senses. What if she stayed and, God forbid, fell in love with him? Every cautious bone in her body went brittle at the idea of trusting her happiness to someone else.

'I…should go back to Auckland.' She was disgusted to hear her tongue change *must* into *should*.

'Why?' He was leaning so close, hanging from tense fingers, that she could feel his breath fluttering on her lashes. 'You told us at lunch that your partner is doing all the paperwork, and that you've had the plans drawn up for weeks. In another few days Simpson will have squared Ian's estate, unchallenged, and you can leave with a full statement of your assets to show your bank manager. Stay until then, Princess…'

At what point had the snide insult become an endearment? Fran wondered as she put a hand flat on his chest to stop herself falling forward into the blue void of his eyes. His chest rose quick and hard against her hand, her fingers sliding through the patch of hair revealed by the opened neck of his shirt.

'I…I can't…' absently, concentrating on the vibrations under her fingertips.

'You can…' The words formed against her lips, his tongue stroking its velvety roughness against their parted warmth, then plunging inside with a suddenness that made her head reel. The muscles of his arms bulged as his hands clenched convulsively against the wire at the inward sway of her body against the open trap of his. The slender, capable hand on his chest slid up around the rigid column of his neck, pulling him down to her, her other hand curving around his hard waist, fingers reaching down to splay against the muscular jut of his buttocks. Ross gave a soft groan in her mouth and arched hungrily into her softness, the powerful thighs supporting the potent thrust of his hips. Fran responded just as hungrily, realising dimly that his refusal to put his arms around her was a deliberate enticement, a sexual challenge that was impossible to resist.

She pushed a thigh between his, and he caught and held it against the centre of his body, letting her feel the rigid proof of his arousal. Yet still he didn't put his arms around her. With a hot surge of mingled power and frustration Fran pushed her rounded breasts against his chest, crushing the taut peaks with a shudder of masochistic pleasure, her mouth widening beneath the silken search of his tongue. Both hands were now clinging to his waist, sliding up under the sweatshirt to find the damp, ridging muscles of his back. Suddenly he tore his mouth away.

'Stay.'

Francesca stared at him with storm-grey eyes, feeling the small tremors that rippled through the powerful male body. The handsome face was flushed, the sensuous mouth full, the blue-hot flame in his eyes both frightening and exciting her. She had never dreamed she could make a man look like that: pleasure-racked from the mere touching mouths and bodies. Hanging there against the wire, he looked as if he was being tortured and she supposed that in way, he was...and she was the torturer. Guiltily she stepped back, but he caught her at last, his fingers white with the marks of the wire, cupping her face, the strain of his gentleness evident in the husky grating of his voice.

'No...stay.' He laid a finger against her mouth and moved it back and forth against the swollen fullness. 'In your own time, Frankie. I won't rush you, I won't hurt you...' And he gathered her delicately into him, his kiss deep and soft and infinitely sensuous. There was none of the tension of moments before, but passion aplenty, smooth and swift-running, freed of the turmoil of Fran's mental resistance. They were so engrossed they didn't hear the tentative electronic tuning from the barn develop into a hard-driving rhythm. Fran was listening to an inner music, far more lyrical. The sound vibrating the timbers of the barn concealed other noises, however, and Fran was highly embarrassed when her eyes fluttered open and she saw Jason and Tessa, hand in hand behind Ross, regarding them with twin expressions of amusement.

'Ross—' She squirmed, trying to push him away.

'Don't get skittish on me now, Princess—' His voice was velvet with sensual threat.

'Unhand the lady, thou blackhearted villain!' Jason grinned, causing his brother to spin around, keeping firm hold of the woman in his arms. 'A gentleman would heed a maiden's protest.'

To Fran's further embarrassment Ross didn't let her go. He scooped her around in front of him, pulling her back against his chest and linking his arms under her breasts so that they presented a united front to his brother.

'Ah, but the lady doth protest too much, and any *man* worth his salt knows what *that* means!' The chauvinistic teasing made Fran struggle to break his implacable grip, but her struggles ceased abruptly as Ross bent his head to murmur throatily in her ear, 'You'd better stay put, Princess. If you move away from me now you're going to embarrass the hell out of both of us.' He eased his hips forward to show her why and Fran felt a slow, tingling blush sweep through her body as an unmistakable hardness was cradled in the cleft of her buttocks. His arms tightened briefly, increasing her breathlessness, before relaxing as he felt her lean obediently back against him.

'Isn't he terrible?' Tessa shook her head cheerfully, embarking on what was obviously a well established family game. 'I mean, women flock to his practice because he has this reputation for being empathetic as well as a damned good doctor. But it's all a sham. He only *pretends* to believe that women are real people with functioning brains as well as bodies, but underneath he harbours these savage sexist fantasies…'

'Thank God you two are going to be married soon!' Ross muffled his laughter in the warm brown curls on

Francesca's head. 'My professional advice, Jase, is bare-foot and pregnant. It's the only way to control that beady-eyed obsession with dethroning the naturally dominant partner…'

'But Ross, I thought you knew, men can't *get* pregnant,' Tess shot back. 'There has to be another way. Fran, you really must do something about this character masquerading as a doctor. He doesn't even know the facts of *life*, for heaven's sake.'

'You mean about women being the naturally dominant partners? I know, I know. He really is incredibly thick,' said Fran, entering into the fray, only to be thoroughly trounced when Ross made a tiny rocking movement against her and said in a low voice, for her ears alone,

'Why, thank you, darling, I'm glad you're impressed.'

She was so flustered she missed the next few moments of lightly insulting banter, and yet it was a confusion she enjoyed. Wrapped in his arms, Fran felt warm and secure and very much at home, wryly aware of how drastically her opinion of him had changed in the short time she had known him. She guessed that women would indeed flock to his practice. Ross was a trifle arrogant, it was true, but it was an arrogance born of confidence in himself and his abilities, and tempered by a lazy charm that was a natural outgrowth of his warm and loving upbringing. It would be a point of pride with him to be the best at what he did, and to treat the whole woman rather than just her condition. Fran had known, and disliked, obstetricians and gynaecologists who used aloofness and medical jargon as a subtle form of intimidation on their patients. But Ross, with his tolerance and humour, would put a woman at her ease, enable her to express her questions and fears about her treatment without being made to feel that she was imposing on a busy man's time. Ross would earn his patient's respect instead of demanding it by virtue of his position…

Fran jumped as a reverberating boom from the barn was followed by a high-pitched electronic whine. Jason winced and said something that was drowned out by another ear-shattering sequence of chords.

'What?' Ross raised his voice to a shout.

'I said,' Jason yelled, 'why don't you invite Tess and I over for a spa this evening in your quiet haven? We'll bring the food if you provide the booze. How about it?'

'Anything to escape the new wave of the future,' Tessa laughed, hands over her ears, nodding towards the barn.

'Perhaps we can make a few waves of our own,' Jason leered, and was teasingly slapped for his pains. 'Shall we bring togs, Fran, or have you both carried on your skinny-dipping tradition?'

'Togs, please,' said Fran primly, ignoring Ross's sensuous chuckle, although she had a suspicion that even if she wore a suit of armour, one look from those sexy blue eyes and she would be naked before him, body and soul!

CHAPTER EIGHT

'BEAUTIFUL, isn't she?'

Faintly amused by Jason's proud parental air, Francesca ran her hand along the stiffened fabric of the lower wing of the biplane and was dutifully admiring. 'Lovely. What is it?'

'Tiger Moth—it was Dad's first plane. These things used to be the backbone of the aerial top-dressing industry in this country, before they started building planes specifically for the job, like the Fletcher there.' He jerked his head towards the corrugated iron hangar across the grassy strip of runway and the small, rather ugly plane they had inspected first residing therein. 'Of course, we don't use Gertie here on the job any more, so Dave took the hopper off. Except for the paint job this is exactly how it looked when it was built in '45.'

Like the rest of the Tarrants, David was a multi-talent—musician, aircraft mechanic, mountain-climber. Naturally he was a flyer, too; even Beth could claim that distinction. Only Florence Tarrant preferred to keep her feet on solid ground, because, she confided to Fran with a twinkle, she suffered badly from motion sickness. She seemed to understand, though, what drove the rest of the family to seek adventure wherever they could find it. 'As long as they're happy' was her serene philosophy. Without it Fran didn't think she could have survived marriage to a man who, having retired early to let his sons run his business, had taken up stunt flying and helicopter search-and-rescue work to 'keep him on his toes'. Fran couldn't help but wonder if there was a price for that outer serenity. How did she endure the waiting?

As Jason guided Fran on a complete circuit of the little yellow and black striped biplane on the pocket-airfield, she couldn't help thinking that she was rather involved in a waiting game herself…thanks to the man sauntering along behind them, hands thrust into the pockets of his faded jeans, wire-rimmed aviator sunglasses masking his expression. Why hadn't he followed through on that promise, that threat, to become her lover? Since Sunday lunch he had surrounded them with his family, and on the rare occasions that he and Fran *were* alone all he seemed to want to do was *talk*…long, lazy, rambling conversations that were fascinating, but pointless.

They began with Ross doing most of the talking, obligingly filling in the blank years, the years of study and striving, of hardship and success, of the crises, big and small, that marked out the progression of his maturity. He even spoke, lightly and whimsically, of his search for love: 'the one area where I have a very consistent failure rate, perhaps because I was looking in all the wrong places', although, he admitted with a crocodile grin, that failure had its compensations.

'I'll bet it has,' Fran had said darkly.

'Now, Fran, you've looked, too, and you should be grateful that I'm not a virgin, after your last experience with one…'

She had blushed at his teasing. His disarming, sometimes embarrassing, but always fascinating frankness had seduced Fran into a similar honesty. She had told him about her abortive affair with the medical student, but not that it had been her first *and* last experience. However, the wryness with which she had described her disillusionment told him far more than she knew. It had made him certain that, however many—or few—men she had been to bed with, none of them had been lovers in the true sense of the word. She had been no closer to love than he, and the passion in her nature was still largely untapped. Fran would need her emotions engaged, as well as her senses, before she gave herself fully to any man.

Fran quite enjoyed the mutual exploration of character, except when Ross spoke with chilling passion of his exploits in competition sky-diving and his growing interest in hang-gliding and micro-lite planes. But each night she went to bed restless and unsatisfied, and amused by her own perversity. Here was a man showing an interest in her mind and all she wanted him to do was hustle her into bed!

'Ready to go up?'

'What? Oh, sure,' Francesca shook free of her indecisive thoughts. 'Which one are we going up in?' She looked back at the Fletcher and the small Cessna beside it.

'Why, this one, of course!' Jason chuckled as he patted the wooden propellor of the biplane.

Francesca blanched. 'You mean, it still *flies*?' Tessa and David, who had been standing to one side discussing invoices—Tessa did the books for this, and other small companies—grinned. Were they all in on the joke?

'Of course it does!' Jason looked mildly offended. 'This is a classic, you know. Dave will keep her flying as long as he can find parts to fit…or can jury-rig them. The RAF used to use these little babies as trainers, you know, because they're so sensitive. Put your hand out into the slipstream and you can make the thing yaw…'

'Really?' Fran didn't know what a yaw was, but it sounded dangerous.

'Waggle to you, darling,' Ross said with an aggravatingly kind smile of condescension. Fran glared at him. She could hardly back down now, with the other three watching expectantly. Turning coward now could cost her a tiny measure of their respect and, she realised, that mattered…

Reluctantly she allowed the two men to help her into the front cockpit.

Immediately she panicked. 'What are all these controls for? I don't have to *do* anything, do I?'

'Not if you don't want to, Fran,' said Jason with a straight face that didn't hide his amusement. 'I don't think you're ready to go solo yet. Ross will do the flying from behind you.'

'*Ross* will?' She squirmed round in the cramped seat to look at the rear cockpit. Sure enough, there was Ross, wearing an old-fashioned leather flying helmet and look- ing for all the world like a vintage fighter ace. Her stom- ach plunged. 'I thought *you* were taking me up!' she wailed to Jason.

'Here, put these on. It can get cold up there, even on a nice day like this.' Jason thrust a warm hand-knitted hat and scarf into her shaky fingers. 'Now sit straight and I'll do your harness up for you. Don't fuss, Fran. Truth to tell, Ross is a better flyer than Dave or I put together, it just wasn't what he wanted to do for a living…'

Francesca closed her eyes for the take-off. The plane was made of wood and wire and what felt like paper…it couldn't possibly fly! When she dared open her eyes her stomach rolled furiously at the angle of their ascent. Re- membering Jason's comment about the plane's sensi- tivity, she sat rigidly still, white-knuckled hands clenched around the safety harness, trying to regulate the great gulps of cold air which kept slipstreaming into her mouth. Gradually, as the engine continued to drone reassuringly, and the wings stayed on, and her stomach adjusted to the sudden jolts of up and down draughts, she began to relax and look about her. After ten minutes she stopped thinking about how far down the ground was and started thinking about how artificial it looked, toy farms and clockwork animals on green-quilted squares. After another ten minutes she was actually enjoying herself and ready to admit that Ross might have done the right thing in tricking her into going up in this jaunty little plane.

She was quite sorry when she saw the corrugated arch of the hangar with 'Tarrant' painted on it in large red letters appear below them. She turned gingerly in her seat and looked back. The ace in the pilot's seat gave her a cocky thumbs-up signal which she returned with a laugh that was snatched away by the wind. Ross made some more gestures with his hand, and thinking that he meant to tell her they were going to land she smiled and nodded and turned to brace herself, excitement and fear gripping her with equal strength.

But instead of tilting down, the nose of the plane tilted up so that Francesca found herself staring straight into the muzzle of a blue sky. There was only one reason she could think of as to why they were going up rather than down, but Fran didn't believe that even Ross would do that to her.

She was wrong.

She screamed for the entire duration of the stunt. When they were upside down she closed her eyes and screamed. She screamed when the loop passed into a series of barrel rolls and the horizon spun dizzily on its axis. She screamed in fear and outrage and sheer, helpless fury. If she hadn't been too utterly terrified to move anything but her vocal chords, she would have climbed over into the rear cockpit and strangled the reckless idiot there before he could deny her the pleasure by killing them both.

The landing was an anticlimax. Francesca climbed out of the tiny torture chamber and stood still for a moment until she was sure that all her parts were in working order. Then she turned to confront the brazen, laughing confidence of the man who had almost caused her heart failure.

'Did you enjoy the roller-coaster ride? Sorry if you got a fright, but I knew that once—'

Her working parts worked perfectly. Her slap nearly took his head off. Throat still raw from screaming, Fran didn't bother to say a single word, she let her back say it for her. She stormed over to Ross's pick-up, which was parked on the roadside next to the hangar, slammed into the driver's seat and took off in a whirlwind of dust along the unsealed road, ignoring the shouts behind her. Let Ross hitch a ride back with his brother. It would serve him right if she wiped this old rust-bucket out doing a few fancy driving 'stunts'!

It wasn't until she was half-way back to the cabin that reaction overtook her and she began to shake, and to have difficulty keeping the car on the road. She almost went straight past the Tarrant driveway, but at the last minute turned in, not really knowing why. Ross's home should be the last place she should run to, but when she stumbled into the warm kitchen to find Florence Tarrant sitting down to a quiet cup of tea she knew why she had come. She might be Ross's mother, but she would understand...

'I won't bother apologising for my son's behaviour, Fran,' the older woman said, plying Fran with a soothing brand of tea and sympathy after listening to her unexpected visitor's disjointed tale of woe. 'He's quite capable of doing that for himself. A pity he's got too big to put over my knee.'

'I took care of that,' Fran confessed, the slight sting in her hand recalling the slap. It probably hurt her more than it did him. 'He *knew* I'd never been up in a small plane before. He *knew* that I was nervous, that I thought Jason was going to take me up in something enclosed and modern and…and…then he leads me like a lamb to slaughter and does those *awful* things…' She shivered at the memory of the rushing wind, the wild, cartwheeling world.

'I know it's no consolation, dear, but Ross is so used to stunting that he probably doesn't think of it as frightening or dangerous. Perhaps he thought you would find it thrilling, perhaps he was just showing off, trying to impress you with his skill.'

'He doesn't *have* to impress me! cried Fran furiously, not realising what she was revealing to his interested mother. Just having him kiss and touch her was breathtaking thrill enough…how much *more* impressive could he be? 'What would you have done, if he had done that to you?'

Florence Tarrant sipped her tea thoughtfully. 'I would have been sick all over him,' she said drily.

Suddenly they were laughing, Fran's high-pitched giggles semi-hysterical with relief. This mixture of sympathy and humour was just what she had needed to restore her perspective. 'I suppose it was rather funny,' she chuckled grudgingly. 'Me, screaming like a banshee, hanging from my shoulder-straps. If I'd seen it in a movie I would have thought it great fun. And you should have seen his face when I took off in his car, leaving him choking in a cloud of dust in the middle of the road. Now *that* was like a movie, *Keystone Cops* variety. I half expected him to chase after me.' That set them off again, until Fran remembered that he might well be chasing after her. She felt too confused and angry to face him quite yet. She pushed her empty cup away and jumped nervously to her feet.

'You won't tell him I laughed?' she said tentatively.

'I think he deserves a good long bit of grovelling first, wouldn't you say?' Florence Tarrant asked, her eyes still filled with serene merriment at her son's expense.

'More than a little,' growled Francesca darkly. 'And if he thinks he can just walk back into that cabin and jolly me into forgetting it, he's got another think coming!'

'I'll make up his bed here,' his mother offered, perfectly understanding, but privately doubting that the bed would be used. 'I take it that you won't stay on for dinner…Ross thought you might.'

Another indication that he didn't want to be alone with her. Fran stiffened at the sharp disappointment that knifed in her breast. 'No, thank you.' The thought of food at this particular time made her feel ill anyway, and the thought of facing Ross in her present state, without knowing what kind of mood he would be in, was enough to make her stutter, 'But…do you think…could you keep him—'

'He invited himself for dinner, he can stay for dinner,' Mrs Tarrant said firmly. 'I'll tell him that you both need time to cool off. And if you take his car and I make sure that he can't get any transport from here, well…that should slow him down somewhat.' She gave Fran a gentle, warning smile. 'But, short of chaining him up, we can't stop him if he's determined. And Ross on a mission is a very determined man…'

'No more determined than *I* can be.' The stubborn line to the young woman's chin reminded Florence so sharply of her eldest son that she had to hide another smile as she bid her farewell. The two of them made an interesting combination, and although Ross had always jealously guarded his bachelorhood a mother could always hope…

The clouds building up in thick, dark columns in the western sky brought an early dusk which suited Francesca's mood. She vented her initial wrath by packing up every stray possession of Ross's that she could find and dumping the lot out on the back porch. She had been right to have her doubts. It was lunacy to imagine that she and Ross could put aside their differences long enough to have any kind of amicable relationship. And to think that she had been on the verge of giving in to lust…no, actually *mourning* the fact that *he* seemed to be having second thoughts.

Funny side or not, what he had done this afternoon was a gross violation of her trust, and she refused to become the lover of a man who threatened to give her a coronary every time she ventured outside with him. Lurking beneath the pleasant, teasing character of the past few days was a daredevil monster champing at the bit to fling himself into another terrifying endeavour. Talk about Jekyll and Hyde…Ross was positively schizophrenic! On the one hand he was a mature, responsible doctor with an admirable reputation, on the other an incurable thrill-seeker. While Fran could imagine herself satisfying the one, she could never, in a million years of trying, satisfy the other. Cooped up here in convalescence, Ross had probably decided that he could 'make do' with Fran for feminine company, but out in the real world no doubt he required vibrant, exciting women, sophisticated and outgoing, the kind of women who make good race-track groupies or knife-thrower's assistants, Fran thought sourly. He was probably sitting at his parents' table right now, eating and drinking and laughing, relieved that he had escaped the toils of staid and boring Francesca Lewis. Perhaps it had been only pity in the first place, and he had merely pretended to want her because she had been so embarrassingly inept at hiding her inexplicable desire for this oh-so-desirable man! Fran cringed at the thought. She needed a drink—a large one. She was annoyed to find her hands shaking as she tried to extract the ice-cubes from the tray, dropping them all over the bench in the process. Perhaps that flight had been a deliberate attempt on Ross's part to frighten her off. Yes, that would appeal to his twisted mind! And now he was congratulating himself at having—

She gave a little scream as the sliding door to the deck shivered violently open. Ross stood there, scowling furiously at her, his hair damp and matted, jaw tense, sloppy sweatshirt showing dark circles under his arms.

'What in hell did you run away for?'

Fran controlled her well stoked fury with difficulty. How dared he make *her* sound like the guilty party? She drew herself up. 'Your stuff is on the back porch.'

'Typical, just typical,' Ross sneered, stepping into the room, big and menacing, breathing hard. 'Ignore a problem and it doesn't exist, huh, Fran? Well, Princess, *I'm* not going to ignore it. We're going to have this out if I have to—'

He was cut short by an ice-cube. It bounced off the hard angle of his chin, slithered down his chest and clattered on to the wooden floor. There was utter silence as the blue eyes narrowed dangerously. Fran swallowed nervously. She shouldn't have done that, but at least it had shut him up.

'That's the second time you've hit me today, lady!' Ross's voice was a purring threat. 'And that's one time too many.' He took another step forward.

'You stay where you are!' Fran squeaked, scrabbling among the ice-cubes, half-excited, half-terrified at her temerity, and still furious with him. She brandished a fistful of hard, icy missiles as she backed away. 'Ross, I'm warning you, I want you to take your things and get out—'

'Warning, Frankie?' he asked softly, still coming. 'Or bluffing…?'

He didn't think she would do it! He thought she'd back down like a frightened rabbit just because he was bigger than she was. He thought he knew her well enough to predict her every move. He had a surprise coming!

Unfortunately the surprise didn't stop him. Fielding the raining chunks of ice, Ross caught her by the back door, ignoring her screams as he manhandled her out of the kitchen, forcing her to dump her last handful of ice-cubes on the floor, where they crunched underfoot as she wriggled helplessly in his purposeful arms.

'Let me go, you big bully!' Fran shrieked, kicking out with her dangling legs. Staggering slightly, Ross's foot came down on a stray ice-cube and skated out from under him. They both landed on the icy floor with a bone-shattering thump. Luckily Fran was on top, but when she caught her breath and tried to move she felt Ross's chest rise against her back in a thick groan.

'Ross? Are you all right?' Another groan. 'Are you hurt?' Carefully she eased herself sideways in his loosening arms and turned to face him, her hands automatically going over him, checking for injuries, anger forgotten in her anxiety. When she felt the rapid thud of his heart her fingers paused over the reassuring vibration.

'Don't stop…'

Her hands stiffened against his chest, but were caught and held by his. 'Ross Tarrant—' she began accusingly, but her words dried up when she tangled with his gaze: soft, blue, gentle…

'Compassion, Princess, it gets you every time, doesn't it? You'd care for the devil himself it he were hurt.'

'I think that's what I'm doing now,' she said drily, in an attempt to resist that melting tenderness.

'Not a devil, Frankie, just a man…and an exhausted one at that.' He sensed her fading anger and was careful not to smile. 'Mum'll never forgive me for leaving dinner on the table, but it suddenly occurred to me that you might take it into that muddled head of yours to run away, so I took off across the back fields. Ran all the way…in pretty good time, too!'

'You *ran*? In the *dark*? But it's *miles*!' Fran was both flattered and appalled. 'You could have fallen and broken your neck and lain there all night! My God, you're a menace to yourself as well as to other people.'

'You and Mum didn't leave me much choice,' he said apologetically. 'She even got Dad to hide the keys to the ride-on mower.'

Fran refused to laugh, and his loosely clasped hands at the back of her waist tightened as she stirred fretfully against his big body.

'Ah, Princess, don't look at me like that,' he sighed. 'I've already been told by Jason and Tessa and David how grossly cruel and thoughtless it was to spring those stunts on you. Tessa said I deserved the right cross. And my mother has subjected me to a harrowing hour of silent reproach. I didn't mean to frighten you, Fran. I just got carried away. You were so obviously enjoying the flight, I just wanted to share the fantastic feeling of freedom I get rolling around the sky—'

'Yes, *you* get. *You*,' Fran said tautly, thankful that she hadn't had that drink after all. He wasn't going to find her so forgiving this time. 'Not me! You weren't trying to share, you were trying to force that feeling on me, regardless of what I wanted. I'm not like you and I don't want to be. If what I am isn't good enough for you, well, that's too bad. I'm not changing my entire personality just to accommodate your whims.' Yes, that sounded good, reasonable but firm, with just the right element of subtle accusation. Perhaps too subtle. 'Your *temporary* whims.'

He could hardly miss that thickly significant look and tone. The sober expression with which he had greeted her unarguable statement of independence sharpened. 'Are you implying what I *think* you're implying?' he asked slowly.

Fran lifted her eyebrows haughtily. 'I don't know. What do you think I'm implying?' The haughtiness backfired, for it made him grin.

'That my wanting to make love to you was just a fleeting whim. My God, woman, are you insane? Whatever gave you that stupid idea?'

A hot, sweet pang pierced Fran's body at his incredulous growl. 'You're the one who turned cool all of a sudden,' she retaliated defensively.

'Cool? Is that what you thought?' He gave a laughing groan. 'Frankie, if my temperature was any higher I'd spontaneously combust! I was *trying* to leave the next move up to you. It was obvious that you had doubts, and I thought you needed a little time to work them through.' He chuckled ruefully at the wild blush that flooded over her stunned face. 'Shame on you, my liberated young businesswoman! Were you only waiting for me to sweep you off your feet? I didn't think there was any mad rush. After all, we do live in the same city...'

Fran felt a squeezing pain in her chest, followed by a

panicky flutter. What did he mean by that? She had been torturing herself with erotic imaginings for days, gearing herself up to a brief holdiay fling and hoping that it would rid her of this dangerous, unreasoning obsession she had developed for him. Wasn't that what he had wanted? What they both had wanted? There had been no mention of a future. The idea of an open-ended affair was slightly terrifying. Could she handle it? Did she dare risk the physical and emotional disruption he would inevitably create in her life? She paused on the brink of a great discovery, but his next words buried it again under an avalanche of riotous sensation.

'You know…what I do up there in the air,' he murmured in a voice that had the texture of cut velvet, 'the "high" it gives me, is the next best thing to sex. Perhaps this afternoon was a subconscious attempt to sublimate my *real* need…to do this…' He slowly eased over until he was braced above Fran's supine body, his hips lowering to grind softly against her thighs until they parted to allow him to lie between, the rough denim weave of his jeans catching against the soft wool-blend of her slacks. '…and I needed you up there, with me, to share the exhilaration, the agony and the ecstasy of subliminal sex. God, Frankie, how much longer are you going to make us wait? Tell me, tell me you want me to touch you, and taste you, and feed your appetite with mine…'

With a cry of need that echoed his own, Fran arched against him. His musky male scent was strong in her nostrils, his tongue knowledgeable and exquisitely familiar in her mouth. In a wondrously compelling feat of strength he stood up, supporting their combined weights without taking his mouth off hers. Then she felt his torso slide and dip against her breasts, and clutched at his

baggy sweater as she felt herself being swept off her feet.
It seemed appropriate.

'No, Ross, put me down…I'm too heavy for you. Your
arm…' her mouth escaped his to plead, even as she rev-
elled in the possessive gesture.

He looked down at her, all arrogant male pride for an
instant, until she saw the softness in the big, blue-grey
eyes. Then he chuckled and whirled her around a couple
of times with a speed that made her gasp and shut her
eyes, it was so reminiscent of her recent flight. When she
opened them they were in the darkened bedroom.

'I love the way you care,' he said with a voice full of
warmth and desire as he nuzzled the opening of her
blouse.' All stiff and starchy and bossy on the outside,
but inside soft and buttery, slightly salty and slightly
sweet…' He licked her skin and Fran's soft and buttery
insides began to sizzle. 'But you're right, after all the
alarms and excursions of today I do feel rather weak.
Shall we lie down together and tend each other's wounds,
heal each other…?' He lowered her to the firm resilience
of the bed, following her down, plucking at the clothes
that suddenly seemed rough and hurtful against her skin,
barriers to his sexual healing. Her own blind touch found
his skin under the sweatshirt, damp and hot to the touch,
a series of smooth undulations of bone and muscle.

'Do I feel cool to you now, Princess?' he growled huskily when her clothes lay discarded on the floor and his
shadowy bulk rose over her, clad only in narrow, dark
briefs. 'Is that why you shiver?' his voice teased her
while his hand explored what he uncovered with erotic
slowness. 'Shall I warm you, Princess…here…and here?'
His delicate touch sent another sighing quiver through
her body. 'Ah, Frankie, at last…after all these years…'

Just as she was sinking beyond rational thought, Ross pulled back and twisted his body to reach up to the light switch on the wall above them.

'No—' Fran caught him just in time, feeling a sudden return of shyness, an echo of the past. She wanted to be perfect for him, and the only way that she could be that was if he couldn't see her as she really was. True, she wasn't plump any more, but the image of herself still remained...

'No?' He let her guide his hand away, but grasped instead the curtains beside the bed and dragged them back so that the pale light of a full moon spilled over the tumbled bed. Its light was enchantingly revealing, yet Fran didn't feel exposed. Moonlight was romantic, kind, silvering away imagined imperfections.

'Ah, Princess, how could you try to deny me the plea-sure of watching myself make love to you?' he murmured with throaty satisfaction, his shadowed eyes running over the moon-bleached smoothness of her body, the breasts that fascinated him with their lush femininity, the pearly sheen of her thighs where they curved invitingly inwards.

Slowly he reached out to cup her breast with an almost reverent desire. He knelt beside her, his other hand join-ing worship of her breasts, the muscles in his belly and thighs tensing as he watched them respond to his flattery, swelling in his hands, the taut nipples beckoning his mouth. As his head dipped in homage, Francesca saw the explicit outline of his need, held straining captive by the thin strip of silk across his loins. She gasped, digging her fingers into the broad, bowed shoulders in a sharp agony of wanting. When she felt his mouth, exquisitely gentle, tasting, enveloping her in warm wetness, violent sensa-tion exploded in the pit of her belly, radiating out through her body in rippling waves of shock.

As he made love to her breasts with his skilful mouth, he nudged her flat on the bed, his hands straying down to twine her legs against him until she could no longer bear the separation and tugged at the silk on his hips with trembling fingers, silently begging him to help her. With an easy flex of muscle he bent and stripped off his briefs, then angled himself against her on the narrow bed to provide them with fleeting relief from the growing pressure in both their bodies.

'Yes, Francesca...God, yes!' he cried gratingly as she moved her thighs restlessly against his velvety hardness, teasing his pulsating desire, finding him with her hands and marvelling at his hot virility. The moonlight played across their shifting bodies, a cool counterpoint to the heat they were generating, and Fran was naïvely astonished at how exciting it was to see as well as to feel what Ross was doing to her, and she to him. Her experience of sex had been of a rushed sense of urgency too soon satisfied...this slow, languid, sensuously thorough journey of exploration was a revelation. Her wide-eyed delight provoked her lover to even greater pleasures and, when at last his strong, gentle fingers lingered, breath-soft on the delicate flesh between her quivering thighs, Fran was stormed by a violent, racking shudder that almost spilled him from his position of dominance. His hand wrapped around her hips, holding her still.

'No...wait, Francesca...' He sucked in his breath. '...slow down...'

'I...can't...' She twisted helplessly, unable to control her body's demand as he groaned against her.

'I don't think I can either...' He thrust her legs apart with a possessive strength that sent a stab of pain to the core of her pleasure. Then, just as he moved between her legs his body clenched. 'Oh, damn...I...I'm not prepared... You are on the pill, aren't you?'

It was a question that had no meaning and the manner of his asking made the answer a mere formality, but Francesca stiffened, her hands balling against his back. The pill? Contraception? Until that instant what they were doing together had had no relevance to anything else, much less to the act of procreation. Sex? Babies? Suddenly the true meaning of what they were risking hit her like a hurricane...

'No!' Babies should be born out of mutual love, not selfish passion. Fran would never, never bring a child into the world unwanted by either parent, as her mother had done. A love child...what bitter irony in the name.

'No?' Ross's voice was hoarse, uncomprehending, his body freezing rigid when his brain interpreted her reply. *'No?'*

'No.' She closed her eyes against the tears, and the terrible realisation, unable to prevent the words tumbling out, 'I'm not used to this sort of thing, you see. I'm not *experienced...*'

'Don't, Frankie—' He rolled off her with a groan and pulled her hard against the length of him, cupping her chin in his hand and forcing her to look at him. 'Don't you think I know that? That's why it's important that this be good for you, why I wanted you to be *sure.*' He gave a short, stunned laugh, blue eyes expressing his bewilderment. 'I can't believe this...I was so busy trying to blind you with the rightness of our being lovers that I didn't even think of the elementary precautions. If this ridiculous situation is anyone's fault it's mine...contraception is part of my *business*, for God's sake!'

'Perhaps it was a Freudian slip, perhaps you didn't really want—'

'Baby, you have to be kidding!' He cut off her attempt to ease away from him with a very definite movement of his still-aroused body against hers and closed his eyes with a slight shudder. 'I'm very, very tempted to ask if this is a safe time for you—' his voice was thick and slow, like syrup '—but we're both too intelligent to deny the element of risk.' He opened his eyes and looked at her and smiled, a slow, sultry smile of resignation. 'Ah, well, Princess, if the path of pleasure is barred to us, I guess we'll have to dally in the by-ways...'

'No, please...can you...just hold me?' Fran put a frantic hand against the deep chest. She knew to suggest that he leave would provoke a confrontation that she couldn't endure, and to have him make half-love to her would be even worse. She held her breath when he studied her flushed face long and hard, her fearful grey eyes and trembling mouth. He protested, but tenderly, with a gentleness that made her ache, and at last acquiesced and held her until the awful tension drained away. They talked of inconsequential things, Francesca desperately willing him to sleep, and when at last the big naked body slackened in sleep she lay there in an agony of guilt for what she was going to do. He had held her, rocked away the pain, acted with supreme consideration in putting her needs above his...all the time believing that tomorrow, tomorrow she would fulfil *his* needs. She was cheating him, and he would never forgive her. But it was for the best...it had to be for the best!

CHAPTER NINE

FRAN was in the bath when the doorbell rang. She groaned. Her nightly soak was the one leisurely luxury she afforded herself in her current hectic, dawn-to-dusk schedule. It was also a necessity, for she came home each night weary, sweaty, grimy and often delicately perfumed with manure. If she didn't love it so much she would bemoan the success of The Garden Company, so completely did it devour her life. But the hard work was worth it. In three short, yet also very long, months she and Christina had built up a booming business, confounding not only their critics but also their own cautious expectations.

Fran towelled herself quickly, grimacing as she caught sight of the bedroom clock. Eight-thirty. The few of her friends who hadn't been driven off by her inhospitable hours knew better than to make social calls after dark. Fran was often in bed at this time, trying to wrest sleep away from regretful, disturbing dreams.

The soft pink and grey tracksuit clung uncomfortably to her still-damp skin, but Fran was too tired to care. She would get rid of whoever it was, heat a quick TV dinner and fall into bed.

She was yawning as she opened the front door of her apartment, leaving the safety chain attached. The yawn froze in her throat.

'Beth!'

Fran fumbled with the chain and threw the door wide, her eyes automatically going past the hesitantly smiling girl to the echoingly empty corridor beyond. Her stomach twisted. What had she expected? She had made it very clear to Ross that she didn't want to see him again, and he had as much pride as she did.

The painful thought must have shown in her face because Beth Tarrant's smile faded and she shifted her bag awkwardly from one shoulder to the other.

'Hello, Fran…I know I should have rung first but… well, Mum did give me your address and said you asked about me when you wrote. She said I should look you up…I was just on my way back to the hostel from the movies, and since I was passing—' The girl shrugged and tried another smile. 'Look, if I've come at a bad time, I can come back…' She half turned away.

'No!' Fran's urgent cry surprised them both. 'I mean, it's lovely to see you, Beth. I was just surprised, that's all.' In those last few golden days at Whaler's Bay she and Beth had become quite friendly, the teenager confiding her firm intention to start her nursing training in Auckland as soon as she was old enough. 'Come on through. Excuse the faint air of neglect,' she apologised, with the guilt of former fastidiousness for the comfortably furnished but untidy lounge. 'I've been so flat out I really only use this place for washing, eating and sleeping…in that order.'

'You live here alone?'

'I used to share with another nurse, but when she moved out to get married I didn't bother to find anyone else. I can afford the rent and I appreciate the peace and quiet.' Fran hoped that Beth didn't notice the slight ring of hollowness. Since the girl looked interested she showed her around. Beth seemed strangely subdued and diffident, quite unlike her usual bouncy self.

'When did you start your training?' Fran asked, as the

tour finished up in the second bedroom and Beth showed the first glimmer of her former animation.

'Three weeks ago today. Of course it'll be ages before I'm allowed near real patients.' She sighed. Was she disillusioned already? Fran could have sworn that Beth had the enthusiasm, determination and resilience to make a good nurse. It was all she had ever wanted to be, she had told Fran, with that Tarrant confidence.

'Would you like some tea or coffee? I was just about to heat myself some dinner...'

'I'm a bit peckish myself,' Beth said with engaging wistfulness. 'I'm paying full board at the hostel, but the meal hours are fixed and if you miss out, you miss out. The biddy who runs it doesn't like us mucking about too much in her kitchen, so other than snacks I don't get a chance to cook the things I like.' Beth had her mother's flair in the kitchen and Fran, having tasted some of her offerings, could appreciate the mournful look.

''I was only going to heat up something frozen, but you can make us some of your fancy omelettes if you like.'

Fran showed her where everything was in the compact kitchen and then set the oval table, listening in amusement to Beth's rapid-fire chatter as she whirled from fridge to bench to stove, her long, dark plait flying around her slim shoulders.

'I would have called ages ago.' Beth raised her voice over the whisking of eggs. 'But I wasn't quite sure of my welcome. I know that you and Ross had some kind of fight...'

'Yes, we did...but you're always welcome to call in, Beth,' Fran managed to keep her voice even. 'A lot of my work involves beavering away on my own, so I appreciate a bit of company.' It was as close as she'd come to admitting she was a little lonely. Success was sweet, but it would be sweeter with someone to share it. Christine, as a solo mother of two teenage children, had a very busy life outside the running of the seven-day-a-week Garden Centre, and the assistant who helped Fran with the contracting was also studying horticulture, so she didn't see much of them in her off-hours. Now that she had begun to adjust to the new rhythms of her life, Fran had the awful feeling that she was going to miss Ross even more...

Ross. To say that they had had a fight wasn't quite accurate. *She* had fought, Ross had reasoned, but Fran had been in no mood to listen to reason. She had been afraid, and as always when she was afraid she had closed up and listened only to the promptings of her fear. In all his sweet seduction Ross had never murmured a word of love. He had been honest. There had been no embarrassing slip of the tongue to encourage false hopes, he had spoken only of mutual needs and desires. Oh yes, Fran had those, but her close encounter with the white heat of her own passion had shaken her deeply. That she was capable of such unreserved feeling was frightening, and realising that she had fallen in love with him against the dictates of her own will was even more disturbing. The strength of her feelings made a mockery of her fond belief that she could handle a brief holiday affair with Ross. Or a long one, that would be even worse...storing up pain for herself day by day, week by week, until Ross got bored with her acquiescence and sought new challenges, new adventures, and returned her love with its legacy of bitter interest. He might demand no more of her than passion, but her own hunger for loving would demand that she give him everything, try and purchase his love with hers. In doing so she would lose a vital part of herself, her self-respect…turn into the kind of woman who pursued passion blindly, relentlessly hopeful, relentlessly disappointed. No, Fran wanted to be master of her own fate, not a mistress in someone else's…

So instead of awakening to a new day with a new lover in his arms, Ross had padded out into the lounge next morning, lazy and sensuous as a cat, to find Fran packing, her defences honed razor-sharp by the fear of what those penetrating blue eyes would see.

He had been justifiably incredulous at her announcement that she had decided that she had been neglecting her 'real life' for too long. At first he had been teasing, then coaxing, then stunningly sincere as he suggested that *he* help her solve her 'real life' problems. Instead of her worrying about probate being settled, why didn't *he* underwrite her loan? Hell, he would loan her the money himself, at a far better rate than the bank allowed her…and that would mean that instead of selling the cabin they could keep it on as a weekend hide-away.

Fran had exploded. So that was what he wanted…a hole-in-the-corner affair, a weekend lover who wouldn't intrude into the rest of his life! Well, he had intruded too far into hers already. It wasn't enough that he had summarily invaded her heart, now he was trying to muscle in on the only thing of her own that she truly and freely possessed…her dream. He was buying an affair, but not with love…with his *money*. Talking as if he had some right to a stake in her future.

She had said bitter things and he had responded with a withering contempt that seemed to see straight through her feverish rejection of any kind of involvement between them.

'My God, is this the way you usually function, Fran?

Slitting the throat of a relationship before it can make any real demands on you?'

'What sort of demands were you thinking of making?' She had meant to make it sound sarcastic, but it came out horrifyingly like a plea.

'Oh, no, Fran.' He shook his head, voice soft and veined with cynicism. 'No free rides. You pays your money and you takes your choice. You'll never know if you don't take the plunge with me. Human relationships don't come with written guarantees.'

'I'm not asking for guarantees,' she denied furiously. 'Certainly not from a man like you. Sooner or later you're going to break your crazy neck in one of your stunts and leave those unfortunate enough to care about you high and dry.'

His eyes narrowed and she turned away, afraid that she had revealed too much. 'Would you have me different, Fran?'

If he had been different she probably wouldn't have fallen in love with him and she wouldn't be suffering now. 'Yes.'

He walked around her rigid back and confronted her with a weary resignation that battered more fiercely at her bruised heart than had his earlier angry contempt. 'What do you want me to do? Make you pretty promises that neither of us would believe? In between last night and this morning, Princess, you misplaced some of that fine courage of yours. Last night we discovered things about each other, elemental things…this morning you act as if that makes us enemies. Is being so close to another human being so terrifying, Fran? You're not running *to* anything as much as away from it. You've locked yourself into one set of options and it has blinded you to others. We all have to live with compromises, Fran, small and large…if we don't bend to life we break. The bottom line here is that *I'm* prepared to take a risk on us, to nurture growth, and you're not. What do you really want, Fran? Do you know? If you get what you think you want, will it be enough?'

'Yes.' Defiant to the last.

So he had let her walk out of his life, speeding her on her way with one last, poison-tipped barb that had pierced her armoured emotions.

'If you change your mind about what you want, look me up. But don't wait too long, Princess. Unlike you, I don't fight what I am—a human being with passions and physical appetites, and a human need for emotional as well as physical intimacy…'

'What's the matter, don't you like it?'

'What? Oh!' Fran blinked at the omelette on the table in front of her and picked up her fork to taste. 'It's delicious, Beth. Sorry, I was miles away.'

Brooding. She couldn't stop herself indulging in the torture of speculation. Where was Ross now? What was he doing? Had he found someone else already to stimulate his wretched human appetite? If he hadn't…

'So, how's life in general treating you?' she asked Beth, firmly crushing her mind's treachery.

'Oh, great, the course is really terrific.' Beth chattered on, but Fran was jolted out of her own jealous self-absorption by the realisation that the younger girl was straining for the right note of cheer, and she mentioned nothing of her personal life.

'Beth, everything is all right, isn't it?' she interrupted gently.

'Sure. Great!' Her cheerfulness wavered under the steady grey stare and suddenly her shoulders slumped.

'Does it show? Oh, Fran...I guess that's really why I came. I just don't know what to do...'

Oh no, thought Fran wryly, *not you, too*. 'Have you discovered that nursing isn't what you want to do, after all? It's nothing to be ashamed of, Beth, better now than—'

'It's not that,' Beth wailed. 'I love the nursing part. It's just that...that...Fran, it's so *awful* living in that *institution*...' It all came tumbling out. Beth had never been away from home and family before, and she was bitterly homesick. 'Don't tell me it'll pass, everyone tells me that and I know it's only a phase, but sometimes I really feel like chucking it all in!' she finished with dramatic misery.

Fran, to whom hostel living had been a pleasant change from the strict discipline and loneliness of home, nevertheless sympathised.

'Couldn't you have gone and lived with Ross?' The name, unspoken for months, stuck to her tongue lovingly and she had to force herself to continue. 'Instead of going to a hostel?''

'Ross lives about forty-three bus changes away from Tech,' Beth exaggerated glumly, 'and we have quite a few evening classes. He works all sorts of hours, too, so I probably wouldn't see any more of him than I do now. He's so busy...and when he does get time to himself I don't suppose he wants a kid sister hanging around to cramp his style.' She clapped a hand over her stricken mouth in horror. 'I'm sorry, Fran, I forgot—'

'I wish I could,' Fran said wryly, and smiled to show her there were no hard feelings. At times, Beth's impulsiveness got the better of her tact.

'Anyway, I made such a terrible song and dance about being able to cope, boasting about striking out on my own, I'm-not-a-baby-any-more and so on, because Mum wanted me to stay with Aunty Celia who is nice enough in small doses but is practically a certified loony on the subject of what 'nice girls' don't do—mainly, have any fun at *all*...that I just *can't* go bawling to Ross. It would be so humiliating, and brothers can be rottenly unsympathetic, you know. Oh, Fran, what am I going to *do*?' A tearful plea, full of such trusting belief in her power to make things right was more than Fran could resist.

She sighed. 'I suppose you could stay here. The second bedroom is—'

'Oh, Fran, really? You life-saver! You darling!' Beth's heartfelt relief clutched at her before the words were out of her mouth. 'Mum'll be so chuffed! I think she was starting to read between the lines a bit...and she likes you and thinks you're really responsible...what a fantastic solution! You really are a darling to come up with it...though I must admit that when I saw that spare room I might have done a teensy weensy bit of subtle angling,' she grinned, her naturally sunny self readjusting to the new situation. 'Oh, Fran, you'll hardly even notice I'm here, I promise, and we'll have such *fun*...!'

The first wasn't at all true, but because of the second Fran found that the loss of her precious peace and quiet was much outweighed by the pleasures of Beth's company. Occasionally, with a look or a gesture or a remark, Beth would conjure up a stinging likeness to her eldest brother that struck Fran into speechless longing, but for the most part she added a dimension to Fran's life that had been missing. Beth was the sister she had never had, someone to take and give advice, someone to listen or moan to, to share small victories and defeats with, to go shopping with and giggle over the differences in taste. Because Fran refused to accept more from Beth than she had been paying in board at the hostel, the girl insisted on doing the lion's share of the housework, particularly the cooking. Fran, in turn, helped Beth with her studies. Passing on the benefit of her knowledge and experience not only appeased her last lingering guilt about forsaking her nursing career, but also the more immediate guilt that she had her own less than altruistic motives for taking the girl under her wing; she wanted to see Ross again.

It wasn't working—trying to forget him. Oh, superficially her life was full and busy and increasingly successful, but there was a hollow ring to it, signalling an inner emptiness that only Ross could fill. She still loved him, after all these months of absence. In her heart, his image was still fresh and bright and vibrant. At times he seemed so close that she almost turned and said, 'Hey, look what I've done, aren't you proud of me?' And he would have been. Ross hadn't been trying to hold her back, or box her in, he had been trying to show her that the parameters of freedom were the ones she created for herself. She had boxed *herself* in by anticipating the worst and thus precipitating the prospect. There was much to be said for Ross's philosophy, which seemed to be a Tarrant trademark, of taking the optimistic approach to life, of believing the best of people rather than the worst.

But how to let Ross know that the decision to cut him unceremoniously out of her life, made in panic and haste, was being repented at leisure? What if he too had changed his mind? Or already moved on? Was that why Beth was being so aggravatingly and uncharacteristically tactful, carefully skirting the subject of Ross whenever his name slipped inadvertently into the conversation? Was that why Ross never visited his sister at the flat, or telephoned? Never passed on regards or even a greeting through the third party of his sister, or his mother? Fran knew that Beth spent some of her afternoons off in Ross's company because the girl was usually unnervingly honest about her doings. On the evenings that she clammed up about her activities Fran knew, with the jealous instinct of one who loved, that she had been with Ross. Knowing that he was out there, existing parallel to yet not touching her life, filled her with restless frustration. The solution, she knew, was in her own hands. She would have to make the first move. Perhaps, she told herself hopefully, this was another example of his determination that she abide by her own choices rather than his…

Her tension inevitably communicated itself to Beth, who became even more tiresomely tactful, until Fran told her tartly one morning to stop behaving as if her brother didn't exist.

'I was just following your lead,' Beth protested righteously, giving Fran's frustrated face an up-and-under look that was suspiciously innocent. 'I thought you weren't interested.'

'Well, you thought wrong,' Fran said pettishly. 'Your mother never mentions him either, when she writes. Is this conspiracy of silence carried out on Ross, too?'

Beth's blue eyes skittered away. 'N-o-o-o. Mum's told him all about The Garden Company and how well it's going, of course, but she said that we weren't to inter-fere…that you two had to work it out between your-selves…'

'It?' Fran's eyebrows rose sarcastically. Did Florence *want* Fran to have an affair with her son? She was always warm and friendly when she rang to check on her daugh-ter…Fran noticed Beth's uncomfortable blush and re-gretted her sarcasm. It wasn't Beth's fault she was frus-trated. 'We can hardly work it out when we never see each other…' She would just have to force herself into action, and the hell with pride. Love conquers all, she reminded herself sternly, and pretended to ignore Beth's furtive excitement.

That evening she was out in her walled courtyard, up to her elbows in potting mix when the doorbell rang. Expecting Beth, getting ready for a night on the town with one of her new-found city friends, to answer it with her usual eagerness, Fran brushed back a sweaty curl with one gloved hand, leaving a streak of dirt on her temple to match the one on her chin, and continued to re-pot. The bell rang twice more and Fran was half-way across the lounge, grumbling testily to herself when Beth popped out of her bedroom, clad in a towel.

'Fran, would you mind—? *Fran!* You can't answer the door like that…what happened to that nice dress you were wearing?'

'I didn't want to get it dirty,' Fran said mildly, looking down at the now extremely grubby stonewashed denims that Beth had persuaded her to buy, insisting that they should be half a size too small 'for effect', and the equally grubby, loose, once-white T-shirt that she had pulled on over her unfettered breasts. 'What's the matter,' she teased 'is it someone special? A man?'

'No, yes…' Beth hissed, looking as if she was about to start ringing her hands in despair as the doorbell sounded again. 'Fran, you don't understand…'

'I promise I won't frighten him off,' Fran said in amusement. Beth was usually terrifyingly blasé about her boyfriends. 'We have to let him in and you certainly can't do it like that. Stop fussing, Beth,' she scolded as the girl let out another anguished protest. 'If he looks down his nose at me I'll excuse myself and change, and if he turns out to be a nice guy he can come out and watch me pot

my plants. Now go and finish dressing…I thought you
were always ready *early* for dates.'

'Fran!' Beth's cry was despairing. 'At *least* take off
the gardening gloves!'

'If he's as prissy as you seem to think I don't think
he's going to want to shake hands anyway,' Fran called
back with playful perversity. Beth was very fond of giving people 'snob tests', especially in up-market dress
shops where she would suddenly lapse into excruciating
country-bumpkinisms. Many a time Fran had been torn
between laughter and embarrassment as she dragged her
companion away. Perhaps tonight she could get her own
back. Pinning a vacant smile to her lips, she threw the
door wide.

It was Ross.

Wasn't it? She blinked. His thick hair was trimmed to
glossy neatness and he was wearing a *suit*. It was dark,
teamed with an immaculate silver-grey silk shirt and ma-
roon tie, his raw masculinity refined into elegant, expensive lines that Fran had a savagely jealous urge to
smudge, to turn him back into the Ross she knew.

'Ross…what are you doing here?' To her horror it
came out almost like an accusation, when he had sacrificed his pride to come and see her…

'More to the point, what are *you* doing here?' he
shocked her by replying. Suddenly she noticed the fine-
grained skin pulled taut around the mouth and nose and
eyes. He was as shocked as she was by this confrontation.
But that would mean… 'I was under the impression that
Beth was living at a student nurses' hostel. I appear to
have been wrong,' he said, his voice coming out dry and
lifeless as he looked beyond her into the flat, and the
untidy signs of Beth's occupation.

Fran closed her eyes briefly as she assimilated his ignorance. Neither Beth nor his mother had told him. For weeks she had been plagued by the assumption that he had known but not wanted to make use of the knowledge. 'I...she moved out of the hostel weeks ago. Didn't she tell you?' She wavered unnecessarily. The sky-blue eyes came back to hers and locked on them relentlessly. Her mouth dried as she watched them change from shock, to suspicion, to wariness, to an unreadable blankness.

'No, she didn't.'

Unnerved by the clipped reply, and the stillness of the big body, Fran found herself babbling out all Beth's troubles, stressing that Beth had come to *her*, not the other way around.

His mask of inexpression flickered at that, and for the first time he looked beyond her pale face. He looked at her hair, crimped by the spring humidity, the dirty streaks on her skin and revealing-concealing casual garb. She felt like a street urchin being looked over by a plutocrat, and unconsciously drew herself up to compensate with a haughty stare. A gleam fleetingly silvered the blue eyes and she stiffened. Did he find her funny? OK, so she was scruffy, but she had seen him look worse. She wasn't going to let him embarrass her, she wasn't ashamed of her body. He obviously noticed, from the way his eyes had lingered on the swell of her hips, that she wasn't as slim as she had been a few months ago, but her roundness wasn't fat. It was smooth, sleekly conditioned muscle. She was more supple and fitter than she had ever been in her life, thanks to the hard manual labour she was putting in.

'No need to get so uptight, Fran,' he drawled, as nervousness drove her on to restate Beth's case. 'I get the message. I'm not to take this as an oblique attempt on your part to fling yourself back into my arms.'

Since that was exactly what it had been, at least in part, Fran found herself flushing faintly. Was that relief she detected? She jutted her chin defensively.

'No wonder Beth never wanted me to run her back to the hostel, and only rang from Tech. I wonder who the secrecy was designed to protect? You or me?' He raised an eyebrow and his mouth curved slightly as he watched her wipe her palms nervously against her denim-clad thighs. Suddenly Fran caught a breathtaking glimpse of the man she knew, and an avalanche of feeling rushed into her hollow heart.

'Don't feel you need to apologise for having taken my sister under your wing, Francesca.' In the midst of that bland softness the drawn-out syllables of her name were an intimate caress that made her heart skip. 'I know that in spite of her brashness and the aura of confidence Beth carries around with her she's still vulnerable, and you're a sucker for vulnerability, aren't you? I have some very fond remembrances of your compassionate breast my-self…' And he stared deliberately at the place where her heart thumped passionately beneath the thin white cotton. Oh, God, that look! Inexorably Fran felt the light, deli-cious tingling that pressaged the tender tautening of her breasts. Quickly she spun around, missing the leaping flare of satisfaction that brought a grimly predatory smile to Ross's lips. So… She was proud, and stubborn and still bristling with defences, but her body and those big, lonely eyes betrayed her. She ached for him as much as he ached for her. His patience had paid off. But, in view of the unexpected circumstances, he would have to take a different, more direct approach from the one he had planned.

'Come in—I'll just see if Beth is ready—' Fran said

nervously, leading him into the lounge and turning towards the bedroom.

'Still running scared, Fran?' His soft taunt stopped her. 'Surely you don't intend to disappoint Beth after she's obviously gone to so much trouble to bring us together again?' When Fran still didn't turn around, he added, 'And it's a little late for a cover-up. If you're embarrassed by your body you only have yourself to blame. Women with breasts as sensitive as yours shouldn't go braless if they don't want their body language read…'

Fran turned proudly, gloved hands clenched at her sides to prevent them crossing defensively over her tingling breasts. 'I never denied that I found you attractive,' she said in a stifled voice.

'Only that it wasn't enough. I didn't agree at the time, but I do now. Not nearly enough.' His eyes glinted at her bewildered reaction to his cryptic remarks. 'You look quite beautiful, Frankie.'

She was taken aback by the sincerity of the quiet compliment. 'I… Don't be ridiculous, I'm a mess…'

He smiled, and a tongue of flame licked out of the blue eyes to singe her body beneath its flimsy covering. 'A beautiful mess…how I always imagined you'd look when you made peace with yourself…earthy, real, the kind of woman a man wants to enfold and be enfolded by…'

A slumberous warmth flushed across Fran's skin. Earthy, that's how she felt, especially when he looked at her like that, and her feelings for him were very strong and real. *Thank you, Beth*, she thought silently. The girl had enabled them to meet without sacrifice of pride on either side. 'I'm afraid I'm earthy in the very literal sense,' she said huskily, holding on to his gaze with difficulty. She *had* made peace with herself, and he was part of the treaty. She lifted her grimy-gloved hands apologetically. 'While you look very…elegant.'

She didn't understand why he laughed softly, until he explained. 'You make it sound like an accusation…after all the times you tried to make me put some clothes on when we lived together.' Fran's flush heated even more at the images his turn of phrase presented and his voice deepened, catching her off guard. 'It's just a skin, and underneath it I'm just the same man…a little more lean and hungry maybe, but the same man. I missed you, Princess. Did you miss me?'

He didn't wait for an answer. His hand reached out to cup the heavy fullness of one breast and exert the pressure which guided her body forward against his as his mouth covered hers, searching and finding her melting response.

As he kissed her his hand massaged her breast in lazy circles until she moaned quietly, and he lifted his mouth to murmur, 'Touch me… You want to, I know you do…'

'I can't—' her hands hovered helplessly in mid-air, '—these gloves, I'll mark you—'

'You already have, indelibly. Touch me,' he commanded huskily, sealing her hesitation with his mouth and she gave in to the need, her gloves catching and pulling at his shirt as she slid her arms around him, up under the tailored jacket, digging her fingers into the rippling heat of his back. When next he raised his head she was trembling against him, her eyes wide and dark with unsated pleasure.

'Oh, yes, you missed me,' he growled with thick satisfaction, and Fran stirred, briefly unsettled by that possessive triumph. But when the warm hands supporting her shoulders slid down to press her shifting hips against the slow rotation of his her resentment died. He, too, was possessed by this blissful torment.

'I wasn't going to wait much longer, Frankie,' he told her, nipping the vulnerable curve of her throat. 'If you hadn't called me some time in the next couple of weeks, I would have come looking.'

'But, you said—'

'I know what I said.' He gave her a small shake. 'I was angry, the way you meant me to be, and my pride was suffering…but you were just being you, resisting the pitfalls of impulse, dealing with one problem at a time. I knew how critical it was to your self-respect that you make this business of yours a success. I estimated it would take you about four months to find your feet, to gain the confidence to look around and reassess your priorities. I made a pact with myself to let you have that time, without the added pressure of my presence. Of course, I didn't know you were going to let Beth in where you feared to let *me* tread…' He stroked his thumb across her lips in wry reproach.

'Beth is different—'

'I should hope so.'

She blushed. 'I mean, she really did need me.

His smile was sombre. 'So do I. Are you happy, Fran? Fulfilled? Or have you found out that success, alone, isn't enough to fill all the lonely crevices in your life?'

'I…I was going to ring you.' She owed him the confession. 'I was afraid you—' He laid a gentle finger across her lips, stopping her rush of words.

'It doesn't matter now. What matters is whether you're willing to make room for me in this brave new world of yours.'

'I think you already know the answer to that.' It was written in every line of the supple body shaped to his.

'I need to hear it, as much as you need to say it. What do you really want, Fran?'

'You.' There was exquisite relief in saying it at last, and a glorious sense of breaking free. 'I want a lover to share myself with…'

'Then you shall have him, Princess!' If he had been triumphant before, he was exultant now. 'And more… everything you ever wanted.' More? How could she want more than this heady feeling of freedom?

'You didn't sell the cabin, after all, did you?' he teased irrelevantly.

'I…no…I just mortgaged it and sold the rest. How did you know?'

'Because my intermediary made the outrageously generous offer that you refused for "sentimental reasons".' He laughed at her blush. 'It kept me going, through the lonely nights, knowing that you wanted to hold on to a piece of our memories. Now we can renew them. I can't think of a better place for a honeymoon, if we can keep my family at bay…'

'Honeymoon?' she echoed faintly and he grinned, misunderstanding her shock.

'Isn't marriage the guarantee that you wouldn't ask for, and I wouldn't give? I wasn't ready then…I was too hung up on saving face. But it's yours for the asking now…'

Marriage? To Ross? A lifetime of playing Russian roulette, wondering when her happiness was going to explode in her face? Fran went weak at the thought.

'Isn't it a bit too soon to be talking about marriage?' She strove for teasing lightness. 'Can't we just enjoy what we have for a while before we get serious?'

To her dismay he must have heard the buried note of panic. He drew back slightly, his eyes solidifying from melting warmth to blue ice at what he saw in her face.

'I thought we *were* serious. I thought that's what the fuss was about...you and I, having to readjust our lives to one another. Was I wrong? Exactly what *do* you think we have, Fran? What is it we should "just enjoy"?'

She stared, afraid to answer, feeling her brief moment of freedom slipping inexorably away. Oh, why were they always out of step? Why did he always insist on demanding more than she felt capable of giving?

'I see...you're dooming us before we even begin, aren't you, Fran?' he said bleakly. 'You'll trust me in your life, but only so far. You want a stud, not a lover. The hell of it is I'm almost tempted.'

'That's not fair, Ross!' Fran cried shakily, freeing herself from the fingers bruising her shoulders. 'Damn it, you spring this on me from nowhere...you said...we never even...marriage was never one of the options!'

'Nor is it now. It's the *only* one.'

Fran couldn't believe it. The conversation had the quality of a weird nightmare. 'But *why*? I thought you only wanted—'

'A slick exchange of sexual pleasures?' he cut in crudely. 'I could have got that from half a dozen women in the last few months.' He saw her wince and that seemed to enrage him even more. 'Do you think I'd have wasted all this time if all I wanted from you was *sex*! And you were willing to *settle* for that?' His incredulous disgust made her bewildered and angry. Just when she had reconciled herself to the rules of the game, he changed them. How did she know that he wouldn't change them again? 'My God, Fran, is that a measure of your own self-worth...or mine? It's an insult to both of us. What in the hell do you *want* from me? You obviously want something I'm not offering. Is it love? I wouldn't be here if I *wasn't* in love with you! You think

I'd put myself through this kind of hell just for masochistic kicks? I love you, Francesca. Does that make a difference? Does that make me a better risk for your cautious soul?'

No! Fran's heart squeezed in anguish. Ross, in love with her? Dare she believe it? And if she did, what an awesome burden of responsibility it would be. His expectations of her were so impossibly high…he expected her to be herself, no barriers, no defences, *herself*, vulnerable to deepest joy and deepest hurt. Oh, God, she would disappoint him, she didn't think she could be that open. Her own suffering she had learned to cope with, but to know that *his* happiness rested with her…

Her hesitation was fatal. The blue flame that had burned so intensely in his eyes flickered and went out. Fran was stricken with the knowledge that already she had let him down. She put out a hand to touch him, wanting to explain, but he had already moved away, distancing himself with space as well as his heart-shattering words,

'No, I can see that it doesn't. I misjudged you, Francesca. It's not only giving love that you're afraid of, it's receiving it. And, coward that you are, I don't think it's a fear that you even *want* to conquer…'

CHAPTER TEN

WHAT am I *doing* here?

The roar inside Francesca's head was almost as loud as the booming rush of air past the open cabin door of the Cessna. Turning her head, weighted by her yellow helmet, she could see the young man sitting stiffly on the vibrating floor beside her. His eyes behind his goggles were tightly closed, his lips moving soundlessly. Fran wondered whether he was repeating the liturgy of the drill or a prayer. She had already said her prayers.

The other three first-time parachutists from her course were sitting in front of them, in the space left by the removal of the plane's passenger seats, facing the jumpmaster kneeling by the door. All too soon they would be over the drop zone and that sergeant-major bawl would be launching them into blue oblivion.

Why on earth am I here?

Because I'm crazy, the answer came. Crazy about a man who was crazy enough to do this for *fun*! Crazy enough to want to understand him, and, through him, herself. Crazy enough to do something drastic about it. This was a proving ground, a test and, if she could confront and conquer this ultimate fear she knew that all others would dwindle in comparison. Heartbreak, rejection, loss…after this she would know she could endure anything.

Poor Beth, she was justifiably bewildered by the events of the past couple of weeks. She had been flabbergasted to emerge from her bedroom that night to find her brother and her flatmate, not locked in impassioned embrace, but silently smouldering at each other from opposite sides of the room. Breakfast the next morning had been spent trying to ferret out the reason.

'Ross nearly bit my head off last night, when I asked him. He was in a foul mood all evening. I pity the poor woman whose baby he got dragged off to deliver halfway through the meal! What happened, I thought you two were nutty about each other?'

'Whatever gave you that idea?' said Fran automatically, staring into her coffee, alternately seething and despairing. How dared he give her something precious with one hand and snatch it away with the other! And because his ego was dented they were further apart now than they had ever been, even during the last few months of limbo that she had discovered last night *he* had decided she needed. And now he wanted to make another decision about *her* life!

'Come off it, Fran,' Beth scoffed. 'I've been in love hundreds of times, I recognise the signs, and I'm not so dumb that I don't know that my being Ross's sister had a lot to do with you letting me move in. Why do you think Mum was so keen? Ross told her he'd fallen for you, that's why. You just needed a little help in getting together—' She subsided, looking so guilty that Fran smiled wanly.

'It's all right. I did manage to figure out that last night wasn't just a startling coincidence.'

'Are you going to chuck me out?' Beth gnawed her lip.

'No, of course not, as long as you promise not to interfere again.'

'Cross my heart,' Beth vowed, but was unable to resist the desire to speculate, 'Did he try and talk you into an affair? Is that why you had a fight? Don't worry, Fran, he'll come round. You can't blame him for being twitchy, though, even if he is in love with you. Women have been trying to back him into corners for years, it's just a conditioned reflex to duck. Believe me, Mum wouldn't approve of Ross messing you around. She really likes you, she wouldn't want you to get hurt. She really thinks that Ross is serious about you—'

It was no use. Fran couldn't let Ross's family go on believing him the villain of the piece when he was being so disgustingly, implacably *honourable*...

'Well, you can set your mother's mind at rest...or I will when I write to her next. It's not Ross who's baulking at marriage. It's me.'

Beth was predictably scandalised. 'Fran!' she screamed, upsetting her coffee. 'He *proposed*? And you turned him *down*?' She hooted. 'Poor Ross, no wonder he looked as if he'd been run over by a concrete mixer!' Then outrage conquered sisterly malice. 'But *why*? Are you *crazy*? I thought you liked us, I thought you'd jump at the chance to be my sister-in-law,' she wailed.

'You marry a person, Beth, not a family,' Fran said drily, although she knew that wasn't quite the case with the Tarrants. They were all lovingly close.

'But what's the matter with Ross? Was it the way he asked or something?'

'Or something,' Fran sipped her coffee broodingly. 'And he didn't ask, he assumed.'

'You can't blame him for that,' said Beth uncertainly, 'I mean...he's got a lot to be confident about, don't you think? He loves you, he's disgustingly eligible, he's kind to children and animals, has a terrific respect for your career. What else could you *want*?' Put like that, it did sound incredible.

'He also likes dangerous sports,' Fran pointed out defensively. 'Specifically, jumping out of aeroplanes in mid-air.'

'Nobody's perfect,' Beth joked. Then, seeing Fran was deadly serious, she protested, 'But, Fran, that accident was a fluke. Statistically speaking, he's far more likely to be killed in a car accident. Or die of cancer, but I bet you wouldn't let *that* hold you back. If parachuting was really that dangerous, do you think Ross would encourage me to take it up? Yet when I was watching him jump last week he helped me sign up for—'

'He's jumping again?' Fran interrupted blindly, and Beth groaned.

'Oh, hell, me and my big mouth! Three times and textbook perfect every time. It's too late to worry now. What you don't know doesn't hurt you.'

She was wrong. Ignorance was the major cause of Fran's fear. By Ross's side or a thousand miles away, Fran was going to worry. Instead of letting her imagination run riot in the dark she should arm herself to the teeth with knowledge. Knowledge was power, knowledge was strength. Already she had let her insecurities dominate her to the point where they were ruling her life.

Beth was right about something else, though. It *was* more likely that Ross would be hurt in an accident on the road than anywhere else, but because Fran drove and accepted that risk herself her fears were proportionately less. An idea, wild and audacious, and worthy of Ross himself, took hold. Why should not the same perspective apply at a higher level of risk, too?

Ross loved her—enough to offer marriage, enough to offer secret assistance by trying to buy the cabin she had flung on to the market in a fit of defiance when the probate was finally settled. She couldn't even drum up any anger at the attempted manipulation, not when she knew it had been motivated by the sweetest of sentiments, the same ones that had led her to take the cabin off the market again barely two weeks later, admitting she would rather mortgage herself to the hilt than sever that precious link with love and Ross Tarrant. And if she loved him, didn't she owe him the best? A woman who was his equal, not one who let doubts and anxieties nibble away at the foundations of love until it crumbled into nothingness. Could she do it? Escape her own limitations, try her wings, literally, to see how high she could soar?

But when she blurted out her idea to Beth, instead of looking suitably impressed by her courage, the girl had been dubious. 'Do you think that's such a good idea? I mean…it's not really your kind of thing…'

'Is that a polite way of calling me a wimp?' Fran's jaw shot out even as Beth hurriedly denied the calumny. Ross had called her a coward too, once too often! She would do it, and to hell with what *they* thought!

'When's the next course?' she demanded, adding grimly when she saw Beth bite her lip, 'And don't you go running to Ross about this. I don't want him to know.'

'But then, I don't see the point—'

'No more meddling, Beth. You *promised*!'

'OK, but I tell you—I think you're crazy!'

That made the verdict unanimous. Christina, too, thought her friend insane.

'I get palpitations when the kids ride their bikes up to the shops, for goodness' sake,' she said, which only served to confirm Fran's theory about perspective. One loves, one fears…it was just necessary to get a proper handle on them, and not impose them constantly on others.

The hardest part, during the two weeks it took for Fran to rack up the required hours of ground-training at the parachute club was resisting the temptation, at Beth's urging, to ring Ross.

'At least give him some hope…tell him you're thinking about it. Please, Fran. He won't ring, you know. A

man has his pride, after all, especially when he's just had
his love and honour thrown back in his teeth as if they
were insults!'

Fran had winced, but she hadn't given in to the
emotional blackmail. Besides, Ross wasn't the kind of
man to cave in at the first sign of resistance or adversity.
If he loved her, he would be back…after his pride had
given her the opportunity to stew for a while, by which
time she would either have been tempered in her trial by
fire or consumed by it. All or nothing, that was what he
had demanded and that was what she was going to give
him. If she wasn't strong enough to love him, she must
be strong enough to reject him. Ironically, acceptance of
her own weakness would require the greatest show of
strength.

'OK?' The jumpmaster's voice was suddenly loud in
her ear as he helped her into position sitting on the door
sill, her legs dangling into a seventy-mile-per-hour slipstream. She had hardly been aware of the others jumping,
but she could see them now, below her, five flowering
canopies drifting on the light breeze.

'*Go!*'

Instantly obeying the command to go had been drilled
into them so often that it was second nature. Fran went.

She pushed off firmly, collapsing into the solid pressure of the air two and a half thousand feet above mother
earth. Without even thinking about it she went straight
into the drill, forcing her body into the 'stable' position,
stomach down arms and legs spreadeagled, head back
against her pack as she shouted out the vital count, 'One
thousand, two thousand, three thousand, four thousand.
Check!'

Even before she had finished counting off the seconds
she felt the disorientating jolt that pulled her into a
vertical position, indicating that the static line attached to

the plane had deployed her parachute. On the word 'check' she looked up to make sure and to her horror she saw that the canopy was billowing out into two asymmetrical lobes rather than a reassuring roundness. She recognised it instantly from their lectures as a 'Mae West'; one of the rigging lines must have caught over the top of the canopy. She looked down towards the other jumpers to judge her speed, and her stomach swooned as she realised that her descent was far more rapid than theirs. She was also starting to rotate in the rigging and knew that it would continue to increase at an alarming rate if she didn't act quickly. *Time*, it had been hammered into them, *is your biggest enemy*. Fran, with years of practice at reacting quickly to emergency situations, had performed the equipment and safety drills meticulously in class and now she automatically went into action, cold clarity of thought smothering her momentary sense of panic.

She reached for the handle on the top of the reserve parachute strapped to her stomach and pulled, holding the pack steady with her other hand and keeping her feet pressed tightly together. The handle came away and she let it go, grabbing the emerging reserve with both hands and throwing it violently down and away. It blossomed up past her, immediately slowing her rate of descent, and she rested her forearms on the reserve rigging lines to keep it clear of the main 'chute which was now beginning to collapse completely. A few seconds later she used the canopy releases to jettison the useless main, and watched it snake groundwards.

She had done it! She had only a brief moment of glorious relief to savour the drifting weightlessness, the beautiful sound of the canopy singing its rushing song of flight, before she was looking for the ground instructor, grasping the steering toggles to obey his hand signals to run and hold according to her position over the target area.

She didn't have time to be scared, even when the ground came streaking up at her—she was too busy. She tucked her arms up, bent her chin on to her chest and rounded her back, holding her knees and feet together to absorb the passive blow from the grassy field, and dissipating the shock of landing with a backward roll to the left.

She was scarcely aware of the congratulations of the instructor as she deflated her canopy and gathered it in, or of the excited chatter of her fellow students. Her hands shook as she removed her goggles. Dimly she heard someone say, 'You did everything right, Francesca, everything right. Here, let's get this off you and you can sit down.' Calm hands unbuckled her harness webbing and pulled off her helmet. 'Are you OK?'

And then there was another voice, abrupt, familiar, aggressively controlled. 'No, she's not OK, she's in shock. I'll look after her, I'm a doctor,' and she was being hustled across the uneven grass, half-dragged, half-carried, past the knot of interested friends and relations and Saturday-morning tourists, through the sagging farm gate to the road where a cluster of cars were parked. She was thrust on to the back seat of the nearest, a long, black limousine which even had a uniformed chauffeur sitting glassily in the front seat, her booted feet scuffing the roadside dust as her head was thrust unceremoniously between her knees. One of the jumpers must have some very rich and very vulgar friends, Fran thought with a semi-hysterical giggle. She stared at the Italian leather shoes, toe-to-toe in the dust with her borrowed boots. Ross! Her shock began to dissipate as she realised that he must have witnessed her spectacular victory over self. Beth must have spilled the beans after all, but no matter,

it saved Fran a trip. She felt drunk with relief. She wanted
to share the bubbling exhilaration with Ross. For a few
minutes up there she had walked the knife-edge, thrilled
to the sharp taste of fear. But this time, unlike that
terrifying flight in the Tiger Moth, she had been prepared
for it…had conquered the fear with her own force of will.
It was like a revelation, illuminating all the shadowy
corners of her psyche. Fran knew now that she could
conquer the world if she wanted to…!

'Ross—'

'Shut up and breathe!' The hand tightened mur-
derously on her neck and Fran squeaked. His tone of
voice was hardly calculated to soothe her shock. Wasn't
he going to congratulate her? He had toasted Beth with
champagne! Fran hadn't gone to watch her friend's
inaugural jump, not only because she wasn't ready to face
Ross, whom she knew would be there, but because she
thought that it would be a psychologically disastrous
move to confront the reality of what all those ground
drills meant until the last possible moment. Coward to
the last…but a brave one!

'Ross—'

Suddenly the weight lifted from her neck and she was
hauled upright, dangling on tiptoe from the jumpsuit
fabric balled in his fists. She gulped as she got her first
look at his expression. Congratulations were definitely
not on his agenda! He looked grey under his tan, the sexy
mouth clamped into a thin line, his eyes two chips of
blue steel.

'What in the bloody *hell* were you doing up there?'
His snarl took the skin off the top of her ears and she
stared at him open-mouthed. The instructor had been
pleased. Had Ross's expert eye seen something that he
had missed?

'It all happened so fast,' she gasped apologetically,

trying to loosen his grip with unsteady hands. 'Should I have tried to clear the canopy? I didn't think there was time to have a go and we were told that if there's any doubt—'

'Not *that*!' he roared, shaking her furiously. 'You know damned well what I mean. I mean, what were you doing up there *at all*? And don't try and feed me that lie you fed Beth about it having nothing to do with me. It has *everything* to do with me. You never showed any sign of being interested in adventure sports before. Why now? What incredibly cretinous theory about us have you cooked up in that tiny little brain that makes you think you have to *prove* anything to me? Goddammit, Frankie, have you any idea what I went through when I saw that malfunction? Well?' he rattled her again. 'Have you?'

The adrenalin still rushing frantically around her body was well shaken up by this time. 'No, but I can make a good guess,' she threw at him. 'At least I didn't land in a tree and break every bone in my body.'

'*What* did you say?' he asked, in a thick and dangerous voice and Fran, still feeling cocky, started to repeat herself with pointed sweetness. She didn't get past the first word. He kissed her with the full force of his anger and, after a moment of recoil from his savagery, Fran kissed him back, with equal force. She was his equal, in every way, and she was through running away from the prospect of loving him.

He broke the kiss as violently as he had begun it, one hand lifting from her shoulder to wipe his mouth. They both stared at the blood which streaked the hard knuckles.

'Is that yours, or mine?' Fran asked shakily and Ross closed his eyes, and shuddered. 'You're not going to faint at the sight of a little blood are you, Doctor?' she murmured as he actually swayed on his feet. He made a raw sound and put his arms around her, not gently, holding her hard against the erratic beat of his heart.

'Don't you ever, *ever*, do that to me again,' he said with quiet violence.

'Parachute?' Fran asked, her voice muffled in his chest. Now that her initial shock and euphoria had died she was realising that she didn't particularly want to make a habit of this kind of thing.

'Shut me out of a decision like this. I need to know, I need to be part of it. Oh, Frankie, I accused you of being a coward, but I'm the coward here, not you. I dismissed your fears as of no account because I was afraid that I would lose you if I admitted that they had any validity. But they do. God, how could I have been such a hypocrite as to say that I love you and yet be willing to put you through the kind of agony I just went through? I never fully realised before how utterly terrifying it can be to watch someone you love hover literally between life and death and be powerless to help them. I had an inkling of it when you swam out to the boat that day, but I didn't know I was in love with you then. I didn't realise it until you walked out on me, and I faced the fact that it wasn't a matter of choice any more. I couldn't just shrug and let you go, I *had* to make you love me, even if it took the rest of my life. But you do, don't you, Fran?' His arms tightened briefly. 'That's *why* you were so afraid and now I understand… But you don't have to be any more. If you want me to give up this sort of thing, I will, with no regrets. I'd far rather have you, just the way you are. You don't have to make any grand gestures to show me how brave you are, I don't care. Just show me your love, that's bravery enough…if you can…'

'I didn't do this for you, Ross,' Fran said, with tender amusement at his anguished humility. 'I did it for me. I wasn't trying to be someone I'm not—just to be a strong *me*. And I am. I'm…free. I needed to know that I could trust myself before I could trust anyone else. And I do trust you, Ross. I know that you would never deliberately hurt me. So don't *you* make any grand gestures, either. Even if you never regretted giving up your racketing around the skies, *I* would.'

He caught his breath and cupped her face, lifting it from the cradle of his chest. The clear, grey serenity of her eyes smote him to the bone. Her love was there, open and unafraid, for him to see.

'Yes, I love you,' she said huskily and watched his skin flush with warmth.' All of you, not just the pieces that I feel comfortable with. And I couldn't bear it if you thought that you had to be less than you are for my sake.' She smiled at his expression. 'I want you to be more, not less. I love you, Ross.'

The long fingers tightened possessively on her jaw, his eyes alight with joy, relief. 'I thought you did, oh, God, I hoped you did, but how good it is to hear you say it. Do you know how wild it drove me trying to work out why the idea of marriage to me was so horrifying? Even if you didn't love me, I thought you'd at least be *flattered*…' His soft laugh held the memory of his frustrated anger. 'When I went to bed that night I was cursing Beth for jumping the gun and myself for greedily trying to take advantage of it. I had been so proud of my damned patience so far, and it all went out the window in a moment when you suddenly looked at me as if I'd sprouted horns, rather than the halo I thought I deserved. Such arrogance…'

'Magnificent arrogance,' she agreed mischievously and he laughed, this time with some of that same, beloved arrogance.

'Like a callow boy I was outraged that you didn't treat

my love like the priceless gift it was, and spitefully I tried to make you feel guilty about it.'

'You succeeded.'

'You got your revenge. When I saw that 'Mae West' I thought it would be my fault if you died. That I'd driven you into believing you had to be some kind of Amazon to earn my respect. But that you always had, and always will...' He tilted his head to the sky and blurted out, 'I still can't believe you did that!'

'I wanted to see what it was like,' she said meekly.

His lips moved silently, very like those of her fellow parachutist before he went out the door. 'And what was it like?' he finally asked, in strangled tones.

'I don't really know, it all happened so fast,' she admitted sheepishly. 'Not as scary as I'd expected while everything was going on and then...sort of quiet but not quiet...rather awesome and fantastic...' Her enthusiasm died a little as she remembered what could have happened. '...I think...'

Ross felt the last of his tension drain away to be replaced by a heavy, sultry sensation of anticipation, spiked with delicious slivers of amusement.

'It gets better,' he said, but didn't make the mistake of grinning at the expression of horror that flitted across her face. No, he didn't have to worry about Fran acquiring an insatiable thirst for adventure, she would continue to express her own quiet courage in other ways. But he would make damned sure that it wasn't over-stretched. She had taught him a lesson that he couldn't unlearn and didn't want to. He frowned, realising that they still hadn't settled the question of marriage. After last time it wouldn't do to take too much for granted. That was another lesson he had learned well.

'Can I give you a lift back to town?'

'I think we're supposed to have a debriefing,' Fran said

vaguely, looking around and realising that they were standing in the middle of a public road and that they were getting a few funny looks from the spectators now trailing back to their cars. She shrugged hurriedly out of the loose encirclement of his arms.

'I think I can take care of your debriefing,' Ross murmured with a wicked look downwards that made her tingle. 'Did you come in the club van with the others?' She nodded. 'Good, then there's no car to worry about.'

He put his hands flat against her shoulders and pushed. Startled, she fell backwards, on to the seat of the limousine she had sheltered in earlier.

'Ross, what do you think you're doing?' she hissed at him as he bent and scooped her legs into the car, thrusting her along the deep leather seat with a sinuous nudge of his hips as he joined her. 'You can't just commandeer—'

'Home, James,' Ross flicked the switch on the small intercom on the padded panel in front of them and the chauffeur, without looking back through the tinted panel of glass, made an acknowledging gesture with his hand as he leaned forward to start the car.

'Ross? Ross, this isn't *yours*, is it?' He was wearing a suit again she realised, on a *Saturday*—looking smooth and suave and stinking rich. She longed to see him in scruffy denims again…or in nothing at all.

He ignored her disbelieving squawk, punching up some numbers on a sleek, cordless phone. 'Nessa? I'm on my way home. Only urgent calls, please…Dr Nugent can take the rest.' He hung up. 'Nessa is my housekeeper. She picks up after me and generally nags me about life in general. Rather like you, in fact,' he added slyly, 'except she's thirty years older and doesn't drive me out of my skull with lust and desire and terrifying elusiveness.'

'I can't believe that you could be crass enough to drive

around town in something like this,' Fran said severely, conscious of the man in the front seat, trying to hide the lurch of excitement she felt at seeing Ross leaning back against the cream upholstery, regarding her with that heavy-lidded sensual amusement. 'After all your sneers about the material trappings of success.'

'He can't hear you, Fran, or see you. All the glass is mirrored.' Ross judged her nervous glance accurately. He grinned lazily at her flush. 'And you're right, I'm not that crass. I rented this to take a very important, wealthy Middle-Eastern patient out to the airport this morning. Just one of the small touches of courtesy and luxury that she takes for granted. I was on my way back home when Beth called, in a panic because she hadn't been able to get hold of me and thought she was cutting it too fine—'

'She wasn't suppose to tell you at all.'

'Wasn't she?' he asked drily, and smiled as Fran's eyes flickered. Had she been setting some kind of test for him as well, without realising it? If so, he had passed with flying colours. 'Anyway, that's why I over-reacted so violently back there. I was shattered by nerves before we even got in sight of the drop zone. Beth said she'd told you about my jumps and you'd closed up and gone "all quiet and fanatical" about doing it yourself. I didn't know what to think. Add to that two speeding tickets and a near-miss with a roadside goat, and that "Mae West" was just a match to the powder keg. It was either beat you or kiss you senseless, and I couldn't do either I was shaking so much.'

Fran cleared her throat. 'The jumpmaster told us that lots of wives and girlfriends of the male jumpers often help as judges in sky-diving competitions. Perhaps I could do that…if I'm not up there myself, of course,' she added bravely to herself, making his mouth twitch.

'Of course,' he murmured. 'We'll wait and see, shall we?' He paused. 'As wife or girlfriend?'

She looked at him and he smiled reassuringly, but he forgot to guard his eyes, which had taken on that steely look again. 'Is that a choice?' asked Fran innocently.

'Yes.' And just as quickly, 'No.' He frowned, and looked unseeingly out at the passing fields. 'Yes. I don't know.' He shrugged impatiently and looked at her with brooding resentment. 'What do you want it to be?'

'What happened to the strong, decisive man I fell in love with?' she mourned gleefully. 'Who is this wishy-washy substitute?'

'Wishy-washy?' Suddenly she was flat on her back against the cool leather seat, laughingly pushing at his wide shoulders. 'You want decisive, Princess? I'll give you decisive—'

And he was kissing her, devouring her with lips and teeth and tongue, and while she was dealing with the erotic shock of his mouth on hers his hands were busily unzipping her flight suit and burrowing eagerly under the tracksuit she wore underneath. The purring hum of the powerful car beneath her, and the tigerish growl of the big man on top of her combined in an exquisite inner vibration that burned from her belly to her brain. He swore roughly at the tangle her clothing created and rolled sideways the better to deal with it, so that they both lay slanted on the seat, their legs entwining, feet jammed against the panelled wood of the door.

'Ross, wait—' Fran shuddered as he found the hard peak of her breast and stroked it lovingly through her silky, seamless bra, making it swell and harden even further.

'I've done nothing else but, since I met you, and if you get pregnant you'll *have* to damned well marry me—'

'I only wanted to say yes.'

'Yes what?' he muttered vaguely, tasting her skin with a connoisseur's appreciation and a starving man's fervour.

'Yes, I'll marry you, even if I *don't* get pregnant.'

'Of course you will,' he purred, moving his hand down her body, pushing under the soft waistband of her tracksuit pants and touching her with mind-bending gentleness and intimacy. 'Your compassionate heart couldn't bear to condemn me to a lifetime of painful frustration. God—' his hips flexed involuntarily as her thigh dragged against his swollen hardness with a convulsive jerk of pleasure, '—you're so hot and sweet and ready for me...how in the hell are we going to work this?' He groaned as he rubbed himself against her, building the pressure for release as he tried to wrestle her out of the restricting jumpsuit.

'Ross, you do remember where we are, don't you?'

'How could I forget?' He cursed as he realised he had no chance of getting the suit off while she still had her boots on.

'Don't you think we should wait for a more appropriate time and place?' Fran asked, quivering with love and laughter at his passionate antics.

'What could be more appropriate, Princess?' he growled. 'We've come full circle. Here we are again, trying to make love in the back seat of a car...except this time we know precisely what we're doing, and why, and nothing and no one is going to separate us again...'

Full circle. A circle of love without beginning or end, and large enough to encompass every dream that Francesca could ever wish for. She began to help him, eagerly...

Anne Weale was still at school when a women's magazine published some of her stories. At twenty-five she had her first novel accepted by Mills & Boon®. Now, with a grown-up son and still happily married to her first love, Anne divides her life between her winter home, a Spanish village ringed by mountains and vineyards, and a summer place in Guernsey, one of the many islands around the world she has used as backgrounds for her books.

Look out for
A SPANISH HONEYMOON by Anne Weale
in Tender Romance™, March 2002.

SEASCAPE

by

Anne Weale

For Barbara, Carol, Dorothy, Lilian, Liz, Margaret and Marie with whom I explored and painted the ancient seaport of Chaniá.

CHAPTER ONE

THE next morning, after telephoning the coronary care unit and being told her employer was sleeping, Kate set out for London.

The object of her journey was to find Miss Walcott's grandson and appeal to his better nature—if he had one!—to come and make peace with the old lady.

Why they were not on speaking terms wasn't entirely clear to her. But, from what she knew of the situation, Kate felt the rift must be his fault, not his grandmother's.

Although still in his early thirties, Alexander Walcott had already made a name for himself as a painter, traveller and lover of beautiful women. Miss Walcott paid a London agency to supply her with Press cuttings about his exhibitions and other exploits. She had several large albums full of reports of his doings, both artistic and social.

His girlfriends had ranged from a British TV presenter to an American lawyer, a beautiful Japanese violinist and the polo-playing daughter of an Australian millionaire. None had held his interest for more than a few months and there seemed to be no shortage of replacements for the girls he discarded.

An illustrated weekly magazine had included him in a feature on a hundred of the world's most eligible men, describing him as 'one of the most elusive of Europe's charmers, whose combination of rugged looks, suave manners, wit and talent compensate for his lack of serious money.'

Not that Alexander Walcott was strapped for cash by most people's standards, Kate thought drily, as she drove away from the village which had been her base for the past six months.

Xan, pronounced Zan, as his grandmother and his intimates called him, made enough from his paintings to pay for a spacious flat in London which had also appeared in the glossies, and to finance his frequent journeys to exotic locations from which he returned with a fresh batch of vividly evocative paintings and all manner of covetable souvenirs to enhance either the flat or his barn-cum-studio in the country.

His grandmother, also a talented painter, made her living by taking groups of amateur artists to picturesque places in Britain and around the Mediterranean and helping them improve their skill with pen, pastel and brush.

Xan travelled alone, or accompanied by his current playmate. His income was probably ten times as much as Miss Walcott's, and earned with far less hassle.

Indeed, it was half a century of hassle—including the distressing estrangement from her grandson—which, in Kate's opinion, had caused Miss Walcott to have a heart attack after supper the previous evening.

The journey to central London took over an hour.

Having lived there for some years herself, Kate had no difficulty in driving to the elegant Georgian square not far from Kensington Gardens where Xan lived.

It was harder to find somewhere to leave the car but eventually she saw a space, parked and put a coin in the meter.

While she was living in London she had had to be smartly dressed with expensive accessories and her hair and nails perfectly groomed. She had had an image to maintain.

Now that she was what Miss Walcott called 'my amanuensis' and Kate herself defined as 'a dogsbody', it didn't matter how she dressed. Jeans and a shirt, with a sweatshirt or padded gilet when the weather was chilly, was the 'look' appropriate to her new role.

And these days a light skin cream, lip gloss and colourless mascara on her naturally dark eyelashes were the only cosmetics she used regularly. It was months since she had dressed up. Most of her London clothes were still in a suitcase, relics of a life to which she would not return even in the unlikely event of being asked to resume her previous job.

Like many of her contemporaries, she had been through the trauma of redundancy, survived it and in so doing discovered that none of the things she had lost had made her happy.

What she needed—had needed all her life and never had—was a family, a sense of belonging somewhere. Which was why she hadn't much time for a man like Xan Walcott who had nothing to do with his closest relation, the old lady now fighting to recover from the destruction of an area of heart muscle.

If she pulled through—and the extent of the damage hadn't yet been established—it would be Miss Walcott's own iron will-power as much as the ministrations in the coronary care unit which would save her. She was as gutsy as they came. A bit set in her ways and opinions, but that was to be expected of someone of her age, born in an era very different from today's world, Kate thought tolerantly.

In the six months they had been together she had become extremely fond of Nerina Walcott and would have been delighted to have her as a grandmother. Why Xan Walcott wasn't—why he never so much as telephoned—was incomprehensible.

As she walked from the car to the house where he lived, Kate knew there was a chance he was not in England at present. She had attempted to telephone him from the hospital last night, only to find that his number was ex-directory. The only reason she could think of for anyone other than a major celebrity's wanting to keep their number out of the telephone book was to avoid recriminatory calls from ex-spouses, partners or lovers. Which tied in with what she knew of Xan's love-'em-and-leave-'em lifestyle.

As she pressed the bell marked 'Walcott', she prepared to mask her instinctive dislike of the man she had come to see. It was no good showing hostility towards someone when you needed their co-operation. But if he refused to play ball—and she wouldn't put it past him—then she might allow her true feelings to show.

'Who is it?'

The question came from an entryphone panel. 'My name is Kate Poole, Mr Walcott. I work for your grandmother. She's in hospital…seriously ill. May I see you for a few minutes, please?'

There was a pause, then a somewhat curt, 'All right…come in. Top floor.' A moment later she heard the click of the mechanism controlling the street door.

Making sure it had latched behind her, Kate entered the long narrow hall common to most terraced houses of this size and period. She had shown dozens of similar houses to prospective buyers during her time as an estate agent on the staff of one of London's most prestigious property agencies.

Casting a professional eye over the fixtures and fittings as she mounted the staircase, she concluded that all the flats in this building were owner-occupied rather than rented to transients.

The staircase and landings had the well-kept appearance of a communal area shared by people who wanted this part of the house to match the standard of their apartments. In buildings where the flats were rented to short-term tenants, there were often signs of neglect.

On the third and last flight the staircase wall was hung with framed drawings. One of them, a pen and ink study of a couple in a four-poster bed, she recognised. It was by Charles Keene, a Victorian artist. She had seen the original in exhibition at the Royal Academy the day before losing her job. The copy here reminded her what a disaster being sacked had seemed at the time.

Eventually her dismissal had proved the truth of the old saying that when one door closed another door opened. Now, unfortunately, it looked as if the new door which had opened for her would itself close before long. Even if Miss Walcott recovered from the heart attack, she would almost certainly have to retire. Kate would be out of a job again.

Perhaps Xan Walcott knew how long it usually took his visitors to climb the stairs, or perhaps one of the carpeted treads of the final flight was fitted with a warning bell. As she was lifting her arm to use the knocker, the door opened.

The photographs she had seen of him in his grand-mother's albums had not prepared her for his size. He was every inch of six foot two and a recent trip to somewhere tropical had given him a deep tan which emphasised the steel-grey coldness of his eyes.

Evidently it was not part of his technique to favour the women he met with a friendly smile. Or perhaps it was her connection with his grandmother that made his expression decidedly unwelcoming.

'I can give you ten minutes,' he said, standing back for her to enter. 'After that I shall have to leave for an important appointment.'

'If your number had been in the book, it would have saved *my* time,' she answered. 'I have plenty to do without driving to London, Mr Walcott. Will you be free later today? As Miss Walcott's next of kin, I think you should be on hand if her condition deteriorates. A heart attack at any age is serious; at seventy, it's very serious.'

Having closed the outer door, he led the way through another into the large, light living-room Kate recognised from a feature about it in *House & Garden*.

'You say you work for my grandmother. In what capacity?'

· 'As her general assistant. I answered an advertisement she put in *The Lady* last winter.' In case the name meant nothing to him, she added, 'The magazine's small ads columns are a well-known marketplace for nannies, housekeepers and helpers. Miss Walcott was beginning to find she had too much on her plate. I've taken over the admin side of the business and I go on the trips as her courier.'

'When did you start working for her?' The question was accompanied by a gestured invitation to sit down.

'Six months ago…at the beginning of April.' Kate seated herself in a cane-backed antique library chair and watched him lower his long frame on to a loose-covered sofa piled with an interesting collection of cushions.

Xan said, 'Long enough, I'd have thought, to be aware that my grandmother and I don't have a close relationship. In fact we have nothing to do with each other.'

'I realise there's been an estrangement, but surely in the circumstances…'

'Has she asked for me?'

'She's still under sedation. She hasn't asked for you yet, but I'm sure she will.'

'What makes you think so?'

Kate told him about the Press cutting albums. 'She's obviously proud of your achievements.'

He glanced at his watch. 'Do you have the hospital's number?'

She unzipped her shoulder-bag and took out a small spiral notebook. Seeing him reach for the telephone on the table at his elbow, she read out the number.

When he had dialled and was waiting to get through, he gave her a swift top-to-toe appraisal and then met and held her eyes as if by staring intently he could also inspect her mind. Kate found his scrutiny disturbing. She hoped when the switchboard answered he would turn his grey stare elsewhere.

'Good morning. My name is Alexander Walcott. I'm related to Miss Nerina Walcott who was admitted yesterday. May I speak to someone who can tell me how she is, please?'

He was still looking intently at Kate, who would have liked to outstare him but found that she couldn't.

Instead she looked round the room, taking in the crowded bookshelves, the equally crowded walls hung with drawings and paintings by other hands than his own, the antique apothecary's chest with its many shallow drawers in which, presumably, he stored his working equipment, and the profusion of interesting old and new objects.

It was—if she were honest—a room which appealed to her far more than the austere simplicity of Miss Walcott's cottage. Kate could see the beauty of those bare white-washed rooms with their simple furniture and absence of all non-essentials. But it was the orderly clutter of this room which drew a stronger response from her; partly, perhaps, because of growing up in a well-run children's home where the staff had been kind, even affectionate, but there had been little chance to acquire a display personal treasures.

She flicked a quick look at Xan, who now was repeating the nature of his enquiry to someone else. To her vexation he was still scrutinising her but with a less austere expression on his face. His appraisal was no longer critical. It had changed to the candid assessment of a connoisseur of women evaluating a candidate for his interest.

Kate didn't like the way he was watching her now any better than his previous appraisal. She had always resented X-ray looks from the opposite sex and for some reason Xan's expression made her especially uncomfortable.

He said to someone at the hospital, 'I'm Miss Walcott's grandson. She has no next of kin other than myself.' A long pause. 'Yes...yes, I see. Has she asked for me, do you know? She hasn't. Thank you. I'll call again later. In the meantime, if she should ask, you can contact me at this number.'

He dictated a central London number, repeated it and, with a crisp thank-you and goodbye, rang off.

To Kate, he said, 'The usual hospital jargon. "Holding her own...stable but still on the critical list".'

She stood up. 'If your grandmother doesn't ask for you, it won't mean she doesn't want to see you. She may not ask because she thinks you wouldn't come. But seeing you could make the difference between her living and dying.'

'I would have thought my reappearance at this stage was more likely to kill her than cure her.' His tone was sardonic. 'It's fifteen years...more...since Nerina and I last locked horns. Our relationship was a running battle from the time I was old enough to think for myself. If your family background is a happy one, it's probably hard for you to accept that many people with blood-ties can't stand the sight of each other.'

She wondered how he would react if she answered, My family background is non-existent. I was left on the floor of a changing-room in a department store when I was six weeks old. My parents were never traced.

But she wasn't about to disclose the facts of her life to

this hard, self-sufficient man who clearly was a loner by choice.

'I'm aware of that,' she said stiffly. 'But there is the expression "blood is thicker than water". I wouldn't have thought the differences between you in your teens and Miss Walcott in her middle age had much bearing on this present situation. She's old and ill and her life has been full of grief. I know losing your parents much have hurt you as well. But children get over such things. Miss Walcott has lost everyone she ever loved. Is it really too much to ask that you find time to make your peace with her? It's not far to go.'

'I'll think about it. Now, if you'll excuse me…'

Instead of seeing her to the door and delaying his own departure until she had left the building, he followed her down the stairs. Judging by the way he was dressed, in a well-cut tropic-weight suit with a formal shirt and silk tie, she concluded his appointment was a lunch date at one of the glitzy hotels or perhaps some important event in the art world such as the opening of a major exhibition.

In the hall, he moved past her to unlock the front door. 'Did you drive or come by train?' he asked.

'I drove in Miss Walcott's car. It's only a meter round the corner.' Before turning in that direction, she held out her hand. 'Goodbye. Mr Walcott. I hope, when you've thought it over, you'll decide to do the humane thing. I happen to know that you are your grandmother's sole beneficiary. If she doesn't pull through, I think you'd feel very uncomfortable inheriting the cottage knowing that you hadn't at least tried to put things right between you.'

As she spoke, she was aware of the latent strength in the long fingers clasping hers. She had noticed his hands earlier, while he was telephoning, and had been reminded of a pair of imitation marble hands, an exact copy of the hands of Michelangelo's famous statue of David, which had been photographed in the colour supplement of her Sunday paper recently.

To her surprise, instead of releasing her hand, he held on to it. Looking down at her, he said, 'You have extraordinary eyes. I'd like to look at your irises through a magnifying glass.'

Then he caught sight of a taxi and, with a brisk, 'Good-bye,' stepped into the street to hail it, leaving her standing on the step between the area railings of the house where he lived and its neighbour.

When she returned to the car, before she switched on the motor, Kate tilted the rear-view mirror to look at her eyes.

Men had admired her legs and her long, thick, honey-blonde hair. They had paid her all sorts of compliments. Whether they had been sincere, there was no telling. *En route,* as they hoped, to bed, men tended to say what they thought girls wanted to hear. But no one had ever remarked on the unusual colour of her eyes.

Miss Walcott had commented on them because, being an artist, she was more observant than most people. She had seen that, if studied closely, the pupils of Kate's eyes were rimmed with gold merging with blue with an outer circle of green so dark at the edge as to be virtually black. This had the effect of making them appear to change colour according to what she was wearing.

A blue sweatshirt would make them seem blue. The dark river-green Indian silk scarf she had bought on a street market made them seem to be green. The amber beads she had worn with smart grey or beige suits in London had made them look golden.

'With those eyes, a few centuries ago they'd have called you a witch…and, for different reasons, me too,' Miss Walcott had said, shortly after Kate had moved in with her.

She was the only person who knew about Kate's origins; not because it was a secret that she didn't know who her parents were but because, except for employers requiring the answers to official questions, no one else had been interested. She was someone to whom people confided *their* life histories and *their* problems without ever being curious about hers.

On her way out of London she made a slight detour to pass the place where some unknown person, probably her mother, had left her wrapped in a blanket with the name 'Kate Poole' pinned to it.

She still had that piece of paper, the only clue to the mystery of her birth and parentage; unless the fact that she had been left in Harrods, one of the world's most famous department stores, was another clue.

Driving past the massive façade of the building where, twenty-six years ago, she had become the subject of a paragraph in more than one national newspaper, Kate felt a peculiar sensation not unlike the disturbance affecting the radio when a car passed under power lines. The feeling had been even stronger when, during her years in London, she had actually entered the store and walked through the fashion departments.

But today, as Harrods fell behind and Brompton Road merged with Cromwell Road, the artery for traffic heading west, it was not her own birth but the possibly imminent death of the old lady in her care which preoccupied her. Ahead of her was a taxi whose passengers might be on their way to Heathrow Airport. But it was from London's other airport, Gatwick, that she, Miss Walcott and the thirteen people who had booked places on the last painting course of the season were due to fly to Crete in two weeks' time.

After disappointing weather all summer, Kate had been looking forward to a fortnight of Mediterranean sun. Now, unless she could find someone to take her employer's place, the trip would have to be cancelled, much to the disappointment and perhaps, in some cases, indignation of everyone who had enrolled for the course.

The situation worried her all the way back to the hospital. There she was allowed to spend a few minutes at Miss Walcott's bedside, inwardly shocked by her appearance but outwardly calm and reassuring.

The doctor she spoke to afterwards was non-committal about the old lady's chances of recovery. Kate knew she would have to wait until she saw Robert to get a franker assessment. Meanwhile she could only pray that the man she had met in London would feel conscience-bound to come.

But did Xan Walcott have a conscience?

At the age of sixteen, after running away, his conscience hadn't prompted him to let his grandmother know he was safe and well. Why should it trouble him now?

From earliest times, artists had tended to ignore the conventions and moral values of the societies they lived in. Xan was not the kind of painter who lived in picturesque squalor. On the contrary, he appeared to be steering his career in the direction of all the rich pickings and public honours the world of art had to offer, thought Kate, on her way to the cottage.

Robert Murrett, son of the now retired doctor who had been Miss Walcott's GP and friend for thirty years, had taken his father's place in the local group practice not long before Kate's arrival.

They had met at a drinks party. A few days later he had rung up to ask her to go to a concert with him. She had had to refuse because the concert had coincided with the first painting trip of the year, a visit to France. But in the intervals between subsequent trips, their acquaintance had advanced to a friendship which might or might not develop into something deeper.

Robert, so she had been told, had had a serious but abortive love-affair with a fellow medical student who, it was said, had attached more importance to her career prospects than to their relationship.

But that was five years ago. As he had never given a sign of being unhappy, Kate concluded he was over it now.

It was Robert who last night had answered her emergency call to the surgery, automatically relayed to the doctor on duty. He had come to the cottage very quickly, confirmed her fear that Miss Walcott was suffering a myocardial infarction and, rather than wait for an ambulance, had taken her to the nearest hospital in his own car.

Later he had run Kate home. Early this morning, before she'd set out for London, he had telephoned to see how Kate herself was bearing up.

'She gave you a nasty fright. You handled it well,' he'd said kindly.

After being on night duty, he had the day off, and not long after her return she saw from the kitchen window his car turning into the parking space at the side of the cottage.

Seeing her at the sink, rinsing lettuce leaves, he waved and entered the kitchen without knocking on the back door. 'Hello. How did it go?'

'Xan was there, but he was going out. So we only had a few minutes. Whether he'll come I've no idea. I shan't be surprised if he doesn't.'

'You didn't take to him?' asked Robert.

Like his father, he was man of middle height and solidly muscular build. Both had kind blue eyes and calm voices. They were not men who would ever flap or lose their tempers. Comfortable men. Reliable. And, in Robert's case, rather attractive, with a good sense of humour.

'I didn't expect to,' she said. 'From everything I've heard and read about him, Xan isn't my sort of person.'

'I never had much to do with him,' said Robert, folding his arms and leaning against the dresser. 'I remember envying his height. I was short for my age until I was about fourteen. He was always noticeably tall…and very much a loner. I was into team games in those days. Cricket and rugger and drilling with the school cadets. I expect I thought sketching a sissy way to spend time. Some of the lads at his school certainly did. Dad was saying at breakfast that he remembers Xan being brought to the surgery, under duress, by his grandmother after several beatings-up. There was a gang of yobs who had it in for him.'

'Miss Walcott wanted to send him to his father's schools, but she couldn't afford the fees,' said Kate. 'She's had a terribly tough life. Being a single mother must always be difficult, but in her case it was really a bad experience.'

'Has she talked to you about it?'

'Only the bare facts…that her lover was killed in World War Two and that both her parents and his wanted the baby adopted. When she wouldn't agree, they more or less disowned her. It seems unbelievable, doesn't it? Like a Victorian melodrama.'

'It's fifty years ago. Nice girls didn't—or at any rate weren't supposed to. Babies born outside wedlock were ''illegitimate'',' said Robert, waggling his forefingers. 'That was still a nasty stigma, even when the fathers had been shot down or torpedoed or whatever and would have married the mothers if they hadn't been killed.'

On impulse, Kate said, 'I was an unwelcome baby. Or did you already know that?'

When he shook his head, she went on, 'Miss Walcott knows and she might have told your father.'

'If she had—which I doubt—he wouldn't have mentioned it to me. I had noticed you didn't talk about your family.'

'I don't have one.' She told him, briefly, about being an orphan. It was better to spell it out now, before their friendship developed…if it developed.

'How do you feel about it?' Robert asked.

'I don't think it's given me any deep-seated hang-ups. When I compare my childhood to what's happening to children in parts of the world now, I feel grateful to have been fed and educated.'

'Are you curious about your parents?'

'I was as a child. Less so now. There's no way I'm ever going to find them, and I might not like them if I did.'

For supper, Kate baked a potato to have with a mushroom omelette. She ate from a tray on her lap while listening to the news on the radio. Miss Walcott disapproved of television.

When Kate had come to live here, the only modern gadgets in the house had been an electric kettle and an iron. The old lady's household laundry had been done by someone in the village. A short time after her arrival, Kate had pressed for the hire-purchase of a washing machine and a steam iron. Reluctantly, complaining about the expense, her employer had agreed to these innovations.

Kate had put the tray aside and was finishing her meal with a russet-coloured pear from the tree in the garden when there was a rap at the front door.

There was no way that word of her employer's illness could have passed round the village yet. Nor would there be a rush of enquiries when it did. Miss Walcott kept herself to herself, declining involvement in any local activities on the grounds that she was too busy.

Mildly irritated at being interrupted in the middle of an interesting programme, Kate uncoiled her legs and slid her feet into the Breton-red espadrilles she wore around the house in summer.

Opening the front door, she was startled to find Xan Walcott outside. She had hoped he might go to the hospital, but hadn't expected him to call at the cottage.

'Good evening.'

Now casually dressed in chinos and a blazer over an open-necked shirt, he still had the air of a sophisticated man of the world rather than the *dégagé* look she associated with artists.

'Good evening. Come in. Mind your head on the lintel.'

'I've been to the hospital,' he said, on the way to the living-room.

'Have you seen your grandmother?'

'No. When I explained the nature of our relationship to the doctor in charge, he agreed it was inadvisable at this stage. Seeing me would be bound to agitate her.'

'I was there myself a couple of hours ago but she was asleep,' Kate told him, switching off the radio and picking up her supper tray. 'I was just going to make some coffee. Will you have some?'

'Thank you.' He glanced round the room. 'Do your duties include keeping the place in order?'

'I do whatever needs doing.'

'It wasn't like this in my day...or not after my mother died. Nerina was never domesticated.'

She said, 'Excuse me. I shan't be long,' and went to the kitchen.

When she had first come to the cottage, it had been in urgent need of a thorough spring-clean. She had assumed that it was her advancing years which had made Miss Walcott tolerate grubby curtains and covers and dust in every corner and crevice.

Kate was not a fanatic about cleanliness but she hadn't been prepared to put up with the state of the bathroom and kitchen. Once they were in order, she had turned her attention to the rest of the cottage. Now it smelt of wax polish and flowers instead of musty neglect.

While she was waiting for the kettle to boil, Xan joined her, his grey eyes raking the dresser and the scrubbed pine drainers on either side of the old-fashioned deep stoneware sink.

'Will you mind being here on your own?' he asked.

The question surprised her. The cottage was half a mile from the village, beside a lane off the main road, but she hadn't, until that moment, thought of it as isolated.

'I shouldn't think so. I'll be too busy. Perhaps you can advise me. How do I go about finding a substitute tutor for the trip to Crete early next month? We have thirteen bookings. To call the course off at this stage is going to be a major disappointment to those people, not to mention a serious loss of income to Miss Walcott. Somehow I have to find a stand-in. But I can't ask her what to do, and my knowledge of the art world is still very limited. Would the Royal Academy be helpful?'

'Probably, given more notice. But maybe not in the time available. Had this been a holiday period, there would have been plenty of professional instructors who'd have jumped at a busman's holiday. But they're back in harness now.'

'What about some of the galleries handling the work of young, up-and-coming painters? Might they know of someone, do you think?'

'If they did, they'd suggest a fat fee plus their commission,' he said drily. 'Nerina used to sell through a gallery. Has that stopped?'

'No, but they haven't had any paintings from her for some time. She was hoping to remedy that situation while we were in Crete. It's been a busy summer. We've done a succession of trips with only short breaks between them. I believe it's become too much for her. Well, clearly it has. That's why she's had this heart attack.'

'I should think the causes go back a lot further than this past summer,' said Xan. 'I talked to a cardiologist attached to the CC unit. It's likely her coronary arteries have been hardening for years. May I carry that for you?'

There had been a reference to his impeccable manners in one of the articles about him, Kate remembered, as he carried the tray to the living-room. She wondered how he had acquired them. His mother might have instilled the fundamentals and, after her death, Miss Walcott would have been quick to stamp on any signs of loutishness. But her influence on him had ended when he was sixteen. Where had he acquired polish of his adult persona?

'I'll make enquiries for you,' he said, as he put the tray in front of the ancient sofa which needed its cushions restuffing. 'Where is the course taking place and what will the stand-in be expected to do?'

'The venue is Chaniá,' said Kate. 'It's a historic seaport at the western end of Crete. As well as the town and the waterfront, there are various picturesque sites in the hills behind the coast. The plan was to paint every morning and every evening, with the afternoons free for swimming and resting. The groups always breakfast and have dinner together, but they make their own arrangements for lunch. Some people picnic. Others go to a café. Every night, before dinner, there's a discussion session led by the tutor. My function is to sort out any practical problems. Miss Walcott takes care of the artistic ones.'

'So, in theory if not in practice, you're both on call most of the time?'

'All the time really…except for the long lunch-break between noon and four, and our two days off.'

'What sort of people go on the courses these days?'

'All sorts. Singles. Couples who both paint. Painters with partners who don't paint. Total beginners. Talented amateurs. A few professionals. The women usually out-number the men, but not always. On the whole, they're exceptionally nice people but sometimes there's a difficult person…someone who doesn't fit in, or complains a lot. But dealing with them would be my province, not the tutor's. I'll give you one of our brochures to take away with you.'

From what had once been a scullery and was now her workroom and the 'office' of Palette Holidays, she fetched the folder containing the brochures for the fortnight in Crete.

On the front was a photograph, taken some years ago, of Nerina Walcott seated at a portable easel on the bank of the Dordogne in France. She was wearing her big-brimmed painter's hat and smiling at the camera with the charm she could exert when she chose. Although white-haired and deeply lined, she had looked a strong, active woman, very different from the one lying in hospital, wired to an electrocardiographic monitor, with a drip-feed attached to her arm and a catheter connected to a bag on the foot-rail of the high white bed.

After a cursory glance at the photograph, Xan looked more attentively at the rest of the brochure.

'This is very good "selling copy",' he said, after skimming the text. 'Who dreamed this up for her?'

'I did…based on what your grandmother told me about Chaniá and my own research,' said Kate. 'Since I lost my job with an estate agency, I've been teaching myself desktop publishing with a view to eventual self-employment.'

He gave her a thoughtful look. 'I wondered what you were doing working with Nerina. I can't imagine anyone staying here unless they had no other option.'

Kate's reaction made her eyes sparkle. 'How can you speak of her like that when she's seriously ill…maybe dying?'

'Because I'm not a hypocrite,' he said equably. 'You've known Nerina for six months. I lived under her aegis for sixteen years. I think that makes me a better judge of her character. She could always charm…when it suited her. But the charm is only a façade.'

Without stopping to think, she shot back, 'The same could be said of you. From what I've read, you have very winning ways, but they seem to cause more pain than pleasure in the long run.'

His right eyebrow lifted. 'What are you talking about?'

Already regretting her unguarded riposte, Kate felt her colour rising. 'I—I was referring to some of the write-ups about you in your grandmother's albums. You've attracted a lot of publicity, not all of it favourable, but—'

'Not all of it accurate either,' he interjected.

'Anyway, it's not my business. I wouldn't have mentioned it if you hadn't spoken in that denigratory way about your grandmother. As far as I'm concerned she's been an ideal employer. I've been much happier here than I ever was in London. Will you have some more coffee?'

'Thank you. By the way, when you wanted to telephone me last night and found my number wasn't listed, the police would have made contact for you in an emergency.'

'I thought of that, but in the circumstances it seemed better to try to speak to you in person today.'

There was a disconcerting gleam of amusement lurking

in his grey eyes as he said, 'Your curiosity being aroused by what you had read?'

'Certainly not!' she said crisply. 'That had nothing to do with it. For one thing I didn't want to advertise that you and your grandmother weren't in touch with each other; and for another I felt I might be more persuasive in person than on the telephone.'

'As indeed you were,' he said smoothly, with an appraising glance which lingered on her slim bare legs exposed to mid-thigh by the denim cut-offs she was wearing with a striped cotton T-shirt.

Because the weather in England hadn't been good and there hadn't been much time for sunbathing in France, for the past week Kate had been experimenting with a spray tan in readiness for the Crete trip. The results were good, and the pre-spraying attention to her legs with a loofah and moisturiser had left them with a silky sheen.

But even if they could compare with the legs of his glamorous girlfriends who had the money to pay for expensive professional waxing and tanning sessions, she didn't care for being eyed in that predatory way.

If he had it in mind to add her scalp to his belt, he could think again.

'It's sad that you needed persuading, Mr Walcott,' she said coldly. 'But I'm very relieved that you came and I hope I can rely on your support while your grandmother recovers...if she recovers. She has no one else to turn to.'

'She has you. I would think you're a pretty good ally when the going gets tough.'

And you are a master of soft soap but it won't work with me, she thought. Aloud, she said, 'I'll do all I can, for as long as I can. But when she recovers, if she recovers, she may need more care and attention than I'm qualified to give.'

'Let's cross that bridge when we come to it. A more pressing problem is finding a replacement tutor.' He drained his second cup of coffee and rose to his feet. 'I'll make some enquiries tonight and give you a call in the morning. Don't bother to see me out. I know the way. Goodnight…Kate.'

CHAPTER TWO

ALTHOUGH Kate had indignantly denied that her visit to London that morning had been motivated by curiosity, after she had gone to bed and was lying awake in the dark, she admitted to herself that there might be a smidgen of truth in Xan's mocking assertion. Perhaps, to be honest, more than a smidgen.

But it was the fact that he was a successful artist, more than his looks or his success with women, which had activated her curiosity.

Although totally lacking in artistic skills herself, she derived great pleasure from looking at other people's works of art. Much of her spare time while she was working in London had been spent browsing in art museums and galleries or poring over costly art books at the public library.

She had often wondered if one of her parents might have been an artist. The only way she would ever be sure—or nearly sure—was if she married and had children. It was an established fact that artistic genes often skipped a generation, as they had in the case of Nerina Walcott and her grandson.

It might be that one of Kate's children would inherit talent from a maternal grandparent, and possibly a physical likeness as well. In the faces of her offspring she might see traces of people whose love had given her existence. For she felt sure she was a love-child in every sense of the term. Why she felt that, she couldn't explain. It was just something she knew.

First thing the next morning, she telephoned the hospital

and was relieved to hear that Miss Walcott had weathered the night.

According to Robert, if she hung on for forty-eight hours the outlook would be more hopeful.

Kate spent most of the day sitting quietly near Miss Walcott's bed in case she should rouse and, alarmed by her surroundings, need the reassurance of a familiar face.

In the event she did wake up a few times, but only briefly and without becoming agitated. When Kate held her hand and repeated quietly and calmly that there was nothing to worry about, she seemed to accept that this was so and slipped back into a doze.

About four in the afternoon, Robert put his head round the door and beckoned Kate into the corridor.

'I'm here on behalf of *your* medic,' he said. 'Fresh air and exercise is her prescription for you. I could do with some too. Come on: we're going for a walk.'

After starting to work for Miss Walcott, Kate had enrolled as a patient with one of the group's two women practitioners, a gynaecologist working part-time while her children were small. So far Kate hadn't needed to consult her.

On the way out of the building, Robert said, 'Have you had any lunch?'

'I brought some sandwiches…brown bread with avocado and fennel,' she added, with a smile, knowing that he attributed many of his patients' ills to the food they ate.

'Excellent,' he said approvingly. 'What have you been reading?'

'A book on what happened in Crete during World War Two. It looks as if I'm not going to need all the information I've mugged up. But it's interesting anyway. I never liked history at school, but now I find it fascinating.'

'It's just as well you are a bookworm, seeing that the old girl won't have TV in the house. How has she been today?'

'Sleepy. We've had a few words, but she hasn't been fussing about the Crete trip, thank goodness. By the way, I had a visit from her grandson yesterday evening.'

'Did you indeed? I meant to ring you last night, but in the middle of supper I was called out to an accident. By the time it was all sorted out, I thought you might be having an early night and I didn't want to disturb you. Was Xan more forthcoming than when you saw him in London?'

'He's going to try to find a replacement tutor for the Crete trip. But even if he can, it still leaves a major problem.' By this time they had reached the car park. 'I'll tell you about it when we get there. Where are we going?'

'Let's go up to the droveway,' he suggested.

This ancient track for driving sheep across country was a place where they had walked before. Following Robert's car out of the hospital grounds, Kate wondered if there would be a message from Xan on her answerphone when she returned to the cottage. Or if he would come in person, calling at the hospital before coming to see her.

Robert's car was a five-year-old Ford. He drove it in the style of someone who had had to deal with the results of fast, careless driving. Kate had not seen Xan's car. It must have been parked in the lane during his visit. But she visualised it as something expensively streamlined with a powerful engine and rapid acceleration. The kind of car which impressed the impressionable. Which she was not and never had been. Not even at eighteen.

Sometimes she felt she had missed a phase in her development: the feckless, frivolous, carefree stage in the late teens when girls spent their money on clothes and make-up and life revolved around dates and discos and fun.

Robert had taken off his sweater and was rolling up his shirtsleeves when she pulled in next to his car at the parking place for the droveway.

'I brought a flask of tea and some of Mum's oatcakes,' he said. 'She's been having a bake-up for a fund-raising do at the weekend.'

Kate knew Mrs Murrett was a mistress of all the domestic arts.

'What did your mother do before she was married?' she asked, as he slung a small knapsack over one shoulder.

'She answered the telephone and franked the post in a solicitor's office until she was nineteen. Then her parents allowed her to marry Dad, who was a junior MO in the Army. Since then she's been a housewife…and likes it that way. So tell me…what's this other major problem that's cropped up?' he asked, as they fell into step.

'Even if Xan can find a stand-in for his grandmother, the group will still need a courier and I can't shepherd them *and* look after Miss Walcott. A nurse told me today that, unless there are complications, most heart attack patients don't stay in hospital long. The inpatient stage could be over in ten days, followed by outpatient treatment.'

Robert nodded agreement. 'But in view of Miss Walcott's age and obstinate temperament, a period of professionally controlled convalescence would be advisable. If you try to keep her in order, likely as not she'll ignore you. She needs to be under the thumb of someone she can't disregard.'

'You mean in a nursing home? But she can't afford to pay the fees of a private one and I think she'd refuse to go to any of the State-run places. She's very antisocial, you know. I've known her to be quite offhand with some of her own painting students if she doesn't like their clothes or their attitudes. On the last trip we did there was one person in particular to whom she was almost rude. I had to make sure the poor unsuspecting *bête noire* didn't sit near her at meals and get her head bitten off.'

'Poor you,' he said, with a grin. 'It can't be restful, being nanny to a mixed bag of strangers. Especially when their instructor is herself a bit of a termagant.'

'That's unfair,' Kate objected. 'She isn't bad-tempered by nature. She just has a rather short fuse when other people are irritating.'

After ten minutes' striding along the droveway with its wide open views and its quietness broken only by the distant drone of a tractor and, nearby, the intermittent buzz of bumblebees, Kate felt refreshed and invigorated.

Later, when they were sitting on the turf, drinking tea from plastic cups and munching his mother's oatcakes, Robert said, 'Some friends of mine are just back from a biking holiday in France. They said it was a lot of fun. They were with ten other people, covering about thirty miles a day with their luggage transported by van. I'm thinking of signing up for the same tour in late October. Depending on how things go here, do you fancy biking round Brittany?'

Choosing her words with some care, Kate said, 'I'm sure I'd enjoy it very much, but in view of Miss Walcott's illness I probably won't be free then.'

Robert was stretched at full length, propped on one elbow while she sat cross-legged.

He said, 'From what you've told me about the painting trips to France, they certainly didn't count as holidays as far as you were concerned. More stressful than restful, by the sound of it. You ought to have a relaxing break before the winter sets in.'

'I'm not that overworked,' she said lightly. 'Not compared with you and your colleagues.'

'Never say that in front of Dad. He thinks our lives are a picnic compared with the hours he worked when he was in practice on his own...on call night and day except for the two weeks a year when a locum took over and we went to a cottage in Cornwall. And even down there he sometimes had to deal with accidents. A doctor may be incognito, but he can't stand by if someone's hurt and there's no one else competent to deal with the situation.'

'Even so, he'd have had more time off than your mother, I expect. Or did she have an au pair when you and your sisters were small?'

She knew he had three older sisters, the eldest a doctor, the middle one a dietician and the youngest a librarian.

'No, Mum never had any help. But she didn't need it. We kept each other amused,' he said, with a reminiscent grin. 'Until I was old enough to rebel, I spent a lot of time being one of Laura's ''patients'' in a make-believe hospital. She even splinted and bandaged the long-suffering cat we had then. What are your earliest memories?'

'Going for walks through a park in a ''crocodile'', holding hands with another little girl.'

As she spoke, Kate was wondering what significance, if any, she should attach to his invitation to join him in Brittany. At the moment their friendship was still on a platonic footing. He had never even kissed her. So it didn't seem likely that he expected them to travel as a pair, sharing a room. But one never quite knew how men's minds worked.

He might feel a bicycle tour would be a chance to test their sexual rapport without incurring gossip. As a doctor he had to be more than usually circumspect. To other men, Miss Walcott's absence might seem an ideal opportunity for them to be private together. But the cottage, although secluded, wasn't so far from the village that what went on there passed unnoticed. Robert's car in the drive after dark, or even for long during the day, would be seen and reported. In no time it would be common knowledge that young Dr Murrett and the woman from London were 'having it off' while the old girl was out of the way.

'More tea?'

The enquiry made her aware that, having answered his question about early memories, she had then missed his next remark.

'Oh…yes, please.' She held out her cup for him to refill it.

'Where were you just then, with that troubled expression? Were you very unhappy as a child?' he asked, in a sympathetic tone.

'No—no, hardly ever,' she answered. 'Young children accept life as it is. It's later on, in the teens, that they start feeling miserable. But I think that's just adolescence… something everyone goes through, whatever their circumstances. I expect your sisters felt unhappy at times.'

'You can say that again!' he said wryly. 'Our parents were fairly strict. All my sisters felt their lives were being blighted by punitive house rules. What with PMT, exam pressures and boyfriend problems, there was usually someone in a temper or tears.'

When they returned to the cars, Kate said, 'A walk was a good idea. Thanks for the tea and your company. Bye for now.'

But as she was turning away, he put a hand on her shoulder. 'And you'll think about my suggestion…biking round Brittany?'

She smiled and nodded. 'Yes, I will.'

His fingers tightened on her shoulder and he came a pace closer. 'I'll see you tomorrow. Try not to worry about things. Most problems have a solution.'

He leaned forward and kissed her, first on the cheek and then, lightly, on the mouth.

It was too brief a caress to tell Kate anything more about their relationship than she already knew. She liked him. She found him attractive. But whether he could supply her deepest needs was still something her instinct questioned. No one ever had. Perhaps no one ever would.

For a moment she thought it would stop there; that Robert's innate patience—one of his most admirable qualities—was going to restrain him from taking things a stage further.

But in that she misjudged him. After looking at her intently, as if trying to determine what she wanted—which she didn't know herself—he suddenly put his arms round her and gave her a kiss that left her in no doubt of *his* feelings.

He wanted her. Wanted her urgently and, in a primitive society, might have taken her there and then. But, because he was a civilised man, he forced himself to let her go.

Perversely, as he released her, she found herself wishing he weren't so civilised, so completely in control of his feelings.

His face flushed, his eyes still ardent, but his inclinations firmly in check, Robert said, 'We could have had dinner tonight, but I've got to introduce a speaker from the Lung Foundation at a meeting of the asthma clinic.'

The clinic was his idea. His youngest sister was asthmatic and the management of the condition, particularly in children, was one of his special interests.

Inwardly rather relieved that he wasn't free tonight, Kate said lightly, 'I ought to stay near the phone anyway in case Xan rings up about a substitute tutor.'

'I'll call you tomorrow. Take care.' He gave her a pat on the arm before turning away.

There was a bottle-green Range Rover standing on the gravel when she got back to the cottage. Kate parked her vehicle behind it. She had no doubt who had left it there but where was he? In the back garden?

Her sneakers making no sound on the brick path surrounding the cottage, she walked round to the rear. Behind
the cottage was an expanse of lawn, then a small vegetable
garden and about a dozen old apple and pear trees, several
no longer fruiting but providing support for climbing roses
and clematis.

Xan Walcott was sitting on a canvas stool, painting his
grandmother's orchard.

'How long have you been here?' Kate asked quietly.

Although he must have been concentrating, he gave no
sign of being startled.

'Hello, Kate. Not long.' He stood up. 'When I found you
out, I rang the hospital and was told you'd been there most
of the day but had left. So I filled in the time doing a sketch.'

'I didn't come straight home. I went for a walk. May I
look?' she asked, eyeing his sketch block.

He held it out to her.

Since coming to work for his grandmother, Kate had seen
scores of water-colours by painters of varying skill. But
even those by the artists who sold their work had not come
up to the standard of this charming picture of the orchard
with the kitchen garden in the foreground and fields and
woods in the background.

Feeling that any expression of praise must sound either
banal or presumptuous, as she handed it back to him she
said, 'Your grandmother showed me a portfolio of drawings
you did as a small boy. Did you always know you were
going to be an artist?'

'It was one of the things I wanted to be. This isn't quite
finished. How about making some tea while I finish it off?'

'Of course. Indian or China?'

'Whichever you prefer.'

While she was in the kitchen, he tapped on the window.

When she opened it, he said, 'If you'll give me the key to the shed, I'll get out a couple of deckchairs.'

After passing him the key, she watched him walking away. With some very tall men their height was mostly in the length of their legs. Others had overlong bodies. She had seen few as well-proportioned as Xan. She found herself wondering what he looked like without clothes and how he kept himself fit. She couldn't visualise him pumping iron in one of the expensive health clubs where City men went to work out. Perhaps regular swimming gave him those limber movements, or he might run in one of the parks or when he was at his country place.

Disappearing into the creeper-covered shed at one side of the garden, he emerged a few moments later carrying two ancient deckchairs in one hand as easily as if they were a couple of lightweight drawing-boards.

Not wishing to be caught watching him, Kate turned away to pour boiling water into the Chinese teapot which was one of her treasures.

Xan, when he tasted the tea, said, 'What is this? It tastes of peaches.'

'Do you like it? If you don't, I can make you some ordinary.'

'No, it's good. Is it herbal?'

She shook her head. 'It's Formosa oolong from Taiwan. When I was about twelve or thirteen, on Saturday mornings I used to run errands for an old man who was housebound. He'd been born and lived in the East. His house was full of things he'd brought back. He drank this tea from cups so fine you could see your fingers through them. He told me oolong comes from the Chinese *wu lung*, meaning black dragon. If I hadn't known him, I'd probably have gone through life using supermarket teabags and not realising there were all kinds of interesting alternatives.'

'Oh, yes, life is full of interesting alternatives. The problem is finding the time to try them all out,' said Xan. 'Talking of problems, last night and this morning I made exhaustive efforts to find a substitute tutor. But no joy, I'm afraid.'

'I was never very hopeful. Oh, well, I'll have to ring round the Crete group and tell them it's had to be called off.'

'No, you won't. I'll come,' he said.

She stared at him. Surely he couldn't mean…?

'It so happens that I don't have any cast-iron commitments between those dates,' he went on. 'And Chaniá sounds an interesting place.'

Kate's eyes widened disbelievingly. Could he be serious? Although the idea had crossed her mind, she had instantly dismissed it as untenable.

There were many professional painters who shared their skills with pupils, but usually they were in the second rank of artists, not major names like Xan. In view of his apparent indifference to his grandmother, his proposal was astounding. Unless, at heart, he was a nicer person than Kate's first impression of him, and Nerina's illness had revived some vestiges of affection for her.

'Well…that's marvellous. That's a huge weight off my mind,' she said eventually.

But even as she spoke she was aware that underlying her relief on behalf of thirteen Palette clients lay a curious sense of dismay. As if somehow their peace of mind, which now would remain undisturbed, had been bought at the cost of her own. Although being responsible for their welfare didn't worry her, the thought of two weeks abroad in the company of Xan Walcott was not a relaxing prospect.

'Do I detect some reservations?' he asked shrewdly. 'Do you doubt my ability to do the job?'

'Oh, no, not at all,' she said hastily. 'I—I'm sure if you put your mind to it, you'll do it brilliantly. I just hope you won't find it…boring.'

'Then you must make sure I don't, mustn't you?' he answered, with a rather enigmatic smile. 'May I use your telephone?'

'Of course.'

While he telephoned, she washed up the tea things, pondering his last remark and what he might have meant by it. She was peeling off the rubber gloves she wore for all household chores when Xan joined her in the kitchen.

'I've booked a table at the Angel. We have a lot to discuss. I said we'd be there at seven which gives you plenty of time to bath and change while I stretch my legs. See you later.'

Ducking his head to avoid a lintel built to clear the heads of most men but not someone of his height, he disappeared out of the back door.

The Angel, ten miles away, had once been an ordinary pub but now featured in most of the guides to good eating places. Kate had never been there. It was expensive, a place where people celebrated birthdays and wedding anniversaries, but where only the rich and extravagant would eat on ordinary occasions. Fortunately for the couple who had built up the Angel's reputation, their 'special occasion' trade was enough to keep them solvent when many of the lavish spenders had to cut back.

While Xan went for a walk, Kate debated disinterring one of her London outfits from the suitcases in the loft. In the end she decided not to bother. She knew local people dressed up to go to the Angel, but sophisticated weekenders wouldn't. Good as the food was, it was still a country pub.

Clean jeans and a new mail-ordered needlecord shirt would be perfectly suitable.

The shirt was the colour of chamois leather, chosen to set off her hair. She cinched her jeans with a silver-tipped belt, tied a silk kerchief round her throat and added silver hoop earrings.

It was ridiculous, she told herself, to be keyed up because she was going out to supper with Xan Walcott. She ought to be thinking about Robert and whether she wanted to continue on the way their relationship was heading.

If she had been dining with him tonight, it was possible he would have asked her to marry him. She could see that coming as clearly as she could see the sun sinking behind the woods to the west of the cottage. A proposal was now as inevitable as tonight's dusk and tomorrow's daybreak.

Robert was past the age for impulsive or trial love-affairs. He was in settling-down mode, ready to start the large family doctors always seemed to have. She wanted that too: a home, children, but most of all one special man to love and be loved by. But was Robert the man for her? Could she be happy with him for the rest of her life? Because when she married she wanted it to be forever.

So did everyone, probably. But some people made crazy choices. She had friends in London whose break-ups had been predictable from the start. They had been in love but they hadn't been friends with their partners. Or they had been compatible, but lacking that extra spark that kept love alive for a lifetime. That was what she was looking for: the special fusion of passion and friendship which was indestructible.

She was sitting on the end of her bed, lost in thought, when she heard Xan calling her from below. She checked the contents of her shoulder-bag and went down to join him.

*   *   *

'I shall go to Chaniá a few days ahead of the rest of you to get the feel of the place and select the most paintable subjects,' he said, an hour later, leaning back in his chair on the opposite side of their table in a secluded corner of the Angel's dining-room.

They had finished their main course and were waiting for the pudding trolley to be brought to her and the cheeseboard to him.

'I'm sorry, it's much too late to change the flight arrangements,' said Kate. 'By booking ahead we get a favourable price. I can't cancel Miss Walcott's ticket at this stage.'

'Whether you can or can't, I shan't be using it,' he said decisively. 'I never fly tourist now. They don't allow enough leg-room for people of my size. When I was young and hard up, I had no option but to sit with my knees rammed against the seat in front. Not any more. But don't worry: I don't expect Palette to fund any extra expenses. I'll pay for my comforts out of my own pocket.'

Although he had told her earlier they had a lot to discuss, this was the first time the trip to Crete had come up.

Since their arrival at the Angel, Xan had steered the conversation in other directions and Kate had found herself enjoying his company as much as the excellence of the food.

He had started his meal with a spicy mango soup followed by lamb cooked in a crunchy crust of yogurt. She had begun with smoked trout mousse followed by artichoke hearts parcelled in filo pastry and served with broccoli and red peppers.

The wine had been his choice: a full-bodied golden Gewürztraminer she had assumed came from Germany but which Xan had discovered while painting in the Vosges foothills. It smelt sweet, but tasted dry and was, she noticed, extremely potent. The label said fourteen per cent alcohol.

When the Angel's proprietor would have replenished his

glass while Xan was choosing his cheese, he shook his head. 'I'm driving.'

He had had three glasses of wine to Kate's two and her glass was not yet empty. Although she liked wine and this one had been a particularly good partner to her fish, she wanted to keep a clear head. To prevent her glass being topped up, she held her fingers above it.

Both men seemed surprised by her gesture.

'You don't like it?' Xan asked her.

'It's delicious, but quite strong. You have to drive back to London and I have some accounts to go through.' As the pudding trolley arrived, she added, 'Tempting as they are, I don't think I can manage any of these after all.'

'But you will have coffee?'

'Yes, please.'

'Are you always so disciplined?' he asked, when they were by themselves again. 'Is that what keeps your skin clear and your waist slim…an iron self-control?'

'Eating and drinking aren't my vices,' she said lightly. 'I binge in second-hand bookshops. I've been known to devour a novel in one non-stop night-long rave-read…knowing it will make me look like a zombie the next day.'

'There are better things to do in bed. What about them?' he asked.

She was taken aback and, for the first time in years, found herself blushing. After a pause, she lobbed the question back at him. 'What about them?'

His eyes were amused. 'Do you like them?'

'You may not mind your private life being made public. I'm more reserved,' she said crisply.

'Your reserve wouldn't safeguard your privacy if your work attracted attention,' he answered drily before the cafetière came, with a dish of chocolates and sugared almonds.

Xan took from the pocket of his blazer a small book and the same type of fine-pointed pen Miss Walcott used for sketching. He began discreetly to draw a couple at another table.

Kate helped herself to a chocolate. Neither she nor Nerina was a sweet-eater and it was a long time since chocolate had melted on her tongue. But not as long as the gap between Robert's recent kiss and the one before it.

Having rebuffed Xan's curiosity about her love-life, she found herself wondering about his. She doubted if it was long since his last experience of sex. He exuded animal vitality and Kate had no doubt that, with his powerful body and long shapely artist's hands, he would be an exciting lover. But would there be any tenderness in his caresses?

The coffee was good, but after one cup he said, 'I'll take you home,' and signalled his wish for the bill.

There was a hint of impatience in the way he dealt with it, as if he wished himself elsewhere. She didn't know why they had come. Certainly not for the purpose he had stated earlier. That had scarcely been mentioned.

On the drive back to the cottage, she said, 'It's a great relief that the trip doesn't have to be cancelled. I'm very grateful to you...as Miss Walcott will be, when she's well enough to think ahead. As soon as she asks I'll tell her. What would be even better would be for you to tell her yourself.'

His answer was clipped. 'Forget it. I've already made it clear she and I have nothing to say to each other. Don't push it, Kate. You could make me change my mind.'

Having snubbed him for trespassing on a no-go area of her own life, she couldn't take umbrage at *his* snub. For the rest of the way she sat silent, the height of the Range Rover's seats enabling her to look over the hedgerows at the moonlit fields.

At the cottage she expected him to drive slightly past the gateway and reverse into it, ready to return to the main road as soon as they had exchanged the courtesies of guest and host. Instead he swung into the drive, parking alongside the cottage. While she fumbled to open an unfamiliar door, he got out and strode round the bonnet to open it from the outside.

'Thank you.' She slid to the ground, thinking it wouldn't be an ideal vehicle for women with short legs or high heels. Fortunately her legs were long and she was wearing loafers.

As he had already demonstrated his punctilious manners, Kate wasn't surprised when he followed her round to the porch and held out his hand for her latchkey. Or when he entered the small hall to press an awkwardly placed switch whose position he hadn't forgotten.

The surprise came when she started to thank him for a pleasant evening and found herself in his arms, her voice fading as she realised she was about to be kissed for the second time that day.

CHAPTER THREE

THE difference between Robert's kisses and Xan's was too complex to grasp while she was still in his arms. Kate felt her mind switching off, abandoning her to her senses.

She could smell the male tang of his skin, hear the throb of his heart, savour the taste of his lips and feel the strength of his arms locking her to him.

With her eyes closed she couldn't see, but that only served to sharpen her other reactions. Excitement coursed through her bloodstream, as potent as the wine at dinner. She shivered, her body yielding, her mouth softening under his, her hands obeying a blind instinct to reach up towards his neck and feel the hard breadth of his shoulders, the texture of his dark hair.

And then, in the subconscious struggle between reason and powerful emotion, common sense came to the surface with a message as swiftly effective as a hosepipe of water aimed at amorous cats.

She struggled to free herself, but only for a few seconds. He didn't try to restrain her.

More angry with herself than with him, Kate said stiffly, 'I'm sorry if you've wasted an evening, but in these back-woods it takes more than an expensive dinner to achieve what you have in mind. When I said I had work to do I meant it.'

She expected his face to darken with the natural resentment of a man unaccustomed to rebuffs being put down by a woman he had thought would succumb to his charm as easily as plucking a pear from the tree in Miss Walcott's garden.

To her surprise he looked amused. 'It was only a good-night kiss, Kate, not an attempted seduction. If and when that's on the agenda, I'll give you plenty of warning. In the meantime don't let your fluster make you forget to lock and chain the door. I'll keep in touch. Goodnight.'

Smiling, he disappeared into the night. Moments later she heard the expensive deep-throated growl of the Range Rover's engine as he set off for London.

It was the consultant in charge of Miss Walcott's recovery who, a few days later, told Kate that, on the instructions of Alexander Walcott, his patient was to convalesce in one of the best private nursing homes in southern England.

'You need have no qualms about leaving her, Miss Poole,' he said kindly. 'Clearly you feel a deep concern for Miss Walcott's welfare. I can assure you she'll receive the best possible attention in your absence. At the appropriate time she'll be moved by ambulance to a very nice private room overlooking the gardens and everything will be done to make her comfortable. Naturally she will miss your visits, but I hope by the time you come back she'll be sketching again. My wife and I have one of her paintings, you know. A delightful study of poppies in a silver jug. Everyone who sees it admires it.'

Kate went home relieved and pleased by Xan's generous gesture, perhaps the first step on the road to a full reconciliation between two people who had so much in common.

She was reading in bed when the phone rang. The clock on the night table showed half-past eleven, an unusual time for anyone to ring the cottage. Unless her employer had had an unexpected relapse.

'Hello?'

'Hello, Kate. How's it going?' Xan took it for granted she would recognise his voice.

'I thought you were flying to Crete today. What went wrong?'

'Nothing. I'm calling from Chaniá. Where else would I be?'

'It's such a good line I thought you must still be in London. From the other end of the Mediterranean I would have expected ''crackle'', or that echo chamber effect one gets on some long-distance calls.'

'It's clear from this end as well. What are you doing? Grappling with your computer?'

'I was earlier. Now I'm in bed.'

'Alone?'

'Yes,' she said shortly.

'You answered too quickly for me to have woken you up. What are you reading?'

'A book about Cretan folklore.'

'That won't keep you awake until dawn,' he said, reminding her of their dinner at the Angel and what had followed. Her insides churned at the memory of his kiss.

Trying to sound businesslike, she answered, 'Is the hotel to your liking?'

'It's fine, and the food is excellent. I've just come in from a stroll on the waterfront.' Without pausing, he asked, 'Why are there no men in your life?'

'I have several men friends,' she said, thinking of former colleagues in London with whom she was still in contact, although not in the way he meant.

'But no one special?'

'This call must be quite expensive. I imagine you rang for a progress report on your grandmother. She's getting on well. They expect to move her to the nursing home you've organised for her any day now.'

'So I've been told.' His tone was suddenly curt. 'I've rented a car to look round the country near here. If you need to contact me between now and your arrival, send a fax and I'll call you back as soon as I can. Goodnight, Kate.' He rang off.

As she replaced the handset, she knew it was her reference to his grandmother which had made him cut the call short. If she hadn't mentioned Miss Walcott he would have gone on teasing her in that deep, attractive voice which sounded even sexier on the telephone.

Kate closed her book and put it aside. She switched off the light and slid down under the bedclothes, but not because she was sleepy. Xan's call had disturbed the calm of her mind like a sudden gust of wind scattering a tidy pile of autumn leaves.

Why had she dodged his question about someone special? Robert was special, wasn't he? He wanted to be special to her. He had rung her that morning, fuming because pressure of work and family obligations had prevented him from seeing her. His mother had house guests and expected him to spend his spare time helping to entertain them.

Turning to lie on her side, Kate tried to fix her mind on the still unresolved issue of whether or not her long-term future lay with Robert. But although she tried to concentrate, thoughts about the immediate future kept intruding.

By the end of the week the cottage would be closed up and she would be far away in Chaniá. While she was there would she find out the reason why, even though he was picking up the bill for the nursing home, Xan still reacted badly to any mention of the old lady towards whom, in the normal course of events, he should have felt a warmly protective affection?

On her last night in England she had supper with the Murretts. Inviting her, Mrs Murrett had said, 'You won't want to use the cooker after you've cleaned it and defrosted the fridge. Robert will pick you up and run you home. It's not pleasant for a girl to go back to an empty house on her own late at night.'

If fact, knowing the Murretts kept early hours, and as she herself would be rising early to drive to the airport, it was only a little after ten when Kate thanked them for their hospitality. Mrs Murrett kissed her goodbye. 'Take care of yourself, my dear.'

Kate felt warmed by her approval but at the same time slightly wary. She sensed that Beryl Murrett would be a very hands-on mother-in-law, especially as all her daughters lived in other parts of the country and she didn't see as much of her grandchildren as she would have liked. When Robert set up his own establishment, she would be a frequent visitor, generous with help and advice. Much as she longed for the security and sharing of family life, Kate wasn't sure she could handle Beryl breathing down her neck for the next twenty years, however benevolently.

Robert invited himself in for a cup of coffee. While Kate was making it, he said, 'The next two weeks are going to seem a long time. I expect you'll be too busy to miss me, but I shall miss you a lot. I love you, Kate. I want to take care of you…make up for all you've missed, not having parents and brothers and sisters. When you come back, will you marry me?'

His proposal was typical of the man he was…kind, unselfish, dependable. She knew it was foolish to wish he had waited until she came back and chosen a more romantic setting than the starkness of Miss Walcott's kitchen. A vision of the candlelit table at the Angel came into her mind.

Robert took her in his arms and kissed her, saying, between kisses, 'I know I can make you happy. I knew you were the one the first time we met.'

With closed eyes and parted lips, Kate waited to be swept away on warm waves of emotion. She did experience pleasure, but not the compellingly sensual undertow she had felt in Xan's arms in the hall. She didn't feel that, if she let go and surrendered her will to Robert's, she would find herself swept up the stairs for a night of passionate lovemaking in the old brass double bed where, long ago, Xan had slept.

When Robert stopped kissing her to ask huskily, 'You are going to say yes, aren't you?' she opened her eyes.

'Have you told your parents about me? That I was abandoned as a baby?'

'I've told Mother. She wasn't surprised. She thought you might be an orphan.'

'What else did she say?'

'That if she and Dad hadn't been able to have children, they would have adopted some babies whose natural parents weren't able to bring them up. Has her reaction been worrying you? You should have known it wouldn't make any difference to the way she feels about you. She's not that sort of person.'

'Most parents would prefer that their children's partners come from the sort of family they can relate to. That's only natural,' said Kate.

'In my experience, in-laws hardly ever really like the other,' said Robert. 'They put on a show, but usually it's just a façade. As a matter of fact Mother's been egging me on. The fact that you haven't a mother is a bonus in her eyes. She loves organising weddings and can't wait to tackle ours. She did a great job on my sisters' weddings.'

'I'm sure she did,' said Kate. 'But I don't know that I'm ready for marriage yet, Robert. Apart from other considerations, Miss Walcott is going to need me. I can't desert her now.'

'Of course not, but we wouldn't be getting married before the spring anyway. There's a house to find…a honeymoon to plan…a hundred and one arrangements.'

Kate felt a sudden thrust of panic. 'You're jumping the gun,' she said hastily. 'I haven't said yes yet. I'm not as sure of my feelings as you are. I have to be honest...I'm not in love with you, Robert. I'm very fond of you... *extremely* fond...but I don't think that's enough. I need more time...a lot more time.'

His face fell. Clearly he had been ninety-nine-per-cent certain she would be as eager as he to set in motion the months of elaborate preparations which, among people like the Murretts, were the proper prelude to a marriage.

Nowadays, even in their conventional world, some things had changed. Kate knew that two of Robert's sisters had shared flats with their husbands before the bond was official. If she and Robert were engaged, Mrs Murrett would not disapprove of their going on holiday together and making love, discreetly, whenever the opportunity offered. But people in love had always done that even when society frowned on it. Miss Walcott had done it and had her life blighted in consequence.

But there would be no unwanted baby if Robert and Kate went to bed together. He would make sure of that. And suddenly she wanted very much for him to scoop her up and, ignoring her half-hearted protests, spring up the stairs to her bedroom and make irresistible love to her.

But of course he didn't. He wasn't that sort of man. In his book it would be not on to put sexual pressure on a woman who wasn't sure of her feelings. Besides which, having been hurt by the girl whose career had been the most important thing in the world to her, this time he would want to be sure of whole-hearted commitment.

After they had said goodnight, Robert going home visibly disappointed but hopeful that she would come back from Crete in a different frame of mind, Kate was glad he hadn't tried to overcome her doubts by physical persuasion.

She felt sure that Xan, in similar circumstances, would have had no such compunction. Although he had claimed that he hadn't been trying it on, she was pretty sure that, if she had been willing, he would have spent the night here. Men like Xan took their pleasures lightly and wherever they found them. If, in Crete, there was no one else to catch his fugitive attention, he might try his luck with her again.

On Kate's first Palette trip to France they had flown to Bordeaux and stayed in a restored citadel overlooking the mid-river islands near the mouth of the Gironde.

On successive trips she had found she could pick out members of the group before the Palette labels on their hand luggage confirmed that they were Miss Walcott's pupils.

Generally speaking, people whose hobby was sketching had an identifiable look about them. Sometimes it was merely an expression of intelligent interest in the world about them. Sometimes it was a slightly 'arty' way of dressing.

The plane to Crete was a Lockheed Tristar carrying almost four hundred passengers and Kate's charges were scattered throughout the main cabin area, so there was no opportunity for them to get to know each other. Nor, with so many people on board and the aisles busy with holiday-makers, many with small children, going to and from the lavatories, was it possible for Kate to locate and chat to them.

She wondered if Xan would come to the airport to meet them and if, while exploring the hinterland behind the sea-port, he had given much if any thought to the people whose enjoyment depended, to a large extent, on him.

It didn't follow that because he was a well-known successful artist he would also be a good teacher. Miss Walcott was an excellent teacher who, whatever she thought of the students as people, was unfailingly helpful with their work. Whether Xan had the ability to deal kindly and constructively with the least talented students remained to be seen.

Flights to Chaniá landed at an aiport which was run by the military with no attempt to smooth the arrival of tourists. The macho scrum for luggage round the badly sited conveyor left Kate feeling battered and breathless and she wondered how the frailer members of the group would get on.

She wasn't able to help them recover their luggage because she had to stand outside to direct them to one of the many coaches waiting to convey tourists to various resorts.

Being tall and strong, Xan would have had no problem retrieving his baggage when he arrived. She felt that a chivalrous man, knowing the airport had neither trolleys nor porters, would have come to help the elderly members of the group with their luggage. Robert would certainly have done so.

To be fair, Xan wasn't to know the party included three widows and an elderly spinster. But even if he had, would he have sacrificed his own pursuits for their benefit? Probably he was painting, putting off as long as possible the moment when he would have to step into his grandmother's shoes.

The final lap of their journey took about half an hour. When the coach was on a straight stretch of road, Kate, who was in the front seat behind the driver, stood up and faced the other passengers. Using the microphone provided for tour guides, she said, 'Good afternoon, ladies and gentlemen. As we only met briefly at Gatwick, let me introduce myself again. I'm Kate Poole. Please call me Kate and come to me with any queries or problems.

'We shall soon be arriving in Chaniá,' she went on, pronouncing the name in the Cretan way, with a silent c, in case there was anyone on board who thought it was pronounced as spelt. 'As soon as we arrive at the Hotel Cydonía, you'll be asked to register and then there'll be time to unpack and rest, or to stretch your legs, whichever you prefer.

'At seven o'clock there'll be complimentary drinks on the roof terrace and you'll be welcomed by Kyria Drakakis, the owner of the hotel, and meet your tutor, Alexander Walcott. Many of you will already know him by reputation. I think you'll agree we're very lucky that, in Miss Walcott's absence because of illness, her famous grandson has agreed to take her place.

'It's rare for an artist of his stature to lead a painting holiday and I'm sure you're going to enjoy watching him work and talking to him. Now I'll just repeat that, if you have any questions, worries or suggestions, don't hesitate to come to me. That's what I'm here for. Thank you.' She switched off the mike and sat down.

Like the outskirts of many large towns, the approach to Chaniá was not particularly attractive, although here and there gardens with orange trees and the vivid purple or deep crimson bracts of bougainvillaea caught the eye.

But when the coach entered the narrower streets of the ancient town, Kate heard exclamations of pleasure and excitement coming from the seats behind hers.

At the Hotel Cydonía two sturdily built teenage maids helped the older people with their baggage. When the formalities had been completed and everyone else had gone to their rooms, the receptionist handed Kate her key.

The rooms had been allocated by the hotel and Xan would have been given the one preferred by Miss Walcott, who had been coming to Chaniá every autumn for a long time. It had a large balcony where she could paint before breakfast when the light was particularly good and, during the afternoon break, lie nude in the sun.

Prepared to find herself in the hotel's worst room, Kate was pleasantly surprised, when she opened the tall shutters, to discover that she was looking out at the sea.

The room was simply but attractively furnished with an icon-style painting of a saint on the wall behind the two single beds and pictures of women in Cretan peasant dress on either side of the window. This, in addition to the shutters left closed by the chambermaid, had inward-opening panes of glass and translucent white curtains hanging from a painted pelmet. In place of a wardrobe there was a curtained recess with two shallow drawers forming a low shelf with space underneath for baggage.

While she was unpacking, there was a tap on the door. When she opened it, a smiling maid handed her a cotton bath mat with what was evidently an apology for disturbing her.

Kate put it on the stool in her small shower-room and then decided to cool off under the shower before she finished unpacking. She was naked when another knock at the door made her wrap a towel round herself.

Expecting to find the maid had come back with something else she had forgotten, Kate was startled and disconcerted to find herself looking up at Xan.

'How was your flight?' he asked, entering the room, taking it for granted that he could come in and talk to her even though she was undressed.

'It was fine...although we could have done with some strong-arm help at the airport,' she added pointedly.

'I did intend coming to meet you, but, today being my last chance to concentrate, I wanted to make the most of it. To get to the airport in time would have meant breaking off in the middle of a picture of some boats which won't be there tomorrow. I'm sure if you'd flashed those eyes, you'd have got all the help you needed. Blondes are popular here,' he said, smiling.

'That wasn't apparent at the airport. It was every man for himself.'

'You've had a long day. What you need is a pick-me-up. I told them to put a bottle and a tub of ice in your room. I'll fix you a reviver. Do you like the room I picked out for you?'

'Yes, very much.' How adroitly he turned the tables, she thought. A difficult man to put down. 'But I hope all the group are equally happy. Our job is to look after them, not put ourselves first.'

'Within reason, yes. But we're entitled to some perks,'

The room being designed to accommodate two people, it had two glasses for toothbrushes in the shower room and two drinking glasses on the tray on the side table. Xan had dropped ice into both, adding generous splashes of brandy before topping up with dry ginger.

'That'll make you feel better,' he said, handing a glass to her.

'I was just about to have a shower,' said Kate.

He glanced at his watch. 'There's no hurry. They don't run out of hot water like some small hotels. Sit on the window ledge and unwind for ten minutes.'

It was where Kate had been planning to sit for a while after her shower. But settling herself in a comfortable position without embarrassing exposures was easier said than done. Luckily, Xan had caught sight of the icon, and while he was looking at it more closely she was able to hoist herself on to the wide ledge between the building's thick outer walls and arrange her legs as decorously as a rather small bath towel allowed.

There were men who, in Xan's place, would have studied the icon out of tact. But she didn't feel that was his reason.

Conversely, with any other man she wouldn't have been so conscious of the towel's skimpiness. It covered more than her swimsuit and she didn't feel shy when she wore that. But somehow Xan made her abnormally aware of her body and her femininity.

Having looked at all the room's pictures, he picked up one of the two upright rush-seated chairs and positioned it near the window.

'This is a delightful place. I could happily spend a month here. There are interesting subjects everywhere one looks— the old buildings, the boats, the fishermen. By some happy chance Chaniá seems to have escaped the massed ranks of expensive motor-cruisers and floating gin-palaces which have changed the character of so many Mediterranean ports.'

'I'm glad you like it. It certainly looks very nice from where I'm sitting,' she said, before taking her first refreshing swallow of ice-chilled ginger.

The kick from the brandy was stronger than she had expected. She didn't often drink spirits, preferring wine. But it proved an effective reviver. Within a few minutes the tiredness resulting from lying awake last night and rising at five this morning had begun to wear off.

As he had during most of their dinner at the Angel, Xan exerted himself to be an agreeable companion, and she found her annoyance at his failure to show up at the airport dissipating.

He drank faster than she did and had only an inch of liquor left in his glass when he said, 'Are you looking forward to this fortnight? Or does having an inexperienced tutor to cope with as well as the paying customers make you feel as if you were starting an endurance test?'

'I'm expecting to enjoy myself. I hope everyone will,' she said cheerfully. And then, impulsively, added, 'I was a bit anxious about whether your grandmother would be happy in the nursing home, but she's settled in very well. It's a lovely place…couldn't be nicer. They moved her the day before yesterday, and yesterday I drove over to say goodbye.'

As she spoke his expression had hardened into the cold indifference which was always his reaction to any mention of Miss Walcott.

'In that case you can stop worrying about her, can't you?' he said curtly. 'You've done all and more than anyone could expect of you. She's receiving excellent care. She's not your responsibility.'

'She'll be my responsibility until you accept yours fully,' was Kate's impetuous retort. 'To pay for her time at the nursing home is going some way towards that, but it's not going far enough. She needs someone to be there for her…and you aren't.'

Xan drained his glass and stood up. 'You're out of line, Kate. I appreciate you mean well but, to put it bluntly, your views are neither relevant nor welcome. So be a good girl and drop the subject. I'll see you later.'

He returned the glass to the tray and walked out of the room, closing the door quietly behind him.

Kate stayed where she was for some minutes, then swung her legs off the ledge and slid to the floor. Putting her drink aside, she went to take a shower.

She was unable to fathom his attitude and perhaps never would find out what had caused this implacable hostility towards the woman he called Nerina, pronouncing her name as if it derived from a poisonous plant instead of from the Latin for sea-nymph.

Five minutes before she went up to the roof terrace where they were to assemble at seven, Kate had another quick skim through photocopies of all the group members' application forms to refresh her memory of everyone's details.

In a fortnight's time she would know a great deal about them—their dispositions and digestions, their best qualities and their foibles. But tonight they were strangers and it was her job to make things jell and establish a convivial mood. How much help would she get from Xan? Would he exert himself to be pleasant to them all, or would his predatory eye single out Juliet as the only one worth his attention?

Juliet Craig—who had crossed out Mrs and Miss, preferring the title Ms—was travelling alone. She had left the space for her date of birth blank but looked to be in her late thirties or possibly early forties. In the section of the questionnaire where applicants were asked to rate their abilities she had ticked 'experienced'. The alternative ratings were 'beginner' and 'intermediate'.

She was tall, slim and self-possessed. Kate had admired the casual chic of her appearance at Gatwick and was looking forward to seeing what she would wear for the initial get-together.

Juliet's manner was rather aloof. She might be shy. She might be unhappy. It wouldn't come as a surprise if there was a divorce in her background.

In the hotel dining-room, a long table had been laid for the Palette group. Kate had written 'Alexander Walcott' on a card to reserve the place at the head of the table for him. She would sit wherever there was a spare chair when everyone else was seated.

As she hung back while they chose their places, she had to admit that Xan had done everything she could have expected of him during the rooftop reception. He had circulated. He had chatted. He had not paid undue attention to Juliet and she had seemed equally indifferent to the fact that the replacement tutor was as personable as he was gifted.

The last seat left vacant was next to Colonel McCormick, one of Miss Walcott's regulars. This pleased Kate because she knew he had used to come with his wife but was now a widower. This was his first painting holiday on his own and she meant to keep a special eye on him.

She had only just sat down when a waitress placed a bowl of green soup in front of her. It looked delicious and Kate was hungry and impatient to try it. But the woman on the other side of her turned round in her chair to shake her finger at the waitress.

'Not…for…me,' she said slowly and distinctly. 'I…will…wait…for…the…main…course.'

'You not like?' The Cretan girl looked surprised. Then, with a shrug, she moved the bowl to the next person's place.

Further along the table a man was signalling for attention. 'May I see the wine list, please?'

Having looked through it, he said in a loud cross voice, 'These prices are outrageous! They're asking the equivalent of a fiver for a bottle of year-old plonk.'

In the hush that followed, Xan, who must have seen the list before him, said, 'The retsina's not expensive.'

'But it doesn't taste nice,' said a woman sitting near him. 'I've only tried it once but I couldn't drink it. A horrible taste, if you ask me.'

'An acquired taste perhaps…like that of many good things,' Xan replied.

There was nothing discourteous in his tone or expression, but Kate's intuition told her he thought the woman a fool and was unlikely to suffer her gladly once this first evening was over.

He rose from the table, passing along the side where she was sitting. To her surprise he stopped behind her chair. Stooping over her, on Colonel McCormick's side, he said quietly, 'Have you tried retsina, Kate? Would you like to share my bottle?'

It had been her intention not to drink while on duty, and tomorrow to buy a bottle of wine from the nearest supermarket and keep it in her room to enjoy in peace and privacy while reading in bed at the end of the day.

Looking up at him, she said, 'Thank you. One glass perhaps.'

Xan nodded and moved on to have a word with Kyria Drakakis, who was keeping one eye on the girls serving the group and the other on the rest of her guests at the smaller tables.

'How long have you been working for Palette, Kate?' the colonel asked.

'Only this summer. I hope you'll tell me if I'm falling down on the job in any way,' she replied.

'You've been most efficient so far. If Nerina had engaged someone to assist her sooner, she might not have succumbed to this illness. She refused to acknowledge her age and over-taxed herself.'

As soon as everyone had been served, Kate sampled the soup. To her taste, it was delicious and, having emptied her bowl, she accepted a second helping. So did Xan, she noticed, and the elderly man beside him. But there were several who didn't finish their first helping.

In confidential undertone, Colonel McCormick said, 'There are always a few faddy people. I don't know why they come abroad if they're frightened by anything different from whatever they eat at home.'

The main course was tender lamb with a strongly herbal flavour served with mashed potatoes and a side salad of tomato and cucumber. Kate had already begun to eat when a waitress filled her glass with pale golden wine from the bottle ordered by Xan.

She found the flavour different from anything she had drunk before but certainly not unpleasant and perhaps, given time, as palatable as good ordinary wine. She looked at the head of the table, found Xan's eyes on her and smiled and mouthed 'thank you'. His response was to nod and make a toasting movement with his own glass.

After the lamb came honey-soaked fritters. When everyone had finished eating, Kate rose, tapping her glass with her spoon to attract their attention.

'For tonight's discussion about tomorrow's programme, Kyria Drakakis has very kindly put her private sitting-room at our disposal for an hour. It's at the end of the corridor on the second floor. Xan will open the discussion at half-past nine.'

On her way down the stairs, from behind her a cool drawling voice said, 'The ten-minute interval being for the benefit of the old and incontinent, I presume?' As Kate looked over her shoulder, Juliet Craig added, 'Of whom we seem to have a rather tedious preponderence.'

Fortunately there was no one to overhear and be hurt by her remark. Kate said, with a touch of crispness, 'At this time of year it's only to be expected that most of the group will be retired people. Younger people tend to come in the main holiday period.'

'I suppose so. Are you and our leader "close friends", as the columnists put it?'

CHAPTER FOUR

THE question took Kate aback. 'We hardly know each other.'

'But you shared a bottle of wine at dinner.'

'That was merely a courtesy on Xan's part.'

'Is he married?'

Kate shook her head, wondering if, even though she was an experienced painter, the other woman's main reason for being here was to have a holiday affair or find a husband.

They moved on down the serpentine coils of the polished wood staircase, its gleaming patina a tribute to generations of good housewifery. The hotel was furnished in the style of a private house and had indeed belonged to Kyria Drakakis's forebears for several centuries.

Her drawing-room—far too grand to be called a sitting-room—was a large, lofty apartment with rugs laid on a stone floor, antique furniture and ancestral portraits hanging on the walls. The sofas and chairs were covered with deep red material, hand-embroidered, and pieces of old embroidery in shades of red and pink covered the many loose cushions.

'These are divine,' said Juliet, picking one up. 'Are embroideries the things to buy here?'

'I believe so. I have a list of the best shops for souvenirs. I'll give you a copy at breakfast.'

Kate watched Juliet sink gracefully on to a sofa to examine the design worked on the upholstery. She looked as if she might be a designer herself. Tonight she was wearing a black jersey halter top with a flowing white linen skirt and high-wedged black espadrilles tied with tapes round her elegant ankles. Her nails and her lips, which she had re-lipsticked at table after declining the sweet, were painted a deep subtle red to match a choker of large red beads at the base of her long neck. Sitting there on the red and pink sofa, she looked as if she were posing for a *Vogue* fashion photograph.

The group had assembled and most were discussing the meal they had just eaten when Xan's entrance quietened the buzz of conversation.

He had an innate air of authority, Kate realised. Perhaps it was an inherited attribute. His grandfather had died while commanding a fighter squadron at Anzio. He had been only twenty-four. At the same age, Xan's father had been the leader of a group of pot-holing enthusiasts and had drowned while attempting to rescue someone trapped by underground flooding.

Standing in front of the drawing-room's massive chimney breast, Xan scanned the faces of his audience before he said, 'Palette Holidays, founded and run by my grandmother, has established an excellent reputation. It's bad luck for you that, instead of enjoying two weeks of her tuition, you're going to have me as your mentor. I'm not used to teaching and, like most practising artists, I haven't much time for the dilettante approach.

'During our working sessions, I'll expect you to work *hard*. The dining-room opens at seven-thirty which gives us all plenty of time to have breakfast, pack our gear and be in the hall, raring to go, sharp at nine.'

Someone put up a hand. 'If I may interrupt, Mr Walcott, we *usually* start at nine-thirty. Nine is *rather* early, don't you think? Especially on the *first* morning when we've had to adjust to sleeping in a strange bed.'

'Does anyone else feel nine is too early?'

His question brought no response.

'Sorry…I'm afraid you're outnumbered by early risers,' he said, with a charming smile at a woman whose face wasn't visible from where Kate was sitting. 'If you drink a small glass of Metaxa brandy before turning out your light,' he added, 'you'll find yourself sleeping so soundly that, unless you've brought an alarm clock, you'd better arrange for the desk to call you.'

The rest of the group smiled or chuckled, but the objector said primly, 'I *always* bring my alarm clock, but I have more respect for my liver than to drink alcohol last thing at night. However if everyone else is prepared to set out at nine, then I must bow to the majority.'

'We'll start with a walk along the waterfront,' Xan went on. 'Then we'll go to the market to buy the makings of our picnic lunches. After that we'll take a break in one of the cafés and I'll ask you to do some sketches so that I can gauge your capabilities and tailor the course to suit everyone's needs. Tomorrow all you need to bring is your sketchbook and a pencil or drawing pen. Any comments or questions?'

Again no one spoke. Xan turned to Kate. 'Anything you want to add, Kate?'

'Only that we shall be having a Cretan breakfast. If anyone wants something different, would they please have a word with the receptionist tonight?'

'What's a Cretan breakfast?' Juliet asked, re-crossing her legs and slanting them both to one side, model-fashion.

Kate had anticipated this question. 'It's fruit with *mizithra*, a white cheese made from sheep's milk, and yogurt and honey and olives. As well as very good bread, the Cretans eat a lot of rusks. To drink, there's mountain tea made from a blend of ten herbs.'

There being no other questions, about half the group rose

to retire to their rooms, leaving the rest drinking coffee and chatting.

'I'm going for a stroll round the town,' said Xan. 'Will you join me, Kate? I might also punish my liver with another glass of wine,' he added, with a glint of amusement.

She would have liked to go out but felt it was wiser to say, 'No, thanks. I want to write a letter.'

She didn't add that it was a letter to Miss Walcott. The hotel had a machine for transmitting facsimiles, as did the nursing home. It would ease her employer's mind to receive a daily report, with the emphasis on the positive side of the trip and no mention of any difficulties which might arise.

Juliet joined them. 'Is it all right for women to wander around here, or is one going to be pestered by Cretan beach boys?' she asked Kate.

'According to Manolis, our bus driver, women are safe here. It's probably wiser to keep to the main part of town and streets with good lighting. Cretan men may not be a hazard, but male tourists might be.'

'I'm going for a stroll if you'd feel happier with an escort,' said Xan. Juliet accepted the offer with no more visible enthusiasm than if it had come from Colonel McCormick. But Kate was almost sure the other woman had overheard her own refusal to join him and been quick to grab the opportunity to replace her.

Early next morning, Kate left the hotel with her swimsuit under her shirt and shorts and her underwear wrapped in her towel.

The beach where Miss Walcott had always swum before breakfast on her visits to Chaniá was some way from the hotel. There were very few people about. Kate enjoyed the walk and the feeling of having the world to herself.

She had left her letter describing the group's arrival on

the desk in the hall with a note requesting it to be faxed to England when the receptionist came on duty. Kate hadn't mentioned that the starting time of the morning painting session had been put forward, to one person's displeasure. With luck there wouldn't be any more objections to Xan's innovations, but she knew from previous trips that suppressed grievances and personality clashes could simmer unnoticed during the first week and boil over during the second.

On one of the trips to France, a seemingly quiet woman had erupted when a man was expounding political views to which she was strongly opposed. At the time, the rest of the group had rather enjoyed the slanging match, but it had led to embarrassment when they were expected to side with one or other of the opponents. Miss Walcott had blamed herself for not foreseeing and averting the row.

However, at this lovely hour of the day, Kate was not going to worry about battles which might break out at a later stage of the trip. Today, provided they had slept well, everyone should be in a mood of happy anticipation.

On reaching the beach, she left her clothes in a neat pile and ran into the sea. As she was by herself, she stayed within her depth and swam parallel to the water's edge. Presently, treading water after an energetic hundred-yard crawl, she caught sight of a snorkel. It was out in the deeper water where the pale jade colour of the shallows changed to turquoise.

As she was wondering what the wearer of the tube was looking at, he did a sudden duck-dive. For a second his wet brown skin and coral bathing slip flashed in the early sunlight and she caught a glimpse of black fins. Then he was gone.

He was under the water so long she began to wonder if something had happened to him. Then, as suddenly as he had gone, he broke the surface, puffing water out of the tube. He was facing the beach now and waved. Turning to see who was there, Kate found it was still deserted. That he had been waving to her was confirmed when he began to swim directly towards her.

She had been floating in a sitting position, but now she put her feet on the sea-bed and stood up. Was she about to be picked up by one of the Cretan beach boys Juliet had mentioned?

Twenty feet away he stopped swimming. But when he stood up he was much taller than any of the islanders she had seen so far. Taller and somehow familiar. He ejected the mouthpiece and pushed up his mask. It was Xan.

'Good morning. I didn't expect to see you here at this hour,' he said, moving closer.

'Good morning.' It was on the tip of her tongue to say, 'I'm emulating your grandmother,' but she changed her mind. Any reference to Miss Walcott always brought on that arctic expression. There was no point in starting the day by annoying him. Instead she said, 'Is the snorkelling good?'

His reply went in one ear and out the other because, as he came closer, she was bowled over by the strength of her reaction to seeing him without his clothes. He was built like the younger gods in classical paintings, every muscle clearly defined under the sleek tanned skin. The breadth of his shoulders was obvious when he was dressed, but now they looked even more formidable. But the latent power of his torso had nothing to do with the overdeveloped beefiness of male strippers. Xan's physique was lithe and graceful. In a word, beautiful.

Kate was aware that it wasn't only aesthetically that his body pleased her. She was also excited at a more primitive level. She did not want to be, but she was. The sensations he aroused were beyond her control. She could only hope no hint of them showed in her face.

'Did you get your letter written?' he asked.

She nodded. 'What was the nightlife like?'

'We didn't stay out late. The cafés were doing good business with locals as well as tourists. Is your bed comfortable?'

'Very.'

'So is mine, but last night an insect disappeared under it which might have caused some agitation had I been a maiden lady of delicate sensibilities.'

'What sort of insect? A cockroach?'

'I don't think so. But I was reading and didn't get a proper look at it. It had disappeared down a crack in the floorboards by the time I leaned over and flashed my torch around.'

'It might be better not to mention it to anyone else. It may have been a one-off and we don't want the women on their own peering anxiously under the beds.'

'Perhaps I shouldn't have mentioned it to you. But you don't look the type to be panicked by spiders and mice.'

'I like mice. I'm not crazy about spiders,' Kate admitted.

'Feel free to call my room if there's anything you can't handle.'

Xan gave her a teasing look, his glance moving downwards to take in first the triangles of wet cotton covering her breasts and then the curlicue of her navel.

Six years ago, at twenty, she would have pulled in her tummy. In her late teens she had been plump, a result of too much stodge in the orphanage diet and a weakness for choc bars. Now she weighed a hundred and twenty-five pounds and could sin occasionally without losing her slim waist and taut thighs. She knew she had a good body, but Xan was a connoisseur and maybe she didn't match up to some of the long-legged beauties who had holidayed with him in places even more beautiful than Chaniá.

'I saw you before you saw me. You're a good swimmer,' he said. 'And sensible to keep in your depth when you thought there was no one around. If I get rid of my flippers, would you like to swim further out?'

'You don't think they might be stolen if you leave them lying on the sand?'

'Not at this time of day. There's no one around but us...Adam and Eve,' he added, with another of his quizzical looks.

Kate stayed where she was while he headed for the beach to shed his gear. As he lifted an arm to pull off the mask, the movement sent a ripple of muscle down his back. She felt her insides turn over in a way they had never done with Robert. But physical attraction was a fever in the blood; not to be confused with love, although it was part of love.

He was in shallow water now and the lines of his backside and long, darkly tanned thighs conjured up visions she didn't want in her mind's eye. Deliberately she turned her back on him, starting to swim towards the pearly horizon. He would soon catch her up even if she swam as fast as she could.

She was almost at the limit of her energy when Xan's shouted 'Whoa!' made her stop. He had been swimming alongside her for several minutes, easily keeping abreast while she flailed through the water, flat out.

'That should have worked up a good appetite for breakfast,' he said, as Kate trod water, panting. He was not out of breath at all. He could probably swim for two or three miles without tiring.

On her own, she wouldn't have liked being so far from the shore. With Xan's broad brown shoulders close by, she felt curiously secure.

Or did, until seconds later, he disappeared under the surface and came up close behind her, slipping his hands under her armpits and pulling her backwards until his chest was touching her shoulderblades.

'Feeling puffed? Have a rest. Let me practise my lifesaving skills,' he said, close to her ear, before starting to tow her shorewards.

There was no way she could release his hold on her. All she could do was keep her feet together, out of the way of his powerful leg strokes, and submit to his latest tease until he had had enough of it.

'Nice out here, isn't it? My favourite time of day…at least in summer which, in effect, this is.'

'Yes, it's lovely,' she agreed.

And it was. A cloudless sky, still tinged with lingering traces of dawn, overhead. The sea like silk on her skin. Strong hands holding her firmly but lightly without hurting the tender flesh under her arms.

'Your hair feels like fronds of fine sea-weed. When I was about twelve I used to dream of catching a mermaid…with a long silver tail and beautiful ripe-peach breasts like the gypsy girls in Russell Flint paintings.'

From the tone of his voice she could almost believe that it wasn't just a line but that, as a young boy, he really had imagined catching a mermaid.

Then his right hand left her arm and she felt the brush of his fingers at the nape of her neck.

'Your bikini top spoils the illusion. If I were to untie it…'

Kate felt an absurd thrust of panic but managed to control it. He didn't mean it. He was only trying to take a rise out of her. Men who undid girls' bras without some encouragement ran the risk of being sued for sexual harassment. Not that she would go to those lengths and probably he knew it. In her view, coping with passes and dealing with gropers was the inevitable downside of being a woman. Always had been. Always would be.

'I've got my breath back now. I'll swim the rest of the way.'

At the same moment that she rolled sideways, his other hand loosened its hold, brushing her ribs and back as she turned over in the water and struck out for the beach.

It was no longer empty. Striding towards the spot where Xan had left his fins propped in an inverted V was Oliver McCormick. He was wearing khaki shorts, with his shirt and one of the hotel's beach towels slung over his shoulder.

'Every inch the military type, isn't he?' said Xan, doing a leisurely side stroke.

Kate murmured agreement. Presently, wading out of the sea, she said, 'Good morning, Colonel. I hope you slept well.'

'Splendidly, thank you. I generally do. Unlike Miss Whatsername, I find a tot of whisky last thing at night a most effective soporific.' He turned to Xan. 'When my duty-free bottle runs out, I'll try your prescription—Greek brandy.' Then, looking at Kate again, 'By the way, I'd prefer you to call me Oliver.'

Xan was towelling his head. His bathing slip was only marginally more concealing than a vine leaf on a nude statue. Kate averted her eyes from the lean hips and long brown legs but they remained in her mind's eye as she left the two men chatting and walked back to where she had left her clothes. From there, Xan's rucksack had merged with the rocks and she hadn't noticed it earlier.

By the time she was dry and dressed, Oliver was in the sea and Xan was sitting on the sea wall, still in his bathing slip, sketching. She walked back to the hotel alone, pepped up by her swim but also disturbed and unsettled by the strength of her desire for him.

* * *

For the group's first exploration of the waterfront and the colourful covered market, Kate dressed conservatively in sand-coloured cotton long shorts and a white short-sleeved shirt.

The youngest member of the party, a seventeen-year-old called Kelly who was accompanying her mother, wore a mini-skirt and a clinging pale yellow top which drew stares from all the young men they passed.

At the mid-morning break most people wanted coffee but Kate asked for a bottle of mineral water.

Standing up and raising her hand to make an announcement, she said, 'Some of you are far more experienced travellers than I. But I'd just like to remind those who aren't that, in this climate, we all need to drink lots of water…at least a litre a day and preferably more.'

Catching Xan's eye, she wondered if she had sounded officious. But it would be her responsibility if anyone became unwell from dehydration.

As she sat down, he took her place. 'I want you all to draw the boat moored to the quay in front of us,' he said, pointing to a small fishing vessel. 'Do the first drawing without taking the point of your pencil or pen off the paper. Then draw it again, using dots and, finally, make a third drawing with a busy scribbly line like this.' He gave a quick demonstration on the pad he was holding.

It had been Kate's intention, while the others were busy, to write cards to Robert and friends in London.

'You as well, Kate,' said Xan. 'You can use this.' He held out a sketch pad.

'But I can't draw for peanuts,' she protested.

'If you can write, you can draw. It's a matter of trying. Don't argue. Have a go.'

It was an order she was unwilling to contest in public. But she would have something to say to him later in private.

While the group were following his instructions, Xan himself sketched the passers-by, mostly wandering tourists but also some locals including short, sturdy fishermen with swarthy faces weathered by years in the sun.

'Don't forget to write your name on your drawing before you hand it in,' he reminded everyone.

When a waiter brought her order, Kate took a refreshing swallow of the cold sparkling water and surreptitiously compared her own continuous line-drawing with those of the people near her. To her surprise she found hers was no worse than some of theirs.

From the café, the party explored some more of the waterfront with Xan stopping to point out interesting subjects. His dark hair and already tanned skin made him look as at home in the sun as the Cretans, unlike some of the group who were visibly flagging in the heat. Only Juliet, her arms and legs hidden from the glare by thin linen trousers and a filmy voile shirt, her face shaded by her straw hat, still looked cool and elegant.

Later, in her room, Kate had a cold shower. Her lunch consisted of two large ripe peaches, bought in the market, and a tub of yogurt from a shop near the hotel. Most of the shops in the town closed at half-past one and reopened from five until seven or eight.

She was naked but for her micro-briefs, about to relax on her bed with a book, when there was a tap at the door. Expecting it to be one of the maids, she pulled on a long loose T-shirt and padded barefoot to answer it.

In the corridor, Xan was carrying a tray with a coffee-pot and two cups on it.

'This seems a good moment to discuss how it's going.'

'Oh...yes...all right,' Kate agreed, standing back for him

to come in. 'Would you excuse me a moment? I was just going to brush my teeth.'

Closing the door of the shower room, she ran the tap while she whipped off the T-shirt to put on the cotton bra she had washed out last night and left hanging over the towel rail.

'You keep your room very neat,' said Xan when she joined him.

She had tidied the bedroom minutes before his knock. The staff in charge of the orphanage had been strict about cleanliness and neatness and that early training had left its mark. She had often been surprised by the mess some of her friends and former clients lived in.

'Your flat looked very orderly from what I saw of it,' she said. As he was already sitting on the bed she wasn't using, with the tray beside him, she perched on the end of her bed.

'A little milk but no sugar—yes?' he said, picking up the coffee-pot.

Kate nodded. Observant of him, she thought. But then observation was his stock-in-trade.

'So what d'you think? Have we started off on the right foot?' he asked. His mouth lifted at one corner. 'I don't mean you and me...we'll get to that later. I mean myself and the others.'

'Apart from the teetotal lady, they all like you very much. How do you feel about them?'

'They're pretty much what I expected. Oliver's the best of the bunch, from my point of view.'

'What about Juliet?'

'What about Juliet?'

'Don't you think she's attractive?'

'I find you more attractive.'

He was passing her cup to her as he spoke, with a look which made her hand shake as she took it from him. The cup rocked on the saucer but he hadn't filled it too full and nothing was spilt.

It wasn't the first time Kate had been told she was attractive but it was the first time she had been targeted by a charmer of Xan's calibre. All the previous men in her life had been nice but ordinary, even the one she had thought herself in love with. Xan was the first high-flyer she had known and also the first man to make her realise she was a lot more hot-blooded than she had previously recognised.

'Is that an early warning?' she asked.

He cocked an interrogative eyebrow.

Could he really have forgotten the kiss at his grandmother's cottage and what he had said to her afterwards?

'When I misunderstood your motives—so you said—the night we had dinner at the Angel, you promised you wouldn't make a pass without warning,' she reminded him.

'I did, didn't I?' He poured coffee for himself. 'But no, that wasn't a warning. Just a statement of fact. What I'd like to do right now is not make a pass but paint you. How about coming along to my room and posing for me? On the balcony…where it's much too public to make passes,' he added drily.

'Now?'

'When we've finished our coffee.'

To be sure what he had in mind, she said, 'As I am now…with my clothes on?'

'As you are now…plus plenty of suncream to make sure you don't get burnt.'

'All right. Why not?' she agreed, secretly rather excited.

There was no denying that, when he was behaving normally, she did enjoy his company. Sunbathing on his balcony, talking to him, was a better way to spend the afternoon break than lying here on her own with a not very gripping whodunnit.

Xan's room, she discovered presently, had been transformed into a studio. He had brought a lot more equipment
with him than the others had. The spare bed, covered with
a sheet of plastic, was in use as a working area. The side
table was also protected and on it, in a tall container, stood
his battery of brushes. But what caught her eye was a small
sketch pinned to the top of a large wooden easel with a
canvas fixed to it. The canvas was primed but otherwise
blank. The sketch was a mermaid with peach-shaped breasts
and Kate's face.

Xan was too busy getting ready to sketch to notice that
she had seen it, and she thought it best not to make any
comment.

Half an hour later, reclining on one of the balcony's two
cushioned sunbeds, soaking up golden warmth, Kate almost
fell asleep.

'Do you want a break?' Xan enquired, from behind the
light metal easel he was using outside.

'No, I'm fine,' she said lazily. 'If I start getting cramped
I'll tell you, but this is an easy pose.'

'Some people can't bear keeping still, however easy the
pose.' Xan dabbled his brush in water and gave it a
dexterous flick. 'I'd like to paint you in oils. Preferably
nude. Would you mind that?'

'Yes, I should. Anyway, neither of us has the time.'

'I didn't mean here. When we get back to England.'

'Surely there you can take your pick from all the professional models who feel comfortable with their clothes
off?'

'But who don't have your skin or your...*je ne sais quoi*,'
he answered. 'An artist, when he's at work, looks at the
human body with the same detachment as a doctor. He's

only amorous outside working hours. You don't feel any embarrassment when you undress for your doctor, do you?'

'My present doctor is a woman. So far I haven't needed to consult her. If and when I do, I'll feel more comfortable talking to someone of my own sex. Would you want a woman doctor if you could go to a man?'

'I'd choose the most able doctor, regardless of sex.'

'I think there are fewer incompetent women doctors because, from the outset, it's harder for them to get started in medicine,' said Kate. 'Even parents aren't always supportive. A girl who wants to be a surgeon has an uphill struggle all the way. If she makes it, she has to be good.'

'You can also argue that, unless she's chosen to stay single, part of her attention will be given to domestic and family matters. She'll never be as single-minded as a man at the top of his tree,' said Xan. 'I've got to stop for five minutes to let this wash dry. Stand up and have a good stretch. Let's have some wine.'

He went into his room and came back with two glasses, each with a cube of ice floating in it.

'I shall need another cold shower to wake me up after this,' said Kate, sipping the retsina. 'How many hours a day do you usually spend painting?'

'Depends. On a bad day, when I have to attend to other things, maybe only three or four. On the best days, twelve or fifteen. When you're engrossed in what you're doing, hours pass like minutes. Most men only experience what I feel when I'm painting when they're making love or eating wonderful food. For women a good comparison would be a spending spree on clothes.' He took up his brush and resumed work.

About fifteen minutes later he took two paces back from the easel, stared through narrowed eyes for some moments and then, apparently satisfied, detached the board to which the paper was taped.

He brought it to where she was lying and turned it round. 'What do you think?'

Kate sat up, feeling a thrill of excitement, both at the consummate artistry of the quick, impressionistic study and at the way he had portrayed her. Could this really be how he saw her? Satin-skinned, lissom, alluring? Or was it a deliberate act of flattery?

'Like it?' he asked.

'It's lovely.'

'You make a lovely subject.'

Her heart seemed to turn in her chest. She looked up to meet his eyes, trying to interpret their expression.

The telephone rang in his bedroom.

'Excuse me.' He rose to answer it, leaving the painting with her.

While he was gone she studied it more closely, unable to relate her own view of herself to this sunlit vision of long limbs and suggested curves. Was this part of his technique? To enhance women's looks, but subtly and therefore more effectively than by obvious exaggeration.

As soon as it became clear that he was taking a long-distance call which might be private, Kate put the board back on the easel, drained the last of her wine and stepped into the bedroom where he was sitting on the side of the bed.

Although he signalled there was no need for her to go, she tapped the face of her watch, mimed taking a shower and waved goodbye.

On the way back to her room, it struck her that she had been in Crete barely twenty-four hours but yesterday's world seemed long ago and far away. Even Robert's proposal of marriage seemed strangely unreal, like something in a dream.

But the life he had offered her was far more real than anything here. This was merely a fleeting interlude…an escape from the everyday things which were the basis of any lasting happiness.

CHAPTER FIVE

AT FOUR o'clock, the group gathered in the hall. Two members wanted to visit an art shop to replace equipment accidentally left behind. Kate said she would go with them, partly to make herself known to the proprietor of the shop with whom Miss Walcott was friendly, and partly to make sure the shoppers didn't lose their way.

'We'll be here,' said Xan, marking a street on her map of the town. 'It's a quiet cul-de-sac with some interesting old doors and windows.'

The next time she saw him, an hour later, he was deep in discussion with Juliet about the work on her easel.

Kate strolled about looking at the paintings in progress but not standing close behind people in a way they might find unnerving. Predictably, several of the least talented people had the most elaborate equipment.

Oliver was sitting on a camp stool with a board on his lap, holding the type of small paintbox called a *pochade* with only a few pans of colour in it. His palette was a white-enamelled tin plate from a camping shop or ship's chandler. But the accurate drawing of a door to which he was applying washes of colour was far better than many of the garish local views she had seen on sale in souvenir shops on the way back from the art shop.

When he glanced up and smiled, she asked, 'Do you sell your work?'

'I've sold a few things, yes. But it was Sophie, my wife, who could paint well. I'm merely a competent draughtsman.'

'An excellent thing to be,' said Xan, overhearing this. 'Come on, Kate. Get cracking. Here's a pad and a pen you can borrow, and you can sit on my stool. I paint standing up and only sit down to snack.'

After fetching his stool and placing it not far from Oliver's, he said, 'Your efforts this morning were better than some of the others'. I can't stand tight, niggly drawing. Yours were admirably loose and free. You'd be surprised what psychological insights one can draw from the way people handle a pencil or brush.'

As she opened her mouth, he added, 'No arguments. See what you can make of that door.'

He walked away, leaving her thinking he had to be the most dictatorial man she had ever or would ever meet. Still, what else did she have to do? The arrangements for tomorrow's outing to a monastery had been checked. She had been in touch with the rep who was coming round after dinner to suggest some excursions for the non-painting partners and for the painters as well, on their days off.

Settling herself on the stool he had lent her, she saw Xan drop to his haunches beside the woman who had objected to early starts. No doubt by the end of the week he would have her eating out of his hand.

Applying herself to the task he had set her, Kate wondered if the door was a remnant of the Venetian occupation of Chaniá. Set in a high whitewashed wall, it had an elaborate architrave worthy of the entrance to an important mansion.

The Venetians had bought the island to expand their maritime empire. They had installed strong and sometimes cruel rulers who during the next four centuries had crushed the numerous uprisings. But they had also reformed and expanded the island's economy. Chaniá had become known as the Venice of the East, and two of the bastions, the shipyards and part of the sea wall built by the Venetians were still in existence. Some of the hotels and guest-houses had once been rich merchants' palaces. This door, now leading into what appeared to be a garden, was a part of that heritage.

As she attempted to draw it, Kate was reminded of a book she had read as a child; a book called *The Secret Garden* about two lonely children with whom, though not lonely herself, or not in the obvious way of lacking companionship, she had strongly identified.

'Do you think it's true that people's drawings reveal their characters?' she asked Oliver.

'Where did you read that?' he asked.

'Xan said it.'

Oliver rinsed his brush in his water container. 'Yes, I think it is,' he said thoughtfully. 'But not until people have developed a personal style, and they only do that when they've been painting or drawing for some time.'

Which must mean that Xan's paintings would be more indicative of his character than those of the amateurs he was teaching, thought Kate. Miss Walcott had catalogues of all his one-man shows, but looking at small reproductions of paintings was never the same as seeing the originals. Kate was curious to see the work he produced while he was here.

An hour before dinner, they assembled in Kyria Drakakis's drawing-room for what was to be a nightly ritual: the assessment of the day's work.

Xan set up his easel and, in alphabetical order, each member of the group submitted a drawing or painting to the comments of their peers before he passed a professional opinion on it.

Knowing that if she tried to exclude herself from the proceedings he was capable of insisting on her participation,

Kate had decided that, if her name was on his list, she would take the line of least resistance. No one was going to sneer if the courier couldn't draw.

Her name *was* on the list and she could tell by his expression that he thought being called would embarrass her. Instead she stepped forward and returned the borrowed sketch-pad, the cover folded back to show her attempt to copy the lines of the door.

'I asked Kate to do this,' he said, 'to support my theory that very few people are totally lacking in artistic ability and too many go through life unaware they're neglecting a skill that could give them a great deal of pleasure. What do you think of this as a first attempt at a fairly difficult subject?'

'Quite good.'

'Not bad.'

Most of the comments were kind until someone said, 'She hasn't got the perspective right, has she?'

'Perspective is a problem for several of you,' said Xan. 'It's one of the subjects I'm going to discuss and demonstrate. In my view this drawing shows considerable promise.' He made some deft alterations to show where it went wrong. 'Thank you for being a good sport and having a go, Kate. I hope you'll have another try tomorrow.'

As her sketch was removed and replaced, Kate knew it was absurd to feel a glow at his praise. Life within Xan's orbit was like being on a seesaw. She teetered between being exasperated and charmed by him.

After everyone's work had been discussed, he produced a large sheet of what she recognised as the heaviest and most expensive type of water-colour paper, almost as thick and stiff as cardboard. When he turned it round and placed it on the easel there was a concerted murmur of admiration.

'I did this the day before you arrived,' he said. 'It was so hot out of doors at noon, the washes were drying in seconds.

I was trying to catch the heat and the somnolent atmosphere.'

And had succeeded, thought Kate. The focal point of the picture was a three-masted sailing vessel moored stern-on to the quay with several others beyond it and, behind them, a line of buildings. But all these were merely suggested and even the largest vessel, her deck shaded by awnings, her white hull reflected in the still water, was not painted in detail.

'How long did it take you?' someone asked.

'About twenty-five years,' said Xan. 'I started my apprenticeship when I was so high—' with an illustrative gesture. Smiling, he added, 'But that's not what you meant, is it? Let's say about ten minutes looking and thinking, and forty minutes painting. Slightly less than an hour altogether.'

His painting was the topic of conversation around Kate at dinner. Nine months ago she wouldn't have known what was meant by 'negative spaces' and 'wet-into-wet'. Now she did, and her understanding of the technicalities was good enough for her to grasp that the apparently simple picture was in fact a very fine example of the difficult art of watercolour.

Tonight's meal began with aubergines fried in olive oil. When one of the group declined them, Xan said, 'You're going to find the garlic fumes from the rest of us rather overpowering if you don't at least try a few mouthfuls.'

Later, for pudding, they each had a large bunch of sweet white grapes. But even these were not to everyone's liking. One person was worried in case they had not been properly washed and another painstakingly peeled and de-pipped the few she did eat.

After dinner, the whole group went out to have coffee in one of the many *kafeneions* along the waterfront.

At this time of day the foreign visitors were outnumbered by Chaniotes taking the air as had been their custom for centuries. It was dark now, with a large moon floating in the sky like a pale Chinese lantern and making the sea outside the harbour glitter.

Kate ordered *kafé skéto*, Turkish coffee without sugar. The group was occupying several adjoining tables and she and Xan were not at the same one. Like him, several others including Oliver and Juliet had brought small sketching-pads with them and were drawing the lively scene around them.

Juliet was sitting next to Xan, wearing the same black top and white skirt as last night but with a wide yellow belt, long amber earrings and half a dozen amber-coloured bracelets sliding up and down her slender forearm as she talked and gestured. It was she who held the floor, and with considerable wit, judging by the frequent laughter at their table. Xan didn't stop drawing to listen to Juliet, nor did he glance at her. But not all his attention was on what he was doing. Kate saw the flash of his teeth whenever what she said amused him.

Gradually the Palette group thinned out as people paid their bills and bade the others goodnight. Sipping the glass of water which had come with her coffee, Kate thought it wouldn't be long before she went back. She still hadn't written her postcards. If they weren't posted soon, they might not arrive before her own return.

Next morning, instead of going to the beach for her early swim, she went up to the pool on the top floor and swam thirty lengths. Then, having the pool deck to herself, she did some stretching exercises, knowing that if anyone joined her it wouldn't be Xan.

When she finished exercising, she went to lean on the

parapet surrounding the pool deck. A movement caught her eye. Three people had come into view. Xan with Oliver on one side and Juliet on the other. All on their way to the beach.

Kate watched them walking away. Juliet was wearing a long indigo robe and carrying her towel and other necessities in a drawstring bag slung over her shoulder.

As she watched them, they all turned to look back towards the hotel, Xan making gestures which suggested he was talking about the play of early morning sunlight on the rooftops and the White Mountains visible behind the town.

Then he spotted Kate leaning on the parapet and waved. Waving back, she wondered if he would signal her to join them. But he didn't. Perhaps because it was obvious from her swimsuit and her wet hair that she had already been in the pool, or because he preferred Juliet's company.

In spite of his telling Kate he found her more attractive, she knew Juliet had more claims to his interest. She was a gifted artist, nearer his height, more elegant than Kate and undoubtedly more experienced in her relations with men. None of the many unusual rings adorning her expressive hands was a wedding ring, but that didn't mean she had never been married.

To a man looking for some uncomplicated dalliance Juliet was a more likely partner than she was, thought Kate, on her way downstairs. Xan's instinct would probably tell him she was looking for love and permanence. If not actually looking for it, hoping for it.

The main entrance to the hotel was at the junction of several narrow streets in the old quarter and the presence of an excursion coach would temporarily block the passage of all other traffic. Manolis, their driver, had asked Kate to make sure they were ready to board with a minimum of delay.

Five minutes before he was due to arrive, Kelly was not down. She and her mother had breakfast in their room. Her mother had come down in good time, but Kelly's elaborate make-up might be delaying her. The lift being in use, Kate raced upstairs to the top floor and knocked on the girl's door.

'Time to go, Kelly,' she called.

'OK…shan't be a tick.'

Kate ran down to the first floor where Loretta, one of the older members of the group, was locking her bedroom door.

'Let me take your trolley,' Kate offered. 'The lift's being used by people with heavy luggage coming down from the top floor.'

If Loretta attempted the stairs with her trolley-cum-stool, she might have an accident. Her sandals were dressy rather than serviceable and she looked as if her bones might be brittle.

When the coach arrived, Kelly was still missing. Oliver, who had sprung to Kate's assistance as soon as he saw her bringing the laden trolley down the staircase, would, she knew, see it safely stowed in the luggage compartment. Although the coach wouldn't be full, the trolley was too bulky to be taken on board.

Kate was ringing Kelly's room from the reception desk and hoping she wasn't answering because she was on her way down when hooting broke out in the street and Manolis appeared looking impatient.

'Two are missing. You and another. Why is she not here?'

'I'm coming. Why all the panic?' Kelly asked, running down the last flight, her full breasts bouncing, her white mini-skirt barely decent.

'We're blocking the street,' said Manolis, his hands in the air.

'Oh…sorry. I didn't know.' She gave him her most melting smile.

'You knew we were going to a monastery,' said Kate. 'You can't turn up dressed like that.'

'What's wrong with the way I'm dressed?'

'Nothing…at Miami Beach or St Tropez. This is Crete and—' Kate broke off as Xan strode in.

'All hell's breaking out. What's the hold-up?'

'Kate thinks I'll shock the monks.' Kelly gave him the look which had mellowed Manolis's scowl to an indulgent grin.

'I doubt if you'll shock them,' Xan said tersely. 'No doubt they're inured to foreigners dressed for the beach. But unless you're prepared to spend the morning sitting in the coach, you'll have to change into something more acceptable.'

'But quickly, please,' said Manolis, as the hooting became more insistent. He dashed outside, muttering what sounded like the Cretan equivalent of, 'All right, all right…keep your hair on.'

Kelly was looking mutinous. 'If there's going to be all this fuss, I'll stay behind,' she said, pouting.

'Right. In that case, we'll see you this evening,' Xan said briskly. 'Come along, Kate.'

As he turned on his heel, there was a wail from behind him and Kelly burst into tears.

'We can't dump her,' Kate muttered, out of the side of her mouth, before she hurried to Kelly and put an arm round her shoulders. 'There's no need to cry. Just hurry upstairs and put on something a bit more covered-up.' To Xan she added, 'The rest of you go ahead. We'll follow by taxi.'

'Good idea, but I'll stay with Kelly. You go with the others.'

Grabbing the girl by the wrist, he hustled her towards the lift, just vacated by an American couple.

'But Kelly's not here,' her mother exclaimed, when Kate climbed aboard and told Manolis to start.

Before leaving the hotel, she had asked the receptionist to call a taxi and to write down where they were going for the driver.

'She'll be coming by taxi,' she explained. 'What she was wearing wasn't suitable for a monastery. Xan's waiting while she changes.'

'Who's going to pay for the taxi?' said her mother.

Kate would have liked to say, You are! You're sharing a room. You must have known her get-up wasn't the 'appropriate' outfit our guidelines advised for visits to churches and monasteries. What she actually said was, 'It will come out of our contingency funds.'

Then she walked to the empty seats at the back of the coach and flopped down for a few minutes' peace.

As Manolis manoeuvred his vehicle through streets and round corners designed for people on foot and mule-drawn carts, she wondered if Xan was in Kelly's room, going through her wardrobe with her.

She and her mother had each brought a massive suitcase and must have enough clothes to wear something different every day. Kate herself was in yesterday's clothes, washed and dried overnight and pressed with her traveller's steam iron on a towel spread over the side table.

She would have loved to be a fly on the wall in Kelly's room at this moment, and in the taxi later. It seemed likely that during his chequered love-life Xan would have had to deal with tearful, temperamental scenes before. No doubt he would handle Kelly's tantrum a lot more expertly than Kate herself could have done.

They had left the town behind, and the coach was picking up speed on a straight road when Juliet rose from her seat mid-way along the coach.

'What happened to our leader?' she asked, sitting down beside Kate.

'Silly little bimbo,' was her comment, when Kate had explained.

'Don't let her mother hear you. She might sue for defamation.'

Juliet shrugged. 'You'd think her mother would realise what a tart Kelly makes of herself. She's wasting her time if she thinks she can turn Xan on. She's got a good body, if she knew how to dress, but there's nothing between her ears.'

'That's rather brutal, isn't it?' said Kate. 'She may not have had much chance to develop her intelligence.'

'That's her problem,' said Juliet. 'Mine has to do with painting and I wanted to discuss it with Xan before we get there. We're here to paint, not to have our time wasted by nitwits like Kelly.'

The sound of a motorist putting his hand on his horn and keeping it there made most people in the coach crane to see what was happening. As Manolis decelerated, a taxi shot past and both vehicles slowed to a halt. A few moments after Manolis had pressed the button operating the door, Kelly climbed aboard, dressed now in a frilled and flounced dress and looking pleased with herself.

Slipping into the empty pair of seats in front of her mother, she must have been hoping Xan would join her there. But he took the single seat immediately behind Manolis where Kate would have sat had it been necessary to make any announcements or give a running commentary.

However, as the Agia Triada monastery was on the Akrotiri peninsula, where the airport was situated, they were on the road they had travelled on the day they arrived.

At the monastery, there was a notice in English—'An

Entreaty. Dress with modesty to come in the church. The monastery is closed 2135 after noon'.

Only a few monks were still in residence and Kate paid the one on duty at the arched entrance for tickets for the whole group. As they passed into the sunlit courtyard surrounding the church, Xan called them together.

'I suggest you have a look round before choosing where to settle down. This morning I want you to use your preferred medium. I'll come round at least twice to see how you're getting on and if you need help. We'll be here until the place closes, and then we're going to a beach taverna for lunch and a swim.'

As they dispersed, he and Kate remained by the entrance.

'Congratulations!' she said. 'I'm sure you accomplished that in half the time it would have taken me.'

'Kelly is the type who responds to the masterful male act.' There was a gleam of mockery in his smile as he added, 'You'd have resisted, wouldn't you? But then you would never have worn that get-up.'

'I've nothing against the masterful male in situations where he's needed,' Kate answered mildly. 'In a crisis such as a fire, I'll be only too pleased for you to take command. I'd only resist if I felt I was being bullied by a man with more muscle than brain. You're certainly not in that category.'

He bowed. 'Thank you kindly, ma'am.'

It seemed to her then, for a moment, that there was real warmth in his smile, not merely the charm she had felt on several occasions.

Juliet reappeared. 'Xan, I need some advice before I get started. Can you spare a few minutes?'

'Of course.'

Kate moved away, taking her camera out of her tote-bag to snap the imposing façade of the church. Erected in the seventeenth century by a family of rich Venetian merchants and supported by vineyards and olive groves on the land surrounding it, the monastery had been laid waste by the conquering Turks. Later it had been rebuilt and now housed a valuable library and several important icons.

She wandered about, inhaling the scent of jasmine. Lemon trees with green lemons on them cast pools of shade, and flights of stone stairs led to archways and walkways at higher levels. On one staircase she found a stone head framed by feathers as exquisitely carved as the neatly brushed and curled hair. Was it an angel? She wondered if someone would paint it.

She had taken a close-up photo and was wondering how old it was and who the carver had been when, from below, Xan said, 'Do you want to relax with a book? Or will you have another go at drawing?' He brandished the pad he was holding.

'I'd like to draw this angel. But I know it's beyond me.'

He came up to where she was standing. 'Not if you simplify it. I'll show you.' He opened the pad at a clean page and uncapped a drawing pen. 'When you start, try to look at the main outlines, not the details. This breaks down into three shapes: the face, the hair and the feathers. They look a bit like an Elizabethan ruff, don't they?' As he spoke, his shapely brown hand moved over the paper in swift assured sweeps. 'There—that's how to begin. Now you have a go.'

He gave her the pad and pen and went down the stairs and, in long-legged leaps, up a wider flight on his way to speak to the people who had set up their easels on an arched loggia at a higher level.

For an hour or more after their arrival, the Palette group had the monastery to themselves. Kate worked hard at her drawing, making many mistakes which she was unable to rub out.

Earlier, while the others were breakfasting, she had sent another long fax to Miss Walcott and shortly afterwards there had been an incoming report on her employer's condition from the superintendent of the nursing home. It had been addressed to her, rather than to Xan, and indeed he had yet to ask how his grandmother was progressing.

Kate found it hard to relate his indifference to his closest relation with the approval he was generating within the group. It wasn't merely that the female members of it responded to his looks and his sexual magnetism which they must feel, even if they didn't recognise it for what it was. The men in the party liked him too. During the morning most of them took several breaks from their own work to stretch their legs and have a look at other people's efforts. All those who paused to have a brief chat with her remarked on how helpful he was.

'I was worried when I heard he was coming with us,' said Heather, one of two retired teachers who had come together. 'Being a complete beginner, not nearly as good as Joyce, I felt quite embarrassed showing him my poor little daub. But he was so nice...so sympathetic, I feel really encouraged.'

'Good. That's splendid,' said Kate.

She wondered what Xan would say when he saw her attempt at the angel and when he would come back to her.

The carving had been in shadow when she started. By the time she had done the best she could, it was in full sun. She retreated to a shady corner of the cloisters where she blew up her inflatable cushion and started to try to draw Oliver while he worked on an oil painting of a corner of the church and a lemon tree.

She was having a drink of iced water from her flask when the first coachload of ordinary tourists arrived. They were of mixed nationalities, some as unsuitably dressed as Kelly had been, and all but a few visibly wishing they had stayed

by the hotel pool. Not content to look at Oliver's painting
from a distance, they crowded round behind him, making
fatuous comments.

'A friend of mine used to deal with rubberneckers by
passing round a hat. It dispersed them faster than a bucket
of water,' said Xan, dropping down beside her. 'How have
you been getting on?'

'Not well, I'm afraid. In spite of your helpful outlines,
my angel doesn't look much like the original.' She handed
over the sketch-pad.

Xan studied it for a moment. 'It tells me a lot about you.'

'Such as?'

'That you generally finish what you start, not getting discouraged or losing interest mid-way.'

'Also that my talent for drawing is practically non-
existent,' she said, with a rueful smile.

'Not at all…merely undeveloped. What this needs is
some shading…like so…' He took the pen she was waiting
to give back to him and began to hatch in shadows behind
the feathers and the hair, which immediately made them
more three-dimensional.

Turning the page, he discovered the start she had made
on a drawing of Oliver. As she watched, alongside it, in less
than a minute and with great economy of line he completed
a sketch which was immediately recognisable as the
straight-backed older man.

'That's an exercise in what are called negative spaces,'
he said. 'Look at the way Oliver's standing with all his
weight on his left leg and his other leg slightly bent at the
knee. The inverted V between his legs is a negative
space…d'you see?'

'Yes, I do.' She hadn't before, but she did now.

'Try it.'

He gave back the pad and watched while she started

again. This second attempt was much better than the first, although not to be compared with his practised sketch.

But she knew it wasn't the almost magical improvement in her drawing which had quickened her pulse. It was the result of Xan leaning towards her so that the negative space between their shoulders must be less than the width of his pen. If it hadn't been for the voices of the tourists, she felt sure he would be able to hear the sudden rapid thumping of her heart.

'Well done…that's much better,' said Xan.

She glanced up at him, sharply aware that merely by bending his head he would be able to kiss her. If they had been alone. If he wanted to kiss her.

'Xan…could you come and advise?' Juliet's voice came from somewhere above them. When they looked up, she was leaning over a balustrade.

'Coming.' In one easy movement he rose to his feet and went to join her.

The beach taverna where they had a late lunch was a simple place with a cement floor and corrugated roof supported by metal pipes painted bright yellow to match the plastic chairs.

In charge was an energetic South African girl wearing short shorts, a black bra top, a cap worn peak-backwards and a profusion of necklaces and rings. Another girl, similarly dressed, was sitting on a high stool at the bar, drinking a can of Coke.

'I wonder what caused that nasty burn on her leg?' Kate murmured to Oliver, after he had asked if he might sit with her.

She had waited till everyone else was settled before seating herself at an unoccupied table. Then he had emerged from the loos at the back of the taverna and had had no choice but to join her or sit by himself.

'An exhaust-pipe,' he told her. 'You see a lot of leg-burns in mainland Greece and the islands where the young hare about on rented motorbikes, the girls riding pillion. They burn themselves as they get off, not realising that the exhaust becomes like the hot-plate on a stove.'

This led her to ask him about his travels in Greece where he had accompanied his wife on a number of art courses. Kate was interested to learn how they compared with Palette holidays and questioned him closely while eating her avocado salad with sesame-seeded bread cubes. Oliver had a pizza, and they each had a litre of water and a glass of white wine.

She found Oliver's company relaxing. He told her about his two sons, one in Africa, the other in Canada. Although he didn't admit to being lonely, she felt he must be and would have warmed to him on that account even if he hadn't been an interesting man…the kind of man she would have liked for her father.

Xan was having his lunch with Juliet and a middle-aged couple who looked staid and conventional but whose union had been the scandal of a Palette trip ten years earlier. At that time, according to Miss Walcott, both parties had appeared to be content with their previous partners. It had been a shock to everyone when they had been seen to be attracted to each other, the more so because neither seemed capable of inspiring an irresistible passion.

'Juliet is very striking, isn't she?'

It wasn't until Oliver said, 'Yes,' that Kate realised she had spoken her thought aloud.

'I find a lot of younger women rather daunting,' he went on. 'My wife was like you, a gentle person. Far from spineless, but not aggressive.'

Kate had never thought of herself as gentle and wasn't sure how to take this reading of her character. Nor was it clear whether he had been referring to younger women in general or had meant he found Juliet daunting.

After lunch, half the group swam and the rest stayed in the shade of the taverna, sketching each other or the view of the beach.

Kate was among those who swam, but she took the precaution of wearing an old T-shirt over her two-piece. The sun was so hot that the arid landscape behind the beach shimmered and the light off the water was dazzling.

Having sun-blocked her face and eyelids before going into the sea, she was lying on her back with her hands clasped under her head and her eyes closed, enjoying the sensation of weightlessness, when there was a disturbance in the water. She lifted her head to find Xan surfacing nearby.

As he raked back his hair, he said, 'How was your lunch?'

'Delicious. I love avocado. What did you have?'

'A toasted ham and cheese sandwich. But it wasn't the food I meant.' When her eyebrows contracted in puzzlement, he said, 'Oliver's not in his dotage. You may think he's past making a pass, but I wouldn't count on it.'

'Oliver!' she exclaimed. Then, remembering how loudly voices could carry across water, she lowered her voice. 'You must be crazy. He's not the pass-making type.'

'Any man is…given enough provocation,' Xan said drily. 'Your signals weren't as blatant as Kelly's, but you were laying on the charm and you could be reminding him of girls he liked when he was young. Don't underestimate yourself—or him. He's fit and virile and lonely…a combustible combination.'

'He's old enough to be my father.'

'A naïve statement if ever I heard one. If older men were immune to the charms of younger women, the gold-digging sorority would go out of business. Men with girls young enough to be their granddaughters are a commonplace sight in every expensive restaurant from here to Hong Kong and back.'

'I wouldn't know. The fleshpots are outside my orbit,' said Kate. 'But I've met a few lechers in my time, and Oliver's not one. He's a thoroughly nice man.'

Whether by design or chance, the slight movements necessary to keep Xan upright in the water had brought him closer to her. There was barely a yard between them as he said, 'Nice men feel the same lusts as lechers. They just control them better. He's been on his own for four years. That's a long time to be celibate. Bear it in mind.'

'I don't believe this,' she said hotly. 'What qualifies you to lecture me, for heaven's sake? My life's been as chaste as a nun's compared with your much-publicised rake's progress. If anyone needs a warning, it's Juliet, not me. Perhaps I should have a word with her.'

CHAPTER SIX

IT WAS his turn to frown. 'You exaggerate. Journalists exaggerate. If they write for the popular Press they give people labels. Housewife…feminist…playboy. In my twenties, I had several good-looking girlfriends, hence the playboy label. It hasn't applied for a long time. Why does it bother you?'

'You're mistaken. Your personal life is nothing to do with me. I wouldn't have brought it up if you hadn't started lecturing me.' She began to swim back to the beach.

It was, as she knew, a futile attempt to end the conversation if he intended to continue it. He could easily outswim her. She might as well attempt to elude a playful sea otter.

Expecting him to shoot past and reach the shallows before her, she was surprised and relieved when he didn't. When she stood up and looked around, he was nowhere to be seen. Then she saw him hoisting himself on to a distant rock looking, for an instant, like an Old Master drawing of the anatomy of a powerfully built man, every muscle in play under the burnished brown skin which a few moments earlier she could have reached out and touched.

She had wanted to touch it, she realised. All through that verbal fencing match, deep down inside her different, less defensive impulses had been urging her to stop talking, to stretch out her hands towards those broad sun-tanned shoulders, to feel his sleek sea-cooled skin under her palms.

As she waded ashore, not for the first time she wondered what it would be like to go through life saying what you really meant, doing what you really wanted to do instead of what convention or cowardice dictated.

She was in her shower room, using a lip-liner, half an hour before the evening critique, when someone tapped on her door.

It was Juliet. 'Sorry to disturb you but I've lost a button and forgotten to bring a needle and thread. I'm sure you've brought everything. Could I borrow the necessary?'

'Of course. Come in. What colour thread do you need?'

'White, please.'

While Kate opened the drawer where she kept her repair kit, Juliet crossed the room to look at the pictures of women in national dress.

'I enjoyed today,' she remarked, without glancing round. 'The monastery was divine and even the beach taverna, though very basic and serving mostly junk food, had a certain rustic charm. Is there anywhere first class to eat in this town, do you know?'

'That's something I'd have to look up,' said Kate. 'With the hotel food as good as it is, most people won't want to spend extra on eating out at night.'

'Xan and I might,' said Juliet. 'He's entitled to some evenings off. He's being incredibly patient with all the group's worst daubers. But he must find it enormously trying to have to spend time with them when he could be painting professionally.'

Kate found herself irritated by the other woman's habit of speaking in superlatives. Or was it Juliet's reference to Xan and herself as if they were set apart from the rest of the party which had a scratchy effect on her normally quiescent nerves?

'He did know what it would be like,' she pointed out. 'He went on Miss Walcott's group painting trips when he was a small boy. It was she who encouraged him to become an artist. He owes her a great deal.'

'I doubt if it would have made the slightest difference if she had actively discouraged him,' said Juliet. 'He would have gone his own way. He's a very powerful person-ality…as the best artists are.'

'Not always. One of my favourite painters is Edward Seago. In his lifetime his gifts were never acknowledged by the art world in London, partly because he was so popular with the public. At his exhibitions, people used to stand in line to buy everything in sight. But he wasn't a self-confident man. He was deeply insecure.'

'I know about Seago,' said Juliet. 'My father used to col-lect him. I've been mixing with artists all my life.'

Kate handed over the zip-bag containing all the repair aids she had thought might be needed. It was on the tip of her tongue to express surprise that, in that case, it was strange Juliet hadn't known Xan was unmarried. Instead, she said, 'How nice for you. Help yourself.'

Juliet sat down on the unused twin bed and turned the bag upside down to shake everything on to the white counterpane. 'You do believe in preparing for all eventualities,' she said, as a trouser clip fell out. 'I suppose you have to. Were you ever a nurse?'

Kate shook her head. 'Why d'you ask?'

'You look frightfully capable…as if you'd know what to do if one of the old dears collapsed or choked or whatever. I thought you might have been a nurse or a policewoman before you took on this job.'

'No, I worked in the property business in London.'

'Really?' Juliet raised her eyebrows. But she didn't ask who Kate had worked for or why she wasn't there now.

After selecting what she needed, she put the rest back in

the bag. As she rose from the bed, she noticed the dress Kate was wearing.

'Where did you find that?' Before Kate could answer, she suggested two nationwide chains selling inexpensive fashions to budget shoppers.

'It's French,' Kate said briefly. Perhaps she was being hypersensitive, but it seemed to her that everything Juliet said was tinged with condescension. 'I bought it from a supermarket on a trip we did in July.'

She didn't add that she had remade the hem, changed the buttons and hunted out a better belt from the days when she could afford expensive accessories.

Juliet was still in her bathrobe, a mannishly cut white silk affair with navy piping and her monogram on the pocket. Catching sight of the clock on the night table, she said, 'Lordy! Is that the time? I'm going to be late. I haven't begun my face yet.'

After she had gone, Kate looked at herself in the mirror and wondered why looking 'capable' should sound tantamount to 'dull'. Was that how she looked?

How else do you want to look?

Ravishing…stunning…a total knockout.

Really? What's brought this on? You've never wanted to be a knockout before.

I didn't know Xan before.

Ah, so it's Xan who's causing all these foolish new feelings. If you don't take care, you'll find yourself falling for him. You'd better watch your step, Kate. Men like Xan spell nothing but trouble for women like you. Juliet can handle him. He won't break Juliet's heart.

Xan came down to dinner in a shirt of deep violet linen and pale dove-grey cotton trousers. Kate took a snap of him talking to Joyce and Heather, both wearing floral silk frocks with beads and earrings carefully chosen to pick up a colour in their dresses.

'Are you keen on photography, Kate?' Oliver asked, as she closed the shutter after quickly taking a second shot, a close-up of Xan's dark head inclined towards the pepper-and-salt perms of the two women.

'Not seriously. I don't develop and print my own films or anything like that. But after my first Palette trip, I had the idea of making a record of who was there and where we went. My first attempt was rather amateurish, but the next one was better and the third one I had colour-copied and everyone in that group wanted one as a memento. Would you like to subscribe to my souvenir brochure of our Cretan adventure?' she asked, smiling to show she was only half-serious.

'By all means. It's a good idea.' His expression clouded momentarily. Instinct told her he was remembering photographs taken of his wife on previous trips.

Juliet was the last to appear, her drawings in a black portfolio under her arm. Tonight she was wearing black silk palazzo pants and a white silk turtle-necked jersey top with a bold silver necklace, probably Turkish, and a pair of large silver hoops swinging from her ears.

'Settle down, please, everyone.' With his height and his distinctive voice, Xan had no problem commanding attention. 'Tonight I'm going to change the way we handle the critique. I noticed last night that not everyone had a good view of the painting under discussion. So tonight I've brought down my easel and I'll ask you to come up in turn and explain what you were trying to achieve and the problems you had. Then I'll say my piece and others can chip in if they want to. Who'll volunteer to be first?'

'I will, if you like,' said Juliet, unfastening her portfolio and flicking through its contents. 'I did several sketches this morning as notes for a proper painting when I get home. While I was doing this one, I was asked if I would sell it by one of the tourists who was wandering about.'

The easel being ready, with a somewhat theatrical flourish she turned the selected sheet of paper face forward and set it in position.

'Like Xan in the painting he showed us last night, I wanted to catch the feeling of somnolent heat.'

In the pause while it was being studied, Kate took another photograph. When the flash made Loretta jump, she said, 'Sorry if that startled you. It made a good shot for our records.'

'How much did the tourist offer you?' Kelly's mother asked Juliet.

'The equivalent of fifty pounds.'

'You missed your chance, love,' one of the men said jovially. 'You could have taken us out for a night on the town.'

Juliet disdained to answer. 'Did I pull it off, Xan, d'you think?'

'I would say so, yes—very successfully. Wouldn't you?' His glance round the group evoked a buzz of agreement. 'One of the most common faults when people start using water-colour is not allowing for the fact that the paint always dries much lighter than it looks when it's wet. Here Juliet's laid on a good strong wash of apricot yellow…'

Kate listened to but didn't take in the rest of his comments. Her mind was focused not on the painting but on the lean brown hand moving from the shapes of the lemons, half hidden by foliage, to the curves of a large clay *pithos*, a traditional container for oil or grain, which Juliet had painted in the lower left corner.

Vaguely aware that Xan was talking about the beauty of its shape and its relevance to the composition, Kate was admiring the articulation of his fingers, the well-scrubbed nails and the strong wrist leading the eye to a sinewy forearm.

When Juliet's painting was replaced by Heather's, Kate forced herself to concentrate on the picture rather than the tutor. He did not, she noticed, dismiss the work of the less talented members with a few cursory comments. They got as good value for their money as the more promising members.

But this was only their third evening here. The course had scarcely begun. By the end of the week would his role have started to pall? Would signs of impatience and boredom begin to show?

The more she was drawn to him, the more Kate was repelled and baffled by his inexplicable cruelty in turning his back on his grandmother. She could think of no reason to justify his living in luxury in London while, not far away, the woman who had brought him up and encouraged his artistic gifts made a precarious living and desperately needed his love and support in her old age.

Juliet, when the work of the members she dismissed as 'daubers' was placed on the easel, visibly switched off, Kate noticed. She even rolled her eyes and gave an audible sigh when it was Loretta's turn to show her painting and Kate had to admit it was strongly reminiscent of a 1930s embroidery transfer.

But when Oliver put up his oil painting and Xan said, 'Notice how much reflected warmth and colour Oliver has worked into the shade cast by the lemon tree,' Juliet's interest revived and she joined in the discussion.

Ten minutes before the time of their evening meal, Xan said, 'Have we seen everyone's? No, we haven't seen your angel, Kate. I hope you brought it down.' To the others, he added, 'I've prevailed on Kate to join in our working sessions when her other duties permit. Did all of you notice the angel at the top of some stairs at the side of the church?'

Reluctantly, she stepped forward. 'This drawing owes more to Xan's preliminary outlines and his finishing touches than to my non-existent skill,' she said.

'You chose an ambitious subject for your first attempt…and didn't make a bad stab at it. Speaking of suitable subjects, several of you were over-ambitious. Until you have a good deal of technical facility, it's best to stick to very simple subjects. Looking round the monastery, I found something I thought very paintable but which the rest of you missed, or perhaps didn't find appealing.'

He opened his own portfolio and placed in front of the angel a small watercolour. Near the edge of the paper he had written, '*A Monk's Washing, Agia Triada*' and the date and his name.

From a line strung between a hedge and a pillar hung a pair of striped socks, some long johns and an old-fashioned vest. Above, casting its silhouette across the white undergarments, was a long spray of crimson bougainvillaea. Below lay sunlit flagstones, here and there barred with deep shadows from the hedge.

What struck Kate about the painting—apart from its technical skill which made even Juliet's and Oliver's work look less good than it had a short time earlier—was the humour and humanity of the picture.

She found it impossible to reconcile his ability to paint this touching insight into the lives of the monks with his indifference to his grandmother's health. Not once had he asked for news from the nursing home.

On the fourth day Kate woke up to find the sky overcast and the sea grey. Beyond the shelter of the harbour wall, the surface was choppy.

At breakfast Xan announced a change of plan. Because rain was forecast, instead of going into the country to paint in a small village, they would spend the morning on the pool deck where he would demonstrate sky-painting.

'How not to make clouds look like floating dumplings,' he added, with a smile round the table.

Most of the group took the change in the weather philosophically, but two people looked put out and complained that they hadn't been warned the climate was unreliable. As only the night before they had been griping about the heat, Kate responded with brisk cheerfulness.

'I expect the sun will reappear before long. Our guidelines did suggest you should bring a light waterproof.'

By next morning the clouds had passed on and the group split up. Eight people, including Kelly and her mother, were eager to see the famous Gorge of Samaria on the southern side of the island. But others thought it sounded too touristy for their liking and opted for a shorter excursion along the coast west of Chaniá.

As the Samaria contingent was going in the bus with Manolis, Kate had arranged a one-day car rental. The car would take only five people in comfort but, if Xan drove, she and another person—preferably Oliver—could travel by bus.

Her reasons for asking him to accompany her were that Juliet, being tall, would need the legroom given by the front passenger seat, and Oliver wouldn't be fazed if the bus turned out to be crowded and rather uncomfortable.

Having telephoned him in his room to check that he was agreeable, she announced these arrangements at breakfast, which had been put forward to seven because the other party had a long drive to the starting point of the gorge walk.

As she explained what was happening, she wondered if Xan would disapprove of her choosing Oliver as her com-

panion. She still felt that his warning about the possibility
of the older man finding her attractive was without foundation. Had Juliet been a less flamboyant personality, Oliver
might have taken to her. But she wasn't his type, and neither
were Heather or Joyce. Although both those two, Kate suspected, would have liked to be singled out for special attention from him.

'Where did you find that useful pack?' she asked him, on
the way to the bus station.

Oliver was striding along with a rucksack incorporating
a folding stool strapped to his shoulders.

'I mail-ordered it from the Royal Society for the
Protection of Birds.'

'Are you a bird-watcher?'

'I was before I took up painting.'

He took her lightly by the arm before they crossed a main
road, but released his hold as soon as they reached the opposite pavement. She felt sure it was only an automatic
courtesy. He would have done the same had he been walking with Loretta or Kelly's mother.

The bus station was crowded with people including an
elderly man in the traditional Cretan dress of baggy trousers,
long boots and a black headcloth fringed with bobbles. He
was sitting on a bench, fingering a string of fat orange worry
beads.

'Why the bobbles, I wonder?' said Kate.

Oliver gave her one of his rare and unexpectedly boyish
grins. 'Perhaps they're the Cretan equivalent of the corks
round the brim of an Australian drover's hat.'

It was he who bought the tickets and found out which
bus was theirs. Kate stood back and let him take charge.
She was enjoying the feeling of not being at anyone's beck
and call for a while. As groups went, so far this one had
given her no serious problems. Yet somehow she was find-

ing the trip more of a strain than the expeditions to France. Was that because of Xan's presence?

Their bus turned out not to be crowded. As they waited for it to depart, Oliver said, 'I shouldn't be surprised if the other lot come back exhausted. They'll be walking downhill but, from what I hear, it's quite strenuous.'

'I gave Kelly's mother some plasters to put in her bag in case anyone had a blister,' said Kate. 'Maybe I should have gone with them. But I'm not awfully keen on visiting famous sights with crowds of other people. I hope they can cope on their own if anything worse than a blister happens.'

'I don't suppose it will,' said Oliver. 'Although personally I wouldn't do even an easy mountain walk in sandals or ordinary trainers. Boots with some ankle support are the safest footwear.'

After a pause, he added, 'I might come back to Crete in the spring for a walking holiday. Last night Kyria Drakakis was telling me about the so-called dew men. I'd like to see them.'

'Who are they?' asked Kate, as the bus started off.

'They're a procession of armed men sometimes seen in late May, just before sunrise, at the ruins of a fourteenth-century castle called Frangokástello. The local people think they're the unredeemed souls of the dead. Because they always appear in the damp early morning air, they're called Drosoulítes, meaning men of the dew.'

'Do you believe in the occult, Oliver?' she asked, in surprise.

He seemed too rational to believe in anything supernatural. But sometimes, after losing someone they loved, even normally down-to-earth people clutched at evidence of life after death.

'No, I don't,' he said firmly. 'And the dew men aren't ghosts. They've been investigated by scientists whose conclusion was that they're a mirage from North Africa. The coast of Libya is only a couple of hundred miles south of Crete, you know.'

'How fascinating. Are the dew men seen every year?'

'Not unless the conditions are right. The sea has to be calm, the humidity at a certain level. Even then the procession is only visible for ten minutes.'

The journey passed swiftly and pleasantly. Behind his initial reserve, Oliver had a keen sense of humour and, if pressed, a fund of interesting experiences. While in the Army he had spent several years in Belize in Central America, a part of the world she had always wanted to visit.

At the village where they were meeting the others, he led the way off the bus and, having stepped down, offered his hand to her.

'Thank you.' She smiled at him, thinking how lovely it would have been to grow up under the wing of a man like this.

The others were waiting in a café only a few yards from where the bus stopped. As she and Oliver crossed the street to join them, the expression on Xan's face reminded Kate of his warning in the sea the day before yesterday.

Obviously he had observed Oliver handing her down. But surely he didn't attach any significance to *that*, Kate thought vexedly. He himself had offered his hand to some of the older women when they were alighting from the coach at the monastery. That she was too young to need helping off buses was immaterial. Oliver would automatically offer his hand to any female.

'How was the bus trip?' asked Juliet, as the circle round the table was enlarged to include two more chairs for the newcomers.

'We enjoyed it, didn't we, Kate?' said Oliver, smiling at

her. 'There were a lot of sketchable types at the bus station.' He showed them his drawing, done before the bus moved off, of the old man in Cretan dress.

The day went well. After painting in the village, the others joined Kate at the nearby beach where she and the woman who ran the beach bar had been managing to chat in a mixture of broken English, rudimentary Greek and a lot of sign language.

They were the only people there and the woman was pleased to have seven customers so late in the season. She kept an eye on their belongings while they swam. Then she fed them with an unexpectedly delicious moussaka cooked in a makeshift kitchen at the back of the bar, next door to the lavatories.

'Loretta would *not* approve,' said Oliver.

'She may have the last laugh when we all go down with Cretan tummy,' said Xan.

'Let's ask for a bottle of *tsikoudía*,' Juliet suggested. 'That should knock out most known germs.'

It was a convivial meal, the other three who were with them being more entertaining companions than the Samaria contingent.

When it was time to go home, Xan said, 'If you wouldn't mind driving back, Oliver, I'd like to see the views you saw from the bus.'

'I'll come with you,' said Juliet.

In the event it was Kate who drove because, after the other two had set off to catch the bus, she realised that Oliver wouldn't be covered by the insurance.

Under the influence of sun, sea air and perhaps the lingering effects of a vinous lunch, the three in the back all dozed off on the way home. Neither Oliver nor Kate felt sleepy but they didn't talk as they had on the outward journey. Oliver seemed preoccupied, perhaps with thoughts of his wife and the lonely interval before dinner when, on other trips, they would have discussed the day's activities or perhaps made love.

Although she thought Xan's warning was absurd, she had to admit that Oliver didn't give the impression of being a man whose virility was in decline. It must be very painful for someone long accustomed to a loving partnership to have celibacy forced on them, she thought sympathetically.

It was hard enough to live without love if you had never been married or had any long-term relationships. Her only and one serious love-affair had not left an aching gap in her life. The only pain had come from her disillusionment, leaving her wondering if her definition of love was unrealistic.

There were some tired and cooked-lobster faces round the table at dinner that night. And some sore feet beneath it. For in spite of Kate's advice, not everyone had taken adequate precautions against sunburn, dehydration and blisters.

Nor, it turned out, had they fulfilled Xan's expectations of them. Because several people were late coming down, he put back the usual pre-dinner critique until afterwards.

When the showing of their day's work—shorter than usual—was over, to Kate's secret surprise and the visible discomposure of some of the group, he revealed himself to be a more exacting mentor than he had seemed so far.

'I'm aware that this visit to Crete is described as a painting *holiday*,' he began briskly. 'But may I remind you that you're lucky to be here? Innumerable people would like to be in your place. There are carers, pensioners and invalids for whom the chance to come here and develop a latent talent must remain wishful thinking.'

He paused to look round the room. 'All human beings with the luck to have health and strength, time and money, are under an obligation to make the most of those assets. If you've come here to draw and paint, then every day you should have a worthwhile output…make some small but significant advance in your knowledge and skill.

'I have now seen enough of your work to know that this group includes some promising artists. What is conspicuously lacking is discipline and application. By application I mean effort and concentration. Everyone who went to the Gorge, excluding the non-painters, should have come back with at least a dozen sketches. They didn't. Even the people with me didn't work as hard as they should. Up to now I've let you off lightly and tomorrow is a free day. But after that I shall be less patient. Goodnight.'

As he strode from the room, Kelly gave Kate a nudge. 'I wonder what's got into him? He's ever so sexy when he's annoyed, isn't he?'

'Is he? I wouldn't know,' Kate said dismissively.

But inwardly she too was wondering what had prompted Xan's strictures and how the group would react to being told they were lazy in that astringent tone.

On all Palette trips lasting two weeks, the fifth day was always a day off for the tutor and courier. By this time, in foreign locations, Miss Walcott considered the group had had time to get their bearings and could look after themselves while she disappeared to work on paintings to exhibit.

In recent years her output of these had diminished. It was no longer enough to merit a one-woman show at the well-known provincial gallery where she had been showing her work for many years past. But she still produced enough work to show in mixed exhibitions.

Kate's days off were usually spent sightseeing. In Chaniá, she had planned to spend the first free day lazing on the beach and perhaps doing some shopping.

She was still in bed, lazily stretching, when her telephone rang.

'I'm re-renting the car and going into the country today, taking a picnic lunch. Would you like to come with me?' asked Xan.

Without pause for thought, she said, 'Yes, I'd love to.'

'Good. The car's being delivered at eight. We'll have breakfast in a café on the way out of town. I'll take care of the provisions. You need only bring your camera.' He rang off.

Kate jumped out of bed, performing a pirouette on her way to the window. Leaning over the wide sill, enjoying the lovely view of calm blue sea and cloudless morning sky, she asked herself why she had felt that burst of elation. Even harder to answer was why Xan should seek her company when he could have spent the day alone, free of them all. Or with Juliet.

Then Kate remembered that, last night at dinner, Juliet had said she was going to enjoy a long lie-in. She was by nature an owl, at her best in the evening, sluggish in the morning.

Thinking about last night, Kate decided not to mention his homily. She knew it had upset some of the group. But, as she had pointed out in response to their aggrieved comments, artists of Xan's stature seldom agreed to accompany parties of amateurs. When they did, the cost was always far higher than the price of the present trip.

By eight-fifteen they were sitting under the vine outside a small bar, breakfasting on cheese, olives and rusks dipped in olive oil.

Across the road two middle-aged women in aprons were engaged in animated discussion. Xan whipped out a sketch-pad and started to draw them, a smile hovering round his firm mouth as he captured on paper their short sturdy legs, brawny arms and graphic gestures.

Intent on his drawing, he was not distracted when Kate rose from the table and moved away to take first a photograph of him and then one of his subjects.

When he had finished, she told him what she had done and that she would like to take a close-up of the sketch.

'By all means,' he said, handing it over.

'If they come out well, the three shots will make an interesting illustration for a future brochure,' she explained, when she had taken the third one.

'Don't you think you should ask if I mind being used as an advertisement?'

His acerbic tone made her flush. 'I'm sorry. That didn't occur to me. Would you mind?'

His a reply was a succinct, 'Yes.' After a pause, he added, 'I'm here as a favour to you. I'd prefer my association with Palette to be confined to this one trip.'

'I'm sorry,' she said again. 'In that case I'll keep the snaps for my private record of the trip.'

She would have liked to ask what had induced him to do her a favour, but she felt this was perilous ground she might be wise to avoid, at least for the present. She confined herself to asking a safe question.

'Where are we going? Anywhere special?'

'Towards Léfka Óri…the White Mountains. I've been reading a book about Crete called *Rare Adventures and Painful Peregrinations*, published in 1632. The author describes the Plain of Chaniá, between the mountains and the sea, as the diamond spark and the honey-pot of the island. He lists all the crops that were growing three centuries ago and calls the area a battle-ground between Bacchus, the god of wine, and Ceres, the goddess of agriculture.'

'Could I borrow the book when you've finished it?'

'By all means.' He took his eyes off the road for a moment to smile at her, his earlier displeasure forgotten.

She resolved not to reactivate it.

CHAPTER SEVEN

DURING the morning they made frequent stops for Xan to do rapid sketches of a wayward shrine, a tethered donkey patiently waiting for the return of its owner, a small barrel-vaulted church in the middle of nowhere and a group of old men playing *tafli,* a form of backgammon, outside a village bar.

The land they passed through was still as fertile and carefully tended as it had been for centuries. But by noon they were in the foothills leading up to the heights of Léfka Óri. Here there were only olive groves and a large herd of browsing sheep watched over by a handsome youth with his crook resting on his shoulders and his wrists draped over the ends.

A mile or so further on, Xan said, 'Time to find a patch of shade and have some lunch, don't you think?'

A suitable spot presented itself a few hundred yards along the bumpy dirt road they were following.

'I borrowed this cooler from Kyria Drakakis,' said Xan, unloading it. He gave Kate a large loaf of crusty bread to carry to the ancient carob tree whose branches would protect them from the scorching midday sun.

In the cooler were some cheese and vegetable pies, a ready-made tomato and onion salad in a plastic bowl, pears and small pots of yogurt for dessert, a bottle of unresinated Cretan white wine and two bottles of water.

While they were eating the main course, spearing the pieces of tomato and onion with a couple of forks Xan had borrowed, he said, 'I hope you haven't been bored, sitting about while I sketch. What have you been listening to?'

In the expectation that he would want to draw, she had brought her headset and a couple of tapes.

'Khachaturian's *Spartacus*,' she said. 'A few years ago the Adagio was used as the theme music for a TV series, *The Onedin Line*. I'm afraid my taste in music is not very highbrow. As to being bored...not a bit. It's nice to have a day doing nothing but looking and listening. But I don't think I'd want as much time on my hands as a shepherd,' she added reflectively. 'I wonder what he thinks about all day?'

'Perhaps he composes *mantinádes*,' said Xan.

'What are they?'

'Two-line rhyming couplets. The name comes from the Venetian word for the serenades which lovers used to sing to their girls in the small hours of the morning. Kyria Draka-kis tells me that not long ago virtually everyone in Crete could make up *mantinádes*. Meeting a friend in the street, they'd do it as casually as the British make comments about the weather.'

'It makes one realise how little most of us know about other people's cultures,' said Kate.

Or about other people, period, was her unspoken after-thought.

This led her, after a pause, to say, 'You once mentioned that being an artist was only one of the things you'd wanted to be. What were the others?'

'They were even more impractical. A master at school was a rock-climbing enthusiast. He taught me and one or two others. But you can't make a living as a climber,' Xan said wryly.

He cut through the loaf until a thick slice was attached

by a thin hinge of crust and offered it to her. When she shook her head, he tore it off himself.

'Nerina would never leave me on my own at the cottage while she was away,' he went on. 'The teenage drug problem was starting and she was afraid I'd get hooked. Not very likely, as I didn't smoke or spend any time at discos with the school's ravers. The year I was fourteen she took a party to Portofino in Italy. One of the non-painting husbands was a yachtsman. He rented a boat and taught me to crew for him. For about six months after that I had dreams of sailing round the world. What did you want to do when you were fourteen?'

'My young-teen ambitions were all wildly unrealistic. I daydreamed of being an opera singer, an actress, a top model. But I couldn't sing, I had no aptitude for acting and I was never going to be tall enough for the catwalk.'

'You may not be tall enough but all your other proportions are right, now that models have breasts,' said Xan, appraising her. 'Although I gather theirs are mainly implants, not the real thing. It's interesting that you let your imagination run away with you. You weren't always as practical and sensible as you are now?'

Was that his impression of her? Were 'practical' and 'sensible' euphemisms for 'down-to-earth' and 'dull'?

To deflect the conversation from herself, Kate asked, 'How did you manage to live after you left school?'

Although she had studied Miss Walcott's albums of clippings about him, there was never any reference to his origins or his early life. Perhaps, when journalists enquired, he was adept at tossing them a red herring.

'I won a prize,' he said. 'The age limits were eighteen to twenty-five, but it was no problem to backdate my birth certificate by two years. Now the prize attracts a lot of publicity, but it didn't then, in its first year. In fact the backers were annoyed because it go so little coverage. At the time the Press regarded art as a minority interest. They take it more seriously now there are several million enthusiastic "Saturday painters".'

'So many that Palette ought to be booked out within weeks of the brochures being mailed,' Kate said, frowning. 'But apart from being hit by the recession, we also have other problems. Art holidays are proliferating. Our advertisements are being swamped by ads for painting holidays here, there and everywhere…often with poor facilities and inadequate tuition.'

'For today, forget Palette's problems,' he told her, with a hint of impatience. 'I want to hear more about you. When did the daydreams stop and practicality set in?'

'The daydreams were only ever a secret indulgence. I always knew I was destined to join the vast army of girls working in offices. That might sound dull to you, but I felt there was a challenge in starting at an ordinary workstation and seeing where those skills might lead. It was chance rather than design that led me to an estate agent's office. Until the bottom fell out of the property market, I was doing rather well…at least in a material sense. I'm actually happier now. This job is much more satisfying. The people I meet are nicer. Before, they were mostly upwardly mobile status-seekers.'

Xan refilled their glasses. 'That was a masterpiece of evasion, Kate,' he said drily. 'It told me almost nothing about you. I recognise the trick because I use it myself when I'm being interviewed. Providing one talks a lot, only the shrewdest inquisitors realise they're being fed superficialities.'

'What do you want? A complete CV?' she asked lightly.

'Yes. Start at the beginning. Where were you born? Where do your parents live?'

'I can't answer either of those questions. I don't know. I was abandoned at six weeks and brought up in an orphanage.'

She wondered how he would react. Not many people were sufficiently interested to find out but, of those who did, the majority said they were sorry and looked embarrassed.

Xan said, 'Do you find it's perceived as some kind of disability? Is that why you avoid mentioning it?'

'I don't avoid it. As soon as you asked me, I told you.'

'Tell me more. Where were you found?'

Later, when he had winkled most of her life history out of her, he said, 'Whoever your parents were, they gave you some major assets. Those remarkable eyes for a start. Which reminds me, I wanted to look at them through a magnifier.'

He sprang up and went to his pack. Having found his magnifying lens, he came back to where she was sitting and went down on one knee beside her, taking her by the chin and tilting her face up. His manner was as impersonal as that of optometrist with a patient.

'Focus on the top of my right ear,' he instructed.

She did as she was told, trying not to blink too often. He was still holding her chin between his finger and thumb and she found herself longing for him to release it and slide his hand down her throat. She forced herself to concentrate on the upper rim of his ear and the thick dark hair growing above and behind it.

'Eyes are an interesting study. I'd like to make some colour notes, but I don't want to give you a crick in the neck. You'd better lie down.' He moved away to unfasten a different compartment of his pack. 'I've got my bathing towel in here. I'll spread it on the ground. You can do without ants or other small bugs in your hair.'

As she lay back, Kate wondered what anyone watching would make of this performance. She had read that although this wild terrain might appear to be deserted, often there were hidden observers—shepherds minding flocks of goats, old women gathering herbs.

Xan set out his paintbox and water pot before stretching himself at full length on the ground beside her, propped on one elbow, the other free to examine her eye through the lens and to paint what he saw.

'Even eyes which aren't noticeably interesting become so in close-up,' he said.

She looked at the tracery of olive branches above her, their leaves stirring slightly in a light current of air. When Xan leaned closer to look at her eyes again, she wondered what he would do if she slipped her arms round his neck and said, 'Kiss me.'

Considering his reputation, this doesn't say much for my kissability, she thought glumly. I might as well be a log with an interesting patch of lichen on it.

'All done.' He rinsed his brush and threw away the painting water.

'May I see?' she asked, sitting up.

He handed over his sketch pad. Beside a small sketch of her eye, showing the shape of her eyelids and the line of her eyebrow, he had painted a diagram of the iris.

'Last month,' he said, 'I was approached by a London publisher with a lot of painting books on his list. He wants a small book of water-colour sketches to bring out at a price which will make it an attractive Christmas present. I've been casting about for ideas and you've given me my theme.'

'I have? How?'

'I'm going to do a page of eyes, a page of hands, ears, noses, feet and so on. Some of the Cretan country people have hands as gnarled as old roots. A baby's hand is like a starfish. Your hands and the way you use them remind me of a ballerina.'

As he said this, he took the one which was lying in her lap and carried it to his lips. 'Thank you for the idea,' he said, before kissing her knuckles.

This gesture, following his apparent indifference to their physical proximity a few moments earlier, took Kate by surprise.

He then surprised her even more by saying, 'I left out lips,' and leaning closer to kiss her.

Compared with his previous kiss, this was even lighter and more fleeting than the brush of his lips on her fingers. He followed it with other gentle kisses round the edges of her mouth, each one a little firmer until suddenly both her lips were pressed firmly under his and she was in his arms, pinioned between his hard chest and sun-baked earth.

Was it one endless kiss, or many kisses merging with each other? Kate lost all sense of time. She had only two sensations: at first the exquisite pleasure of what his mouth was doing to hers and then, steadily growing more urgent, the longing for a more complete syntheses with the powerful body holding her a willing captive.

It was ended by Xan, not by her. She had her arms round his neck, one hand in his thick dark hair, and his hand was unbuttoning her shirt when he stopped short and rolled away.

She opened her eyes and saw him sit up, turning from her so that she could only see his bowed shoulders and bent head. Instinctively she knew he was wrestling with the same fiery need which had been sweeping through her and that fighting it was painful for him.

She waited, her shirt half open, her breasts aching for his caresses, her body melting and quivering with unsatisfied desire. But her mind knew that he was right. This was not the time or the place for that lovely taking and giving which surely must be the outcome of this unfinished embrace.

She was sitting up, fastening her shirt, when Xan straightened and said, 'Time to move on, I think.'

He sprang to his feet and held out a hand to pull her up. Then he busied himself with packing their picnic things.

As they made their way back to the car, Kate wondered if he knew how complete her surrender had been. Perhaps not.

Or it might be that he did know and had every intention of carrying on from where they had left off as soon as a more appropriate setting offered itself.

'I'm hoping we can return to Chaniá without backtracking,' he said when, back at the car, he opened a map of the region borrowed from Kyria Drakakis. 'Yes, there's a road which winds round through several small villages. If one of them has a likely-looking bar, we'll stop for refreshments. On a day as hot as this, the more cold liquid we can pour down our throats the better. Would you like to take over the driving?'

'Not unless you've had enough of it,' said Kate. 'You're a better driver on these rough, twisty roads than I should be.'

'That statement would be vigorously repudiated by the politically correct lobby,' he said, switching on the engine.

'Oh, sucks to them,' she said cheerfully. 'I think "anything you can do, I can do better", or even equally well, is a silly attitude. I'm not an experienced rough-country driver. I assume you must be or you wouldn't run a Range Rover. I know some people have them more as status symbols than for practical reasons, but I wouldn't include you in that group.'

'Thank you, ma'am…no, I'm not. I have it because I often paint in places where I need a four-wheel drive. Judging by your general efficiency I should think you're an excellent driver. I wonder how long these hire cars stand up to being hammered over country roads by tourists who are rotten drivers?'

The first small village they came to seemed not to have a bar. But a few kilometres further on there was a larger village where the bar had a vine-shaped *plateía* outside it. At present all the tables and chairs were occupied because a party was in progress.

As Xan slowed the car to see what was going on, Kate caught sight of a bridal couple. 'It's a wedding party.'

As she spoke, a young man stepped into the roadway, grinning at them.

'Are you lost?' he asked, in English.

Kate smiled and shook her head, but Xan put on the hand brake and swung himself out of the car. Speaking across the roof of it, he said something in Greek.

The young Cretan responded in Greek. While they were talking, an older man came to the fence surrounding the *plateía* and shouted something.

Reverting to English, the young man said, 'My uncle says as you speak Greek, you are welcome to join us.' Taking their acceptance for granted, he opened the passenger door for Kate to climb out.

Kyria Drakakis had told them that away from the coastal areas there was still a warm welcome for *ksénos,* the term used to mean stranger, traveller or guest, as distinct from *tourísta* with its somewhat unflattering connotations.

The truth of her statement was demonstrated by the way they were drawn into the happy throng and pressed to eat, drink and share the general enjoyment.

Yorgo, as the young man was called, was not the only one there who spoke good English. There was also Yannis, who had gone to America to make his fortune and now, in his sixties, was back to his native village. But he hadn't resumed the Cretan dress worn by most of the older men present: the baggy *vraches* tucked into long black boots, the black cummerbund and the piratical black *mandilli* wrapped round the forehead.

'She asks if you are also newly-weds?' Yargo translated, when an old lady in black came to peer at the foreigners, one of her eyes showing the opacity of a cataract.

Xan bent to speak to her in Greek and whatever he said made her give a cackle of laughter. But Kate had no chance to ask him before she was taken under the wing of the bride's proud mother.

The *nyphítsa* herself was a sturdy, cheery-faced girl with eyebrows that joined in the middle and several moles on her face. But her burly bridegroom in his cheap city suit looked delighted with his choice.

The only beauty present was one of the bridesmaids who, presently, sang a traditional wedding song which Yorgo translated for Kate in a loud whisper.

I beg you, Fate,
Send me a rich husband.
Let him have flocks and shepherds and cheesemakers,
A garden full of bees, with beekeepers,
Twenty yoke of oxen, grain both old and new.
But cotton plants, my Fate—not those.
I want to have soft hands.

Her performance was received with applause and approving comments, punctuated by more of the shots they had heard earlier while they were driving towards the village.

Then it was time for more feasting which Kate gathered had begun soon after the wedding and would continue for the rest of the day. Most of the men had a handmade knife, the handle shaped like a goat's leg. With these they cut slices from the lamb cooked with lemon, oregano and thyme.

Watching Xan standing with a group of men while she did her best to converse with some of the women, Kate thought how well the traditional costume would become his tall, long-legged figure.

If Fate had ordained that his life should be spent in a village in Crete, he would be a *pallikári,* the name given to a brave man. He might even be a *kapetánios* or captain, the title of a man of power and, fifty years ago, of the guerrilla leaders who had held out against the last occupation of the island.

As she watched him, he looked towards her and, excusing himself to his companions, came over to where she was standing.

'No wine for you, Kate?' he asked, looking at the glass of some sugary cordial she was holding.

'I thought it would be easier for me to stay on the wagon than for you,' she explained. 'It would probably be seen as very unmacho for you to decline the hard stuff, but it's all right for me...and from here on the road should improve.'

'That's very thoughtful of you. Don't worry. I shan't get smashed. I'm sticking to wine and resisting the lethal doses of *tsíkoudia* all these old boys are knocking back. That stuff's real firewater. There'll be some sore heads tomorrow.'

Presently one of the men sang a song. At the end, Yannis stepped forward and made a brief announcement. He then turned to Xan and Kate. 'I have told them I am going to sing it again...for you two. This song is called *"Kalopéra-si"*, meaning ''The Good Life''.' He signalled to the musicians that he was ready to begin.

Little by little the Lord sends the rain,
Then comes the quiet snow,

Cold in the mountains,
Snow on the hills.
But the man who has a well-roofed house,
Fruit in his storerooms,
Oil in his jars,
Wine in his barrels,
Wood in his yard,
A girl to kiss as he sits by the fire,
He doesn't care what the north wind brings,
Rain or snow.

Kate thought it a beautiful song. She wondered what Xan was thinking as he joined in the applause.

Then the musicians struck up for dancing. The man with the pear-shaped *lýra* propped on his thigh, had his bow strung with hawk's bells to accentuate the rhythm.

'This village has fine musicians. They make their own instruments and keep them on pegs in the bar to make music together,' explained Yorgo.

One old man was playing an *áskavlos,* a double flute with a bag made from an animal's skin. It sounded like bagpipes.

Kate would have preferred only to watch the dancing but found herself forced to participate in some of the simpler measures. A glass or two of wine would have helped her to feel less self-conscious, but she doubted if wine had much to do with Xan's relaxed performance.

He was revealing himself as one of those fortunate people who were at ease in any company. That he spoke more Greek than she did was a help, but it wasn't only his superior vocabulary that made him at home among these simple, hospitable country people. It was something in the man himself, something she had failed to register at the beginning of their association. Every day, one more of her preconceptions about him was proved false. The only thing left to dislike was his attitude to his grandmother. How was it that he could strike up an immediate rapport with all these black-clad Cretan grannies and not feel the slightest affection for his own?

It was dark when they left the celebrations.

As they were saying their goodbyes, Kate had wondered if, in spite of the many glasses of wine he had drunk, Xan would insist on driving. But although he seemed perfectly sober, he handed over the car keys and opened the driver's door for her.

Their departure was marked by another fusillade of shots from pistols and rifles.

'Trigger-happy lot, aren't they? But nice people. That was fun,' he said as the car moved off. 'Did you enjoy it, Kate?'

'Very much. I wonder what the others have been up to?'

'Oliver was going to paint a Turkish house in the old quarter. As soon as we get back, I want to do some sketches of the wedding party while it's fresh in my mind. I'd have liked to do them on the spot, but that would have been impossible. Fortunately I have a pretty good visual recall.'

Kate felt a twinge of disappointment. Although they were not in need of any more food, she had hoped he would suggest ending the day with a stroll along the *paralía* and coffee at one of the quieter cafés.

She said, 'I want to write down the songs before I forget the words.'

It took about an hour to get back to Chaniá. At the hotel, when they had collected their keys, she said, 'It's been a lovely day. Thank you.'

He looked down at her with an expression she couldn't interpret. For a few moments she thought he was going to

change his mind about doing sketches of the wedding fes-
tivities.

But then he said, 'Yes, it's been a day to remember,
hasn't it? Goodnight, Kate. See you tomorrow.'

'I'm a bit worried about Kelly. She's been out with Manolis
three nights running,' her mother confided to Kate, a few
days later. 'I've warned her not to let him take her anywhere
lonely, but she doesn't listen. Her father could keep her in
order, but she pays no regard to me. You can't put an old
head on young shoulders, can you? I wish you'd have a
word with her, dear.'

Kate felt the time to instil some sense into Kelly was long
past. She suspected it might be a case of like mother, like
daughter, with the mother conveniently forgetting the flight-
iness of her own youth.

Later, Kate reported her conversation to Xan.

'Could you have a tactful word with Kelly? She'd ignore
me, as she does her mother. But advice from you might sink
in.'

'I doubt it,' he said sardonically. 'Kelly can handle Manolis. I'd guess that where sex is concerned she's a lot less
dumb than she looks.'

'I hope so,' said Kate. 'If she led him on and then panicked…'

'Are you worried about Kelly's welfare? Or the effect on
Palette if a scandal blew up?'

'Both,' said Kate. 'I don't want anything unpleasant to
happen. It would spoil everyone's holiday.'

Secretly she was counting the hours to their second free
day, hoping it would resolve all the unanswered questions
left by their day in the country.

Since then they had had no more time alone together. Xan
was spending his lunch-breaks painting the waterfront from

the steps of the lighthouse. In the evenings the coffee and chat sessions in the waterfront cafés tended to go on later.

He could, if he wished, have come to her room even later, but he hadn't, and she was relieved. For in spite of the ardours under the carob tree, there was still a barrier between them. She had forgotten about it while she was in his arms, but it was still there and must remain there until he changed his unfeeling attitude to his grandmother.

'All right: if it worries you, I'll put my oar in,' Xan said, in a resigned tone. 'But not by tackling Kelly. I'll drop a hint to Manolis that she could spell trouble. My guess is he values his job with the coach company too much to put it at risk for a roll in the hay. But you can't blame a guy for trying if he's given a come-on.'

Later, thinking over his comment, she wondered where he would set the parameters of a come-on. Surely he must have known that, when he was making love to her, she would not have stopped him from going a lot further than he had, might even have abandoned herself to him totally?

Why had he failed to make the most of that opportunity?

Because making love on a hillside like a lusty young shepherd and a willing village girl wasn't his style?

Because he had enough decency to resist making casual love to a girl who might take him seriously and be hurt by him?

Or because he was beginning to feel seriously tender towards her and, having never loved before, was as unsure of his feelings as she was of hers?

If only the last explanation could be the correct one, Kate thought wistfully. But she didn't have much hope that it was.

In the event the second free day wasn't free in the usual sense because Kyria Drakakis invited Xan and Kate to accompany her on a visit to her bachelor brother's house in the country. It turned out that her brother had been a famous musician, giving concerts all over the world until illness forced him to retire.

It was an interesting excursion but, not surprisingly, their housebound host monopolised Xan. Kate was left chatting to his sister, which she enjoyed, but not as much as being on her own with Xan.

Only at the very end of the visit did they have a few moments alone when, as she was starting her car, Kyria suddenly remembered something she had forgotten to tell her brother's housekeeper.

In her absence, Xan, who was in the front passenger seat because of its greater leg room, turned round and said, 'Will you have dinner with me?'

Kate's heart gave a leap of excitement and pleasure. But she tried not to show those feelings as she said pleasantly, 'Yes, I'd like to…thank you.'

'There's a place I've read about, overlooking the sea, which sounds rather nice. Let's meet in the lobby at seven.'

He turned to face forwards, giving her a quarter-profile view of his cheekbone and jawline.

When they were back in Chaniá, she asked Kyria Drakakis to drop her near the shop where she had some photographs to collect.

'Thank you for including me in a most interesting visit, Kyria,' she said, before she got out.

'It was a pleasure to have you with us,' the hotelier said kindly. As she prepared to drive on, Kate heard her say, 'What a nice girl she is.'

But whatever reply Xan made was lost as the car moved forward.

He was waiting for her in the lobby when she stepped out of the lift. The others would still be changing. Only the receptionist saw them leave the hotel together.

'We'll walk there and take a taxi back, if that's all right with you?' He glanced down at her shoes.

She was wearing low-heeled white loafers with a white cotton skirt and a pale blue chambray shirt. Not a glamorous outfit, but cool and fresh-looking, with a skein of small silver beads and a matching bracelet to add a touch of pizazz. She had bought the beads after collecting her photos. They were not as dramatic as Juliet's silver necklace but they appealed to Kate's less flamboyant sense of style. She wondered if Xan would notice them.

He did, but not until later when they were drinking their first glasses of retsina in as romantic a setting as she could have wished for.

'Did you buy that here?' he asked, reaching out to slip his finger between her wrist and the bracelet.

His touch revived all the feelings she had felt when he started to kiss her under the carob.

'Yes, it's my souvenir of Chaniá.'

'I was going to give you a water-colour sketch I did of you as a souvenir. If you'd like to have it?'

'I'd love to.'

'When I get back to London I'll frame it for you. I learnt to do my own frames as an economy when I was young and broke. I still do the mounts and frames for pictures I'm giving as presents.' His finger was sliding back and forth round her wrist in a subtly intimate caress which was tying her insides in knots.

Just then the waiter came back to ask if they were ready to order. Xan withdrew his hand and replied with a smile that they would now give their full attention to the menu and have their decisions made in a few minutes' time.

He didn't touch Kate again while they were in the restaurant, but at times his eyes conveyed messages which sent *frissons* of excitement down her spine as she wondered what he had in mind for later.

It was her suggestion that they should walk back, partly to prolong the delicious agony of waiting to feel his mouth take command of hers, as surely it would before the evening ended. Partly because she loved walking by moonlight and lamplight along the winding esplanades skirting the sea and the harbour.

'I've always hankered to live by the sea,' she told him, as they were strolling back. 'I sometimes think my father was a sailor and that's why I'm drawn to the sea. I used to wonder if he had been lost at sea and my mother couldn't cope on her own and left me in Harrods hoping somebody rich would find me and want to adopt me. But I expect the real explanation is far more prosaic.'

'There's a town called Poole on the south coast of England. You don't think your surname might be a clue to your origins?'

'Maybe? Who knows? I don't really care any more. The here and now is what matters.' She looked up at the sky. 'Those stars. The smell of the sea…'

'You and the night and the music…'

As she turned her face to his, Xan swept an arm round her waist and began to dance her along the esplanade in time to some Forties music being played in a bar they were passing.

She knew that the words he had spoken were not his own, but the title of a long-ago love song on an old-fashioned wax record in a dusty box in the loft at the cottage. There was also an ancient gramophone up there, on which once, when Miss Walcott was out, Kate had played the scratchy-sounding music of her employer's youth.

Xan must have done the same thing and the title had

stayed in his mind as it had in Kate's. Did he also remember
the words? Something about 'burning desire' and the girl to
whom the song was being sung setting the singer on fire.

Several old men sitting at tables outside the bar turned to
stare at the foreign couple whirling in each other's arms to
steps which reminded Kate of equally long-ago movies star-
ring Fred Astaire and his dancing partners. But although
Xan was inventing the dance as he went along, she found
she could follow him perfectly.

'You're crazy,' she said, laughing and breathless when,
too far from the bar for the music still to be audible, he let
her go.

For a moment he didn't answer but stood looking down
at her with a curious intensity. She had a strong intuition
that the reply in his mind was, Yes—crazy for you.

But it must have been wishful thinking. What he said was,
'I have crazy moments. Doesn't everyone? Hey, there's a
taxi. Let's grab it.'

The taxi whisked them back to the Hotel Cydonía in a
matter of minutes. In those few minutes in the back of the
cab Xan took her hand in his and gave it a gentle squeeze,
the meaning of which was very clear to her.

Unless she withdrew her hand, he would take it as tacit
permission to come to her room and pick up where they had
left off under the carob tree.

At the hotel he paid the fare, adding a tip which the driver
accepted with a look of surprise and delight.

Xan's hand was under Kate's elbow as they went to the
desk for their keys. Her heart was pounding like the pile-
driver at a building site they had passed on their way out
of town with Kyria Drakakis that morning.

The proprietress was in the office behind the reception
desk.

'Ah, Kate…you are back. There's a gentleman to see you.

He's come all the way from Iráklion and arrived just a few minutes after you went out. Unfortunately, I couldn't tell him where you had gone because I didn't know. He's waiting for you in the bar.'

'A gentleman for me…from Iráklion?' Kate echoed, baffled.

'His name is…' Kyria Drakakis paused to refer to a note she had made '…Dr Robert Murrett.'

CHAPTER EIGHT

'WHAT the hell is he doing here?' Xan said, in a savage undertone.

In Kate's mind there was only one reason for Robert coming to Chaniá. She was seized by an icy apprehension.

At that moment Robert himself came out of the bar and saw them. 'Kate!' he exclaimed, hurrying towards her. 'I've been hanging about for hours. Where have you been?'

'Oh, Robert, she isn't…dead?'

It seemed to take him a moment to grasp what she meant. Then he said, 'No, no…of course not. That's not why I'm here.'

Something of her inner distress must have shown in her face, for his next words were, 'You'd better sit down. You look a bit shaken up…and no wonder, if that's what you thought. Come into the bar and I'll ask them to fix you a brandy.' He put his arm round her shoulders and steered her towards the small bar adjoining the lobby.

Kate did feel badly shaken up. In quick succession she had experienced intense sexual excitement, mystification, dismay and lastly the painful shock of believing that thousands of miles away someone she cared for had died without her being there.

'Why *are* you here?' Xan demanded, when Kate was sitting down.

'To see Kate of course,' said Robert. 'As it happens, Miss Walcott has had a bit of a set-back, but there's no cause for alarm.'

'What do you mean, set-back?' Kate asked anxiously.

'Oh, she took a dislike to one of the staff and had one of

137

her stroppy outbursts. Then she didn't feel well and panicked, thinking she had set off another heart attack. She
hadn't, but it's taught her a lesson. She won't lose her temper again in a hurry. There's nothing for you to worry
about.'

Xan brought Kate a glass of brandy. 'If you've come to
see Kate, I'll leave you,' he said to Robert, as he handed
her the glass. 'I'll see you tomorrow, Kate.'

His tone was briskly businesslike. His eyes had the frosty
glint she remembered from their first meeting. The man
who, less than half an hour ago, had said, 'You and the
night and music…' had vanished as if she had dreamed him.
She felt like bursting into tears.

'Where were you when I arrived?' asked Robert, after
Xan had gone. 'Nobody seemed to have any idea where you
might be.'

'I was having a meal with Xan. Today's our second day
off. We've been out in the country mostly, with Kyria
Drakakis, the owner. Then we went to try a small restaurant
Xan had heard about. Robert, what on earth possessed you
to come to Crete? Without any warning…when the trip is
more than half over? We'll be flying back in a few days.
You're the very last person I expected to see.'

'I've been missing you like hell. I had some holiday ow-
ing to me. I thought we might stay on here after the others
have gone. You don't *have* to fly back with them, do you?
It was actually Mother's suggestion. The weather's been
lousy in the UK ever since you left and she said, ''Why not
hop on a plane and get yourself some sunshine?'' So I did.
But the only flight I could get was to the main airport at
Iráklion, which meant renting a car and driving here.'

'You ought to have let me know you were coming. Is
there room for you? I thought the Cydonía was full up?'

'It is tonight and tomorrow. After that there'll be room.
Mrs Doodah rang up another hotel for me. It's very near

here. Drink some brandy, pet. You're still looking a bit shattered. It should have occurred to me you might jump to the
conclusion I was bringing bad news.'

'Yes, it should,' she said shortly. 'My heart dropped into
my boots. What else would I think? It's so unlike you to
fly off to places on impulse.'

She knew that part of the reason she was cross with him
was because she felt deeply guilty at putting him out of her
mind; indeed, scarcely giving him a thought, when he and
his proposal should have loomed large in her thoughts.

'I know it isn't, but being in love changes people. I was
in love once before, but it was never like this,' he told her,
with a rueful smile.

Don't I know it! she thought. For those were her feelings
too.

'I'm sorry, I didn't mean to snap at you. It's been a long
day and I'm tired. Could we leave everything till tomorrow?
We've had several rather late nights and I need to catch up
on some sleep. I should think you must be fairly tired too,
aren't you?'

'Not really...but if you are I won't keep you up. I'll join
you for breakfast tomorrow.'

Kate said, 'We don't eat at separate tables. We eat as a
group. Why don't you come round after breakfast? I don't
have to be at the morning painting session until after the
coffee-break. Come round about quarter-past nine. The others will have gone by then.'

'All right. Nine-fifteen tomorrow. Goodnight, my dear.
Sleep well.' Before he rose from the sofa where they were
sitting, Robert leaned forward to press a kiss to her forehead.

In her room, Kate collapsed on the bed and wept. It was
not often that she shed tears. She could only remember crying twice in her adult life, once when her first love had
ended with a crashing let-down, the second time when she
had lost her job at the estate agency.

In time she had recovered from both those disasters. Perhaps tomorrow would put this one in a less ruinous perspective. But right now she felt like a child from whom a long-promised present had been snatched away at the very moment of undoing the wrapping paper.

Tonight had been the most perfect evening of her life, an unforgettable memory of the kind women treasured forever. But then it had all gone wrong and perhaps might never come right again.

Xan was angry with her. Robert was going to be angry with her. And she was angry with herself for letting this catastrophe happen. If she had had the sense and the courage to tell Robert she could never marry him, this predicament wouldn't have happened. But in trying to keep her options open she had upset them all.

'I'd like a word with you, Kate.'

Xan's tone as he grasped her arm and stopped her from entering the dining-room for breakfast—not that she felt like breakfast—would have sounded no different from his normal pleasant way of speaking to anyone overhearing him.

But his grip on her arm was not the caressing pressure of the night before. The bite of his fingers was custodial. And when he opened the door of the small room next to the dining-room and propelled her inside, she knew that when she looked up at him his expression would be glacial. As it was.

'I think an explanation is called for, don't you?'

He stood with his back to the half-glazed, lace-curtained door, preventing anyone from intruding on them.

Without giving her time to answer, he went on, 'You led me to believe you were free, without any commitments. Clearly that isn't so. You lied to me by default. I don't like being duped.' His eyes were hard with contempt.

'I did *not* lie,' she answered fiercely. 'I'm not committed to Robert. He would like me to be…but I'm not. I told him before I left that I wasn't in love with him and wasn't ready for marriage.'

'But not too convincingly, it seems. He believes that you'll change your mind. That's why he's here, isn't it? He wouldn't come all this way, paying the cost of a scheduled flight, unless he had grounds for believing he could persuade you to change it. You've been playing a double game, Kate…fooling around with me while keeping him on a string. He may be so besotted that he's prepared to put up with it. I'm not. I don't take that kind of treatment.'

She had had hardly any sleep and her nerves were already over-strung before he began his tongue-lashing. Keeping her cool was impossible. She said, with an outward defiance completely at variance with the contrition she felt, 'What are you going to do about it? Beat me up?'

The flash in his eyes was like watching distant forked lightning. It was not going to strike her down but the zigzag of lethal force was awesome. She knew he would never be brutal, no matter what the provocation. He wasn't that kind of man. But he wouldn't let her get away with—as he saw it—playing a game with him. The rage she had glimpsed in his eyes had to find some kind of outlet.

An instant later it did. He stepped away from the door and wrapped one arm round her waist, his other hand forcing her face up to meet the fury in his.

'I should have done what I wanted when *you* wanted it too,' he said, in a low, fierce voice. 'It would have been something for you to remember five years from now, when the only sex you'll be getting with Robert is once a week with the light out.'

Kate gave a gasp of rage and struggled to wrench herself free. But his hold on her was unbreakable. She had no more hope of freeing herself than from a strait-jacket.

'Why didn't you, then?' she challenged, her own eyes flashing rebelliously.

'For reasons you probably wouldn't begin to understand. Your generation of women know less about men than any generation before you. You're so busy competing with us, demanding your rights, reviling us for our unfairness, that when someone puts your interests first, ahead of his own, you don't even recognise it.'

'I don't know what you're talking about.'

'I didn't think you would,' he said scathingly. 'You've been brainwashed by feminist dogma into seeing half the male sex as predators and the other half as wimps. So I'll have to explain it to you.'

He let go his hold on her chin, his hand sliding round to her throat, his thumb and forefinger under the angles of her jaw, his other fingers on the side of her neck.

'Contrary to your preconception that I'm a dedicated stud, I actually like and respect women—when they deserve it. I liked and respected you—until last night. The reason I didn't make love to you after our picnic was partly because of where we were—not in the most comfortable or private surroundings—but mainly because I thought *you* might regret it.'

He paused, and when she didn't speak, continued coldly, 'I had no reason to hold back and every reason to go ahead. But I thought, after you'd cooled down, you'd probably change your mind and feel bad about it. At the time, I was under the impression that you hadn't too much experience. Maybe only one guy before me, two at the most. No doubt that's something else I was wrong about.'

By this time Kate was so angry that, if it hadn't been impossible, she might have vented her temper by throwing something at him. Trapped in the vice of his arm, her only weapon was sarcasm.

'Your chivalry knows no bounds! Who would have

guessed you were modelling yourself on St George, the slayer of dragons and champion of helpless maidens? The group have been asking me what to give you as a token of their appreciation. Shall I suggest a red cross, like the one on St George's banner? But hang on a minute…why don't I quite believe in all those right-minded motives you've been professing? Could it be because any man with a nature even half as noble as you claim to have wouldn't be so contemptible to his only living relation? You're picking up the bills for her now. But what about all the years when you ignored her? If you'd done your duty by her then, she might not be where she is.'

Xan's face, already a mask of anger, from the narrowed glitter of his eyes to the clenched muscles at his jaw, was now suffused by a dark flush. He looked as if he would have been happy to strangle her.

But instead of the long fingers holding her throat slowly tightening, they slid round behind her head, delving into her hair and cupping the back of her skull.

To her shock and fury, she found herself being kissed with a savage sensuality which should have repelled her, but which almost instantly revived all the unfulfilled lust he had roused in her under the carob tree.

Robert walked into the hotel as the antique clock in the lobby was striking the single chime which marked the quarter-hour.

By then Kate was outwardly composed. Inwardly, she felt it might take her days, even weeks, to recover from Xan's behaviour in the little writing-room. The appalling thing— for which she could never forgive him—was that by the time he had finished kissing her she had been reduced to wanting him so badly that he could have made love to her there and then and she would only have resisted because of the door being glazed and people coming and going to the dining-room. If it had been somewhere private, and he had chosen to, he could have gone on to what poets called 'the right true end'.

If she hadn't experienced it, she wouldn't have believed that any man could, with his lips alone, command so complete a surrender. But he had. And he knew he had.

'Feeling better after your sleep?' Robert asked, as he joined her.

'Yes, thank you. Did you sleep well?'

'Like a log.'

'I missed breakfast this morning,' said Kate. 'So I thought, if it's OK with you, we'd go to a café and I'll have some coffee and rusks, and you can catch some sun while we talk. It's a good time of day to start working up a tan.'

'You've got a glorious tan,' said Robert, with an admiring glance at her arms and legs. 'Why did you miss breakfast?'

She had a white lie ready. 'I forgot to set my alarm and overslept.'

As she spoke, she wondered again how many of the group had glimpsed that prolonged embrace through the meshes of the coarse lace curtain. Some of them must have seen her locked in Xan's arms, which was among the reasons why she hadn't been able to face them at breakfast, instead fleeing back to her room to fling herself on her bed, alternately pounding the pillow with impotent rage, cringing with mortification and rolling around in a frenzy of unassuaged hunger.

As to the latter, she hoped that Xan—damn him!—would feel the same way, and have a harder time hiding it from the observant eyes of his pupils.

'This is a super place,' said Robert, looking round from his chair in the café near the sponge-vendor's stand. 'Must you join the group today? Can't you spend it with me? Surely they don't need much looking after at this stage of the trip?'

'I want to be with them,' she answered. She had to face Xan again some time, and life had taught her that anything difficult was better confronted sooner rather than later. 'You really shouldn't have come without contacting me first. If you had, I'd have told you not to come. I've made up my mind about us. I'm afraid my decision isn't the one you want, Robert. I'm truly sorry to disappoint you, but I know I'm not the right wife for you.'

He received the statement in silence, absently plucking a loose thread on the checked cotton tablecloth. Kate could empathise with his feelings, having once been rejected herself, but at a far more painful stage of the relationship.

Xan's conjecture that she had not had many lovers was accurate. There had indeed been 'only one guy' before him. The traumatic end of the affair, after more than two years together, had left her wary of starting another relationship which might end equally painfully. But that was a long time ago and now she was in love again, which made her doubly aware of the hurt she was inflicting on Robert.

'Why not, Kate? *I* think you're right for me. Why don't you?'

'For one thing I don't want the same life you want…a quiet, steady life in the country.'

'What sort of life do you want, then?'

'It's not easy to explain. What I *don't* want is to settle down and do pretty much the same things every year for the next fifty years. I want a life of adventure. Oh, not expeditions to faraway, dangerous places,' she added quickly, as he seemed about to expostulate. 'Not that kind of adventure. But I'd like to go on doing this—taking groups to paintable places—and to broaden my mental horizons. Somehow coming to Chaniá has made me aware of myself in a way I wasn't before.'

She turned to look at the sea. 'I think my genes have been sending me signals that I'm someone different from the person I thought I was. When you don't know who and where you came from, it's harder to know where you ought to be heading. Am I making any sense to you?'

'If you ask me,' Robert said slowly, 'it's not your genes sending signals. It's your hormones acting up after two weeks of close contact with Macho Walcott.'

She was about to deny it when she realised that, even if she didn't like the way he expressed it, in essence he was right. The fundamental reason why she could never marry him *was* Xan and what he meant to her.

'That guy has been making trouble as far back as I can remember,' Robert went on. 'One of the times he was roughed up at school was because he'd snaffled someone's girl. He's no good for you, Kate. He'll only make you unhappy. You're one of a long line of women he's given a whirl…and you won't be the last. If that's in your mind, forget it.'

He sprang to his feet and walked off along the waterfront.

At lunchtime Kate returned to the hotel before the group, whom she had not joined after all. She ate some fruit and a rusk and wondered where Robert was. It was not impossible that he had packed and driven back to Iráklion. But would he do that without saying goodbye?

She had taken a couple of paracetamols for a headache when there was a tap on her door. She opened it, half expecting to see Robert. But it was Juliet.

'May I come in and talk to you?'

'Of course. Is anything the matter?' Kate asked, closing the door.

'You could say that.' Juliet replied, with a hollow laugh. 'Nothing to do with the course, or only indirectly. Nothing you can put right for me. But I need to unbottle to someone and you'll understand because you're in the same boat.'

She had walked to the window to look out at the sea, but

now she swung round to face Kate. Leaning back against the wide sill, she said, 'You've fallen for Xan, haven't you?'

Instinctively, Kate hedged. 'What makes you think that?'

'Only intuition. You're hiding it well. No one else would have guessed it…least of all Xan himself. For all his experience with women, I don't think he knows what to make of you. I've seen him watching you…trying to deduce what lies behind that unflappably capable façade you present to the world. He isn't sure how to deal with you and he's not used to uncertainty. It bothers him. As for the man I fancy…he'd run a mile if he knew the way I feel about him. I'm definitely not his kind of woman.'

Kate said in a puzzled tone, 'Isn't Xan the one you fancy? I would have thought you were exactly his kind of woman.'

'Xan? Oh, God, no—not him!' Juliet exclaimed emphatically. 'I may have fancied him slightly, at the beginning…or at least pretended I did. I didn't want to acknowledge what was really happening. One feels such a fool, falling in love like a schoolgirl…and especially with someone as inaccessible as Oliver.'

'Oliver?'

'Who else? Of course he's much older than you are. Old enough to be your father. But surely you can see what a heart-throb he would have been at Xan's age.'

'Yes, I can…and he's so nice too. I think he's lovely,' said Kate. 'But I didn't know *you* did. I thought you disliked each other, except as artists. I know he admires your paintings.'

'It's the only thing about me he does admire. He disapproves of the way I dress and my make-up. I expect his wife was one of those intrepid women who don't mind washing their hair in meltwater and cooking over a campfire. He makes it clear he thinks I'm appallingly decadent.'

Since this was Kate's own impression of Oliver's attitude to Juliet, it was difficult to find anything positive to say to her. Indeed, Kate was still digesting Juliet's statement that Xan had no idea she was in love with him and appeared to find her as inscrutable as she found him.

'Are you sure it's love, not just a passing attraction?' she asked. 'This is a very romantic place and when people are thrown together, spending days in each other's company—'

'Is the way you feel about Xan going to wear off when you get home?' Juliet asked bluntly.

It seemed pointless to deny the truth. 'No, but I think Xan will forget me as soon as he's back in his normal milieu. You don't detect any signs that he's *seriously* interested, do you?'

'Xan isn't the type to wear his heart on his sleeve,' said Juliet.

Kate knew a diplomatic evasion when she heard one. 'If he has a heart,' she said drily.

'Oh, he has one,' Juliet said, with conviction. 'He couldn't paint as he does if he didn't have a soft centre. But don't forget, he wasn't always a devastatingly attractive thirtysomething. Maybe when he was younger and more vulnerable, something happened to make him wary of exposing his deeper feelings. Perhaps you've been keeping your cards too close to your chest. Why not give him a glimpse of your hand? What have you got to lose?'

When Kate didn't answer, she went on, 'Last night I lay on my bed feeling lonely and randy—a deadly combination—and fantasised sashaying along to Oliver's room and making a heavy pass at him. But I couldn't muster the nerve to do it in real life.'

'You've just asked me what I've got to lose,' said Kate. 'I might say the same thing to you.'

'Yes, you might…and the answer is "face". My impression of Oliver is that while his wife was alive he would have been totally loyal and, since her death, equally faithful to her memory. There are men like that. My guess is he's one of them. It's going to take more than a blatant proposition from a war-painted wanton—which is evidently how he sees me—to revive Oliver's interest in a close relationship. Either he'll soldier on alone, or he'll meet a sympathetic widow who reminds him of his wife and offer her decorous companionship. It's a shame because I'm sure he still needs and wants love. Who doesn't?' Juliet said, sighing.

Strangely, now that Kate knew Juliet wasn't interested in Xan, she felt quite differently towards her. Sympathetic. Concerned. Anxious to help in any way she could.

'Perhaps you should revise your fantasy. I wonder what would happen if you left off the war-paint and went to Oliver's room, not to make a heavy pass but to tell him how lonely you are? Not as baldly as that. You'd need a pretext. Perhaps a problem with a painting.'

'He'd refer me to Xan,' said Juliet. 'And you don't know what I look like without a careful maquillage—not good. My skin never was like yours and my eyes, in their natural state, look like raisins in a rock-cake.'

'I don't suppose they really do. Anyway it's the expression in people's eyes, not their size or colour or sparkle, which is important,' said Kate. 'If you let Oliver see you in rock-cake mode, it might change his attitude…break down his misconception that women who cut a dash dress-wise have to be hard-boiled bitches.'

Juliet looked unconvinced.

Later in the afternoon, a note was slipped under Kate's door. Opening the envelope, she read the typed message.

Ariana Drakakis requests the pleasure of your company in her private dining-room for dinner this evening. 8 p.m. Dress informal.

Underneath was a hand-written postscript. 'I have invited your friend Dr Murrett to join us and he has accepted. Also the Colonel and Ms Craig.'

That Xan would be there went without saying.

At a quarter to eight Maria, the receptionist, rang to say, 'Your friend Dr Murrett is here, Miss Poole. He would like to speak to you privately before you join Kyria Drakakis.'

'I'll come down right away.'

There was no one else in the lobby but Robert. To her surprise and relief, he greeted her cheerfully, as if nothing had happened.

'You look nice.'

'Thank you.' She had put up her hair and was wearing some cheap but effective dull gilt jewellery to give a bit more panache to a lemon-yellow cotton frock picked up in the summer sales.

'Listen, Kate, I've had time to think things over. I'm not taking your answer as final. Let's see how things go. I'm not giving up hope. I accept that you're not in love with me, but being in love never lasts anyway. It's friendship that lasts. When my first love-affair went wrong, I was very upset. Now she means nothing to me. It was a fever in the blood…not enough to sustain a permanent partnership. If, in time, you realise I'm right, I'll still be there for you.'

He spoke so kindly and sincerely that she felt her eyes brim with tears and had to blink them away. Her voice unsteady, she said, 'You're being incredibly nice.'

As she spoke Xan appeared round the bend of the staircase and went to speak to Maria. He was wearing a dark blue button-down cotton shirt and cotton gabardine trousers the colour of clotted cream. A dark plaited leather belt with a silver buckle and tongue was slotted through the loops on the waistband.

Turning to join Kate and Robert, he took in her dress, the

upswept hairstyle and the imitation gold torque circling her throat. But, unlike Robert, he didn't compliment her.

'Good evening, Robert,' he said pleasantly, holding out his hand.

While the two men were making small talk, Kyria Drakakis appeared, majestic in flowing crimson voile printed with swirls of black. Skeins of black beads draped her generous bosom and black combs restrained the coils of her steel-grey hair.

'You look magnificent, Kyria,' said Xan, kissing her hand. 'You realise that Dr Murrett is Nerina's physician.'

'Welcome to Chaniá, Doctor,' said Kyria Drakakis. 'I'm sorry I can't accommodate you till tomorrow. Do tell me the latest news of my dear friend Nerina.'

While Robert was answering her questions, Xan turned to Kate. 'I like the Roman torque.'

His gaze moved down from her throat to the soft hollow revealed by the neckline of her dress. Her face flamed with colour at the memory of their last encounter. After a stilted, 'Thank you,' she could find nothing to say and pretended to be listening to the others, knowing that Xan was still watching her, amused by her discomfiture.

She was thankful when Oliver came down the stairs, reaching the lobby just as Juliet stepped out of the lift. She was wearing a long, clinging slither of tobacco silk with slits in the narrow skirt and a great deal of bosom on show. As she went to leave her key on the desk, Kate watched the men's reactions.

Oliver was scowling slightly. Robert was looking uneasy, in the manner of many nice, conservative men when confronted with glamour laid on with a trowel. Xan's expression was inscrutable.

'I'm not late, am I?' Juliet asked, as she joined them in a gust of expensive scent. She didn't wait for an introduction.

'Hello. I'm Juliet Craig. Who are you?' she said, giving her hand to Robert.

'I wish we had another week here,' she remarked, during dinner. 'I'm not looking forward to returning to grey skies and the onset of winter. This town teems with tempting subjects. Given more time, I'd like to paint that staircase supported by a half-arch behind the cafés looking out at the mouth of the harbour. When are you next taking off for foreign parts, Xan?'

'I may spend Christmas in India,' he answered. 'An American travel company wants me to illustrate a lavish brochure advertising a holiday for the mega-rich staying in maharajahs' palaces. Considering how many fine artists there are in the United States, I'm surprised and flattered to have been asked. By the way, have you found the tape of Cretan folk music you want to take back, Juliet?'

It was they and Kyria Drakakis who kept the conversation flowing. Neither Robert nor Oliver had much to say, and Kate had completely lost her tongue. Emotionally, the past twenty-four hours had been very draining, and it was difficult to recover her equilibrium when every so often Xan would glance across the table at her with a look which left her self-possession in shreds.

CHAPTER NINE

THE next day Robert attached himself to the group, and they naturally assumed he was Kate's boyfriend. If anyone had witnessed the scene in the writing-room, which would have thrown doubt on that conclusion, they were keeping it quiet.

During the lunch-break he moved his luggage to the Cydonía. In the evening, to Kate's dismay, she found the Palette dinner table had been extended, giving everyone a little more elbow-room and enabling him to sit beside her.

What with Robert dogging her footsteps, and Xan looking sardonically at them both, Kate was glad when the day was over. Although they had been within arm's length of each other at various times, she and Xan had had no conversation. She felt he was deliberately cutting her.

Since their inception, Palette painting holidays had always wound up with an exhibition of the students' best work on the penultimate evening, followed by a celebratory dinner and prize-giving on the last night of the trip.

The prizes were vouchers donated by manufacturers of art equipment and publishers of art books. Judging was done by the group, using a secret ballot system. When, as sometimes happened, two paintings tied for a prize, the tutor had the casting vote.

The last but one day's painting session ended earlier than usual to allow people extra time to tidy their rooms and arrange their exhibits on their beds. Not being involved in the ballot, Kate went round the exhibition with her camera, taking at least one snap of everyone's work and, in some cases, several.

Xan's paintings were also on show in his room, although

not for sale as Miss Walcott's displays of pictures always were. On trips to France they had sold well, but her prices had been far below what Xan, or rather his London gallery, could charge.

He had also put on a sketchbook containing many quick studies of members of the group. Leafing though it, Kate found herself caught unawares with a range of different expressions from laughter to deep thought.

It happened that for a few minutes she was alone in the room, giving her a chance to photograph a page with two sketches of herself on it, and also to read the titles of the neat pile of books on his bedside table.

Most of the group had brought thrillers and other current bestsellers with them. His night-time reading was a fifty-year-old classic *The Colossus of Maroussi,* and the Cretan journals of Edward Lear, an artist and traveller who had visited the island in the nineteenth century.

There was still so much she didn't know about Xan, she thought, as she left his bedroom. Most people in their thirties had developed as much as they ever would. But he was the kind of man who all his life would continue to widen his perspectives and become increasingly interesting. It was impossible to imagine being bored by him. But what kind of woman would it take to keep him interested?

Before dinner, while the others were having complimentary drinks, she collected the ballot papers and took them upstairs to be totted up later. A quick flick through suggested the results would tally with her own judgement of who had won each of the several awards.

Then she went back to the others, bracing herself for a difficult evening.

Several hours later, when someone knocked on her door, Kate closed her book and put it on the night table, next to her small alarm clock. It was ten minutes past midnight; not as late on a warm, starry night on an island at the eastern end of the Mediterranean as in an English village where, with the nights growing colder, people would be switching on electric blankets before going to bed.

All the same, for anyone to disturb her at this time of night suggested trouble in some form. So far the trip had been remarkably trouble-free, at least in the ordinary sense. No one had been badly sunburnt, drunk too much wine or had a bad tummy upset.

Slipping a cotton robe over her thin summer nightie, Kate wrapped it round her and tied the belt.

When she unlocked and opened the door, she was taken aback to find Robert standing outside.

'May I come in?' he whispered.

After a slight hesitation, she stood back for him to enter.

Speaking in a low voice which wouldn't be heard through the walls, he said, 'I've been for a walk to the far end of the esplanade. I saw your light was still on as I was coming back.'

She wondered if he had been drinking. She had a feeling he might have stopped off at a couple of bars during his walk. Not that he gave any obvious sign of having drunk too much. But he looked on some kind of high.

'It's very late, Robert,' she said. 'I was just about to put my light out.'

'You don't look tired. You look lovely in this soft light. Good enough to eat. Oh, Kate, you're driving me crazy. You've got me lying awake, dreaming about you like a schoolboy…wanting you…longing for you…' The words came out in a rush as he moved towards her.

Caught unprepared and unready to deal with the situation, she found herself pinioned, unwilling to be kissed and equally reluctant to repulse him with a vigour which would hurt his feelings.

But as soon as his lips touched hers and began a passionate kiss, she found it deeply repellent to be kissed in this way by anyone. Anyone but Xan. Forgetting about wounding Robert's pride, she attempted to push him away.

He was strongly built and her push wasn't vigorous enough to break his tightening embrace, or even to make him realise she wanted him to let her go. Rather than struggle with him, Kate opted for passive resistance. In a moment or two, her lack of response must get through to him.

Unfortunately it didn't seem to. Although her body didn't yield to him, he appeared not to notice. To her dismay, she felt his excitement mounting and was anxiously conscious of how little she had on. Only two thin layers of cotton between her naked flesh and the heat of his hands. They hadn't started roving yet, but she felt they might at any moment.

She was bracing herself to give a more vigorous shove when there was a rap at the door and, seconds later, a voice said, 'Did you realise you'd left your door unlatched?'

Robert stopped kissing Kate to raise his head and glare angrily across the room.

Kate gave a gasp of mingled relief and consternation.

Xan who, when he entered, would have been momentarily hidden by the wall of the shower room where it formed a short passage between the door and the bedroom proper, looked at them both with raised eyebrows.

'Sorry to butt in...I didn't expect you to have someone with you.'

The smoothness of his apology was belied by the look in his eyes. They were like chips of granite.

'What the hell are *you* doing, bursting into Kate's room?' Robert demanded.

'I did knock. If you want to be private, you should make sure the door is properly closed...preferably locked.'

'That doesn't answer the question,' Robert said belligerently.

By this time he had released Kate and moved back a pace. He had been flushed before. Now, either from arousal or anger, his colour had risen.

In contrast, Xan's expression was as cold as Kate had ever seen it.

He said, 'I was sitting up talking to Kyria Drakakis when there was a call from the UK. I'm afraid I have bad news, Kate. Nerina's taken a turn for the worse. She's asking for you.'

Immediately she forgot her chagrin at being caught in misleading circumstances. Her only concern was for the stricken woman far away in England.

'Is it another heart attack?'

'Apparently not, but she's unwell and asking for you. They feel it's advisable for you to get there as soon as possible.'

'I'll run you to Iráklion,' said Robert. 'If you tell them I'm a doctor and it's an emergency, they'll give us seats on the first flight out in the morning.' In a matter of moments he had changed from importunate lover to Nerina's physician and Kate's friend.

'There's a better expedient,' said Xan. 'Kyria Drakakis is arranging for Kate to fly out tonight on a private plane owned by a friend of hers. He's a shipping millionaire from mainland Greece who has a holiday house here. Luckily he's in residence at the moment. They were once very close, I gather, and if it's within his power he'll do anything she asks.'

At this point there was another tap on the door and Kyria Drakakis herself appeared, carrying a tray of tea-things.

'I thought you might feel the need for a cup of tea, Kate. This is very worrying news, but thanks to a dear friend of mine we can get you to England quite quickly.' She looked faintly surprised to see Robert in the room. 'I'll fetch another cup for you, Dr Murrett.'

'No, no, please don't trouble. A cup of tea will do Kate good, but not for me, thank you.'

Xan took the tray from her while she moved the dressing-stool close to one of the chairs. As she sat down, he placed the tray on the stool.

'Thank you.' She gave him a warm smile before turning to Kate and saying, 'While you're drinking your tea, there's something I should like to read to you. Then I'll help you to pack. Phaedon is sending his own car to pick you up and take you to his private airstrip.'

She poured out three cups of tea before putting her hand in the pocket of the loose silk jacket she was wearing over her dress. After putting on her glasses, she unfolded some paper with handwriting on it.

'I had this letter from Nerina in the summer. The first part deals with business matters, but then she writes, "I've had the good luck to engage a young woman to help me who has every quality I could wish for. She works hard, gets on well with the students, is cheerful, tactful and resourceful. I like her very much and thank my stars she answered my advertisement. She doesn't appear to have any admirers, but I fear it can't be long before that changes. As you'll see when you meet her, she has a subtle beauty which, although unlikely to strike those whose taste has been formed by the cinema and television, must appeal to anyone with a more discriminating eye. Her name is Kate Poole. She makes me feel as if I had been blessed with a long-lost and delightful granddaughter."'

As the hotelier took off her spectacles and refolded the letter, it took all Kate's self-control not to break down in tears. Her eyelids prickled and her lower lip quivered. But she managed to master her voice sufficiently to say, 'Thank you, *kyria*. It's nice to know Miss Walcott feels that way. But the good luck is mostly on my side. Working for her has been more rewarding than anything I've ever done.'

Robert said, 'I'll go and get packed. I have something to help you sleep during the flight, Kate. Otherwise you'll be worn out. How long have we got before the car arrives, *kyria?*'

'I'm afraid it won't be possible for you to go with her, Dr Murrett. But you can be sure Kate will be in excellent hands. My friend flies all over the world. He can afford to employ the best pilots and mechanics. He owns two aircraft, one for the longer journeys, and this smaller one for flying around Europe. It has room for only two passengers and naturally, being Nerina's next of kin, Xan is the one who must go with Kate.'

By the time Kate was ready to leave, the car was outside the hotel. Robert bade her an anxious goodbye.

'I wish I were coming with you. I'll drive to Iráklion first thing in the morning and hope to be back in the UK by tomorrow afternoon or evening. Here's the stuff to help you sleep.' He handed her a small plastic bottle containing a few pills.

Xan was taking leave of Kyria Drakakis and somehow the two men contrived not to shake hands with each other.

Kate was beginning to suspect that even as boys they hadn't liked each other. If they had, being sent to different schools wouldn't have ruled out a friendship during the holidays. There must always have been some innate antipathy between them. Now, on both sides, this had been exacerbated by their relationship with her.

In the car, Xan exchanged a few words with the driver but said nothing to her. He might have been on his own for all the attention he paid to her. She wondered if, now that his grandmother's life was at risk again, he was regretting his obdurate attitude to her.

When they boarded the aircraft it was immediately apparent that Robert could have come with them.

'Was it your idea to prevent Robert from coming with us?' she asked Xan.

'Why should I want to do that?'

'I don't know. But clearly he could have come.'

'I agree. I'm as puzzled as you are. But I don't think we should send the car back to fetch him. By now he'll have gone to bed. Waiting for him could delay us by over an hour, and we also have quite a long drive at the other end, don't forget.'

'I wasn't suggesting we should wait for him. I'm just baffled by why Kyria Drakakis thought there wouldn't be room for him.'

'A misunderstanding, I suppose,' Xan said indifferently, fastening his seat belt.

Not many minutes later they were airborne, with the peaks of the White Mountains pale in the moonlight as the small aircraft soared off the end of the airstrip and, gradually gaining height, turned westwards.

It was the strangest and longest night of Kate's life. She offered Xan some of the sleeping pills Robert had given her, but he shook his head.

'No thanks. I never take that stuff.' He leaned back and closed his eyes.

Kate didn't like the idea of taking pills either. But after a couple of hours of wondering how ill Miss Walcott was, and if they would get there only to find she had died, she decided to swallow a couple. They put her to sleep for several hours and then she woke up with a bad headache which was still throbbing when the co-pilot came back to tell her they would soon be landing and to wake Xan who seemed to have slept as soundly as if he had been in bed.

Before they set out on the final lap of the journey, in the kind of luxurious car only very rich people rented—this too had been laid on for them by Kyria Drakakis's friend Phaedon—Xan telephoned the nursing home and returned with the news that Miss Walcott was 'no worse, but still very poorly'.

They had been on the road for half an hour, and Kate's headache had abated slightly, when he suddenly said, 'What exactly goes on between you and Robert?'

'Nothing goes on. We're still friends, but that's all.'

'Come off it, Kate. What I interrupted last night wasn't a friendly chat. He was all fired up to make love to you. If looks were lasers, I'd have a hole between the eyes.'

'It wasn't like that. You exaggerate. It was just a kiss…an unexpected goodnight kiss. A few minutes earlier, he wouldn't have been there. A few minutes later, he'd have gone.'

'Not willingly,' he said sardonically. 'And if you didn't intend or want him to stay, how come he was there in the first place?'

'He knocked on my door. He asked to come in. I—I thought he must have a reason for wanting to speak to me.'

'Would you have let me in? At that time of night? With you in your nightie?'

'With a dressing-gown over it.'

'That doesn't answer the question,' he said, echoing Robert. 'Would you have let me in, given that I had no valid reason for coming to your room at that hour?'

'I'd have assumed that you had, as I did with Robert.'

'Never assume,' he said drily. 'It can lead to embarrassing complications. As it would had done last night, but for my intervention. Judging by your expression when I walked in, you weren't as carried away as our worthy doctor.'

The implied scorn for Robert's prowess as a lover made her say bitterly, 'He wasn't forcing himself on me as sadistically as you did the day before yesterday.'

There were road works ahead. Xan's gaze flicked to the mirror before he changed down and then braked. He handled the luxurious car as smoothly as if it were his own.

'Sadistically, Kate?' he said, turning to look at her while the warning stop light glowed red. 'I don't think I inflicted any physical pain on you, did I? Some mental discomfort perhaps. But it's hardly my fault if you can't come to terms with the fires smouldering under that cool, collected surface you present to the world.'

Deliberately, he put his hand on her thigh. It couldn't be described as a lecherous gesture. His fingers were closer to her knee than the top of her thigh and they didn't move in that direction. But there was a possessive intimacy about his touch which made her tremble inwardly.

She said nothing, turning her face away and staring blindly out of the window until the temporary traffic light changed to green and he took his hand away to put the car back in gear.

The rest of the journey passed in silence until, as he swung the car through the gateway of what once had been a private mansion, she said, 'Are you coming with me to see her?'

He took so long to answer that she thought he might be ignoring the question. But eventually, when they were half-way along the drive, he said, 'Yes...since you wish it, I will.'

'You may find her rather confused. Her mind has been wandering,' said the sister on duty that morning, as she led them to Miss Walcott's room.

'You have some visitors, dear,' she announced, making Kate flinch at the thought of her proudly independent employer being forced to endure kindly meant but unacceptable familiarities.

Nerina Walcott opened her eyes. She seemed to have shrunk since Kate had said goodbye to her. She looked very old and frail, as if she were letting go her once strong grasp on life.

Her gaze rested vaguely on Kate, as if she didn't recognise her, and they drifted up to the face of the tall man with her.

'Neal…' she said. 'Neal…is it you?'

Xan moved to the side of the bed, taking her out-stretched hand. 'No, it's not Neal, It's Neal's grandson…Alexander. But you always called me Xan. I've been away a long time. But now I've come back to see how you're getting on. They tell me you've been overdoing it, Nerina. That's nothing new, is it? You always did and I dare say you always will. Are you comfortable here?'

His tone was matter-of-fact, more like an old friend's greeting than an emotional reunion after a long separation.

Miss Walcott's reaction was astonishing. As his long fingers gripped her veined and age-spotted hand, it seemed to have the effect of jump-leads recharging the battery of a broken-down car.

In a matter of seconds she was struggling to sit up, her eyes brightening, her life-force reviving.

'Xan! I didn't expect *you* to come. I knew Kate would. I never thought you would. I suppose you think I'm about to fall off my perch, that you'd better get back in my good books in case there are any rich pickings. But I'm not on my way out yet, my boy. You're looking well…very fit. How did it go, the Crete trip…?'

About half an hour later they got back in the car and drove to the nearby village and the small hotel where visitors to the clinic often put up for the night. There Xan arranged for use of a bedroom, explaining that he wasn't yet sure if they would be staying overnight, in which case they would need two rooms.

'After breakfast, I'll have a shave and a shower and you'll go to bed for a couple of hours. You look bushed,' he told

Kate, while they were waiting for the full English breakfast he had ordered.

'Did you really sleep as soundly on the plane as you seemed to?' she asked.

'I've slept on park benches before now. When I was in my late teens, I dossed down in all kinds of weird places.'

Kate was too exhausted to do justice to the orange juice, muesli, mixed grill, croissants and wholewheat toast which was Xan's idea of a restorative breakfast. She was half asleep when he went up to shave and fast asleep in a chair in the lounge when he came down.

As if she were ten years old, he marched her upstairs, turned back the eiderdown on the double bed, told her to sit down on the edge, took off her shoes, said, 'Lie down,' and covered her up.

'I'll be back before lunch. Sleep tight.'

In fact it was mid-afternoon when she was woken by the manageress coming in with a tray of tea and a message from Xan. She had been so deeply asleep when he looked in at lunchtime that he had decided to leave her undisturbed. At six o'clock he would fetch her for an early dinner with his grandmother.

Kate drank the tea, had a leisurely bath and took her time doing her make-up. She was downstairs, looking at a magazine, when Xan came for her.

'Feeling better?' he asked.

'Yes, thank you. A new woman.'

'Good. Let's have a drink. What would you like? A glass of wine?'

She nodded. 'Red, please.'

He rang the bell for service and said, 'I've decided that, having deprived the group of their last-night party and prize-giving—although I expect they'll have some kind of rave-up tonight—we should make it up to them by laying on a late lunch party at one of the airport hotels. In fact it's already arranged. There's nothing for you to bother about.'

'Are you staying here tonight?' she asked.

'I am, but don't worry. We shall be in separate rooms. And you will be chaperoned,' he said, with a mocking gleam.

'Chaperoned? By whom?'

'Robert. Who else? He hopes to be here by eight and will join us at the clinic.'

'You've spoken to him?'

'No, to Kyria Drakakis. She also wants to speak to you. She'll give you a call early tomorrow morning, before we leave for the airport. I think we should both fax letters of thanks to Phaedon and I'm also going to give him one of my paintings of Chaniá.'

When their drinks had been served, Kate asked the question which had been preoccupying her ever since she woke up.

'What made you change your mind?'

'About what?'

'About a *rapprochement* with your grandmother.'

He tilted his gin and tonic, making the ice cubes clink softly against the glass. 'You did,' he said, looking at her. 'But we won't go into that now. I've been talking to the clinic's consultant physician and he thinks Nerina's recent deterioration was largely psychological. She decided she didn't want to go on and was willing herself to fade out.'

Kate sipped her wine and kept silent.

'The estrangement between us may have something to do with it,' he continued. 'But the principal reason was, as she's admitted to me, that even with you doing the donkeywork, running Palette is now beyond her. She doesn't want to let down her regulars by shutting up shop, but that's what she'd like to do. She has a plan for the future she wants to discuss with you. I don't know what it is. She hasn't told me yet.'

When they returned to the clinic, they ran into the consultant to whom Xan had talked earlier. He introduced him to Kate.

The physician said, 'I've heard a lot about you, Miss Poole. You're Miss Walcott's right hand, I gather. Well, you'll be pleased to hear that in my opinion she's going to be around for some time yet. She's a very strong-willed old lady. For a while she gave up the struggle, with alarming effects. But now she's decided to press on, although taking life a lot more easily, it wouldn't surprise me if she made eighty or ninety. The human will is a very powerful force.'

Miss Walcott was out of bed and sitting in a chair when they joined her. She was wearing a long blue silk garment, bought in Morocco, and dabs of blue shadow on her eyelids.

'Kate, my dear, have you recovered from the shock and fatigue of being fetched back in such a rush? Yes, I can see you have. What it is to be young. A few hours' sleep and you look as fresh as a daisy.'

It was not until after they had eaten a meal which seemed very bland compared with the Cretan dishes of the past two weeks that Nerina leaned back in her chair and announced, 'I have something important to discuss with you both.'

Before she could go any further, an auxiliary came in to clear away. Tapping her finger on the arm of the chair, Miss Walcott cast an exasperated glance at her grandson, who responded with his characteristic half-smile.

'Oh, you are so like your grandfather...my darling Neal,' she told him. 'He had just the same trick of curling up the corner of his mouth when he thought I was being too impatient.' Her smile held a hint of coquetry, giving a glimpse of the charming, flirtatious girl she must have been fifty years ago.

Earlier, while they were eating, Kate had been aware that

apart from her greeting, her employer had scarcely spoken
to her. All her attention was on Xan. Which was natural
enough, Kate supposed. They had a great deal to catch up.
But it was slightly hurtful to feel that, now he was back,
her only importance was as what Americans called a 'gofer'.

'I've thought it all out and I'm definitely going to retire,'
Miss Walcott began. 'You two can take over Palette. Kate
to handle the day-to-day running and you, Xan, to be the
figurehead and to give Kate advice when she needs it. I've
had my name down for some time for a flat in a complex
of sheltered housing for old ducks like myself. I shall live
there on my pension and paint and perhaps give occasional
classes. Kate can have the cottage and a salary and anything
over will be yours, my dear boy.'

She looked at him for agreement, taking Kate's consent
for granted.

Xan said, 'I have no objection to your scheme, but Robert
may not be agreeable.'

'Robert? What has it to do with him?'

'He has an interest in Kate,' Xan said drily. 'He wants to
marry her. He's not taking no for an answer. He pursued
her in Crete and in half an hour he'll be here, still in pur-
suit.'

'Oh, but that's splendid,' said Miss Walcott. 'Why didn't
you tell me, Kate? You and Robert are ideally suited. I
hoped this was in the offing and I know Beryl Murrett will
be delighted. You're just the type of daughter-in-law she
wants.'

'But I don't want to marry Robert,' Kate said quietly.

'Of course you do. He's a dear thing. You won't find a
better husband. He'll be faithful and kind and devoted. You
can run Palette with one hand and manage him with the
other. It will be a piece of cake,' she said, using the slang
of her youth. 'You are cut out to be a doctor's wife, my

dear. You have all the qualifications. I can't think why you didn't accept him the first time he asked you.'

'I'm sure he'll ask her again…perhaps tonight,' Xan said smoothly. 'I've booked him in at the hotel. You can show him the way, Kate, and have a long tête-à-tête. He deserves it, poor guy. I expect he's had a rotten day hanging about the airport at Iráklion, wondering what dastardly treatment I've been meteing out to you.'

'Robert was always jealous of you,' said his grandmother. 'He was rather small as a boy. I think he envied your inches.'

At this point there was a knock at the door and Robert came in, visibly startled to see his patient sitting up and looking animated. As Xan had foreseen, he had had an extremely trying day, although that didn't emerge until he had satisfied himself that Miss Walcott and Kate had come through their ordeals in good order.

'I suggest you take Robert back to the hotel, see that he gets a good meal and lend a sympathetic ear to his difficulties in getting here,' said Xan presently.

'An excellent idea,' he grandmother seconded. 'Off you go, the pair of you.'

This time it was Robert who drooped over the dinner table at the hotel, until Kate packed him off to have a quick shower and fall into bed.

She sat in the lounge for a while, hoping Xan would come in. But he didn't. Eventually she went bed, her thoughts going round in circles.

Next morning, while she was dressing, the bedside telephone rang. It was Kyria Drakakis. She was on the line for twenty minutes.

*　　*　　*

Xan was already at breakfast when Kate entered the dining-room. He rose to draw out a chair for her. They exchanged good mornings.

'Where did you go last night?' she asked. 'Robert went to bed early and I'm sure you didn't stay with your grandmother very late.'

'No, I went for a drive. Did you tell Robert about Nerina's plan? How did he react?'

'He was worn out by all the hassle at the airport and then having to deal with an emergency on the flight. It was lucky for the man taken ill that he was on board. I'm sure the cabin staff are extremely competent but it's not the same as having a doctor in attendance.' After a pause, she added, 'I'd be grateful if you wouldn't refer to the future of Palette when he comes down. I don't want to talk about it this morning.'

'As you wish.'

'Are we going back to see your grandmother before we leave for London?'

'No, I think not. Visitors aren't really welcome before eleven. They interfere with routine.'

'I had a long call from Kyria Drakakis just now. I'll tell you about it later. Here's Robert. How did you sleep?' she asked, as the other man joined them.

'Like the dead,' he replied. 'What time did you turn in?'

'Not very long after you. Xan stayed up late, he says.'

Robert gave him an offhand, 'Good morning,' which Xan returned equally coolly. He then asked if they would mind if he read the review of an important art show in the morning paper. Breakfast passed almost in silence until, swallowing the last of his toast, Robert asked Kate, 'Will you be home tonight?'

'I should think so, yes.' She turned to Xan. 'How long will the party go on?'

'It should be over by five. Some of the group may leave earlier, if they've a long way to go.'

Robert said, 'I suggest you spend the night with us, Kate, and re-open the cottage tomorrow. Or, if you give me your keys, I can do it for you. And have a hot supper waiting. Mother always had plenty in the freezer. I can heat something up in your oven.'

'It's very kind of you, Robert, but I may spend the night with Juliet, at her flat in Chiswick.'

'Oh, I see…well, I'll see you tomorrow then.'

'Probably, unless she asks me to stay for a second night. I'll give you a ring.'

'Did Juliet ask you to stay with her, or was that an invention?' asked Xan, as they set out for London.

Ignoring the question, she said, 'I was going to tell you what Kyria Drakakis told me…the reason she made up a white lie about there being no room for Robert on Phaedon's plane.'

'Another woman who's adept at invention, it seems,' he said drily.

Kate let that remark pass, saying, 'Phaedon wasn't always a millionaire. When he was young, they were in love, his prospects seemed non-existent. Her parents disapproved of him and pressed her to marry Andreas Drakakis. Eventually she did and has always regretted it. It was obvious to her that Robert was keen on me, and she wanted to stop me making the same mistake—marrying for security rather than doing what she knows now what she should have done; trusted her heart.'

She turned to look at Xan's forceful profile, waiting for his reaction.

CHAPTER TEN

AFTER a pause, Xan said dampeningly, 'I think she did the best thing in marrying Drakakis. If she didn't love Phaedon enough to trust her future to him, she wouldn't have been the right wife for him. Luck plays a large part in the making of fortunes. If his luck had gone the other way, Kyria D. would now be wishing she'd followed her parents' advice. Men who take chances, or choose chancy careers such as mine, need strong, self-reliant women as their partners.'

'What makes you think Kyria Drakakis lacks those qualities? She runs the hotel on her own, now her husband is dead.'

'He got it going. She admits she couldn't have done it alone.'

'I expect it was a joint effort and she underestimates her contribution. She didn't strike me as a feeble personality. I wonder why she and Phaedon didn't get married after Andreas died? Did you ask her that?'

'Because he couldn't have her, Phaedon didn't stay single. He married and had a large family. His wife's still alive. In Greece, the ties of marriage aren't broken as lightly as elsewhere. Family life takes precedence over everything.'

'Do you think she and Phaedon are lovers?'

'In the physical sense?' he said, glancing at her. 'Possibly. For her age, she's still attractive. She has the air of someone who enjoys all the sensual pleasures. But some women have that aura and when it comes to the point they have inhibitions and hang-ups which conflict with their appetites.'

Did he think she was such a woman? Kate wondered. She couldn't bring herself to ask him. Instead, referring to his earlier remark, she said, 'I wouldn't have thought your career was particularly chancy. Like aspiring actors, the current crop of students at art schools may be chancing their luck in an overcrowded profession, but you're established. What could go wrong with your career?'

'Many things. An accident to my hands or my eyes. The kind of pictures I want to paint losing their appeal for the people with money to buy them. Paintings are luxuries: the demand for luxuries fluctuates. Creative people have a good life—if they're lucky. But things can go badly wrong for them. They live on the edge, a precarious place to be. It's a lot more secure being a lawyer or an accountant…or a doctor,' he added drily.

At three o'clock that afternoon, he announced the final award resulting from the ballot in Chaniá two nights ago.

'Ladies and gentlemen, there are two paintings in the exhibition which you considered outstanding.'

Xan looked down the double row of expectant faces. 'I agreed with your verdict and found it impossible to place one above the other. They were Juliet's atmospheric watercolour of the interior of the church at Thériso, and Oliver's very powerful mixed media study of the Venetian arsenals on the waterfront.'

There was a burst of applause and murmurs of congratulation before he went on, 'I foresaw that this problem might arise and therefore I have much pleasure in inviting the two joint winners to be my guests at a gala evening at the Royal Academy next month.'

After more applause, he held up his hand to make another announcement.

'I expect it will come as a surprise to her, but we've all been very impressed with the way Kate has handled the tour. A good courier needs to combine the abilities of a sheepdog, a kindergarten teacher, an agony aunt and a translator. Kate has filled all those roles *par excellence*, in addition to coping with an inexperienced tutor.'

He paused to look down the length of the table to Kate's seat at the far end.

'We know it's your job, Kate. Nevertheless we're grateful for your tact and your patience. The group has clubbed together to show their appreciation.' Picking up an envelope, he beckoned her to come and fetch it.

To another burst of clapping, Kate made her way to the top of the table to shake hands and receive the money collected for her. It was not the first time this had happened, but previously the presentation had been done less formally.

She was mentally preparing a few words of thanks, when Xan surprised her again by tightening his hold on her hand and stooping to kiss her, first on one cheek and then on the other.

Even in public, the brush of his lips was disturbing. She was vaguely aware of some mildly ribald remarks, laughter and more applause.

Disengaging her hand and turning to face the others, she said, 'Thank you all very much. Actually, being a Palette courier is one of the best jobs anyone could wish for. People who paint tend to be exceptionally nice. I've enjoyed myself every bit as much as I hope you have. I look forward to seeing you all again on one of next year's courses.'

'You're ever so poised, aren't you, Kate?' said Kelly, when she returned to her seat.

'Poised? Me?'

'I couldn't make a speech like that. I wouldn't have known what to say.'

'Saying thank you is easy,' said Kate. 'It's being witty, like Xan, which is hard.'

'Oh, yeah, isn't he gorgeous? I could fall for him in a big way, but it'd be a waste of time. He's a bit too old for me, really, and I'm not his type anyway. If you ask me he fancies Juliet and that's why he's fixed up to take her and old Olly to this posh do in London. I wonder what she'll wear? She's got some smashing outfits.'

Wondering how Oliver would react to hearing himself called 'old Olly'—probably with a good-humoured laugh— Kate listened to Kelly prattling on about clothes. There had been a time when Kelly's theory about the gala would have troubled her. But even when Juliet had seemed a rival for his interest, Kate's common sense would have recognised that it would have been easy for Xan to give his casting vote to Juliet and invite her to the gala by herself. Could he have guessed how Juliet felt about Oliver? Could he be trying to help her by setting up a romantic evening?

Kate dismissed the idea. Matchmaking was a female activity.

Presently, the main purpose of the party being over and while people who wanted to get home were starting to say their goodbyes, Juliet came to talk to Kate.

'If I hadn't arranged to spend tonight with my mother at Reigate, you could have stayed with me in Chiswick. Coming home from a trip is always an anticlimax, and particularly so in your circumstances. But I can't disappoint my mother. She's been very lonely since Pa died and my brothers are too far away to visit her regularly. But I'd love to have you to stay another time. I'll call you next week to find out how things are going.'

Juliet, in spite of having plenty of money and an easy life, was almost as lonely as her widowed mother, Kate surmised.

'Yes, do. I'd like to hear from you…and to see you again,' she agreed.

But she knew, from what others had told her, that friendships made on these holidays, however enjoyable at the time, seldom lasted once people were back in their normal environment.

'I was bracing myself to say a final farewell to you-know-who,' Juliet said, in a confidential tone. 'But, thanks to Xan, I've been reprieved. That's if Oliver doesn't find some excuse to get out of coming to the gala.'

'I'm sure he won't.'

'He doesn't like London…detests it. He lives in the wilds of Wiltshire. It wouldn't surprise me if he didn't possess a dinner-jacket. When he was in the army he would have worn mess kit for anything formal.'

'That's no problem. He can hire a dinner-jacket.'

'He may not think it worth the effort. Unlike us, men don't like dressing up. Not men of his sort anyway. Here he comes now.'

'I'm off, Kate,' said Oliver, holding out his hand to her. 'I'll look forward to seeing you again at the gala…and you too, Juliet,' he added, smiling at her in a way which should have boosted her morale, Kate thought, watching.

'I don't think I'll be there,' Kate said. 'Xan hasn't mentioned it to me.'

'I expect he takes it for granted,' was Oliver's parting remark before he strode from the room.

'Men!' said Juliet, with feeling. 'But no doubt he's right—that Xan does intend you to be there. I'll go and ask him, shall I?'

Without waiting for Kate's affirmative, she drifted away, pausing to chat to other people on her way to speak to Xan.

She was one of the last to leave. As she bade Kate goodbye, she said, 'The answer was yes. He's expecting you to make up the foursome. See you on the night—dressed to kill. Bye for now, honey.'

For the night of the gala dinner at Burlington House in Piccadilly, home of the Royal Academy of Arts, Kate booked a room in an inexpensive hotel.

Talking to her on the telephone, the week before, Juliet

had said, 'I would ask you to stay with me, but it just might happen that you could be highly *de trop*. I don't suppose things will work out that way, but I'm going to give what I want to happen every possible chance. And anyway Xan may have post-gala designs on you.'

'I doubt that,' Kate had answered despondently.

Since the party, her only contact with him had been short talks on the telephone relating to Palette matters such as the design and printing of next year's brochure, normally mailed in January. True, he had rung up most days, but always in a businesslike manner, never saying anything personal.

Nor had she seen much of Robert, whose visits she had discouraged, telling him firmly that it wasn't fair to him to continue a friendship which, on her side, could never develop.

'For better or worse, I'm in love with Xan,' she had admitted to him. 'I hate hurting you, Robert, but that's the way it is, I'm afraid.'

It was mid-afternoon when she arrived at the hotel and, after unpacking and hanging up her dress, went out to buy the sheerest tights she could find and contain her impatience by browsing in her favourite bookshop.

They were meeting at Xan's flat for drinks at seven o'clock. By a quarter to seven she was ready. Her dress was a one-off extravagance from the days when she'd been earning good money: a long sheath of lustrous *dévoré* velvet, a luxurious fabric with a pattern formed by the velvet pile in places being eaten away by the application of acids, leaving only the thin silk ground to give a very subtle see-through effect.

The colour was one Xan used a lot in his paintings. It was called *terre verte*, a pigment made from green clay. During one of his talks in Crete, he had told the group it was found in several parts of the world, but the one he preferred came from a blueish-green clay from near Verona in Italy. Kate's dress was also Italian, designed by Giorgio Armani. It had cost her almost a whole year's clothes' budget. But, as soon as she'd put it on, she had known that she had to have it. The middle-aged assistant had clinched the sale by saying, 'It's what I call a forever dress. You'll be wearing it when you're my age…and it's *wonderful* with your eyes.'

Would Xan think so too? she wondered, surveying her reflection in the mirror on the door of the hotel wardrobe.

She arrived at his flat at a quarter past seven, hoping to be the last comer. This time, when she pressed the bell, there was no curt, 'Who is it?' The door was unlocked immediately, but it was Juliet, looking glamorous in carnation-red silk jersey with a sequined top, who was waiting for her at the head of the top flight of stairs.

Kate had already taken off her cashmere-lined midnight-blue velvet evening jacket, another expensive investment in her prosperous years. They appraised each other with mutual approval.

'Very chic, Kate. That should knock a certain person sideways,' Juliet said, smiling. 'Will my Scarlet Woman outfit have a scaring-off effect, I ask myself? Xan has vintage champagne on ice, but we've been waiting for you.'

She stood aside and Kate preceded her into the large room she remembered so clearly from her first visit here. Tonight, with the curtains drawn, many lamps alight and a fire burning on the hearth, it looked even more attractive. But, as she walked in, it was the taller of the two men, both slightly unfamiliar in their immaculate evening dress, who caught and riveted her attention.

Xan in a dinner-jacket made her heart lurch inside her. She forced herself to greet Oliver first, offering her hand and cheek and receiving a light but affectionate hug.

Xan, when she turned to him, took her hand and kissed it. 'That's a fantastic dress…perfect for you.'

When, a few moments later, they all had glasses of champagne in their hands, Juliet said, 'This is far more my style than the last-night party in Chaniá. In the absence of you two, the rest of us went to a bar where they play Cretan folk music. It was mildly amusing for the first hour or so. But I grew out of that sort of place—upright chairs on a cement floor and bottles of beer on the tables—a long time ago. Those who've led sheltered lives, like Heather and Joyce, found it tremendously exciting. Especially when they were given the eye by some moustachioed fishermen who, in spite of minimal English, obviously make a good thing out of chatting up the foreigners *d'un certain âge.*'

Later, after Juliet had asked if she could touch up her lipstick before they left for the gala and the two women were alone in the bedroom used by Xan's visitors, she said, 'You were attractive before, Kate, but now…for a moment as you came up the stairs I almost didn't recognise you. It's not just the dress and the new way you're doing your hair. It's as if you were lit up inside.'

'I am,' said Kate. 'It's the effect Xan has on me. When I'm with him, the world's a different place. Even if it's only for a few hours and there's no future in it, I feel on the threshold of heaven.'

As Juliet uncapped a lipstick that matched her dress, she added, 'So Oliver didn't opt out, as you were afraid he might. Do you still feel the same way about him? Have you had any contact with him since you rang me last week?'

'No, but the fact that he's here, and is staying in London till Friday, is encouraging,' said Juliet. 'Before you arrived Xan was telling us that he might take a Palette group to Bali next year. I'm definitely going to sign on for that, and I think Oliver may, even though it will be expensive.'

'Really? He hasn't mentioned it to me.'

'Perhaps he's planning to discuss it with you later,' said Juliet. 'This do at the Academy won't go on till the small

hours. It'll be probably be over by eleven. I came in my car
and I'm going to say I hate night-driving and ask Oliver to
drive me home to see a big painting I've done—a montage
of the Chaniá experience. If he wriggles out of it, I'll know
I'm wasting my time yearning for something that's never
going to come right.'

After carefully painting her lips, she said, 'Xan's different
too, tonight. I sensed that as soon as I saw him. He's more
open, more approachable. He was always charming, but
there was a certain reserve…some part of his mind one
couldn't penetrate. Didn't you feel that?'

'I still do,' Kate answered wryly. But she knew what
Juliet meant, and she thought it must have to do with the
resumption of good relations with his grandmother.

'Anyway, whether or not I succeed in luring Oliver to my
lair, I'd bet serious money that you'll find yourself back
here before the night's over,' said Juliet. 'Clearly, he thinks
you look ravishing and is panting to ravish you. Are you
going to let him?'

The question was in Kate's mind all through a magical
evening. Her answer when Juliet had asked it had been, 'I
don't know.' But inwardly she did know. Xan already held
her heart. Whatever else he asked of her, she would give,
freely and gladly, without counting the cost to herself if his
heart was not involved.

But the way he kept looking at her kindled wild hopes
that it might be.

At the end, when the women had collected their wraps
from the cloakroom and were rejoining the men in the gran-
deur of the building's entrance hall, Juliet said, 'Would you
do me a great favour, Oliver? Last week someone was
mugged near the lock-ups where I keep my car and I'm a
bit scared of going home. I should have come in a taxi. If
I organise one for your return journey, would you be a
knight in white armour and run me home? You can have a

look at my masterpiece at the same time. I'd like your opinion of it.'

Without hesitation, Oliver said, 'By all means. Where is your car?'

The four of them walked to the meter where Juliet had left it. As they were saying goodnight, Juliet gave Kate a discreet wink and a covert thumbs-up. 'Good luck,' she breathed in her ear, as they kissed goodbye.

As the others drove off, Xan said, 'It's not late. Would you like to come back to the flat and see the paintings of Crete I've been working on? There are also one or two things I'd like to discuss with you.'

Trying to sound casual, Kate agreed, and he hailed a taxi.

On the way, they discussed the evening. She was trembling slightly inside, but not as nervous as she had expected to be. At the house, he preceded her up the stairs to unlock the door of his flat. Catching sight of the Charles Keene drawing of the couple in the four-poster, Kate wondered what Xan's bed was like—it had not been included in the photographs in the glossies—and if, very soon now, she was going to find that out.

The log fire was still alight behind a protective screen of fine chain mesh which stopped sparks from damaging the beautiful Tibetan rug in front of the fireplace. Xan opened the screen and put on another log.

'Make yourself comfortable while I make some coffee.'

'Can I do anything to help?'

'No, thanks, everything's ready. I thought the others might come back but then it became obvious that Juliet had other plans. I'm sure she made up that story about the mugger. The question is, does Oliver know the score?'

Was this his oblique way of warning her that by coming back here she had put herself in a similar situation? Kate wondered, remembering his promise that he wouldn't make a pass without prior warning.

'I'm sure he does,' she answered. 'A man as attractive as Oliver must have had lots of passes made at him. But I happen to know that Juliet's intentions are honourable, as they used to say. She wants to fill the gap left by Sophie McCormick. Not to replace her—she knows she could never do that. But to give him the loving companionship he still needs. With their painting as a common interest, I think, in spite of the disparities between them, it could work out well.'

'Let's hope so. I shan't be long.' Xan disappeared.

When, some minutes later, he came back with a tray, Kate was sitting on the sofa, enjoying the atmosphere of the room but feeling increasingly jittery as the crucial moment drew nearer.

As he poured out, Xan's hands were as steady as when he was painting. When he put a cup of coffee where she could easily reach it, and a glass of brandy beside it, she would have liked to swallow a mouthful of the latter straight away but restrained herself.

However, when he sat down it was at the other end of the sofa, not close to her.

'You've told me what little you know about your antecedents,' he said. 'I think it's time I told you about mine...and the reason why Nerina and I were estranged for so long. That always worried you, didn't it?'

'Yes, it did,' she agreed. 'I couldn't imagine how that situation had come about. It made you seem...hard, even cruel. I couldn't relate those characteristics to your good qualities.'

'I'm glad you did credit me with some good qualities. That wasn't always apparent,' he said drily. After a pause, he went on, 'Emma—my mother—died when I was eleven. I had to call her Emma because Nerina didn't approve of my calling her "Mum". She has some fairly archaic ideas about acceptable behaviour. We lived by her rules because she paid the bills. Even as a very small boy I knew Emma was afraid of Nerina.'

'Had your mother no family of her own?'

He shook his head. 'She was an only child, brought up by her mother's father after her parents split up. Her father was a surfing champion, her mother a university drop-out who became a surfing groupie. They were never married, although later her mother—my other grandmother—did marry a rich American. At the time I'm talking about she didn't want to be encumbered with the product of her wild youth. The old man—my great grandfather—had been a famous pot-holer. That was how Emma met my father. She herself was afraid of caves, and of water. By the time I knew her she was afraid of a lot of things.'

When he paused, Kate noticed a tight knot of muscle at the angle of his jaw and took it as a sign of repressed anger or pain.

'For the last two or three years of her life she had an undiagnosed illness,' he went on. 'It may have been ME— myalgic encephalomyelitis. Even now there are doctors who either deny its existence or know next to nothing about it. At that time it was barely recognised. Anyway, whatever was wrong made her very listless and depressed. She also had dizzy spells. She might have been dizzy and disorientated when she stepped into the road in front of a petrol tanker. Or she might have decided she had had as much as she could take.'

Kate stifled an exclamation of shock and distress. She had had no inkling of a tragedy of this order in the not so distant past.

'I had no idea,' she said. 'No one has ever mentioned this to me.'

'People who have no friends are quickly forgotten,' Xan said, with a shrug. 'Emma was discouraged from taking any part in village life. She was, in effect, an unpaid servant.

Her only pleasures were books and her child, but even our relationship was spoilt for her. If we spent too much time together, Nerina accused her of turning me into a mummy's boy. I hated Nerina. She made my mother's life unbearable…perhaps literally. For a long time I found it impossible to forgive her for that. Later I began to understand her behaviour.'

His paused to swallow some coffee, but as if he were not really tasting it.

'For one thing she obviously felt Emma's generation had less excuse for accidental pregnancies than her own. In her view, Emma should have known more about avoiding an unwanted baby than she herself had done at a time when young men were snatching everything life had to offer in case they were killed, but sex and contraception weren't discussed and written about as freely as they are today.'

'Even our mothers' generation weren't all that clued up,' said Kate, who felt sure her own conception had been unintentional. 'You would think that Nerina's experience would have made her *more* understanding.'

'She may have become more tolerant latterly, but in those days she had very little time for anyone's shortcomings.'

Thinking about it, Kate could remember several recent examples of Miss Walcott's intolerance which, before, she had excused as the tetchiness of old age.

'She also felt that Michael and Emma were unsuited,' Xan went on. 'In that respect, she was right. Everything I've learned about my father, and everything I remember about my mother, points to major incompatibilities which, had he lived, he would have found exasperating. He was tough, adventurous, brave…a replica of Neal, my grandfather. Emma was physically and morally timid. She was frightened of spiders and thunder, frightened of being alone at the cottage when Nerina was away. If Michael hadn't died and had married her, the marriage was bound to have foundered. Nerina was right about that.'

He paused, his expression bleak as he called up the past.

'Having survived on her own, without any support, Nerina despised Emma's helplessness. She thought her lacking in character and clearly she was. I never knew her to defend herself. But I loved her very much and resented my grandmother's bullying.'

Reading between the lines, Kate guessed that what he had left unsaid was that Emma hadn't defended him either. Perhaps Nerina had bullied the little boy too—until, taking after his father, he had learned to fight back.

Suddenly she saw the whole situation from a new perspective. Everything became clear to her. And with understanding came a great rush of love which she could no longer hide, nor had any wish to.

It was in her eyes as she looked at him. In her voice as she murmured, 'Oh, Xan...' In the involuntary gesture of her hands stretching towards him.

For a moment he sat very still. Then, like someone released from a cage, he sprang towards her, pulling her into his arms, holding her painfully close.

'But it's you I love now,' he said huskily, into her hair. 'I do owe the old girl that. But for Nerina, I might never have found you. Darling Kate, will you marry me?'

A long time later, in his bedroom, Kate said softly, 'What time is it?'

Lazily, Xan raised himself on one elbow to look at the clock.

'Half-past twelve. I'd better ring your hotel to tell them you've been detained and will be collecting your things in the morning.'

She felt the conventional reflex, but so faintly and briefly that it was like the momentary sputter of a damp match.

What did it matter what the people at the hotel thought? Why should she give up a night of tenderness and passion for the cold propriety of the hotel bed? There had been too many lonely nights in her life. But not any more.

The call made, Xan turned back to her, smoothing a stray lock of hair from her forehead with gentle fingers.

'Tomorrow I'll take you down to my country place. It's an old tithe barn where a tenth part of the harvest used to be stored. There's another smaller barn near it which I was going to offer you as a home and an HQ for Palette if things hadn't worked out the way they have.'

'What I don't understand,' she murmured, 'is why, if you felt this way, you didn't put me out of my misery sooner.'

'I've been crazy about you from day one. Why else do you think I agreed to go to Crete? It wasn't out of duty to Nerina. It certainly wasn't because I wanted to waste time teaching people like Loretta whose mind isn't open to new ways and new techniques. It was solely because a girl with eyes like opals had marched in here and given me a ticking off.'

'Oh, Xan, I didn't!' she protested mildly. 'I was at pains not to show how anti-you I was then.'

'You were?' he asked, raising an eyebrow. 'You may not have said so outright, but the message I was receiving was that I was at number one on your "hates" list. I wanted to change that. I wanted to make you purr for me, instead of threatening to scratch if I came anywhere near you.'

'I've been purring madly ever since you carried me in here,' she said, smiling. 'I'm purring now. I expect to be purring for the rest of my life.' She slid her arms round his neck. 'Oh, my love, you don't know how wonderful it is to let go of all those inhibitions and hang-ups you were talking about the day we discussed Kyria Drakakis and Phaedon. I felt sure those were digs at me...that you thought *I* was tied up in knots.'

'At the beginning I did. You changed my mind about that under the carob on our picnic. Things were going well for us then. But then Robert turned up and I thought you'd been leading me on as a kind of revenge for my attitude to Nerina. There's a lot of hostility coming from women in general towards men in general these days. You didn't look or act like an aggressive feminist but those attitudes lurk behind some misleading exteriors. Several friends of mine have been taken to the cleaners by wives and partners who suddenly turned into harpies after the split.'

'Yes, I think something's gone badly wrong with the way men and women should interact,' said Kate. 'Most of the people I know don't believe any more that there's any chance of being ''happy ever after''. I don't think it ever was something that happened very often. But sometimes it did. I believe it will happen to us.'

'I was never more sure of anything,' Xan told her quietly. 'I've waited for you a long time, but we're going to be together a much longer time.'

For the second time that night, he began to make love to her.

Catherine George was born in Wales, and early on developed a passion for reading which eventually fuelled her compulsion to write. Marriage to an engineer led to nine years in Brazil, but on his later travels the education of her son and daughter kept her in the UK. And instead of constant reading to pass her lonely evenings she began to write the first of her romantic novels. When not writing and reading she loves to cook, listen to opera, browse in antiques shops and walk the Labrador.

Look out for
LEGALLY HIS by Catherine George
in Modern Romance™, December 2001

REFORM OF THE RAKE

by

Catherine George

CHAPTER ONE

LOWRI gave her distinguished, grey-haired male customer a friendly, courteous smile, her amusement well hidden as she gift-wrapped expensive scraps of sexy underwear so very obviously intended for someone other than his wife. When he'd gone she exchanged a grin with her nearest colleague.

'End of the lunchtime rush?' She cast a hopeful eye round the suddenly deserted underwear department.

'Give it five minutes, then it'll be the afternoon surge of mothers and daughters.'

'Plain cotton for school,' agreed Lowri, tidying a rack of lacy silk teddies. 'I wish I hadn't taken early lunch—I'm starving already.'

'Then you'd better have tea with me later,' said a voice with a familiar, attractive lilt, and Lowri looked up in astonishment to meet a pair of blue eyes bright with accusation.

'Sarah!'

'In person. And I hope that blush is guilt, Lowri Morgan,' said her cousin, plainly incensed. 'What on earth are you doing here?'

'Working,' said Lowri lamely.

'I managed to puzzle that out for myself,' retorted Sarah. 'When did all this happen, may I ask? And why didn't you let me know?'

Lowri cast a hunted eye at some approaching customers. 'I meant to soon, cross my heart. Look, I can't talk now. I get a tea-break at three. Could you meet me upstairs at the coffee-shop?'

'You bet I could—ask for extra time.' Sarah fixed her

5

young cousin with a steely eye. 'You've got some explaining to do, young lady. In the meantime I'll take one of these in thirty-four. And I'll come back to collect you at three. Be ready.'

Lowri found the required size quickly, wrapped the purchase and took her cousin's money, promising to see her later, then dealt with a pack of skinny, black-clad girls in leather jackets, all demanding the same make of maximum-bounce, minimum-price bra. For the next hour or so Lowri sold underwear of every category from sensible cotton sports to shameless see-through numbers of the type she'd never possessed herself nor ever dared to. It was some time before she got the chance to beg an extra ten minutes to add on to her tea-break. She hurried back to her post afterwards to attend to a tall man who was contemplating a display of astronomically pricey trifles with no hint of the dogged embarrassment most male customers displayed in the same circumstances.

'May I help?' said Lowri, in her usual friendly manner.

He smiled down at her, gold-flecked hazel eyes glinting under a pair of thick, ruler-straight eyebrows. 'I'm sure you can,' he said in a deep, drawling voice which flowed over Lowri like warm honey. He waved a hand at the exquisite lace bras. 'I want two of these things, and the other bits to go with them—one set in thirty-six C, the other in thirty-two E.' He cast an assessing eye over the display. 'The first lot in that pinkish colour, I think, and the other one black. Mmm, yes, definitely black.'

Lowri swiftly located the required sizes, riven with envy for the recipients. 'The knickers come in two styles, sir, the brief and this type.' She pointed out a sexy lace G-string.

He grinned lazily. 'The brief in pink, the non-existent one in black.' He raised one of his distinctive eyebrows. 'You approve?'

Lowri nodded, pink-cheeked. 'A popular choice, sir. Would you like them gift-wrapped?'

Her customer, as she'd expected, not only wanted them gift-wrapped, but clearly marked as to which was which, a male request familiar to her after four hectic weeks in the underwear department. And normally Lowri prided herself on deftness and speed at gift-wrapping, but under the bright, amused scrutiny her fingers changed to thumbs, a condition which worsened as Sarah bore down on them, tapping the watch on her wrist.

Lowri threw her an apologetic smile, but Sarah was staring at the man tucking his credit card back into his wallet.

'Adam!' she said in surprise. 'What are you doing here?'

The man grinned and kissed her on both cheeks. 'What do you think I'm doing, Sarah? I'm buying underwear.' He shot a look at Lowri. 'And damned expensive it is in this place.'

Sarah raised an eyebrow at the tempting packages. 'I bet I know exactly what you chose, too.'

'The same stuff Rupert buys you, I imagine,' he said, the grin wider, and looked at his watch. 'Let me ply you with tea and sinful cakes upstairs.'

'Not today, thanks, Adam. I'm just about to feed my young cousin, Lowri, here. Lowri, this is Adam Hawkridge.'

Adam Hawkridge turned the bright gold eyes on Lowri again and held her hand rather longer than necessary as he gave her a white, mega-watt smile. 'How do you do, Lowri—a pleasure dealing with you. Let's all have tea together.'

To Lowri's intense disappointment Sarah refused briskly, telling Adam this was a girls-only bun-fight and she'd take a raincheck for another time. Wistfully, Lowri murmured something polite as Adam took his leave, then raced after him with the packages he'd forgotten.

'Your parcels, Mr Hawkridge!'

He swung round, smiling. 'Thank you. Pity about tea,' he added in an undertone. 'Another day, perhaps?'

Lowri blushed again, said something incoherent and hurried back to Sarah.

'Wow!' she said breathlessly. 'What a gorgeous man.'

Sarah shook her head emphatically. 'Not for you, love. Gorgeous he may be, but he's a notorious heartbreaker.'

'I wasn't thinking of *marrying* him,' said Lowri tartly. 'I'll just get my bag.'

Once they were settled at a corner table in the coffee-shop Sarah fixed her cousin with a commanding blue eye.

'Now,' she ordered. 'Talk! When did all this come about? Have you quarrelled with your father? Why haven't you been in touch—where are you living?'

Lowri bit into a profiterole with enthusiasm. 'I came up here a month ago, but no quarrel with Dad, since you ask. I'm squashed in with four other girls in a flat in Shepherds Bush *pro tem*, and I intended making contact soon, Sarah, really I did, but I—I wanted to get my bearings first.'

'Which doesn't explain why someone with perfectly good secretarial skills is selling underwear to earn a crust, Lowri Morgan,' said her cousin severely. 'I thought you had a steady job in Newport.'

'So did I. But my boss took early retirement, and bingo, no place for little Lowri.'

'Surely you could have found something in the same line?'

'Not easy. Besides—' Lowri shrugged, smiling wryly. 'It gave me the ideal excuse to get away. Right away.'

Sarah poured tea, frowning. 'You said no quarrel, but *are* there problems at home?'

'Only for me. Dad's in seventh heaven.' Lowri sighed guiltily. 'I keep telling myself my father's only forty-seven and very attractive and perfectly entitled to a second wife only a few years older than me. And I adore Holly. Really I do. But sharing a house with two newlyweds who can't keep their hands off each other—particularly when one of them is your father—is pretty hard to take, Sarah. I got a nice little cheque from my old firm in Newport, Dad gave me a bit more, and one of the girls I worked with knew someone who needed another flatmate up here, so I left the land of my fathers and managed to get this job pretty quickly, thank goodness. It's only part time, but it's financing me while I do some serious job-hunting.'

Sarah eyed her narrowly. 'And are you enjoying life more?'

Lowri pulled a face. 'I didn't at first. I was even feeble enough to feel homesick for a while. But I'm settling down now.'

'How did my favourite uncle take to the move?'

'Torn between objections to the idea, and euphoria at the prospect of privacy and solitude with Holly.'

'Are you jealous?'

Lowri thought it over. 'Not of Holly,' she said slowly. 'Only of what they've got together, I think. And Mum's been dead a long time. Dad deserves his happiness. Only I just couldn't stand playing gooseberry.' She smiled cheerfully. 'Anyway, enough about me. Tell me about Dominic and Emily—and that scrumptious husband of yours.'

'Rupert's the same, only more so.' Sarah smiled wryly. 'Up to his ears in his latest book and prone to vile moods when the flow doesn't flow, as usual. My son seems to have some of his father's brains, but a far sunnier disposition, thankfully, while Emily sails through life happy in the belief that everyone loves her.'

'Which they do!'

'Up to now,' agreed Sarah. 'But she starts proper school in the autumn, so things may change.' She gave Lowri a

militant look. 'I shall expect you for the day on Sunday—
no excuses.'

Lowri smiled happily and got to her feet. 'Try to keep
me away! Sundays in London can drag a bit.'

'Then why on earth didn't you get in touch before?'

'I didn't want to cadge, Sarah.'

'You, Lowri Morgan, are an idiot. But I understand—no
one better,' added Sarah, and kissed her. 'I was just the
same when I first came to the big city. Right, I'm off. Come
any time after breakfast on Sunday—or even before, if you
like.'

Lowri shook her head, chuckling. 'I'll come in time for
lunch—but thanks, Sal. I'll look forward to it.'

As she fought claustrophobia in the Underground on her
way home, then battled for tenancy of the bathroom later
that evening, Lowri's mood remained buoyant as she
thought of Sunday with the Clares in St John's Wood. Her
cousin Sarah, one of the three beautiful daughters of the
Reverend Glyn Morgan in Lowri's native village of
Cwmderwen, near Monmouth, was the wife of Rupert
Clare, a novelist bankable enough to sell film rights to his
books. Sunday would be fun. And she would enjoy it all
the more because she hadn't given in and invited herself
as she'd longed to do ever since her arrival in London.

The Clares' house in St John's Wood was a large, light-
filled house with a sizeable walled garden at the back, and
a converted coach house which housed the family cars on
the ground floor and provided a self-contained flat on the
floor above for Rupert's constant stream of secretaries, few
of whom stayed for long. After a heartwarming welcome
from Dominic and Emily, Lowri looked up to see Rupert
loping down the curve of the graceful staircase, hands out-
stretched, Sarah close behind him.

'Who's a sly one then, little cousin?' he said, shaking

his head, then gave her a hug and a smacking kiss. 'Escaped from the claws of the dragon, I hear!'

'If that's your way of saying I've left home, yes.' She grinned up at her cousin's charismatic husband. 'Hello, Rupert, nice to see you.'

'You wouldn't say that if you'd had to live with him this week,' said Sarah with feeling. 'Mrs Parks is not only the least efficient secretary Rupert's ever had but also the most timorous, which brings out the sadist in him. She's driving the great author mad. And I flatly refuse to take over from her—but you don't want to hear about that. Come into the conservatory. We'll picnic in there to enjoy the April sunshine.'

With Emily clinging to her hand, and Dominic telling her all about the new school he was going to shortly, Lowri basked in the glow of Clare hospitality as she leaned back in a comfortable wicker chair, sipping happily from a tall frosted glass decorated with mint and slices of fruit.

'Pimms for us, fruit juice for the small fry,' said Rupert, handing a beaker to his daughter. 'You, Dominic, are promoted to the dignity of a glass.'

'Gee thanks,' said his son with sarcasm. 'Couldn't I have just a sip of Pimms, Dad?'

'No fear,' said his mother, smiling to soften the blow. 'There's the doorbell. Off you go to answer it, please.'

'Mummy says you live in London now,' said Emily, beaming up at Lowri. 'Why aren't you living with us?'

'I've got a flat,' said Lowri hastily, and Rupert snorted. 'Fifth share of one, I hear.'

'One girl is moving out next week, thank goodness.' Lowri pulled a face. 'Which means my rent will rise, but at least I'll get a room with a wardrobe, and more chance of the bathroom.' Her eyes narrowed suddenly at the sound of voices in the hall. One of them was vaguely familiar. She threw a questioning look at her cousin.

'We've got two other guests today, love,' explained Sarah. 'After I met Adam Hawkridge in your shop the other afternoon he rang up and invited us out to something he calls brunch today. I told him we had company and asked him here instead, which meant including the current girl-friend, as usual.'

As Dominic showed the new guests into the conservatory Lowri got to her feet politely, wishing she'd worn something smarter than jeans and a striped cotton shirt as she shook hands with a leggy, narrow-hipped blonde encased in a ribbed white cashmere dress which drew all eyes to her startlingly prominent breasts. Adam Hawkridge, Lowri was relieved to see, wore jeans older than her own, plus a sweater over an open-necked shirt. He smiled at Lowri in gratifying recognition.

'Well, well—the little cousin!' He clasped her hand warmly. 'This is my friend, Fiona Childe.'

Lowri murmured something suitable, then watched, amused, as the girl gushed over the house to Sarah, cooed at the children briefly then turned the full battery of her charms on Rupert.

'Miss Thirty-two E, black lace,' murmured a deep voice in Lowri's ear, and she stiffened, swallowing a giggle.

'Not today,' she couldn't help whispering. 'It would show through.'

'Really?' Adam grinned down at her as he accepted a drink from Rupert. 'How very interesting.'

'What's interesting?' demanded Emily.

'You are,' said Adam promptly and sat down with Emily on his knee, stretching out a hand to Dominic at the same time. 'Right then, you two, tell me what you've been up to.'

This man is preposterously attractive, thought Lowri as she watched him charm the children. Taken feature by fea-ture, his heavy eyebrows and wide, slightly crooked mouth had no pretensions to good looks, and his forceful nose had suffered a dent at some time, but somehow the sum of it all added up to something irresistible. And quite apart from his looks Adam Hawkridge possessed effortless charm all the more powerful for the hint of steel under it all. Rake he might be, but a potently attractive one in every way, thought Lowri as she listened to the inanities Fiona was burbling about her hairdresser.

'That's a frightfully clever cut—where do you have yours done?' she asked, eyeing Lowri's boyish crop with interest. 'Is the colour natural or do you have it tinted?'

'Sloe-black, crow-black Welsh hair like Sarah's,' Rupert informed her.

'There's a man in the hair salon where I work,' explained Lowri. 'He did it half-price for me.'

'You're a hairdresser?' exclaimed Fiona, flabbergasted.

'No, I sell underwear.'

'In the West End, not door to door,' added Rupert, poker-faced.

'How fascinating,' said Fiona blankly, losing all interest in Lowri on the spot.

Adam Hawkridge, however, more than made up for the deficit. During the meal he installed himself next to Lowri, asking her all kinds of questions about herself in between telling Dominic and Emily about his recent trip to Japan.

'How's your father?' asked Rupert later, refilling wine-glasses.

'Retiring soon,' said Adam, sobering a little.

'Does that mean you'll be in charge of the company?' asked Sarah.

'Afraid so. All good things come to an end, so no more globe-trotting for yours truly. I'll be a desk-bound sober citizen at last.' He grinned challengingly. 'Did I hear someone say ''about time''?'

Fiona tossed back her hair, pouting. 'Does that mean no more Ascot and Henley and so on?'

'Afraid so—to the first two, anyway.' The hazel eyes gleamed suggestively. 'I might be able to fit in a bit of so-on now and again, perhaps.'

Fiona gave a little scream of laughter. 'O-o-o-h, Adam!'

Sarah and Lowri sprang up simultaneously to clear away, avoiding each other's eyes. They refused offers of help from the men, who went out into the garden with the children to play cricket, while Fiona remained firmly where she was, reclining on a wicker chaise with a pile of magazines.

'What does he see in her?' said Sarah in disapproval as she loaded the dishwasher.

'Oh come on, Sal, two reasons hit you in the eye! She's the black lace thirty-two E I sold him that day. Adam told me.' Lowri grinned as she stored salad in a plastic container. 'Mind you he's got someone else on the go, too. He bought the same things in angel blush, thirty-six C.'

'Typical! Next week he'll probably be back for more of the same in two quite different sizes.'

'Why do men go unfailingly for sexy underwear, I wonder? Does Rupert?'

Sarah nodded. 'Pretty pointless, really.'

Lowri eyed her cousin curiously. 'Why?'

'Because the minute a man sees you decked out in that stuff he wants to take it off, of course!'

Lowri blushed to the roots of her hair.

Sarah eyed her narrowly. 'Ah! You've already discovered that for yourself.'

'Only once.'

'Not a happy experience?'

'No. My social life was pretty uncomplicated up to then, just enjoying dates with blokes I'd been to school with, and one or two men I'd met through my job. Then disaster struck. I got emotionally involved.'

'What happened?'

'Not a lot. The object of my affections forgot to mention he was married, the pig. It put me off men for a while. And since I've come up to London I haven't met anyone at all.' Lowri smiled ruefully. 'I hoped I would, to be honest. But so far the streets of London aren't exactly paved with eligible males eager to buy me romantic dinners.'

'Oh, dear, oh, dear, we'll have to do something about you,' said Sarah, the light of battle in her eye. 'I'll ask Rupert—'

'No, you won't,' interrupted Lowri promptly, 'I came up to London to manage my own life, remember. Let me have a go at it for a bit on my own, please, Sal.'

Sarah patted her cheek. 'Sorry—interfering again. Come on, let's drag Miss Thirty-two E into the garden for some cricket.'

But Fiona refused to budge, too careful of her hairdo to set foot outside the conservatory. Sarah and Lowri left her to her magazines and went to join in some energetic fielding while the menfolk batted, bowled and kept wicket in turn.

'How about you, Lowri?' asked Adam, offering the bat to her. 'Fancy your chances?'

'I don't mind having a try,' she said demurely, and let him show her how to grip the handle correctly. She winked at Dominic, who grinned from ear to ear as Adam jogged down the lawn ready to deliver a nice, easy ball to the beginner. Rupert, hunkered down behind her to keep wicket, smothered a laugh as Lowri danced down the wicket to the tame delivery, smashing it away into the shrubbery with a perfect forward drive.

Adam stared, open-mouthed as Dominic raced to retrieve it. 'I see, I see,' he said ominously, scowling at Lowri.

'Having me on, were you?' He put up a hand to catch the ball then came sprinting down the wicket in earnest, letting fly a full toss which Lowri swiped over his head with ease to wild applause from the four Clares. She dealt with his three successive deliveries with equal disrespect, until she grew careless and lofted a ball which Dominic sprang up and took spectacularly with one hand, winning concerted applause all round, loudest of all from the bowler.

Adam came sprinting towards Lowri, his eyes hot with accusation. 'Don't tell me that was beginner's luck!'

'Nah!' said Dominic scornfully. 'Her Dad's captain of the village cricket team where Lowri comes from. He taught her to play cricket when she was littler than Emily.'

'No son, you see,' said Lowri apologetically. 'Dad had to teach his skills to me. Not,' she added, 'that I get to use them much.'

Adam grinned. 'Did he teach you to bowl, too?'

'Only tame medium pace stuff.'

He handed her the ball. 'Right. Come on, then.'

'It's my turn to bat,' pointed out Rupert, aggrieved, as Adam took his stance in front of the wicket.

'Later—I want my revenge first!'

But Adam, swiping mightily at the third ball Lowri delivered, sent it straight through the window in the coach house office in a hail of broken glass, bringing the match to an early close.

Astonished by the howls of laughter from her hosts, Fiona burst from the conservatory to hurl recriminations at Adam, winning her deep disapproval from Emily, who slid a small comforting hand into his large one in consolation as he apologised profusely.

'Don't worry—Mrs Parks can type in the conservatory tomorrow,' said Rupert, clapping him on the shoulder.

With promises to settle the bill for the damage, Adam took reluctant leave, prompted by a petulant reminder from

Fiona that they were expected for dinner elsewhere that night. Despite her urgings he took his time in parting from Dominic and Emily, even contriving a private word with Lowri while Fiona went upstairs to make unnecessary repairs to her face.

'For a pint-sized lady,' he said, his eyes glinting, 'you pack an almighty wallop, Lowri Morgan.'

'It comes in useful from time to time,' she admitted demurely.

'For beating off importunate lovers?'

'Not too many of those around,' she said candidly.

Adam Hawkridge shook his shiny brown hair back, frowning. 'Why not?'

'I wish I knew,' she said without thinking, then regretted it as she saw the gleam in his eyes.

'It's not personal preference, then? You don't have anything deep-seated against my sex?'

'Not too deep-seated, no,' she said warily.

'Splendid.' He smiled and shook her hand. 'I'm very glad Sarah invited me here today. Goodbye, little cousin.'

Lowri, pressed to stay for supper once the others had left, accepted with alacrity. She helped Emily get ready for bed, read her a story, then gave Sarah a hand with the meal, which Dominic was allowed to share before he too went off to bed and left the other three alone. Lowri found herself listening with shameless avidity when Sarah and Rupert discussed Adam Hawkridge's future destiny as they lingered over coffee round the kitchen table.

'A bit of a playboy, our Adam,' mused Rupert, 'but a brilliant electronics engineer just the same, with a definite flair for marketing. He'll fill his father's shoes very ably—far more than his brother would have done.'

'Rupert was in school with Peter Hawkridge,' explained Sarah.

'I often spent part of the holidays with his family,' added Rupert. 'Adam was only a kid in those days, of course. Can't be much more than early thirties even now. He's packed such a lot in his life that one tends to forget his youth.'

'Why isn't his brother taking over the business?' asked Lowri.

'He's dead, pet. Smashed himself up in his car when his wife went off with another man. Adam was at Harvard Business School at the time.'

'Gosh, how tragic. What sort of business is it?' added Lowri, trying not to sound too interested.

'Hawke Electronics rents software to a worldwide clientele. Adam's father built the company from scratch, and believes in ploughing back a fair percentage on research and development.' Rupert held out his cup for more coffee. 'And since Adam's return from the States the number of software programmes they provide has tripled. He's one bright cookie, our Adam. Dan Hawkridge is damn lucky to have such an able son to follow in his footsteps.'

'Adam switched off a bit at the prospect at lunch, though, wouldn't you say?' said Sarah, joining her husband on the sofa.

Rupert put his arm round her. 'The weight of future responsibility, I suppose. Once Adam's in charge, Dan's taking his wife off on the world cruise he's promised her.'

'In the meantime Adam will work his way through as many Fiona types as possible, I suppose, before he knuckles down,' said Sarah acidly.

'Does his taste always run to brainless blondes?' asked Lowri, chuckling.

'I don't think our Adam specifies hair colour, precisely. His women do tend to be leggy and well endowed in the bosom department, now I come to think of it. Why?' added Sarah in alarm. 'You're not thinking—?'

'No, of course not,' said Lowri promptly. 'I'm neither leggy nor blonde, remember. I like Adam, that's all. Dominic and Emily like him, too.'

'They dote on him,' agreed their mother. 'Adam will make a good father when he's ready. Retired rakes always do.' She smiled up at Rupert. 'As I know from experience!'

CHAPTER TWO

LOWRI had very little time for daydreams about Adam Hawkridge next day. The department was short-staffed due to influenza, and she was run off her feet during working hours. When she got back to the flat, weary and footsore, she forced herself to do a thorough cleaning job on the room vacated that day by the outgoing occupant, spent the evening arranging her things, then took a much needed shower before allowing herself the luxury of something to eat.

As Lowri emerged from the bathroom, Barbara, the owner of the flat, told her she was wanted on the phone. 'Man. Very attractive voice.'

Lowrie flew to the telephone, blushing unseen at her own disappointment when she heard her father's resonant tones. She assured him she was fine, told him about her day with Sarah, promised to ring more often and sent her love to Holly, at which Geraint Morgan coughed, hummed and hawed and finally blurted out the reason for his telephone call. Holly was pregnant. Lowri would soon have a little brother or sister.

Lowri congratulated her father enthusiastically, assured him she was overjoyed, then put the receiver down feeling rather odd. Deciding it was lack of food, she made herself scrambled eggs in the poky, chaotic kitchen, added a pot of tea and took her tray back to her room, in no mood now to join the others in the communal sitting-room. Later she rang Sarah to share the news.

'You sound shattered,' said Sarah bluntly.

'I am, a bit. I'm really very happy for Dad, but it was a bit of a body-blow, just the same.'

'Only natural. You two were so close after your mother died. Not your usual father/daughter arrangement.'

'Sorry to moan at you, but I had to talk to someone.'

'I'm glad you did—I can moan at you in exchange. Rupert's Mrs Parks threw a wobbly today.'

'Why?'

'It started with the broken window in the office and the move into the conservatory while it was mended. Then Rupert topped it off with twice as much work as usual this morning because he was struck with inspiration last night and dictated into his machine into the small hours—'

'Sarah, can't you think of a way to keep him in bed?' gurgled Lowri. 'I'll get you a sexy nightie at cost, if you like.'

'Don't be rude!' Sarah retorted, then sighed heavily. 'Anyway, Mrs Parks has taken herself off, vowing never to darken our door again, and I'm saddled with the typing, heaven help me. I don't know how I ever coped with working for Rupert in the old days before we got married—too besotted with him to mind all the fireworks, I suppose.'

'Can I help? I get Friday and Saturday off this week. I could lend a hand then, if you like.'

'Oh, Lowri, *would* you? Rupert pays well—'

'I don't need money!'

'Of course you need money. Don't be a goose. Anyway we'll sort that out when you come.'

In the end Sarah insisted Lowri come for a meal on the Thursday evening and stay the night, fresh for work in the morning. Lowri needed little persuasion. A couple of days' typing for Rupert was a small price to pay for a stay in the airy, comfortable house in St John's Wood.

The coach house window was intact, and the comfortable little office behind it in perfect order when Lowri settled

down to start work on Rupert Clare's current novel a few
days later.

'First of all,' advised Rupert, 'read through the draft so
far. Sarah's printed the disks Mrs Parks typed, so spend
this morning familiarising yourself with the characters and
the plot. There's a kettle and coffee and so on in the other
room when you take a break, but come over to the house
for lunch before you start on any typing.'

Lowri, long one of his most ardent fans, smiled happily.
'Right, boss. I'm looking forward to a sneak preview of
the latest Rupert Clare bestseller—nice work if you can get
it!'

'It may not be a bestseller,' he said gloomily. 'I'm tackling a new period for me in this one: dark deeds in fog-
bound Victorian London.'

Lowri breathed in a sigh of pleasure. 'Sounds great to
me.' She rustled the sheaf of papers on the desk. 'Right
then, eyes down and looking for the next hour or so.'

The story gripped her so completely from the first paragraph that Lowri hardly noticed Rupert leave, and looked
up at Sarah blankly when her cousin appeared a couple of
hours later to announce that lunch was ready.

'Lunch?'

'Yes, you know—soup, sandwiches, stuff like that,' said
Sarah, laughing, then frowned. 'No cups? Didn't Rupert tell
you to make yourself some coffee?'

Lowri bit her lip guiltily. 'He did, but I forgot. I was so
absorbed I didn't notice the time.'

'That's a novelty! Mrs Parks could never work for more
than half an hour at a time without a dose of caffeine to
keep her going.'

Lowri stood up, stretching. 'Sounds as though the lady's
no loss.'

'She will be to me if I have to stand in for her,' said
Sarah with emphasis. 'Come on. Dominic's in school,

Emily's gone off to spend the afternoon with her chum, and Rupert's having lunch with his agent so it's just the two of us.'

It was pleasant to gossip with Sarah over the meal but Lowri was adamant about returning to the office after half an hour, eager to finish the first portion of the draft so she could start on the real work of typing up Rupert's next tapes. The novel, which bore all the hallmarks of Rupert's style in the vivid characterisation and complex, convoluted plot, was an atmospheric story of revenge.

'It's riveting,' said Lowri, as she finished her coffee. 'All that underworld vice simmering away behind a façade of rigid Victorian respectability. I can't wait to find out Jonah Haldane's secret!'

Lowri's enthusiasm resulted in more progress in one afternoon than the less industrious Mrs Parks had achieved in the two previous working days. When Rupert came to blow the whistle at six that evening he was deeply impressed, and obviously found Lowri's reluctance to call a halt deeply gratifying.

'Enough's enough for one day, nevertheless, little cousin,' he said firmly. 'Sarah says you're to pack it in, have a bath, then if you can bear it, read a story to Emily. We had to promise her that to keep her from storming your citadel hours ago.'

'Of course I will,' said Lowri, stretching. 'Though something a bit different from yours, Rupert.' She shivered pleasurably. 'It's a bit terrifying in places.'

'Sarah says you like it.'

'Like it! I can't wait to see what happens next.'

'You're very good for my ego, Lowri,' said Rupert as he walked with her across the garden. 'A little sincere encouragement does wonders. Writers get bloody depressed some days.'

'You needn't,' returned Lowri with certainty. 'This is

your best ever, Rupert. And I should know. I've read every book you've written.'

He gave her a friendly hug and pushed her into the kitchen, where Emily and Dominic were eating supper while Sarah clattered saucepans on hobs set into an island which gave her a view of the large kitchen while she worked. At the triple welcome showered on her Lowri felt suddenly enveloped in something missing in her life since her father had married again: a sense of belonging.

'About time you knocked off,' said Sarah, waving a wooden spoon. 'The idea was to help Rupert out a bit, not work yourself to death, Lowri Morgan.'

When Lowri was packed and ready to return to Shepherds Bush, Rupert fixed Lowri with a commanding green eye.

'Sarah and I have a suggestion to make. Feel free to refuse if you want, but hear me out.'

Lowri looked from one to the other, her dark eyes questioning. 'I'm all ears.'

'It's about the work you've been doing for me—'

'Something wrong?'

'Wrong!' snorted Sarah. 'The exact opposite, Lowri. I'm the only one who's ever worked so well with Rupert. Though you haven't seen him in a tantrum yet,' she warned.

'Tantrum?' said Rupert, incensed. 'I may be subject to the odd mood—'

'Your moods are not odd, they're horrible,' corrected his wife flatly. 'Anyway, Lowri, the gist of all this is that if you're not totally dedicated to selling knickers Rupert wondered if you'd fancy working for him full time.'

Lowri's eyes lit up like stars. 'You mean it?'

'You bet your sweet life I do,' said Rupert emphatically. 'And what's more, you can pack in that flat and come and live here with us.'

'But I couldn't impose on you like that,' said Lowri swiftly.

'Not even in the coach house flat?' said Sarah, smiling. 'You can be as private as you like over there, live entirely your own life as much as you want, or be part of ours whenever the fancy takes you. We'd even take a small rent for the flat if it would make you feel any better.'

'Are you doing this because you feel sorry for me?' asked Lowri suspiciously.

'Don't talk rubbish!' Rupert patted her shoulder. 'It's you who'd be taking pity on me. I'm offering you the job, Lowri, because you do it so well. Better than anyone since the reign of my lady wife here. *And* you won't have hysterics if—when—I shout at you. Because shout I will when things go wrong, believe me. So before you answer you'd better think that bit over. But if you can stand my moods, and you fancy the job, how about it?'

From the day she moved her possessions into the Clares' coach house life was transformed for Lowri. The bed-sitting-room adjoining her little office was a comfortable little apartment, complete with bathroom and a minuscule kitchen just large enough for Lowri to cook a meal for one occasionally. After the flat in Shepherds Bush the privacy was wonderful, unmarred by the slightest tinge of loneliness, since at any time Lowri knew she could stroll down the long, beautiful garden to a warm welcome in the house. This, however, was a privilege Lowri rationed herself strictly from the start.

But there were definite advantages for the Clares in the situation, nevertheless, since Lowri was happy to act as baby-sitter when the busy social life of the Clares demanded it. Since the retirement of Mrs Dobson, Rupert's original treasure of a housekeeper, Sarah had taken on Brenda, who came in daily to help with the house. But

Brenda enjoyed a hectic social life, and wasn't keen on
baby-sitting too often in the evenings, which left a gap
Lowri was only too glad to fill.

As the horse-chestnuts came into bloom and a green
smell of spring came floating through her open office window, Lowri felt that fate had been very kind to her indeed.
She sniffed at the heady vanilla scent of trees in blossom
and heaved a contented sigh as she applied herself to the
work which grew more absorbing by the day. The novel
was now in its third quarter and working up suspensefully
to the climax which Rupert flatly refused to reveal to Lowri
in advance. Not even Sarah was any wiser, which apparently was nothing unusual. Rupert liked to keep his plot to
himself until the very last sentence was recorded on tape.

Then one weekend Lowri's presence as a guest was commanded at one of Sarah's parties. And the tempo of life
quickened again.

Lowri had helped out during the day, mainly by taking
charge of Emily while Sarah concocted delicious cold
dishes for the party meal, but once Dominic and Emily had
eaten supper and the latter was settled in bed with a story
Lowri dashed back to her flat to get ready, tingling with
anticipation. She had a new, flattering black dress to wear,
bought with her first cheque from Rupert, but, most important of all, Adam Hawkridge would be one of the guests.

The party, as always at the Clare home, was a lively,
entertaining occasion from the start, and Lowri, circulating
with platters of canapés, no longer felt shy as she mingled
because so many of the guests were already well known to
her by this time. Sarah, stunning in a plain white dress with
turquoise and diamond hoops in her ears, her black hair
coiled high on her head, was in her element at Rupert's
side as they welcomed their guests, most of whom had
some literary connection. But the guest who had none was
nowhere in sight. Adam Hawkridge was late. Lowri found

it hard to stop watching the door, but when he finally put in an appearance her heart sank at the sight of his tall, blonde companion. When he noticed Lowri his face lit with the familiar, blazing smile, and he threaded his across the crowded room towards her, leaving the voluptuous blonde with Rupert and Sarah, and another man new to Lowri.

'Hello, Lowri!' He squeezed her hand and took the silver dish from her, dumping it unceremoniously on the nearest table. 'How's the little cousin? Are you enjoying the new job? Is Rupert a despot to work for?'

'Hello—Adam,' responded Lowri shyly. 'I'm fine, the work is fascinating, and so far Rupert's very kind.'

'And so he should be.' He kept hold of her hand to take her across the room. 'Come and meet Caroline.'

'Where's Fiona?'

'Haven't the foggiest,' he returned carelessly. 'Out partying with some other guy, at a guess.'

When they joined the others Adam barely had time to make introductions before the man with Caroline moved in on Lowri with practiced expertise.

'I'm Guy Seton, Caroline's brother,' he announced, and took Lowri by the hand. 'Afraid I'm a gate-crasher. The delightful Mrs Clare assures me she doesn't mind.'

Lowri gazed into a pair of narrow, hot dark eyes under hair almost as fair as the sexy Caroline's, and felt an odd pang of apprehension. Guy Seton exuded such restless energy that he made her feel uneasy.

Rupert, who obviously did object to the gatecrasher, smiled warmly at Lowri. 'So there you are, little cousin,' he said, with emphasis on the relationship. 'Having a good time?'

'Too busy handing round food for that,' said Sarah, and flapped a hand at Lowri. 'Leave all that now. Brenda will help with supper.'

To her annoyance Lowri found herself neatly separated

from the rest by Guy Seton. Adam, who had momentarily deserted Caroline for a delighted redhead on the far side of the room, spared a disapproving frown for Guy's manoeuvre, Lowri noted wistfully, as the latter hurried her through the open French windows on to the terrace outside. The slim, restless man perched on the stone balustrade, one leg swinging as he patted the place beside him.

'Come. Tell me your life story, little Welsh cousin. Was your father a fan of matchstick men—is that how you got your name?'

Lowri perched uneasily beside him, not at all happy about finding a constricting arm round her waist. 'No. Mine's spelt with a final "i"—Welsh for Laura, nothing to do with Lowry the artist. And my life-story isn't interesting in the slightest.'

'You interest me a bloody sight more than the so-called literati in there.' His arm tightened. 'What's a nice little Welsh maiden like you doing in the big city, Lowri with an "i"?'

She sat rigid in his clasp, disliking the innuendo he managed to inject into the word 'maiden'. 'I work for Rupert.'

'Lucky Rupert.'

Lowri shifted uncomfortably, but Guy Seton held her fast. 'Don't be frightened, poppet,' he said, chuckling. 'I shan't eat you.'

'Which reminds me—there's a perfectly good supper waiting inside,' she said firmly, and disengaged herself. 'Shall we go and sample some of it?'

Guy Seton possessed a thick skin, she found, quite impervious to her unsubtle hints that his monopoly of her company wasn't welcome. He stuck to her side like glue, and short of causing a scene there was nothing she could do about it. Something about his hectic, almost feverish attentions filled her with unease. Lowri had no illusions about her looks. She was more rounded than she would have liked for her lack of inches, and regarded her large, dark eyes as her only redeeming feature. Besides, she had good reason to distrust a sudden rush of attention like Guy Seton's, wary of men who came at the gallop after only one glance. And by staying so close all the time Guy was destroying her hopes of a chat with Adam at some stage. Not, she noted, depressed, that there was much chance of that. Adam had now returned his attentions to the sultry Caroline, who was smouldering up at him in a way which made it obvious she wanted him to round off the evening in her bed.

'Are you a friend of Adam's?' she asked Guy, her eyes on the absorbed couple across the room.

'Not a friend, precisely,' said Guy. His mouth thinned as he followed her gaze. 'I was in school with him. He's Caroline's "friend". She's crazy about him. Women flock round Hawkridge in droves. Can't think why. He's no oil painting.'

'No,' agreed Lowri. 'He's not.' But he's twice as attractive as you, Guy Seton, she added silently, because he's got warmth. You're a cold fish, I think, for all the burning glances and febrile charm.

'Caro's so blatantly panting to share Hawkridge's bed I'm amazed she insisted I came with them tonight. But I'm glad I did.' Guy gave her a smile of confident intimacy. 'Instead of playing gooseberry to those two, I can take you home instead.'

Lowri's answering smile was frosty. 'No need. I live here.'

'Hell.' He scowled. 'That's a blow.' He eyed her up and down, his eyes undressing her. 'Rupert Clare's bloody lucky, having two gorgeous women at his disposal under the same roof.'

Enough was enough. Lowri glared at him. 'I'm very fond of Rupert, but I live in the coach house to be precise, not under his roof. Nor am I at *anyone's* disposal.' She thrust her empty glass in his hand. 'Goodnight, Mr Seton.' And without another word she hurried through the hall to the kitchen and slammed the door shut behind her.

'What's up?' Brenda looked up from loading the dishwasher in surprise. 'Someone ruffle your feathers out there?'

'Someone certainly did,' said Lowri, seething. 'Any coffee going, Brenda? I'll give you a hand to clear away.'

'Coming up, love,' said Brenda, filling the kettle. 'Won't say no to a bit of help. Terry's coming for me in half an hour—mustn't keep him waiting.'

'Terry?' said Lowri, laughing. 'What happened to Wayne?'

Brenda winked, thrusting a hand through her spiky blonde hair. 'What he doesn't know about he won't grieve over, eh?'

A few minutes later Lowri stole along the pergola lining the path which led to the coach house. She gained her little sanctum with a sigh, partly of relief for eluding the disturbing Mr Seton, but mostly of regret for having so little opportunity to talk to Adam. Which was stupid, she told herself as she hung up the black dress. Any time he'd had to spare from Caroline had been spent on the redhead with the cleavage. She cleaned off her make-up irritably, rubbed some moisturiser into her olive skin, gave her lengthening hair a good brush and got into a nightshirt and the vividly embroidered black silk kimona her father and Holly had given her for Christmas, by which time she felt ominously wide awake. She slid into bed and reached for a well-thumbed copy of *Northanger Abbey*. Jane Austen's dry wit rarely failed to soothe, and with a sigh Lowri banked up her pillows, settled herself comfortably and put thoughts of Adam and the annoying Mr Seton firmly from her as she settled down to read.

She was halfway through the first chapter when a knock on the outer door brought Lowri bolt upright. She sprang off the bed, startled, and went out through the office, certain it must be Sarah or Rupert with some emergency. She unlocked the door then screeched in fright as Guy Seton pushed her back inside the office, slammed the door shut and stood with his back to it, a wild look about him which scared her rigid.

'Now, now, Lowri,' he said menacingly. 'This isn't at all friendly, is it? I need some comfort, some tender loving care, sweetheart.'

'Well, you won't get it from me!' she snapped. 'You shouldn't be here.'

'Why not? I asked if I could see you home. And here you are, and so am I. Let's party!' He stalked towards her, the restless, feverish aura about him now so pronounced that Lowri could have kicked herself for not recognising the cause sooner. Her unwanted visitor was obviously high on something a lot more dangerous than champagne.

'Guy, please,' she said, backing away. She tried to smile. 'It's late and I'm tired—'

'Then come to bed,' he said hoarsely, and reached for her.

Lowri fought him off savagely, but despite his slim build Guy Seton was strong; deceptively so. He managed to drag her, kicking and struggling, into the bedroom and on to her bed. Beside herself with rage, Lowri twisted and turned like an eel, her nails raking down his face, her teeth sinking into the mouth crushing hers, and Guy let out a howl and drew back, face contorted, clenched fist raised. Then suddenly he was flat out on the floor, felled by a savage blow from Adam Hawkridge, who stepped over the unconscious man without a second look, and hauled Lowri into his arms.

'Are you all right? Did that bastard hurt you?' he barked.

Her teeth were chattering so much Lowri found it hard

to reassure him that apart from the odd bruise and the fright of her life she was fine.

'How—how did you know—?' she gasped.

'Caroline was ready to go home and insisted her blasted brother go with us. When I couldn't find him I made an educated guess. Thank the lord I did,' he added harshly, and tipped her face up to his. 'Were you saying the truth? He didn't—harm you?'

Lowri's face flamed. 'If you mean did he rape me, *no*! And I didn't lead him on, either—I swear I didn't.' Tears of reaction slid down her face. 'I just don't understand it. He stuck to me like glue all evening. In the end I got so fed up I escaped and came back here. But—' she gulped. 'He followed me. That's it, you know the rest.'

Adam held her close, patting her as though she were Emily. 'There, there, it's all over now. Shall I fetch Sarah?'

'No! And for heaven's sake don't say a word to Rupert, either.' She grimaced at the thought. 'His explosion threshold's a bit low, as you know. Let them finish the party in peace.' A convulsive shudder ran through her. She swallowed a sob and Adam's arms tightened.

He cursed under his breath and turned her face up to his. 'Don't, little one,' he said urgently, 'you're safe now.'

As her tear-wet eyes met his Lowri's heart gave a sudden thump and she breathed in sharply. For a moment they were utterly still, then Adam bent his head involuntarily to kiss her, the inflammatory effect of the contact so unexpected it took both of them by surprise. Lowri's lips parted to the sudden seeking of his tongue and Adam's arm tightened, his free hand cupping her head to hold her still as he kissed her with a fierce heat quite different from the comfort she knew was all he'd intended.

When he let her go, several earth-shattering moments later, Lowri almost staggered.

'Hell and damnation!' he said bitterly. 'I'm no better than Seton.'

Lowri blinked, dazed, trying to smile. 'Don't say that. You—you were just comforting me.'

Adam's eyebrows rose. 'Was I, Lowri?'

She flushed, and looked away, biting her lip in sudden disgust as she caught sight of Guy Seton, still out to the world on her bedroom floor. 'Ugh! What shall we do about—about that?'

For answer Adam bent down and slung the unconscious man over his shoulder with negligent ease. 'I'll just dump him in the back of the car and collect Caroline. I'll have to put her in the picture, I'm afraid, but no one else need know.' He manoeuvred Guy Seton's body through into the office, motioning Lowri to open the outer door. 'Is the coast clear?'

She peered around outside, nodded, then smiled up at him ruefully. 'I'm deeply grateful to you, Adam. I rather fancy you saved me from a fate worse than death.'

Adam gave her a sombre look. 'I feel responsible. I brought the bastard here tonight, after all. I'm very sorry, Lowri. For everything.' He paused a moment, a sudden, irrepressible gleam in his eyes. 'Well perhaps not *quite* everything,' he amended, grinning, and hefted his unconscious burden more securely, waved his free hand, then made his way down the outer stair and disappeared through the gate in the wall.

When he was out of sight Lowri locked her door and shot the bolts into place, then stripped her bed and put clean sheets on it, thrusting thoughts of Adam's kisses from her mind by concentrating fiercely on the debt she owed him. Without his timely appearance there could have been a great deal more to put right in her life than a mere change of bedlinen.

CHAPTER THREE

AFTER a restless night Lowri slept late next morning, and awoke at last to loud knocking on the office door. She jumped out of bed, pulling on her kimono.

'Coming!' she called, wincing at the pounding in her head, and went to the door to admit Dominic.

'Mum says will you come over? You've had a telephone call.' He eyed her in surprise. 'Gosh, Lowri, what a shiner! How did you get that?'

Since Lowri could barely see out of one eye, the question came as no surprise. 'I bumped into something,' she said with perfect truth. Guy Seton's elbow had rammed her eye while she was fighting him off. She smiled at Dominic. 'Tell Mum I'll be there as soon as I've dressed. I've been lazy this morning.'

One look in the bathroom mirror told her that trying to keep last night's events from Sarah would be a complete waste of time. The truth, Lowri thought, resigned, will out whether I want it to or not. She frowned, realising she'd forgotten to ask Dominic who'd rung her.

Later, dressed in jeans and an old checked shirt, Lowri put on dark glasses to shield her eye from the bright sunshine and crossed the garden to join Sarah and Rupert in the kitchen.

'Good morning,' she said, smiling brightly. 'Where's Emily?'

'Dominic's keeping her amused until you've told us about the black eye,' said Sarah promptly, pouring coffee.

Rupert plucked the glasses from Lowri and whistled.

'Hell's bells!' his eyes narrowed dangerously. 'Right. Tell me who did that, Lowri—now!'

'First tell me who rang,' she said quickly to divert him.

'It was Adam,' said Sarah, 'He's coming round later to take you out to lunch.' She eyed Lowri militantly. 'But never mind that—how on earth did you get that shiner?'

Lowri, trying to appear unaffected by the news that Adam intended taking her out, drank some coffee and gave a terse account of the encounter with Guy Seton. 'So you don't have to do battle for me,' she told an incensed Rupert at the end of it. 'Adam knocked Guy Seton cold last night on the spot. The man probably looks—and feels—far worse than I do this morning.'

'I should bloody well hope he does,' said Rupert savagely.

'Is the eye the only damage?' demanded Sarah urgently.

'Yes. Adam arrived on the scene before Guy could have his wicked way with me.' Lowri held out her cup for more coffee. 'But it beats me why the wretched man should have been so intent on getting it. I'm not the type who drives men wild, now am I!'

'You obviously appealed to Seton.' Rupert scowled. 'He took one look and kept sniffing round you all night. I would have done something about it, but he's quite attractive, I suppose. You might have wanted it that way.'

'I told you she wouldn't,' said Sarah with scorn. 'Guy Seton's bad news where women are concerned.'

'Another heartbreaker, like Adam Hawkridge?' asked Lowri slyly.

'Adam would never be so crass as to assault anyone,' said Sarah indignantly. 'Guy was in school with Adam, I admit, but otherwise he's not in the same class.'

'Beats me what he was doing here at all.' Rupert's jaw set. 'I'll have a word with Adam, find out why the devil he brought the chap along in the first place.'

'Caroline's idea, probably—Adam seems fairly smitten in that direction from what I could see,' said Sarah, and pushed a toast-rack towards Lowri. 'Eat something.'

'I'm not hungry.'

'Possibly not, but if you drink any more black coffee on an empty stomach you'll rattle like a castanet.'

Lowri gave in, and felt a little better afterwards, though angry with a fate which gave her a black eye for her lunch date with Adam Hawkridge. Any other time she'd have been on Cloud Nine at the mere thought of it. Even if he was smitten with Caroline.

'Go and change your clothes, slap on some lipstick,' advised Sarah, reading her mind. 'You'll soon feel more enthusiastic.'

Duly attired in a newish pair of cream denims, long pink cable sweater and dark glasses Lowri both looked and felt a great deal better by the time Adam arrived. She opened the office door to his knock, her smile wobbling slightly at the sudden, vivid memory of his kisses the night before.

'Hello, Lowri,' he said, smiling, and took her hand. 'I've rather press-ganged you into this, I'm afraid, but I wanted time alone with you to explain the drama last night.'

'It's very kind of you to take the trouble,' she said sedately, and took her time in locking the door to the flat.

'I've had a swift word with Sarah and Rupert to put them in the picture.' He ran down the stairs in front of her then turned at the bottom to hold out a steadying hand. 'Not unnaturally, Rupert feels responsible for you. He came down on me like a ton of bricks about my part in the affair.'

'But I told him you came to my rescue,' Lowri assured him as they left the garden by the side door.

'Rupert pointed out that if I hadn't brought Guy Seton no rescue would have been necessary. And he's right.' Adam's wide mouth twisted in disgust, then he smiled at her. 'Let's say goodbye then make for the open spaces. I've brought a picnic.'

Lowri gave him a delighted smile. 'What a brilliant idea!'

Adam suggested Runnymede, and a quiet spot near the river for their picnic lunch.

'The "banks of the sweetest river in the world" according to John Evelyn,' he told her later. He spread a rug for her, then opened a picnic basket to serve her with smoked trout pâté, cold chicken savoury with rosemary and garlic, a small bowl of green salad and crusty fresh rolls to eat with fierce farmhouse cheese.

'How did you manage all this on a Sunday morning?' asked Lowri, impressed. 'I bet King John didn't do nearly as well the day he signed the Magna Carta here.'

Adam's eyes danced beneath the heavy, straight eyebrows. 'My mother saw to it. I told her I needed to feed a very charming young lady from Wales. When she'd expressed her surprised approval—my usual female company tends more to smart nightspots than riverside picnics—she gave me some of the goodies intended for my father's lunch. Don't worry,' he added, as she gave him a startled look. 'There was more than enough left over—for them and several others. My mother's catering is generous.'

'Please thank her warmly on my behalf, and tell her how much it was appreciated,' said Lowri, surprised to find her appetite alive and well after all. 'This is lovely. All of it,' she added.

Adam leaned forward and gently removed the sunglasses, his eyes hot with sudden anger as he examined her eye. 'Exactly how did that happen?' he asked harshly, giving her back the glasses. 'If the swine hit you I'll go back and break his jaw this time.'

Lowri hastily explained her accidental contact with Guy Seton's elbow. 'He was obviously high on something.

Wouldn't take no. Heaven knows why—I never gave him the slightest encouragement,' she added irritably.

Adam looked grim. 'He didn't need any. The girl he lives with gave him the push yesterday. She delivered an ultimatum. He was to see sense about his cocaine habit or she was leaving. Seton objected. She could take him with all faults or not at all, since, I quote, he could pull any woman he wanted any time, and would prove it.' Adam's jaw tightened. 'He stormed round in a state to Caroline, who's always adored him. She was terrified to leave him on his own, and, knowing I'd refuse if she told me why, she insisted we take him with us to the party. You were the obvious choice for Seton to make good his boast. I'm sorry. I should never have let the bastard anywhere near you, Lowri.'

'It wasn't your fault,' she assured him, and smiled. 'Now let's forget about Guy and just enjoy the sunshine. We don't get enough to waste it, and tomorrow I'll be back at my desk. Not that I mind,' she added happily, 'I can't wait to find out what happens next in Rupert's novel. We're approaching the climax of the story.'

'He's a master of his craft, I agree.' Adam smiled. 'And damn lucky to find someone willing to work so hard for him.'

Lowri shook her head. 'The luck's all mine. When I left home I never dreamed I'd find something so interesting to do, especially with a flat thrown in. I owe such a lot to Sarah and Rupert.'

He eyed her curiously. 'Why were you in such a hurry to leave this home of yours?'

Lowri looked away. 'Dad and I have been closer than most, but now he's got Holly it's only fair to leave him to his new life without me in the way. Especially now Holly's pregnant.'

'Ah. Do you mind that?'

'No—at least not now. It was a bit of a shock at first. Though I should have expected it; pretty obvious really from the way—' She stopped, flushing.

'I take it your father's very much in love with his new wife,' said Adam quietly.

'Exactly. And she with him.' Lowri turned away to investigate an insulated jug. 'Mmm, wonderful—coffee. Want some?'

They fell silent as they drank the dark, fragrant brew provided by Mrs Hawkridge. After a while Adam leaned over and took her hand.

'Never mind, Lowri. One day you'll marry and have a baby of your own, and no more regrets about your new little stepbrother—or sister.'

She withdrew her hand swiftly. 'My regrets were very short-lived, Adam.'

'Sorry.' He lay flat on his back, hands linked behind his head. 'Nevertheless I meant what I said. You're exactly the type for marriage and babies, Lowri Morgan.'

'Because I'm not blonde and voluptuous and a frequenter of fashionable haunts—like Caroline Seton and Miss Thirty-two E?'

Adam opened a disapproving hazel eye. 'That's not what I said. Those two are just to play with. You're the sort men marry.'

Lowri grinned impudently. 'Whereas you blench at the mere thought of marriage, I suppose!'

'How right you are. I've got too much to do to get married. When Dad retires, Hawke Electronics will be wife, mistress and family rolled into one. I'll have no time left over for the normal kind. All my energies will be concentrated on the company.'

Such a waste, thought Lowri, her eyes on the powerful, sprawled figure.

'Besides,' said Adam, his eyes closed, 'I've good reason to be allergic to the sanctity of marriage.'

Lowri sat very still. 'I heard what happened to your brother, if that's what you mean.'

'I do. I keep thinking I could have prevented what happened if I'd been home. Stupid really. Peter was always a highly strung, sensitive sort of chap—nothing like me. But to end it all just because his wife walked out on him! Damned if I would—but enough of that.' Adam leapt suddenly to his feet, holding out his hand. 'Come on, let's pack this stuff back in the car and go for a walk.'

As Lowri strolled with Adam Hawkridge through the sunlit afternoon, it suddenly occurred to her that she was finally living out the fantasies she'd indulged in before coming to live in London. She was actually wandering over watermeadows with a tall, devastatingly attractive man, a thought which added such sparkle to her mood Adam showed gratifying signs of reluctance when he parted with her in Hamilton Terrace.

'I won't come in, Lowri,' he said, as he stopped the car. 'I should have been somewhere else half an hour ago, so give my best to Sarah and Rupert and tell them I took great care of their little cousin.'

'It was a lovely day. Thank you, Adam.'

He smiled at her and patted her hand affectionately. 'My pleasure too, Lowri. You're very sweet—take good care of yourself.'

Lowri hesitated, then gave him a funny little smile. 'Can I ask you a very personal question, Adam?'

He grinned. 'Feel free.'

'Is Caroline the thirty-six C angel blush?'

Adam threw back his head and roared with laughter, then squeezed her hand, winking at her. 'Actually, no. You haven't met Miss Thirty-Six.'

Lowri shook her head, laughing, waved him off then reported in to Rupert and Sarah. She took herself off to her own little domain later to reflect on the day and wish, rather irritably, that Adam thought of her as something more exciting than the Clares' nice little cousin. She'd hoped against hope that he'd kiss her again, so she could show him she was all woman as well as just 'sweet'. Sarah was right, she thought moodily, as she lay in a hot bath. Adam Hawkridge was a heartbreaker of the most dangerous type of all—totally unaware of his own power.

Lowri buckled down to work with a will next morning, determined to put Adam Hawkridge firmly from her mind. Rupert had almost finished dictating his novel. In a day or two he would have given her all the tapes and by the end of the week Lowri hoped to finish typing the first draft.

'Then you'll have to type the whole thing all over again, and not just once but several times, probably,' warned Sarah. 'Rupert's rarely satisfied with it until about the fourth or fifth draft. Do you think you'll cope?'

'Of course I will,' said Lowri cheerfully, then raised an eyebrow. 'What happens when it's finally finished? Does that mean I'm out of a job?'

'Of course not! Rupert's already got the next book in mind. You'll be needed to research for ages before he actually starts on it. Which, I warn you, means long hours shut up in libraries, or lugging home weighty tomes to search for some obscure detail Rupert can't do without.'

Lowri beamed, delighted. 'Sounds great to me. History was my best subject at school.'

Rupert finished dictating his novel by mid-week and Lowri finished typing it late on the Saturday evening, ignoring all protests from the Clares about working on a weekend.

'I just have to know how it ends,' she said firmly, and refused to budge from her desk until the last line was typed. She sat back with a sigh at last, her mind buzzing with

Jonah Haldane and his triumphant victory over his adversaries.

'Well?' demanded Rupert, when she went over to the house later to say she'd finished. 'What do you think?'

Lowri heaved a great sigh. 'It's utterly magnificent, Rupert.'

'Not recycled Dickens, then,' said Sarah with satisfaction.

'Sarah! What a horrible thing to say.'

'Rupert's description, not mine. I haven't even read it yet.'

Lowri turned on Rupert in fury. 'Don't you dare say that, Rupert Clare! I've never dared admit it because I seemed to be in a minority of one, but Dickens always bored me rigid. Whereas your book—' She waved her hands, searching for the right word. 'I can't express myself like you, Rupert, but what I'm trying to say is that when I came to the last line I wished desperately that I hadn't finished it, that I was starting at the beginning again. And this is just the draft—think of the impact when you're finally satisfied with it!'

Rupert threw his arms round her, laughing. 'All right, you little spitfire. Every novelist should have a champion like you. How long will it take you to print the last bit?'

'By Tuesday, I should think—Monday if I work tomorrow.'

'Definitely not,' said Sarah firmly. 'Rupert's giving you a treat tomorrow. At least I hope it's a treat—Dominic's sure you'll be thrilled.'

'Would you like to watch some Sunday cricket at Lord's?' said Rupert. 'Sarah's taking Emily to some birthday party, so how about coming to see Middlesex play your beloved Glamorgan with Dominic and me?'

Lowri was just as thrilled as Dominic had predicted. Lord's cricket ground was within such easy walking distance of the house she'd been longing to get to a match there ever since moving to St Johns Wood.

'Dad will be green with envy,' she said with a sigh of pleasure.

Sarah smiled affectionately. 'Not every girl's idea of a fun day!'

'But then,' mocked Rupert, 'Lowri's a Morgan like you, by no means a run-of-the-mill type of female.'

After her week of gruelling work it was an enormous pleasure to Lowri to sit between Dominic and Rupert at the famous cricket ground, applauding with partisan enthusiasm as she watched the Glamorgan eleven pull out all the stops against Middlesex.

'This is my second picnic in the space of a week,' she commented happily as they shared the picnic she'd helped Sarah pack earlier. 'Only this time I've got cricket as well and I adore one day-games. Dad's such a purist that he looks down on Sunday cricket, but I think it's exciting. Thank you so much for bringing me, Rupert.'

'I want to be a professional cricketer,' said Dominic indistinctly, wolfing a pork pie. 'I hope I'll be picked for the first eleven when I get to Shrewsbury.'

'Of course you will,' said a familiar voice, and all three turned round to see Adam Hawkridge laughing down at them. 'Make a few more catches like the one you saw Lowri off with and you can't fail. Greetings, everyone. May I join you?'

Rupert sprang to his feet to welcome the newcomer, Dominic beaming as he made room for Adam between himself and Lowri.

'You were lucky to find us in this crowd,' said Rupert, offering him a sandwich.

'I rang Sarah—she told me roughly where you'd be.' Adam smiled down at a suddenly shy Lowri. 'I gather this is your reward for working so hard.'

'Not every girl's idea of a treat,' said Rupert indulgently.

'Actually I rang up to see if you were free tonight,' said Adam, accepting a second sandwich.

'Me?' enquired Rupert blandly.

'No, thanks, you're not my type!' Adam grinned, then turned to Lowri. 'It was this lady I was after. I realise it's short notice, but I wondered if you'd care for a meal tonight somewhere and a film afterwards?'

Lowri bolted an unchewed morsel of sandwich whole, eyes watering. There was nothing in the whole wide world she'd have liked better, but that was hardly the point. Caroline, or Fiona, or Miss Thirty-Six C or one of probably a dozen others must have let him down at the last minute, leaving him at a loose end. She smiled politely. 'How very kind. But I'm afraid I'm tied up tonight.'

Adam stared in surprise, the wind very obviously taken out of his sails. He pulled himself together, smiling rather stiffly. 'My bad luck. I suppose it was a bit optimistic to expect you to be free. Another time, maybe?'

Lowri returned the smile non-committally, then rummaged in the picnic basket, conscious of the narrowed look Rupert turned on her. 'Anyone for an apple?'

When they got back to the house Lowri listened to a spirited account of the birthday party from an excited Emily, volunteered to put her to bed and read a story, declined supper on the excuse of the large picnic tea, and took herself off to mope in her own quarters.

An hour or so later Sarah knocked on her door and asked if she could come in for a while.

'Of course.' Lowri, glad of relief from her own morose company, went to put the kettle on for coffee.

'You can tell me to go away, if you like.'

'Of course I don't mind.' When Lowri returned with a tray she eyed her cousin sheepishly. 'I suppose Rupert told you Adam asked me out tonight.'

'He did, indeed.' Sarah ran a hand through her long dark hair thoughtfully. 'His account of the afternoon was very interesting. Adam obviously expected you to consent with maidenly—but prompt—gratitude and, I am told, seemed a bit put out when you refused. And since I know perfectly well you had no plans for this evening, unless you count washing your hair, or a date with a good book, I'm agog to know why you turned Adam down.'

'I thought you'd have worked that one out for yourself.' Lowri smiled ruefully. 'He was so confident I'd say yes, you know! Besides, he's dangerous—he frightens me.'

'You're not worried he'd behave like that beastly Seton man!'

'Of course not. But you were the one who warned me, remember. The first time I laid eyes on Adam Hawkridge you told me he was a heartbreaker. You were right. I could like him a lot—far too much for safety. If I see too much of him I could get my fingers burnt a second time. So I refused. Besides,' added Lowri tartly, 'I objected to the way he breezed up at the cricket match, expecting me to accept with humble gratitude because somebody else stood him up tonight.'

'How do you know that?'

'What other reason could there be? I've got my pride, Sarah. It was pretty obvious he expected me to drop everything and run.' She sniffed. 'No chance.'

'Rupert was deeply impressed,' said Sarah, smiling. 'Adam's such a charmer that at a guess I'd say no woman's ever said no to him in his life before, unless it was his mother, who's absolutely lovely, by the way. A nice polite little no from you probably did him the world of good.'

'I hope it did—because it didn't do *me* any good at all,' sighed Lowri despondently. 'It quite spoiled my afternoon—and to cap it all Glamorgan lost by one measly run!'

CHAPTER FOUR

LOWRI soon learned she'd hit on the one tactic likely to secure her Adam Hawkridge's interest whether she wanted it or not. Next day she answered the newly installed telephone extension in her office with a chuckle.

'Rupert, you must be psychic—I was just going to ring you. These hieroglyphics of yours on page thirty—'

'Sorry—I'm not psychic and I'm not Rupert either,' said a deep, satin-smooth voice. 'Adam here, Lowri. Rupert put me through to you. How are you?'

Lowri blinked. 'Adam! What a surprise. I'm very well, also very busy. How are you?'

'Offended. I spent a very lonely evening last night after you turned me down.'

'How sad.'

There was a pause. 'Lowri,' said the caressing voice. 'Was your refusal some kind of dressage by any chance?'

'Dressage?'

'Playing hard to get,' he said indulgently.

'Oh, but I'm not. Playing at it, I mean.'

Another pause.

'I thought we got on rather well together,' he went on, the banter suddenly gone.

'If you mean we had a pleasant time by the river, of course we did.'

'Then have dinner with me. How about Saturday?'

'Sorry. My weekend's booked.'

She heard him breathe out slowly.

'I won't give up,' he warned. 'You'll say yes to me sooner or later, Lowri.'

Don't hold your breath, she thought. 'Thank you for ringing, Adam. Goodbye.'

Lowri put the phone down with an unsteady hand, her heart beating like a drum. The mere sound of Adam's voice was more than enough to throw her off balance, which only confirmed how sensible she was to refuse him. It just wouldn't do to get involved with Adam Hawkridge. Not, she thought wryly, that she required a man to declare himself eligible before she'd have dinner with him. Not normally, anyway. And with any other man in the world it wouldn't matter. There was no danger of falling in love with someone else because… Her teeth sank into her lower lip as she stared in sudden dismay at the computer screen. Because she was already in love with Adam Hawkridge? Rubbish! She'd only met the man a few times. Not that it made a blind bit of difference, it was true just the same. She ground her teeth impotently. What a bird-brained idiot, to fall for a man allergic to emotional commitment!

Lowri took in a deep breath and pulled herself together. Now she'd faced the truth she'd get over it eventually, which meant avoiding Adam like the plague. Without fuel a fire would go out. She'd make it go out. And this time there was no white lie involved. She *was* booked for the weekend. Rupert was giving a lecture at a literary seminar, and she'd volunteered to move into the house to stay with Emily and Dominic so that Sarah could go with him.

Once they'd waved their parents off, Emily and Dominic helped Lowri get supper, ate it happily with her at the kitchen table and helped clear away afterwards with such conscious virtue that Lowri couldn't help laughing.

'Don't try to be *too* good, you two, or you'll burst by the time your mother gets back on Sunday.'

'Daddy said I must be an angel,' said Emily with a worried frown.

'Some hopes,' said her brother scornfully. 'You've got to die before you can be an angel, silly.'

Emily stared at him in horror, her lower lip jutting ominously. 'I don't want to die,' she quavered. 'Not before Mummy gets home.'

'Absolutely no chance of that,' said Lowri briskly, 'not with me around. Now then, *cariad*, race you up to the bathroom—if you win you choose the story.'

Some time during the protracted process of getting Emily to bed Lowri heard the telephone ring a couple of times, but left Dominic to answer it. Later, after she'd allayed Emily's fears about growing wings, and settled the little girl to sleep, Lowri went down to find Dominic just coming in from the garden.

'Who was on the phone?' she asked him.

'Sorry—didn't hear it ring. I was out in the practice net Dad put up for me. I'll check the answering machine.' Dominic went off, whistling, while Lowri checked that all the doors were locked.

'Two for you,' he reported, coming back to the kitchen. 'One was your Dad and the other was Adam.' He eyed her pink cheeks with interest. 'Do you like Adam, Lowri?'

'Of course. He's very nice,' she said sedately.

'I think he fancies *you*! All right if I watch television now?'

Lowri nodded, rather touched that he was asking her permission. 'I'll join you in a minute.' She went into Rupert's study to listen to the messages. Her father's voice enquired if she were well, but Adam's message made her bristle by ordering her to ring back immediately.

Lowri had a chat with her father and Holly, but ignored Adam's orders. Pleased with her iron self-control, she went off to join Dominic in front of the television, and when Sarah rang later Lowri made no mention of Adam's call.

'I hope the weekend won't be too tiring for you, or too dull,' said Sarah.

'Of course it won't. Stop worrying and have fun!'

After breakfast next morning Lowri drove Emily to her ballet class, dropped Dominic off at a friend's house for the morning, then went back to make the chocolate cake she'd promised as a treat. As she was sliding the tins into the oven the phone rang.

'At last!' said the spine-tingling voice. 'I've found you, Lowri Morgan.'

'Who is this?' she answered calmly.

'Adam—as you well know. Why didn't you return my call last night?'

'By the time I heard the message it was late. I assumed you'd be out.'

'I'm not out every night,' he cut back. 'In fact I was working my socks off until very late. It occurs to me that you could have meant you were just booked up in the evenings this weekend, so how about lunch today—or tomorrow?'

'Sorry.' Lowri explained the situation. 'I really must dash, Adam, I've got a cake in the oven. Bye.'

'*Lowri*—!'

She put the phone down swiftly before her resolve weakened, and rushed back to the kitchen to make herself a cup of extra-strong coffee. As she drank it she tried hard to quiet a small voice which asked her why she was giving Adam such a hard time. You might be the very one, it said insinuatingly, to change his mind about commitment, even marriage. In a pig's eye, she told it scornfully. I'm nothing much to look at. My face wouldn't launch so much as a dinghy, let alone a thousand ships. And Adam likes his women glamorous and skinny—except around the chest, whereas my shape's more the other way round. And if he does ask again—not that he will—I've just got to keep saying no.

When Lowri got back to Hamilton Terrace after collecting Emily and Dominic there was much excitement when they found a familiar convertible parked outside.

'Great! That's Adam's car,' said Dominic as Lowri drove into the garage.

'Is Adam coming to lunch?' clamoured Emily, and raced after Dominic towards the man reclining on the garden seat under the rose arbour. 'Adam, Adam!' she squealed, and launched herself into the arms held at the ready to receive her.

'Good morning, Miss Clare.' He said laughing and swung her round in a circle, then aimed a playful punch at Dominic.

'Mum and Dad are away.' Dominic grinned at him impudently. 'Lowri's looking after us.'

'Aren't you the lucky ones!' said Adam, smiling smugly as Lowri reached them. 'Nice to see you, Lowri—at last. I was just passing so I thought I'd call in.'

'Hello, Adam.' Conscious of the children's eyes on her, she managed a cool smile. 'I don't suppose you've time to come in, I know how busy you are.'

'All the time in the world—it's my day off,' he assured her, eyes dancing irrepressibly.

Emily tugged him by the hand to follow Lowri into the house. 'Come and have lunch with us—*please*, Adam. Lowri's made a cake.'

'I know,' he said, then laughed as Dominic's eyebrows shot to his hair.

'How? She hadn't started it when she took us out this morning.'

'I confess I rang up,' said Adam, unabashed. 'When I heard she was baking a cake, nothing could keep me away.'

'You rang her up last night, too,' pointed out Dominic.

'No law against it,' said Adam cheerfully. 'Tell you what, I'll give you a few balls in that net out there while Emily, like a perfect little angel, helps Lowri put lunch.'

'Emily doesn't want to be an angel,' said Lowri with a warning look, and gave the child a cuddle. 'Which is a very good thing. We like her just the way she is.'

'Who wouldn't!' said Adam swiftly and swept Emily up in a hug. 'Never did care for angels myself anyway—all that twanging about on harps!' As he put the child down Adam gave Lowri a straight look.

'*May* I stay for lunch?' he asked.

'Of course you can,' said Dominic impatiently. 'Come *on*, Adam!'

'I was asking Lowri. She's in charge.'

She gave him a fulminating look, then shrugged. 'If you've a taste for pasta and chocolate cake, by all means join us.'

'That's settled, then,' said Dominic and gave Lowri a conspiratorial wink. 'Adam can clear away afterwards instead of me.'

Once Adam's company was inevitable Lowri decided she might as well relax and enjoy it. Both children very obviously adored him—it would be a shame, she assured herself, to spoil their pleasure in the unexpected visitor.

During the meal, which Adam praised with extravagance, there was a heated discussion on how to spend the afternoon now it was raining. Dominic wanted to go swimming, while Emily pleaded for the rare treat of a trip to the cinema. With all the skill of a career diplomat Adam settled the argument by the simple expedient of agreeing to both.

'We'll all go off to see *Beauty and the Beast* this afternoon, then you and I, Dom, will bring the ladies home and go for a swim on our own.' Adam smiled at Lowri challengingly. 'We'll fetch a takeaway back with us—give Lowri a break from catering.'

'You're staying to supper too?' Dominic let out a war-hoop of delight.

With Emily cuddled on his lap Adam eyed Lowri warily as she loaded the dishwasher. '*Do* you object?'

'Since you've won the majority vote, how can I?' she said tartly, then smiled at Emily. 'Go and wash the chocolate smudges off your face, darling. You too, Dominic, please.'

Emily slid off Adam's knee obediently, then looked up at him with cajoling green eyes. 'Can I sit by you at the cinema, Adam?'

'You certainly can.' He ruffled her black curls. 'Only hurry up. Nearly time to go.' He smiled at Lowri as the child trotted off happily after Dominic. 'Imagine the havoc that young lady will wreak when she grows up. One look from those eyes of hers and she'll have every man in sight at her mercy.'

'A bit like you, really,' observed Lowri, putting the remains of the chocolate cake in a tin.

Adam glared. '*What*?'

'Your eyes aren't green exactly, but aren't most women at your mercy when you smoulder at them?'

'Rubbish!' His mouth twisted in distaste. 'Besides, if that's the case why am I so bloody unsuccessful where you're concerned?'

'You're just not my type.' She smiled at him sweetly. 'You're so much older than me, for a start.'

His eyes narrowed dangerously. 'I'm not quite over the hill yet, Lowri Morgan—on any count!' He sprang to his feet and stalked towards her, then stopped dead as Dominic came rushing into the room with a packed sports bag. The boy halted, looking from one to the other.

'Were you two quarrelling?'

'Certainly not,' said Lowri, and went off to fetch Emily. At the cinema Lowri managed to arrange things so that

Emily was between herself and Adam, with Dominic on his far side. But before the film began Emily asked to go to the cloakroom. When Lowri took her back to the others Adam quickly installed Emily between himself and Dominic, forcing Lowri to take the seat next to him.

Once the award-winning music began, Emily was entranced. Even Dominic, who'd been rather superior about indulging his sister with her choice of film, was soon engrossed, something which Lowri was thankful for when Adam's hand captured hers and retained it in a relentless grip impossible to loosen without making a scene.

No fan of cartoon films herself, Lowri found the afternoon very long, deeply conscious of the warm dry clasp which never slackened throughout the entire film. To her relief Adam released her hand before the lights went up, but not quickly enough to escape Dominic's astute green eyes, one of which drooped in a knowing wink as he grinned at Lowri.

Adam drove them back to Hamilton Terrace, deposited Lowri and a tired, excited Emily at the house, then whisked Dominic off for a swim at a surprise location.

While they were gone Lowri supervised Emily's bath and sat quietly with the child afterwards, reading to her on the sofa in the small sitting-room the family used in preference to the rather formal drawing-room kept for entertaining. Emily burrowed against Lowri's shoulder drowsily, and dozed off for a while, but woke up with a start when Dominic came rushing in, blazing with excitement.

'*Guess* where we went—Adam's place! It's in this block of flats by the river, and there's this fantastic pool in the basement—there was no one there, we had the place to ourselves. I did *ten* lengths!'

'Fantastic! In that case you must be hungry. Where *is* Adam?' inquired Lowri.

'We stopped for a takeaway. Fried chicken and chips and things—he's just coming.'

Adam appeared in the doorway. 'I've dumped it all on the kitchen table, Lowri, will you come and supervise?' He bent over Emily. 'Hello, poppet, want some chicken?'

Emily shook her head. 'No. Thank you,' she added belatedly.

'Aren't you hungry, my angel?'

Emily glared at him and burrowed against Lowri. '*Not* an angel,' she sobbed.

'No, of course not, sweetheart,' said Adam, wincing as he met Lowri's glare. 'Shall I go and switch on an oven or something to keep the stuff hot?'

Lowri managed to soothe the child's sobs, motioned Adam to sit down and transferred Emily to his lap. 'You cuddle Emily, Dominic and I'll see to supper. We'll have it in here, for a treat.'

Once Adam exerted all his considerable charm on Emily she was soon laughing with him, though too tired to eat much.

'I think I'll take this young lady up to bed,' Lowri said after a while. 'Dominic, there's ice-cream or cake if you want pudding, and some cheese if you'd prefer, Adam.'

Adam sprang to his feet, holding out his arms for Emily. 'I'll carry her upstairs for you.'

'Thank you.' Lowri hurried up the curving staircase to Emily's small, pretty bedroom, then took the drowsy child from Adam. 'I don't think we'll bother with a bath tonight.' To her surprise Adam insisted on staying to help her undress the little girl, holding Emily on his lap while Lowri sponged her face, then watching as the child was tucked up in bed.

'She looks like a little angel, lying there,' he whispered.

Lowri shook her head, laying a finger to her lips as she went out of the room ahead of him. 'Never mention the word "angel" again, for heaven's sake. Emily discovered one's obliged to die before getting to be one, something she objects to violently, particularly before Mummy gets home.'

'Oops!' Adam grinned ruefully. 'I don't know much about children. I obviously put my foot in it.'

'Your famous charm soon won her round,' Lowri assured him tartly. 'I'd better clear up the remains of our supper—which I haven't thanked you for, by the way.'

He gave her a gleaming, complacent look as they went to join Dominic. 'I told you I'd get you to dine with me, didn't I! Not that I envisaged such a bizarre way to gain my ends.'

'Quite a change for you.' She gave him a crooked little smile and went into the sitting-room, where Dominic was glued to the television among the greasy remains of their impromptu meal. He jumped up guiltily, but Adam waved him away.

'My turn to help Lowri, old son.' He smiled at Dominic's open relief as the boy returned eagerly to his television programme.

Their disposable feast took very little effort to clear away, and once Sarah's kitchen was restored to its usual immaculate condition Adam volunteered to make coffee while Lowri checked all was well with her young charges.

When she got back she found Adam had mugs of instant coffee ready, instead of brewing Sarah's best Blue Mountain beans as Lowri had intended. She drank gratefully, just the same, feeling suddenly bone-weary.

'Right.' Adam's bantering manner dropped away like a cloak, his eyes steely as they challenged hers. 'Now that I've gone to such lengths to secure your company, Lowri, tell me the truth. Why did you turn me down?'

She eyed him curiously. 'Do I take it no one ever has before?'

Adam thought about it, then shook his head. 'Not that I can remember,' he said candidly.

Lowri decided to tell him half the truth. 'If you must know, Adam, I couldn't for the life of me think why someone like you should be interested in a girl like me.'

'Why the devil not?' he demanded, amazed.

'Oh come on,' she said scornfully. 'I've only met two, I admit, but Sarah says all your girlfriends run true to type.'

'What type?'

'You know perfectly well what I mean! Clothes, background, gloss, totally unlike me in every possible way. I'm a small-town girl, unsophisticated, and years younger than the women you usually go for. So it seemed only sensible to keep my distance from a notorious heartbreaker like you.'

Adam stared at her in blank distaste. 'Heartbreaker! What the blazes are you talking about?'

Lowri sighed. 'That's just it. You don't even know you do it. You turn that smile on a female, and give her that look that makes her feel she's the only woman in the world, say sweet nothings in that sexy dark brown voice of yours, then when she's putty in your hands you stroll off in search of the next conquest. You should carry a government health warning, Adam Hawkridge.'

CHAPTER FIVE

COLOUR flared in Adam's face then receded, leaving him pale and dauntingly grim.

'You're wrong!' he said cuttingly. 'My health is something I take great care of. In every way. I may enjoy the company of women but I'm no health risk to any of them, including you.'

Lowri blushed to the roots of her hair, her eyes bright with dismay. 'I had no intention—I mean the health warning bit was a joke, a stab at flippancy. I was referring to the heart trouble you inflict, nothing else!'

'Were you really?' He smiled sardonically. 'About time you grew up, Lowri. Hearts don't break. And I've never misled a woman in my life. I admit I enjoy the company of your sex, make the most of any privileges I'm offered— and I do mean offered—but always on the strict understanding that the arrangement's temporary. No strings and eyes wide open are the rules of the game. Permanence is out for me. At least for a good few years yet.' His eyes narrowed. 'You know, Lowri, if you expect some kind of commitment from every man who wants your company, you're likely to get pretty lonely.'

'I'm not that stupid!'

Adam gazed at her thoughtfully, an assessing gleam in his eyes. 'If you were any other woman I'd suspect your tactics.'

Lowri stiffened. 'What do you mean?'

'Frankly I'd take it as a ploy to arouse my interest, maybe even a bid to change my point of view.'

'Dream on!' she said scornfully.

The amusement faded. 'Then what is it, Lowri? Why won't you spend time with me?'

She smiled pityingly. 'Is it so hard to believe that I might just not want to?'

'Yes,' he snapped. 'It is. You enjoyed the picnic the other day.'

'Of course I did.' Lowri got up and cleared away the coffee-mugs. 'But I didn't realise it committed me—if you'll pardon the word—to come running any time you were at a loose end.'

Comprehension dawned in Adam's eyes. 'Ah, I see. The truth at last. You were annoyed because I asked you at such short notice.'

'That's right,' said Lowri glibly, glad he'd accepted her explanation at its face value. 'Now I'm sure you have other things to do tonight. Thank you for the trip to the cinema, Adam.' She held out her hand with deliberate formality. 'Perhaps you'll pop in on Dominic as you go out. I'll say goodbye here.'

Adam looked at the hand, then took it to pull her into his arms, holding her cruelly tight as he kissed her open, protesting mouth. Lowri struggled instinctively at first, but soon found Adam was a very different protagonist from Guy Seton. Adam was taller, broader, fitter, and even more intent on getting his own way. But his greatest advantage was Lowri's realisation that the pleasure she was experiencing was so intense it seemed a shame not to savour it. She yielded, and Adam took full advantage of it, kissing her until they were both shaken and breathless.

When he raised his head Adam's eyes glittered in triumph.

'You see?' he demanded, panting.

'See what?' she said unsteadily, thrusting her hair back from her flushed face.

'You asked what I saw in a girl like you. If I'm honest,

Lowri Morgan, I think it's a lot to do with sexual chemistry.'

The words damped Lowri down like a cold shower.

'You don't like that,' he said, eyeing her warily.

Lowri shrugged and said nothing.

A smile played at the corners of his mouth. 'You'd prefer I was enamoured with your mind?'

Lowri looked at him steadily. 'It doesn't really matter, Adam. Either way I've no intention of adding my name to your list of conquests.'

Adam's lips compressed. 'Always supposing I'd any intention of suggesting that,' he said with heat.

She nodded, unruffled. 'True. Goodnight then, Adam. It was very good of you to help entertain Dominic and Emily. They had a lovely day.'

'Up until a few minutes ago, so did I,' he said bitterly, and with a curt goodbye he turned on his heel to go in search of Dominic.

Lowri passed a restless night in the Clares' guest-room, spending a major part of it convincing herself she'd done the right thing. In the long run, she told herself stringently, she'd be glad she'd resisted temptation and made her position clear to Adam. If she gave in and spent whatever time with him he wanted it was obvious he'd take it for granted they'd become lovers—a prospect which sent a slow, cold shiver down Lowri's spine. But eventually, probably sooner than later, Adam would grow restless and take off to seek pastures new. As he always did.

When she heard no more from Adam for a while Lowri tried hard to convince herself she was happy about it. The fact that she wasn't went unnoticed, mainly because she was working harder than she'd ever done on draft after draft of Rupert's novel. He was proving just as hard a taskmaster as Sarah had warned, but his moods had no effect on Lowri.

She was glad of the work, just as determined as the author to arrive at a final jewel of a novel, cut and polished to the standard Rupert Clare's readers had come to expect.

When Rupert finally professed himself satisfied enough to let his impatient editor see the manuscript Lowri heaved a great sigh of relief and went home to Cwmderwen for the weekend, as she'd promised she would once her contribution to the book was finished.

'You realise the manuscript may come back for revision?' Rupert warned as he drove her to Paddington. 'For one thing the damn thing's probably too long. Tom Harvey will want me to cut it.'

Lowri stared at him in dismay. 'Oh, *no*—you can't! It's perfect as it is.'

'Did I ever tell you I loved you, Lowri Morgan?' said Rupert, chuckling. 'Only don't let my wife know I said that.'

'Sarah wouldn't mind a bit.' Lowri gave Rupert a wry smile. 'She knows you've got no eyes for anyone else in the world.'

'True. But it took quite a bit of persuading to make her believe that at one time.'

Lowri eyed her cousin's handsome husband consideringly as he brought the car to a halt in the station approach. 'I can well believe it.'

Rupert gave her a wry green look. 'Even the wildest rake settles down in time, Lowri, given the chance.'

'Always assuming he has the slightest inclination to do so,' she retorted, well aware he was referring to Adam. She took her grip from him. 'Thanks for the lift. I'll see you on Tuesday.'

Lowri enjoyed her weekend of peace and quiet, with nothing more demanding on the programme than watching her father play cricket and helping Holly prepare meals. And to her own secret relief she found she could tease

Holly about her approaching motherhood with no trace of qualms about the advent of a new little Morgan. It made for a happy holiday all round, particularly since Geraint Morgan was well aware of the fact and grateful to his daughter for her reaction.

'You look a lot better,' said Sarah, when Lowri returned to St Johns Wood. 'Hardly surprising. A spell away from Rupert is a necessity now and again.'

'Not for you!'

'That's different. If Rupert and I fight we can make up afterwards—and enjoy it. But anyone who works for him needs a break from the famous temperament now and again. Come and have some lunch before you unpack.'

Over the meal Lowri gave the news from Cwmderwen, frank about her relief at feeling happy about the new baby. 'But I didn't go to church,' she added diffidently. 'It's not the same without Uncle Glyn.'

Sarah's face shadowed. 'No. The sudden shock of having my mother die first soon did for my father, and now he's gone I don't suppose I'll ever set foot in the church there again.' She blinked, and smiled brightly. 'But to change the subject, and cheer us both up, would you groan if I enlisted your help on Saturday?'

'Party?'

'Just a dinner. Ten of us. One of which,' added Sarah firmly, 'is you. And before you trot out your usual excuses, you won't be an odd female, Tom Harvey's coming.'

'His divorce came through recently, didn't it?'

'That's right. It's your job to cheer him up.'

'Thanks a bunch!' Lowri pulled a face.

After a few days deep in the fourteenth century, researching the Peasants' Revolt, Lowri thoroughly enjoyed a Saturday morning spent in helping with preparations for the dinner that night. Brenda was going through the rest of the house like Sherman through Georgia, and Rupert had volunteered to take his children swimming, followed by lunch in the restaurant of their choice.

'Which means cheeseburgers and milkshakes and the devout hope that Emily won't be sick afterwards,' said Sarah, as she concocted a sauce to serve with the salmon they were to eat later. 'What are you wearing tonight?'

Lowri pulled a face as she looked up from scrubbing tiny new potatoes at the kitchen sink. 'The black dress I wore to the last Clare soirée I graced, I'm afraid.'

'No afraid about it.' Sarah grinned. 'Beside, Tom was missing that night, so he won't have seen it.'

'I don't suppose he'd notice if he had.' Lowri pulled a face. 'What do I talk about to cheer him up, for heaven's sake? He's tremendously witty and erudite, according to Rupert. I'm frightened before I've even met the man.'

'All you do is mention Rupert's book and you're up and running.'

'I hope you're right!'

Lowri's evening began with a series of surprises, the first of which was the pleasant discovery that she'd lost a pound or two. The black dress was far less struggle to get into. Then while she was doing her face Rupert knocked on the door of the flat and presented her with a package.

'A small token of appreciation for all your hard work, Lowri.'

Deeply touched, she opened a box containing a silver filigree brooch shaped like a butterfly, with coral insets in its wings. 'Rupert, this is so lovely! But you had no need—'

'A bribe to ensure future labours,' he assured her, kissing her cheek. 'Hurry up. Come and have a drink before the others arrive.'

When he'd gone Lowri added a few more touches to her face than she usually bothered with, then pinned the new brooch just below her collarbone, delighted to find it quite transformed her plain little dress.

The third—and biggest—surprise confronted her in Sarah's drawing room. When Lowri saw Adam Hawkridge chatting with Rupert near the open french windows she stopped dead in her tracks, heart thumping as she fought the urge to turn tail and run.

Rupert beckoned her over with an affectionate smile. 'There you are, Lowri. Come and say hello to our unexpected guest. May I say you look ravishing this evening, little cousin?'

'You can say it any evening,' she returned flippantly, and walked towards them hoping her turbulence wasn't showing behind the bright, social smile she gave Adam. 'Hello there. I didn't know you were coming tonight.'

Adam took her hand and held it for a moment, his answering smile accompanied by the familiar gleam in his eyes. 'Hello, Lowri. Rupert's right. You look wonderful. And I'm afraid I'm a sort of gatecrasher—again.'

'Nothing of the sort,' said Rupert, handing Lowri a glass of champagne. 'Adam came round to consult us about the cricket bat he's giving Dominic for his birthday, so Sarah insisted he stay for dinner. One extra is never a problem to my wife.'

'You're a lucky man,' said Adam with feeling.

'I second that!' Rupert raised his glass.

Lowri joined in the toast with enthusiasm, then excused herself to go off in search of Sarah, who was running down the stairs, looking her radiant best in a narrow midnight-blue dress. Lowri thanked her for the gift, lifting one shoulder to emphasise how good the butterfly looked on her dress.

'I thought it would. I helped Rupert choose it. I suppose you know we've got an extra guest?' added Sarah warily as they went into the kitchen together.

'Yes—shall I lay another place?'

'I've already done it. Do you *mind* having Adam here, Lowri?'

'Of course not. Besides, Madam Hostess, it's your dinner party. The guest-list is nothing to do with me.'

'Oh dear. You do mind.' Sarah sighed. 'I didn't ring the flat to tell you in case a mysterious malaise suddenly struck you down. Are you sure you didn't have a fight with Adam that weekend?'

'He was a bit miffed because I wouldn't go out with him.' Lowri tasted the consommé appreciatively. 'His ego took a blow, that's all.'

'Do him the world of good,' said Sarah callously.

Having an extra man at the table was no drawback to the success of the evening—quite the reverse, Lowri discovered, from her own point of view. Sarah's table was round, which made for ease of both seating and conversation, and placed between Tom Harvey and Patrick Savage, a fellow writer friend of Rupert's, with Adam directly opposite, Lowri settled down to enjoy herself rather more than she'd expected.

Far from being glum about his newly divorced state, Tom Harvey seemed in a mood to celebrate it, and proved so entertaining Lowri forgot his renowned intellect in simple enjoyment of his conversation. Patrick Savage, too, was an easy dinner partner, though his conversation, to Lowri's amusement, centred more on his newly born son and small daughter than literature. They chatted comfortably about babies, Lowri telling him about the new arrival due in her own family, and the pleasure she took in Dominic and Emily's company. The blond, attractive man was so engrossed in the subject that she looked up at one point to find Adam's eyes fixed on her in deep disapproval. He turned away instantly to talk to Carey Savage, Patrick's wife, and Lowri quelled a very human little gush of satisfaction as she plunged back into discussion of Rupert's book with Tom Harvey.

When the men returned to the drawing-room later Adam detached Lowri the moment she'd finished handing round coffee. He drew a couple of chairs up near the cool breeze coming in from the windows and installed her in one firmly.

'Neat. Just like one man and his dog,' she commented.

Adam laughed. 'Which one am I?'

'Oh, the man,' said Lowri promptly. 'I'm the nice woolly sheep the dog cuts out from the rest of the flock.'

'A wonder I'm not the dog. Lord knows I'm in the dog-house where you're concerned.'

'Nonsense,' she said lightly, and smiled up at Rupert in refusal as he offered her brandy.

'I won't either,' said Adam with regrets. 'If I'd known I was staying to dinner I'd have come by cab.'

'You're law-abiding, then,' said Lowri, as Rupert moved on to another group of guests.

'Too much at stake for me to be otherwise.' Adam drank his coffee and put their cups down on a nearby table. 'Soon I'll be in the driving seat at Hawk Electronics. My parents are off on a world cruise and I'll be left minding the baby.'

'But this baby is just your cup of tea—far more than the usual kind, I fancy.'

Adam smiled at her. 'Frankly, yes. I know where I am with electronics. Hand me a real live squalling baby and I'd run a mile.' He paused. 'I would have rung you last weekend, but Rupert said you were away.'

Why had he wanted to ring her? 'Yes,' she said serenely. 'I went down to Cwmderwen once Rupert's manuscript was on Tom Harvey's desk.'

Adam's face darkened. 'You were getting on remarkably well with Harvey.'

'Yes—though I've never met him before. He's a very interesting man.'

'And only recently loosed from the chains of matrimony. Be careful, Lowri.'

'I make it a habit to be, Adam,' she said sweetly, and got up. 'Forgive me, I must circulate.'

For the rest of the evening Lowri took good care to avoid privacy with Adam. It was by no means difficult, since Tom Harvey seemed to have taken a fancy to her, and, just as Sarah had predicted, was only too happy to discuss the autumn launch of Rupert's novel all night. It was well after midnight before the party showed any signs of breaking up, and Tom was last to go. Adam, to Lowri's intense disappointment, had been first to leave. Going on somewhere else, of course, she thought in secret fury.

Brenda had left the kitchen spick and span and gone off on the back of her Wayne's motorcycle by the time Lowri said goodnight to Sarah and Rupert.

'Did you have a good time?' asked Rupert, putting an arm round his wife. 'You were talking nineteen to the dozen with Tom Harvey.'

'He's nice. Not so frightening after all,' admitted Lowri.

'How about Adam?' asked Sarah. 'I saw you talking together at one stage.'

Lowri nodded. 'He seemed rather irritated because I got on so well with Tom Harvey.' She exchanged a little smile with Sarah, then said goodnight and left them to lock up as she crossed the moonlit garden to her flat. As she reached the flight of wrought-iron stairs leading to it a figure emerged from the shadows, startling her.

'It's me, Adam,' said the familiar, velvet voice as he moved out into the moonlight.

She breathed out audibly. 'I thought you'd left.'

'I did. But I decided to wait for you, so I walked round and let myself in by the side gate.'

'I was just coming to lock it.'

'Talk to me for a while first.'

'Why?'

'Does there have to be a reason?' he said irritably.

'You must have some reason for coming back at this time of night,' she pointed out.

'I came back to see you. Which,' he added harshly, 'you know perfectly well.'

Lowri battled for a moment with common sense, and lost. 'Then you'd better come up. I'll make coffee.'

He followed her up the stairs with alacrity, eyeing her face as she switched on the lights in her flat.

'I don't want any coffee,' he said bluntly.

Lowri gave him a very straight look. 'Coffee's the only thing on offer.'

'You think I don't know that? I'd decided I just wasn't going to bother again,' he said morosely. 'But one look at you tonight changed all that.' He looked at her slowly, feature by feature. 'Your hair's grown a lot since I first met you. I like it. And you looked so full of life tonight; your eyes shone like lamps when you were talking to Harvey. What the hell was he saying to switch you on like that?'

'We were merely discussing Rupert's book.' Lowri sat down in the adjustable chair at her desk, waving him to the small sofa. 'Won't you sit down?'

Adam shook his head. 'I shan't stay. Not,' he added bitterly, 'that you've any intention of asking me to. Hell, it's so hard not to put a foot wrong. Though it would make it a bloody sight easier if I knew how to put a foot right where you're concerned. I don't usually have this trouble with women.'

'Which says it all, Adam.' Lowri's eyes held his. 'As I said before, I don't want my name on any list of Hawkridge cast-offs.'

'Even if there were a list, which I deny, that wasn't what I had in mind.' He frowned, eyeing her belligerently. 'Can't we just be friends? Looking at you tonight, it suddenly dawned on me why I enjoy your company, why you're so different from the rest.'

'I believe you said something about sexual chemistry,' she said distantly.

'There is that, yes,' he said, pacing up and down restlessly. 'But there's a lot more, too. The other girls I know get bored so easily, but boredom doesn't seem to exist where you're concerned. You enjoy life whatever you're doing, playing cricket with Dom or reading to Emily, working for Rupert or enjoying an evening like tonight. You're involved all the time. It's refreshing, and I like it a lot.'

Lowri looked at him thoughtfully, undecided whether his statement was the simple truth, or some new line he was casting after the one who got away.

'What, exactly,' she began slowly, 'do you mean by "friends"?'

Scenting victory, Adam turned the full battery of his smile on her. 'I want to share my final fling of freedom with you, Lowri. I could get tickets to any show you fancy, take you to Ascot, Wimbledon, Henley.' The familiar gleam danced in his eyes. 'I'll even throw in a test match at Lords.'

Lowri looked at him in silence for a long time. How damnably attractive he was, she thought hopelessly. She'd been doing so well until tonight, too. And just one look at him had been enough to have her hooked again, utterly and completely. It didn't matter whether he took her to Ascot or Lords or just stayed here in her little room with her all the time they were together, she realised in self-revelation. What mattered was just being with Adam, and if this final fling of his meant he wanted to be her lover, then so be it. It was what she wanted too, if she were honest. She knew his reputation, he'd made no bones about being averse to commitment, but suddenly it seemed silly to deprive herself of a summer idyll she knew would never come her way again.

'Temptation indeed,' said Lowri, at last. She smiled at him whimsically. 'What woman could resist such blandishments?'

'You mean you like the idea?' said Adam, starting towards her.

Lowri held up a hand. 'Wait a minute. Clarify. While you're indulging in these wholesome activities with me, would you also be out partying with Caroline and Co.?'

He shrugged. 'Not if it's an obstacle to your agreement.' He smiled wryly. 'There's been precious little partying lately, anyway—until tonight. My usual social round seems to have lost its charm. In the end I gave up trying to kid myself and called round this evening in the hope of seeing you. The cricket bat was just a flimsy excuse. My hopes rose when I was invited to dinner, but I hardly saw anything of you during the evening. So I came back.'

'So you did.'

They looked at each other for a moment.

'It's a deal then?' said Adam at last, and held out his hand. Lowri got up and shook the hand gravely.

'Deal.' She smiled. 'Would you like that coffee now?'

And suddenly they were back to the day of the picnic, easy with each other as Adam watched her make coffee in her cupboard of a kitchen, talking about his company and how life would be very different for him once his father abdicated.

'That's his word for it,' he explained as they sat down together. 'My mother's always teasing him about giving up his crown.'

'Sarah says your mother's lovely,' said Lowri.

'Sarah's right, even if it is conceited to say so. I'm supposed to be exactly like her.' He scorched her with the hot gold gaze. 'Especially about the eyes.'

Lowri shook her head. 'You just can't help it, can you?'

'Help what?' he demanded innocently.

'You know perfectly well, so stop it.'

Adam grinned. 'All right.' He drank his coffee in one swallow. 'Tell me what happens with you now Rupert's book is finished.'

'I'm already researching the next one.' Lowri chuckled ruefully. 'Which isn't as easy as I thought. I get so involved in what I'm reading I forget to take notes.' She yawned suddenly, and Adam jumped to his feet.

'I've kept you up too late.'

'Not to worry. I get a lovely, lazy lie-in on Sundays.' Lowri stood up, smiling, and held out her hand. 'Goodnight.'

Adam took the hand and bent to kiss her on both cheeks. 'Goodnight. Come down and lock the gate after me to avoid any further nocturnal visitors.'

'You only got in tonight because it was left open for Wayne to collect Brenda on his Harley,' explained Lowri, her cheeks hot from the casual caress.

By the time she'd explained the identity of Brenda and Wayne they were at the gate in the wall. Adam paused, looking down at her in the moonlight.

'I'm glad I yielded to impulse and came back.'

'So am I,' said Lowri honestly.

'Can I take you out to lunch tomorrow?'

'All right. The weather forecast's good. I fancy some fresh air, so my turn to provide the picnic this time.'

CHAPTER SIX

SOMETIMES, when Lowri looked back on the hectic period with Adam, it seemed as though the sun always shone and she was always happy, except for the niggling uncertainty about Adam's feelings. She was never sure whether he was sincerely attracted to her, or merely thought of her as the Clares' little cousin, a playmate whose obvious crush on him was entertaining to indulge. One thing he made very clear was that their weekend expeditions into the country together would have bored his other playmates rigid.

'Playmates!' snorted Lowri as he drove her back from a perfect day in the Cotswolds.

'Just a term to show that none of them meant anything more than a decorative companion for the evening,' he explained. 'The only thing any of the recent ones had in common with you was their single status.'

'Ah! No married ladies?'

Adam shook his head. 'Only one. I avoided citation in a divorce case by the skin of my teeth.' He grimaced. 'Never again.'

Lowri glowered at him. 'I must be mad to associate with a rake like you! You were born in the wrong century—I can just picture you as a Regency buck, gambling and carousing and cuckolding husbands.'

Adam turned indignant eyes on her for a moment. 'It was only one husband—and you can hardly call a bet at Ascot a passion for gambling. Besides, I work damned hard for my living, remember.'

Lowri subsided. 'I'll grant you that.'

'Thank you. And, just for the record, I don't think of *you* as a playmate.'

'Good. I don't look the part.'

'Stop putting yourself down!' he said, exasperated. 'I think you're cute.'

'*Cute!*' she exploded.

'So how would you like me to describe you?'

Lowri thought about it as they reached the Chiswick flyover. 'Interesting? Good company?'

'Both of those,' he agreed, and gave her a sidelong glance. 'And hellish sexy, too, in those shorts.'

She blushed to the roots of her windblown black hair, utterly silenced.

'Cat got your tongue?'

'No one's ever called me sexy before,' she muttered.

'How can you possibly know?' said Adam, grinning. 'Men don't always come out with their private thoughts. Good thing, too,' he added with feeling, thinking it over.

Lowri tugged surreptitiously at the denim shorts, wishing they exposed rather less of her tanned thighs.

'I shouldn't bother,' advised Adam. 'You're only calling my attention to those parts of you I've been panting to touch all afternoon.'

Lowri glared at him. 'You're deliberately trying to embarrass me!'

'Not at all. I was stating the simple truth.'

She breathed in deeply, eyeing his profile with disquiet.

'Do me a favour, Lowri,' he said, exasperated. 'Stop behaving like a virgin sacrifice waiting for the knife! I promise you're safe as houses—at least until we're out of this blasted traffic. The entire population of Britain seems to be converging on London.'

Adam drove the rest of the way to St John's Wood whistling through his teeth with a nonchalance which set Lowri's nerves on edge. When they arrived at the house she unlocked the side gate and marched up the stairs to her flat, leaving Adam to follow her with Sarah's picnic basket, borrowed for the day.

When she'd unlocked her door she put out her hand for the basket, but Adam shook his head.

'No point in telling me you're busy this evening, because I know the Clares are away for the weekend. I'll take you out to supper.'

'I'm not hungry,' lied Lowri.

Adam laughed down at her. 'Is all this maidenly panic because I said I wanted to touch? Lowri, sweetheart, we've had a perfect day out in the sunshine among some of the most beautiful scenery in the country. I looked at your shiny nose and untidy hair as we lay on that hill counting sheep, and I was so pleased with life I suddenly thought how it would crown the day if I took you in my arms and gave you a hug and a kiss. But I didn't. Because I know damn well that if I put a foot wrong again you'll shut yourself up in your little retreat here, and I won't be able to do a damn thing about it because you're safe on Rupert's property.'

Lowri looked at him uncertainly, then suddenly her sense of humour came to the rescue, and she chuckled. 'Sorry! I'm an idiot.'

'True,' agreed Adam, 'but a very *cute* idiot, Lowri Morgan.' He ducked as she aimed a punch at him, then dumped the picnic basket and caught her to him, her flailing arms imprisoned at her sides as he looked deep into her eyes, all the banter suddenly missing. 'Would it be such a death blow to friendship if we did exchange a kiss?'

Despite a strong conviction that it would, Lowri hadn't the will to say no. As his mouth met hers her lips parted in such instinctive response that she felt Adam stiffen against her. Without taking his lips from hers he reached out behind her and opened the door, then lifted her by the elbows and carried her inside. He set her on her feet and stared down at her, breathing unevenly.

Lowri thrust a hand through her hair, gave him a wobbly, shy smile, then she was back in Adam's arms as he kissed her again.

'Might as well be hung for a sheep as a lamb,' he muttered against her mouth and pulled her down on his lap on the sofa, his hand stroking the smooth brown skin of her thigh as he went on kissing her with such undisguised pleasure that she was utterly disarmed. He raised his head a fraction and saw the astonishment in her eyes.

'Any minute now,' he said hoarsely, 'you're bound to throw me out and tell me to get lost again. So while you're still struck dumb I'll make the most of it.' He thrust his hands into her hair and kept her head still as he kissed her with such unexpectedly clumsy ardour that Lowri couldn't control her response. Here was something very different from the smooth, practised lover she'd expected, and somehow it made him all the more dangerous. A good thing, she thought, dazed, that he had no idea that this was what she'd yearned for all along. And now it was happening she didn't want it to stop. Which was where the real danger lay. If Adam really set out to breach her defences he'd find out she didn't have any at all where he was concerned.

When he raised his head at last she stared up at him mutely.

'I thought you'd be blacking my eye by now,' he whispered.

She cleared her throat, heat rushing to her face at the look he gave her.

'I'm surprised you're not.' His mouth twisted wryly. 'The usual Hawkridge finesse went right out of the window.'

'I don't know what that's like but I don't think I'd prefer it,' she said honestly.

His eyes blazed. 'In that case—' He bent his head and ran his tongue over the contours of her lips before suddenly crushing them with a hunger which made her tremble. His arms tightened in a rib-threatening grip but after a while he freed one hand to stroke her thighs again. His long fingers moved upward slowly to find the curves of her breasts, but when he began undoing her shirt buttons in smooth, rapid succession she stiffened and drew away.

'Now that *was* practised,' she said tartly, and slid off his lap, doing up her shirt again.

Adam locked his hands behind his dishevelled head, his teasing eyes gleaming. 'Lowri, I'm a lot older than you, and I've knocked around the world a bit. I'd be lying if I said I hadn't undone a fair few buttons and quite a lot more than that. I like women, and I revel in making love to them, but I make sure that in the process none of them suffer by it, mentally or physically. So my only apology is for letting the sheer pleasure of having you respond so unexpectedly turn me into a crass amateur, like a schoolboy who's never kissed a girl before.'

'That's a long speech,' said Lowri sedately. 'Would you like some more coffee?'

'I'd rather take you to bed.'

She stared at him, startled. 'You don't beat around the bush!'

'Normally there's none to beat around.'

'You mean you'd have already made it to bed by now with anyone else.'

Adam nodded, utterly matter-of-fact. 'Yes. You're the exception.'

'Really?' She got up and took their cups into the kitchen, Adam following behind. 'I like that.'

'Being an exception?'

'Yes.'

Adam shrugged wryly. 'Not that it would have progressed further anyway—at least not tonight.'

'Why, exactly?'

He rubbed his nose, eyeing her warily. 'Because of the nature of our relationship, Lowri, I didn't come prepared for such a contingency.' He smiled as colour flooded her sunburnt face again. 'And somehow I don't think you pop your little Pill like the other girls do.'

Lowri gave him a taunting look over her shoulder as she filled the kettle. 'You're wrong, actually.'

Adam stared in such shock that she swallowed a giggle as she spooned coffee into their cups. 'Are you telling me that all this maidenly reluctance on your part was a front, Lowri?'

'The reluctance, no. But if you mean have I had a lover the answer's yes.' She scowled at him. 'What's so funny about that? I'm twenty-one soon, Adam. A decade or so behind you, of course, but still a bit long in the tooth for maidenly purity.'

He shrugged, his eyes blank. 'I don't know, I just assumed you were—'

'A virgin,' she finished, resigned.

'Yes. I suppose I did.' Adam took the mug of coffee from her and swallowed some of it so convulsively it burnt his mouth.

Lowri handed him a glass of cold water. 'Here. I wouldn't have told you if I'd thought you'd be so shocked.'

'Surprised, not shocked.' His bright eyes narrowed under knitted brows. 'So why have you been handing out the touch-me-not routine?'

'My limited experience has rather made me wary.' She gave him a wry little smile. 'Pity I blurted the truth. I think you'd have been happier if I'd kept it to myself.'

He smiled, suddenly very much in command again. 'Pointless, Lowri. I'd have found out the moment I made love to you. Which I'm going to, I warn you,' he caught her in his arms, 'one day—or night—*very* soon, Lowri Morgan.' He kissed her long and hard before releasing her so suddenly she rocked on her heels. He smiled down at her victoriously. 'But I can be surprisingly patient when I want to be. Sweet dreams, darling. Come and lock the gate after me. If you must stay here alone tonight I want you safe and sound behind locked doors before I leave.'

In bed later Lowri cursed herself for shying away from Adam at the crucial moment. She was so much in love with him by now that she longed for him with an almost physical ache. She tossed and turned, forcing herself to face the truth. As she'd told Adam, it wouldn't be the first time. And last time she'd been hurt. She knew she would be this time, too, when it ended, but in a very different way. Adam was utterly honest about his no-strings, non-commitment policy. Philip Garfield had conned her from the first.

When Philip had been seconded from London to the Newport office, Lowri, knowing she was the envy of her female colleagues, had been utterly dazzled by the clever, confident man who'd pursued her openly from the moment they met. He flattered and courted Lowri, taking her out to dinner and the theatre, and finally away to a remote little hotel in mid-Wales for a secret, romantic weekend, with veiled promises of an important question to ask. Convinced Philip meant to propose, an excited Lowri had rushed off to what she believed was her destiny. In actual fact Philip had taken her to bed the moment they arrived, stampeding her swiftly and disappointingly into her first encounter with what she recognised instantly as mere sex and nothing to do with love. The moment it was over Philip confessed he was married. He told a shattered Lowri that he was separated from the wife who refused to divorce him. But for the brief period of his secondment there was no reason why he and his darling little Lowri couldn't enjoy a nice, intimate little relationship, as long as they were discreet.

Lowri, furious and disillusioned told him exactly what he could do with his neat little plan, repacked her bag and hitchhiked home to Cwmderwen. Life was one long, dull torture for a while afterwards as she came in contact with Philip Garfield daily at work. He made a very public show of ignoring her completely, giving rise to all kinds of comments from her colleagues, but Lowri hid her humiliation, refused to rise when she was teased, and greeted news of her subsequent redundancy with euphoria.

With Adam it was different. She was going into this with her eyes wide open, willing to share his final fling and prepared to cut her losses when responsibility finally overtook him. Or even sooner if he got tired of her first—or she of him. Lowri gave a mirthless little laugh in the darkness. Who are you kidding? She asked herself. You'll never tire of Adam if you live to a hundred.

All next day, through the flurry of welcome when the Clares returned, and the time she spent typing the notes she'd made about life in the fourteenth-century reign of Edward III, Lowri waited, strung tight as a violin string, for Adam to ring. When he did it was so late she'd given up all hope of hearing from him, and gave him a cool response.

'I've only just got back to the flat—sorry it's late, Lowri. Hope you aren't in bed.'

'No. I've been over at the house, chatting to Sarah.'

'I detect a hint of frost.'

'Certainly not.'

'Good. I would have rung earlier, but I spent most of the day with Dad and the rest of the board. Things are hotting up now his retirement's looming closer.'

'And at your age you must get tired so easily!' she said, mock solicitous.

'You little devil,' he hissed. 'If I had you right here in my arms this minute I'd show you exactly how old and tired I am!'

The laughing intimacy in the deep, caressing voice tightened muscles Lowri wasn't usually much aware of.

'No response?' he asked, amused.

'Yes. But I'm not telling you what it is,' she said demurely, and heard a sharp intake of breath.

'Witch! When can I see you again? Tonight?'

Summoning all her willpower, Lowri tried to postpone seeing him for a couple of days just to convince herself she was in control, but Adam wouldn't hear of it, telling her bluntly he intended to spend as much of his free time with her as he possibly could.

'You're seeing quite a bit of Adam these days,' said Sarah a couple of days later. 'He's staying the course with you far longer than he usually does with the Carolines of this world.'

'Probably because we're just friends,' said Lowri, not altogether truthfully.

'Or maybe because you're the only one who's ever held out against the famous Hawkridge charm.' Sarah eyed her young cousin challengingly. 'I take it you *are* holding out?'

Lowri grinned. 'Since you ask, yes. I am.'

'I'm amazed. Rupert says—'

'You and Rupert discuss me?'

'Of course we do! We're not just fond of you—we feel responsible, too.'

'Oh, Sarah!' Lowri blinked hard.

'Now don't go all mushy and sentimental on me, but it's the truth just the same,' Sarah pulled a face. 'I wouldn't put it past Rupert to corner Adam and demand his intentions!'

'He'd better not!' said Lowri in alarm, then shrugged. 'Besides, I know exactly what Adam's intentions are—a good time, no strings and no recriminations when we go our separate ways.'

Sarah snorted. 'He doesn't want much, does he? Are you happy with that?'

'Yes,' fibbed Lowri firmly. 'Adam's great fun, and I enjoy his company, but he's the last man I'd think of settling down with. When I get to that stage—which won't be for years yet—I'll find me a man who doesn't run a mile at the thought of commitment and babies.'

It was a thought which sustained her through dinner at an Italian restaurant in Putney the following Friday, an outing to seventeenth-century Ham House near the Thames below Richmond Hill the day after, right through an evening at the theatre watching the new Tom Stoppard play and up to the moment when Adam saw her through the Clares' side gate late on the Saturday night. At the foot of her stair Lowri stood firm, baulking any attempt on Adam's part to see her inside the flat.

'You're not letting me come up tonight,' he stated wryly. 'Is that because the family's in residence over at the house this weekend?'

Lowri thought about it, and nodded. 'I rather think it is.' It was the truth. Inviting Adam to share a bed which actually belonged to the Clares didn't seem the right thing to do. She reached up a hand to his face. 'You probably think I'm silly.'

'No—just very, very sweet.' Adam kissed the hand and held it tight. 'How about tomorrow? The weekend isn't over yet.'

'Right. Where do you want to go?'

'I thought a swim and a picnic—my turn to provide the eats.'

Lowri nodded happily. 'Sounds lovely. Where?'

Adam grinned. 'Wait and see.' He bent swiftly and kissed her gently. Then kissed her again, less gently, and suddenly they were locked in each others' arms careless of the fact that they were in full view of anyone who cared to stroll in the garden in the scented, summer darkness.

Adam put her from him at last, breathing hard. 'I'd better go,' he said unevenly.

She nodded wordlessly, reached up for one last kiss, then went inside her little flat and shut the door before she could change her mind.

Adam had been gone for half an hour before it suddenly dawned on Lowri that the only decent swimsuit she possessed was at home in Cwmderwen. Swimming hadn't featured in her life since her arrival in London.

'No problem,' said Sarah cheerfully next day over the lazy, once-weekly ritual of breakfast Lowri usually shared with the Clares. 'You can borrow one of mine.'

'It wouldn't fit,' said Lowri, depressed.

'Rubbish. I'm not the sylph I was since Emily's advent, and you've lost a few pounds lately, I fancy.'

'Am I working you too hard, Lowri?' demanded Rupert, emerging from a screen of Sunday papers suddenly.

'No, of course not.'

'I don't want Geraint on the rampage because I'm wearing his daughter to a shadow!'

'If anyone's wearing her to a shadow, darling, it's Adam, not you,' said his wife.

'Geraint might not be too pleased about that, either,' he said darkly, and eyed Lowri in suspicion. 'Everything all right?'

'Of course it is. Adam's just a friend, Rupert.'

'Hmm.' Rupert retreated behind his paper, unconvinced, and Sarah took Lowri upstairs to choose something for the swimming expedition.

Firmly rejecting brief two-piece trifles Sarah offered her, Lowri seized on a plain, beautifully cut black one-piece maillot which flattered her shape very satisfactorily and showed off the tan she'd acquired during lunchbreaks spent lying in the recent sunshine they'd been blessed with.

When Adam arrived to collect her it was an hour before they got away, due to offers of coffee from Sarah, and pleas to stay from Emily and Dominic. When they heard he was taking Lowri swimming, the longing on both young faces prompted a promise from Adam that he'd include them both in the next swimming expedition.

'But not today,' said Adam, as he drove Lowri away later. 'Today I want you all to myself.'

Smiling happily in agreement, Lowri asked where they were headed.

'You'll see soon enough,' he said mysteriously. 'I hope you've brought something to swim in.'

Lowri assured him she had and sat back, letting her hair blow in the wind, her face to the sun as Adam's roadster took her through London on the way to the mysterious destination. When they eventually arrived she stared in surprise as he drove into the underground car park of a large block of flats.

'Why are we stopping here?'

'Because this is where we're going swimming, my pet.' Adam grinned at her as he switched off the ignition. 'Wapping, home of rising young electronics wizard Adam Hawkridge.'

Lowri stared at him, then began to laugh. 'I'd rather expected Brighton.'

'Too unoriginal. You'll like it much better here in Wapping.'

He was right. The indoor swimming-pool attached to the building was a surprisingly luxurious affair, with pillars and concealed lighting, greenery in tubs, and not another soul in sight.

'Where is everyone?' asked Lowri later, when she emerged in her borrowed bathing suit.

'In bed—or in Brighton, probably,' said Adam with a grin, and gave her a swift, all-encompassing scrutiny from head to foot. 'Very nice indeed, Miss Morgan.'

'Likewise, Mr Hawkridge,' she returned serenely, her colour a little high. But impressive was more the word, she thought secretly, one swift look enough for an indelible impression of broad shoulders and slim hips, long, muscular legs. And without any fuss she dived neatly into the water and set out for the far end with the efficient crawl she'd learned at school. Adam dived in after her and passed her without effort, treading water until she joined him, then turned with her to swim effortlessly at her pace for several lengths before suddenly disappearing beneath the water. She looked about her nonplussed for a moment, then suddenly Adam shot up out of the water, imprisoning her in his arms, laughing. Just as abruptly he let her go again, and for a few minutes they ducked and dived and splashed like children, before Lowri took off at the fastest speed she could manage, only to be caught long before she reached the far end of the pool.

'All right, all right,' she gasped. 'You win.'

Adam heaved himself out of the water and leant down to pull her up out the water in one easy movement, not even short of breath as he wrapped her in her pink towelling robe.

'That was fun,' she said breathlessly, rubbing her hair with a sleeve. 'So where do we go for the picnic?'

'Not far. You don't even have to change first. Just bring your bag with you and we can go up in the service lift as we are.'

Lowri eyed him narrowly. 'You mean you're taking me to your flat?'

He nodded, grinning from ear to ear. 'Bullseye. If you're *very* good I may even show you my etchings.'

Adam's home was high up in the modern, pyramid-shaped building, with a bird's eye view of the Thames from the terrace outside his living room. It was a white-walled, sparsely furnished place, a very masculine air about its stripped wood floors, and furniture covered in glove-soft Italian leather the colour of vintage port. The windows had louvred blinds instead of curtains, and the only wall free of bookshelves was hung with a variety of artwork ranging from a pair of small oils to a series of pen and ink sketches. Adam's kitchen was clinically white and businesslike, but his bathroom had a touch of the sybarite about the coral-red walls and black and white chequered floor, the claw-footed Victorian bathtub and huge gold-framed mirror sporting cherubs at each corner.

'Gosh,' said Lowri, awed. 'So this is how the man-about-town lives.'

'Only very recently,' he assured her. 'I still have my bedroom at home with my parents. And after that and before this—when I came home from the States—I had a rather scruffy place not far from here in a less upwardly mobile part of the community.' He indicated a pile of striped black and white towels on a wooden stand the same vintage as the bath. 'Help yourself—plenty of shampoo and so on. I'll get lunch ready.'

'Don't you need a hand?'

'Not for my type of catering!'

Lowri had a swift bath, washed her hair free of chlorine and dried it vigorously on one of the huge towels. Afterwards she added a touch of colour to her lips, flicked on some mascara and resumed the yellow cotton dress she'd worn earlier. When she emerged, damp hair caught back from her face with a yellow towelling bandeau, Adam was in the kitchen, wearing a fresh white cotton shirt and jeans, his bare feet in espadrilles and his hair still damp.

He looked up with a smile. 'I hope you're not allergic to lobster.'

'Only to the cost,' she assured him.

Adam led her to a glass-topped table on the small terrace, seated her in a red leather chair and served her half a lobster with lemon mayonnaise, crisp green salad and hot Italian bread. They drank dry white wine with the meal, then took a rest for a while before Adam produced a Sachertorte frosted in smooth dark chocolate too alluring for Lowri to resist.

'Catering's easy if one patronises a certain well-known chain-store foodhall,' said Adam, grinning. 'A half-hour shopping session yesterday morning before I came for you and hey presto, lunch for two.'

'It was wonderful,' said Lowri with a sigh, gazing out at the Thames.

'Would you like some coffee?'

'Not at the moment.' Lowri slid lower in the chair. 'I just want to sit in the sunshine and gaze at the view for a while. I'll help you wash up later.'

'No need. I've got a machine for that.'

Lowri chuckled. 'Have you got a machine for everything?'

'No,' said Adam softly. 'Some things a machine can't do for a man.'

She shot him a look, but his bright eyes were bland beneath the thick straight brows.

'Adam,' she said bluntly. 'Is this the one day soon you were talking about? Have you brought me here to seduce me?'

He threw back his head and laughed. 'When it comes to a bush you don't beat around it much yourself, Lowri Morgan.'

She took off the bandeau and shook out her hair to dry in the sunshine. 'You must admit this has all the hallmarks—the surprise trip to your flat, the exquisite meal, the wine. The works, in fact.'

Adam got up to collect plates. 'You've forgotten something I once told you, Lowri. I only take what's freely given. Does that answer your question?'

'I don't know.' She yawned, suddenly sleepy after the swim and the wine and the sunshine. 'I'll think about it.'

'You just sit there while I see to this lot. When I come back you can tell me exactly how you'd like to spend the rest of the day.'

She nodded drowsily. 'Right.' When she was alone Lowri relaxed completely, only dimly aware of the drone of traffic somewhere in the distance below. Her eyelids felt weighted, and soon all her thought processes ground to a halt and she fell asleep.

Lowri woke with a start, disorientated, to find herself on a wide bed in cool twilight in what was obviously Adam's bedroom. A swift look at her watch told her it wasn't late evening, as it might well have been from the light. It was a mere three hours since lunch. She shot upright in dismay. Taking a long nap—or any nap at all—was hardly good manners for a guest invited to lunch. She slid off the bed rapidly, opened the blinds and went into Adam's bathroom to spend a few necessary minutes there. Her bag, she saw, touched, had been left by the side of the bed where she would find it easily. After a touch of lipstick and a vigorous session with her hairbrush she went in search of Adam to apologise.

He was out on the terrace, deep in the Sunday papers. As she stepped out from the living-room he jumped to his feet, smiling.

'Better?' He ran his eyes over her. 'You look all flushed and rested—good enough to eat.'

'I've slept for ages. I'm very sorry,' she said penitently.

'Why?' He held out a chair for her. 'I'm flattered you felt at home enough here to relax.'

'I don't imagine women usually fall asleep on you,' she said drily.

He grinned. 'Not over lunch, anyway.'

Lowri flushed. 'I'd quite like that coffee now.'

'Coming up,' he said promptly. 'Or you can have tea, if you like.'

'Oh, yes, please! Shall I—?'

'No. You just sit there and read the paper.'

When Adam brought a tea tray he'd added a plate of cookies. 'I thought you'd like something to nibble with the tea—all from the same reliable source.'

'I know. They're my favourites.'

They drank tea together, ate a few cookies, talked about some of the news items Adam picked out from the paper. Then Lowri flipped through the pages of the magazine, showing him several pages of the latest beachwear.

'None of them comes within streets of that black affair you were wearing,' said Adam.

'Borrowed plumes from Sarah. Mine's at home.'

'Wherever it came from, you looked good in it. Very good,' he added with emphasis.

'It must be the cut.'

'No, sweetheart, it was the shape inside it.'

Adam's eyes met hers, and held, and at last she looked away, seizing on the book review section from the pile of papers in front of her. She studied it furiously, suddenly so intensely aware of the man beside her the paper shook in her hands.

Adam cleared his throat. 'We'd better go out,' he said gruffly and got up, holding out his hand to her. 'Come on, we'll go for a drive, walk in a park somewhere.'

Lowri nodded blindly and dropped the paper, then bent to pick it up just as Adam did the same. Their heads cracked together and she gave a little shriek and Adam caught her in his arms and held her close.

'Darling, did I hurt you?'

Lowri shook her head.

'Look at me,' he ordered. 'Look at me, Lowri!'

Slowly, reluctantly, her lids lifted until she met the question in his intent, brilliant eyes. She answered it without words, melting against him, rubbing her cheek against his chest, and Adam picked her up and carried her through his living-room and along the hall, with a slow, measured tread like a sleepwalker, giving her every opportunity to change her mind right up to the moment when he lowered her to his bed and stretched himself out beside her.

They lay face to face, as still as their mutual, thundering heartbeat allowed, then Adam bent his head and Lowri met his kiss with a fire which dispensed with questions. The spell abruptly broken, they surged together, hands and lips seeking and urgent, and at last, breathing laboured, Adam took off her clothes with unsteady hands rendered clumsy by need. As before, Lowri's response to such lack of skill was so heated that Adam tore off his own clothes and pulled her naked body close, his breath leaving his lungs with a rush at the contact. Hard, muscular angles and soft, buoyant curves fitted together with such exquisite exactitude that Lowri's hips moved involuntarily and Adam gave a smothered sound, his kisses suddenly famished and desperate as he caressed her to a fever-pitch of longing. And at last, vanquished by the need overwhelming them both, he buried his face against her throat and their bodies flowed together in such harmony that there on a sunny Sunday afternoon, high above the Thames, they achieved a miracle that for Adam with all his experience, and for Lowri with virtually none, was as near perfection as two humans could ever hope to achieve.

CHAPTER SEVEN

IT WAS almost dawn when Adam drove Lowri back to St John's Wood.

'I'm glad it's so late,' she said drowsily. 'I don't want to run into Sarah or Rupert—or anyone in the world to-night.'

Adam ran a caressing hand over her thigh. 'Why not?'

'Because I rather fancy that what's happened is writ large in my face, Adam Hawkridge. One look at me and Sarah will know how I spent a shamefully major part of my Sunday.'

He gave her a questioning, sidelong glance. 'Regrets, Lowri?'

She thought about it for a moment. 'Theoretically I should have some, I suppose. But I don't. At least I now know what all the fuss is about. I didn't know it could be like that.'

'Neither did I.' He smiled wryly at the disbelieving look she turned on him. 'It's God's truth, Lowri. I've made love to a lot of women. I admit it. But until today I thought of lovemaking as—well as a sort of appetite, like eating your dinner, or enjoying a fine wine. With you it was different. Surely you realised that?'

'It was certainly different for me,' she agreed. 'But my former brush with the subject was a disaster, so almost anything halfway pleasant would have been better.'

'Thanks a lot!' His hand tightened cruelly on her knee. 'Who was he?'

'No point in telling you. You wouldn't know him. And

the whole affair finished before it started, almost, when I found out he was married.'

Adam brought the car to a halt near the gate in the Clares' garden wall. 'I'm coming in,' he said brusquely, as he helped her out.

Lowri gave him a startled glance, and without a word unlocked the gate and ran ahead of him up the stairs to her flat. Once inside he took her in his arms and kissed her, and went on kissing her until their hearts were pounding.

'I know it's illogical,' he said through his teeth, 'but after what happened today I can't stand the thought of other men, past or present. I won't share, Lowri.'

'Does that work both ways?' she demanded.

'Of course it does,' he said roughly. 'Rules of the game.' His eyes darkened. 'What the hell is it about you? I want you again, right now.'

Lowri stared at him, her breathing quickening. Colour flooded her face as he caught her to him and began kissing her again, all over her face and down her neck until she pushed him away with shaking hands. 'Adam, I need breathing space. This is all a bit—sudden.'

'Sudden!' He gave a bark of laughter. 'I gave you due warning days ago.'

Her eyes locked with his. 'So was lunch at your place part of an overall plan for what happened?'

Adam's eyes gleamed irrepressibly. 'Of course it was. Thoughts of taking you to bed were keeping me awake at night.'

Lowri's eyes softened at his honesty. 'I confess to the odd girlish fantasy on the subject myself.' She smiled a little. 'Not that any of them were a patch on the reality. It's easy to see why all the girls are mad about you.'

He seized her shoulders and shook her. 'Don't cheapen it, Lowri. It's never been like that with anyone else. Nor do I know why it is with you. You're not conventionally pretty or a sensational shape—'

'Like the others,' she snapped.

'Will you stop banging on about the others? Just believe me when I say that our experience together was a rare and beautiful thing. For me, anyway,' he added roughly, and pushed her away.

Lowri pulled him back, sliding her arms round his neck. 'It was for me too—and you know it.'

Adam kissed her long and hard, then released her with reluctance. 'Time I let you go to bed,' he said, touching a hand to her cheek.

'I probably won't sleep.' She gave him a half-embarrassed little smile. 'I've spent too much time in bed today already!'

Sleep soon came last on Lowri's list of priorities, since Adam demanded they spend every possible moment they could together, making no secret of the fact that once he was in charge at the firm his time would no longer be his own.

'We'll still see each other as much as I can manage,' he assured her, 'but it might have to be just weekends for a while until I settle into the new job. But until then,' he said, smiling in a way which made her heart turn over, 'I want to see as much of you as I can, starting right now.'

'Which means get your clothes off and come to bed, I suppose,' said Lowri cheekily, then gave a squeak as he yanked her into his arms and slid down the zip of her dress almost in one movement.

'I'm more than willing to do it for you,' he assured her as they fell, laughing together, on his wide, welcoming bed.

Sarah and Rupert were worried, Lowri knew, but refrained from interference with a tact she deeply appreciated. She told Sarah so when her cousin came up to the office one morning with a covered dish of pasta for Lowri's lunch.

'Whatever it is you do with Adam, it can't include food much,' said Sarah bluntly. 'You're losing weight, and you're all eyes. Can't you sleep?'

'Oh, yes, when I get the chance—' Lowri stopped dead, blushing vividly.

Sarah sighed. 'Go on, eat this up while it's hot. I'll make us some coffee.' She came back with two mugs and perched on the arm of the sofa, eyeing Lowri while she ate.

'You couldn't hold out, then.'

'No.' Lowri met her cousin's beautiful eyes squarely. 'As must be perfectly obvious.'

'Since you mention it, *cariad*, yes, it is.' Sarah hesitated. 'Does your father know?'

'I told him I've got a boyfriend.'

'Is that how you think of Adam?'

Lowri smiled wryly. 'I don't think Dad would appreciate being told I've got a lover. It's such an emotive sort of word.'

'But pretty apt, just the same. You're head over heels in love, aren't you?'

'You know I am. I have been from the moment I first laid eyes on Adam, if we're into truth here.'

'In that case it's a miracle you held out so long!' Sarah examined her fingernails intently. 'How does he feel about you?'

Lowri hesitated. 'It never ceases to amaze me that he wants to take me to bed the minute we're together, if that's what you're asking. And even out of bed we enjoy each other's company. Adam's a lot of fun to be with. But beyond that your guess is as good as mine.'

'Rupert's making noises like an anxious parent, you know.'

'That's very sweet of him. But tell him not to worry. I went into this with my eyes wide open.'

Sarah got up to go. 'Just remember we're here if you want us. Any time at all.'

Lowri smiled. 'Thanks Sarah. By the way, Adam suggests we take Emily and Dominic over to his place on Saturday morning for a swim in the pool, then out somewhere for lunch.'

'Which means straight to the nearest burger bar, of course.' Sarah looked pleased. 'It's very good of Adam—in the circumstances I'm surprised he can spare the time!'

Then to her dismay Lowri caught a stomach bug and had to spend a couple of days in bed, precious time she begrudged away from Adam. Marooned in her bedroom, feeling wretched both from the malaise and the antibiotics she was given to cure it, Lowri had more cause than ever to feel grateful to Sarah, who looked after her without fussing, and kept Rupert and the children away until the patient was on the mend.

Adam was refused admittance until Lowri felt confident she'd stopped throwing up, but he came to see her the moment he was allowed, complete with flowers and books, and adamant she needed a breath of country air to complete the cure.

'My parents own a cottage a few miles from Hereford,' he told her. 'I'll drive you down there this weekend for some peace and quiet far from the madding crowd.' He sat on the edge of the bed, smiling into her eyes. 'I'm suffering too. It's a hell of a long time since I held you in my arms.'

'You can't want to the way I look now,' she said, slight colour tinging her face.

'Wrong!' And to illustrate his point Adam drew her up against him gently, and kissed her at length. 'I'll come for you on Friday afternoon.'

Lowri recovered as quickly as she'd succumbed. Probably, she told herself, because the prospect of a weekend away with Adam was a more effective cure than all the pills she'd swallowed.

The cottage was a long way from anywhere, reached by an unadopted road which led up past a few isolated houses to a common which stretched for miles with no sign of human habitation.

'Nothing to disturb us here,' said Adam, as he led the way down a steep garden to a cottage with glorious views across a valley from its front windows. 'Peter and I loved it here. He was a lot older than me, but he let me go with him to roam over the common, go shooting for rabbits, pick hops, too, in September. And sometimes we'd sneak out at night and lie low in the garden for hours for a glimpse of the local badger family.'

Lowri gazed at the view with a rapturous sigh, then held out her arms to Adam. 'It's utterly perfect. Thank you for bringing me here.'

He hugged her close, kissed her, then put her away from him firmly. 'Supper first, then an early night. You must be tired.'

Lowri smiled invitingly. 'I'm not in the least tired, but the early night sounds good.'

'If you smile at me like that it'll be earlier than you think,' he warned, grinning. 'Come and help me put supper.'

Later, as they lay together in bed, tired at last after love-making all the more impassioned after the period of abstinence, she marvelled at the sheer quiet of the place after London, and stared wistfully into the darkness which was so much more intense here, far away from any city lights. This was such a perfect place for a honeymoon. She knew beyond all doubt that she wanted to belong to Adam for the rest of her life, but if he felt the same way he never said so. He made love to her as though she were food and he starved for her, talked to her on every subject under the sun, and laughed and teased and paid her extravagant compliments. But he never said a word about love. Lowri curved her body closer to his, making a fierce, silent vow to convince Adam once and for all that marriage was their mutual destiny.

Lowri got her wish, but, like the one granted by the monkey's paw, it was in the last form she wanted. After a couple of weeks' panic Lowri secretly bought herself a pregnancy testing kit, got in an even worse panic at the result, and felt sick with apprehension as she went to meet Adam at the flat one Friday night. When he let her in he looked drawn and haggard himself, with dark smudges beneath his eyes, and for once looked every one of the years she teased him about so often. For a moment she was tempted to keep quiet, to wait for another more propitious time. But, afraid there'd never be one, she blurted out the news the moment he'd closed the door behind him.

'You're *what*!' said Adam, his eyes narrowed to appalled slits.

'I'm pregnant,' she repeated baldly.

'How?'

'In the usual way, Adam. With your help,' she added, feeling cold.

He flung away to pace round the room like a caged tiger. 'I suppose you forgot to take your Pill,' he threw at her.

'I did not!' Her eyes flashed. 'I take it religiously, always. But I had a stomach bug, remember. I took antibiotics, and the Pill didn't work this time. It's not infallible.'

Adam stared at her in brooding silence for so long Lowri shivered, despite the warmth of the evening. 'Are you telling me the truth, Lowri?' he said slowly at last. 'Or did you by any chance engineer this little ''accident'' deliberately, to trap me?'

Lowri's heart gave a sickening thump against her ribs. The silence in the room lengthened again cruelly before she said in a flat, wooden voice, 'No. I didn't do that. I'd better go.' She turned away to pick up her overnight bag.

'Don't be so stupid,' he said brusquely, looking more like a grim stranger than the rakish, laughing Adam she'd fallen in love with. 'We've got some sorting out to do.'

Lowri shook her head, her face blank. 'No. We haven't. You've just made it patently clear I'm to blame. In which case any sorting out is my business, none of yours.' She made for the door without a backward glance, but his hand came down hard on her shoulder before she reached it.

'Lowri, wait.' Adam's tone was slightly more conciliatory. 'I suppose I shouldn't have said that—but hell, surely you can appreciate the shock you gave me. Let's talk things through, go over the options.'

'Options?' She gave him a look of such glacial distaste angry colour rose in Adam's face.

'Yes, options!' he snapped, and forced her down into a chair.

'If you're about to give me the address of a nice private clinic, don't bother,' she flung up at him. 'It might do for your other women, but not for me.'

'None of my so-called ''other women'' ever put me in this position,' he hurled back, his face white with anger.

'It's the first time for me, too! Do you think I'm enjoying this?' She jumped up, but Adam shoved her back again ungently, then bit his lip, thrusting his hand through his hair.

'Sorry—didn't think.'

'That makes two of us,' snapped Lowri. 'A bit more thought on my part and none of this would be happening.'

'Don't be stupid. It is happening, so something must be done about it,' he said forcefully.

'First,' said Lowri coldly, 'let me make two things very clear. I intend both to have the baby, *and* to keep it.' She gestured at him regally. 'Now you can have your say.'

Adam stared down at her, his eyes oddly blank. 'I see. It's ultimatum time.' He shrugged. 'All right. You leave me with no choice. We get married.'

'Oh, *please*,' she said scathingly. 'Spare me the histrionics. Right from the beginning you made it clear that marriage and a family are the last things you want. Besides, shotgun weddings are a bit out of date, Adam. Please don't trouble yourself. I'll manage on my own.'

'Who's into histrionics now?' Adam's mouth tightened. 'You're being stupid again, Lowri. There's nothing else for it. I'll arrange a quiet wedding as quickly as possible—'

'To hide my shame?' she said derisively. 'Get real, Adam. Times have changed.'

Adam's jaw set. 'It's nothing like that. I meant that we have to get it done quickly before—before my time's taken up with the changeover at Hawk Electronics.'

'Ah, yes, Hawk Electronics—your *real* baby.' Lowri stared blindly at her feet for a long time, her mind working at a furious rate. 'Right,' she said at last. 'But with one proviso.'

He sighed irritably. 'What now?'

'We keep the entire thing, wedding included, secret until it's done. Then to the world a quick, quiet wedding was just our rush to tie the knot before you take over the firm, as you said. But no word about the baby until absolutely necessary.'

Adam looked impatient. 'It's not a secret you can keep for long, Lowri.'

'Long enough to give me—and you—a bit of breathing

space; time to adjust to the idea,' said Lowri firmly, and stood up. 'Now I really must go.'

Adam's eyes softened slightly for the first time since she'd broken the news. 'Why? You look exhausted. Anyway, I thought you were staying tonight.'

She gave him a scathing look. 'Bad idea, in the circumstances.'

'I'll sleep on the sofa out here, if you prefer,' he offered.

Lowri stared at him, wondering why a man of his famed experience with women couldn't tell that she yearned for him to take her to bed and hold her in his arms all night. The last thing in the world she needed was a night in his bed alone while he slept on his rotten sofa.

'No, thanks. I'll just ring for a cab—'

'Don't be stupid, I'll drive you,' he snapped angrily.

'If you call me stupid once more I'll hit you, so stop it!' she bit back, cut to pieces because he hadn't insisted she stay.

'I will when you stop talking like an idiot!' He seized her arm to march her through the hall to the door. 'I'm driving you home, whether you want me to or not.'

Afterwards Lowri could never look back on what followed without shuddering. From the moment she broke the unwelcome news Adam changed from a laughing, demanding lover into a humourless, businesslike stranger who condemned her insistence on utter secrecy as both juvenile and irritating.

'Nevertheless I insist,' Lowri said obdurately. 'We can get it over with while your mother and father are away on their cruise.'

'*Your* father's not on a cruise,' Adam pointed out curtly. 'Won't he think it a touch odd when you present me as a *fait accompli* after the deed is done?'

'Dad's very much taken up with his own affairs at the

moment,' said Lowri flatly. 'Holly's not too well. No point in adding to his worries.'

Adam eyed her morosely. 'I trust you'll tell him it wasn't my idea when the time comes.'

'Don't worry, I'll take the blame.' Lowri smiled at him disdainfully. 'I'll make *sure* he knows *none* of this was your idea.'

Their relationship changed so completely it was hard sometimes for Lowri to remember Adam as someone she once had fun with, let alone as a demanding lover. To keep the change from Sarah and Rupert, Lowri asked Adam to avoid St John's Wood for the time being.

'Let's keep to neutral ground until—until afterwards,' she said firmly. 'Restaurants will do.'

'Bloody waste of money.' Adam eyed her barely touched dinner grimly. 'You hardly eat anything. We might as well stay at home and have a sandwich—I could save money for my approaching commitments.'

'Perhaps it might be better if we don't meet at all until the wedding,' she said stonily.

'Don't be—' Adam caught himself up in time. 'Look, Lowri, why won't you come back to my place? I promise not to lay a finger on you until after we're married if that's what you want.'

What utter idiots men could be, thought Lowri bitterly. Adam's obvious distaste for laying a finger on her was precisely why she preferred to give his flat a wide berth. News of forthcoming fatherhood had been the kiss of death to his famed libido as far as she was concerned. He gave her impersonal goodnight kisses, it was true, but they were perfunctory gestures unworthy of the word caress. They spent less and less time together as the date of their nuptials approached.

'Might as well get as much work in beforehand as possible,' said Adam in extenuation. 'My parents leave next week, remember. And while we're on the subject I still think you should meet them before they go.'

'No!' Lowri was adamant. 'Let's leave it until they get back.'

One evening, shortly before the date set for the secret wedding, Sarah surprised Lowri in tears, and proceeded to extract the entire story from her, then took her over to the house to repeat it to Rupert. Lowri talked with them into the small hours, glad at last to confide in someone, and feeling it was only fair that they, at least, should know the truth. Her gratitude was boundless when they hugged her close and reiterated their pledge of help and support as they walked her back to the flat through the starlit garden.

The wedding-day dawned as bright and sunny as any bride could wish for. Lowri looked up at the sky with a wry smile, had a bath, washed her hair and dried it carefully, a process which took longer now her hair had grown. She took almost as long over her face, dressed with care, added the last bits and pieces to the luggage waiting near the door. Afterwards she went over to the house and bade a rather emotional farewell to Sarah and Rupert, and hugged Emily hard, grateful that Dominic was playing cricket, and spared the embarrassment of seeing her cry.

When the taxi came she was ready and waiting, her tears dry, and her face composed. With one last round of good-byes she got in the cab, waving to the others as it moved away, then turned in her seat to stare straight ahead, feeling that one chapter in her life was well and truly over. She hadn't wanted to leave Sarah and Rupert to face the music, but Rupert was adamant. When Adam Hawkridge came storming round to the house, as he was certain to do, not only would he find the bird flown, he'd have Rupert Clare at his most formidable to contend with.

Lowri stared out of the window, feeling no qualms at all about leaving Adam in the lurch. In fact, she discovered, it satisfied some deep, primeval need in her to think of him pacing up and down waiting for the bride who never came. Do him good, she thought fiercely. Who said revenge wasn't sweet? In her mind's eye she could just picture him jamming coins in a callbox to ring her, then driving like a maniac to St John's Wood to pick up the terse letter Rupert had ready and waiting for him.

Dear Adam,

You're saved. My pregnancy was a false alarm, after all. Put it down to panic, or maybe a faulty testing kit. Either way, the hole-and-corner wedding isn't necessary. Not that *I* ever insisted on it. You did—probably afraid it would tarnish your image to be seen as shirking your responsibilities. You've got so many of these now you must be glad of one less. Especially this one.

This is not an apology for standing you up at the register office, by the way. I did that deliberately—my little gesture of retaliation. You were not kind, Adam. And lately you've become a stranger. One I don't want to know any more.

Goodbye,

Lowri.

CHAPTER EIGHT

Lowri locked the shop door with a sigh of relief, stretched mightily, then called down the stairs to the basement.

'Everything all right, Jenny?'

'Fine,' came the answer. 'Just tidying up a bit.'

'Could you hang on a few minutes while I nip to the supermarket? We were so busy at lunchtime I never got out to buy food.'

'Take as long as you like, Boss. We're perfectly happy down here. I'm in no hurry.'

'Great. Won't be long.'

Lowri let herself out of the shop, took a quick, proprietary look at the window display, made a mental note to rearrange some of it, then got in her car to drive quickly through rush-hour Pennington. She eyed the clock, calculating another five minutes to the supermarket, a ten-minute dash round the store to do her shopping, five minutes for parking, another five to get back—suddenly she gasped and jammed on her brakes hard as the back of the car in front loomed close. She wasn't quick enough. There was a grinding impact and she was flung back and then forwards, held by the seatbelt. To an accompaniment of irate tooting of horns a man leapt out of the car in front to inspect the damage, ignoring the traffic damming up behind them.

Groaning in horror, Lowri fought to release the seatbelt, then got out to discover she'd driven into the back of a large, very expensive-looking car. The man bending over to inspect his property straightened and turned to confront her, his face grim with anger but so unmistakable under the street-light that the blood rushed to her face, then receded so suddenly that she felt sick as she sagged against her car in shock.

'What the devil were you playing at?' he demanded, incensed. 'Didn't you see the bloody lights change?' He stopped short as he reached her, his eyes narrowing in abrupt incredulity. He stared at her for a moment then shook his head in disbelief. 'Good lord, *you*, Lowri? I don't believe it. Lowri Morgan, as I live and breathe!'

Before she could find a word to say two policemen arrived on the scene, one of them directing the traffic, the other questioning Adam Hawkridge about the mishap.

'Just one of those things, Officer,' said Adam quickly. 'The lady and I were together. She was following me and I stopped too quickly. My fault entirely.'

On inspection Adam pronounced his car virtually unscathed, unlike Lowri's modest little runabout, which was very much the worse for wear.

'I'll ring my garage,' she said quickly. 'They'll tow it away.'

'Can we leave it here, Officer?' enquired Adam. 'I'll give the lady a lift.'

Minutes later, with the help of the police Lowri's car had been pushed down a side street ready for collection, she'd rung her garage on Adam Hawkridge's car phone and she was sitting in the passenger seat of his Daimler, making a belated effort at apology to a companion whose aura of hostility was almost tangible now they were alone.

'I'm very sorry,' she said as he drove away. 'I was in a panic to get to the shops. I just didn't stop in time.'

'I can't say I'm altogether sorry myself,' he said coldly. 'I always hoped I'd bump into you again one day—though not quite so literally, it's true.'

'I'll give you the name of my insurance company—'

'Unnecessary. I shan't hound you for the sake of a scraped bumper and a new rear light.'

'Thank you. That's very good of you.'

'Good?' he retorted savagely. 'I think I'm being bloody magnanimous for a jilted bridegroom, if that's what you mean.'

'I don't,' she flung back, her penitence vanished. 'I meant that I'm to blame for the accident just now.'

'From my point of view you're culpable for a damn sight more than that!'

Lowri'd had enough. She gestured towards a row of parking spaces at the end of the gardens lining the main street. 'Stop here please. I'll walk the rest of the way.'

'If you've got some idea of disappearing again, forget it,' he said forcibly. 'I'll come with you, then drive you home. I'm not letting you out of my sight until I know where you live.'

Lowri breathed in deeply, struggling for calm. 'I'd much rather you didn't do that.'

He gave her a cold, encompassing glance. 'I take it there's someone who'd object if you came home with a strange man in tow.'

'Yes, there is,' she assured him. 'You can drop me here. Thank you for the lift. My apologies again for running into you.'

'I'll park here for a moment, but you're not going any-where yet.' A long, sinewy hand grasped her wrist. She eyed it, then looked up at him with hauteur, stiffening as Adam's teeth showed in a brief, frightening smile.

'Not so fast,' he said softly. 'I'm entitled to some expla-nations. You did quite a lot of damage to my life, Lowri Morgan. It's time you repaired some of it.'

Her mouth tightened. 'The main damage was to your ego, Adam, and since that's obviously alive and well I feel no obligation to give you any explanation at all.'

He eyed her from head to foot without haste. 'You've changed, Lowri.'

'You mean I've grown up,' she retorted. 'I'm not the vulnerable, stupid little girl you once knew, Adam Hawkridge. It may be less than two years in actual time since we last met, but in other ways it feels like a lifetime.'

They stared at each other in open antagonism, each one taking stock of the changes wrought in the other since their last meeting.

During the halcyon days of their relationship Adam had looked younger than his age. Now he appeared more than the mere thirty-four Lowri knew him to be. Responsibility and leadership had etched lines on the familiar, striking face. There was a vertical crease between the heavy straight brows, strands of grey among the brown of his hair, but his eyes were as bright and searching—and cold—as ever.

They took their time in moving over her from the glossy black hair, long now and tied back with a yellow scarf, to her face, which she knew was thinner, its contours emphasised skilfully with make up she hadn't bothered with much in the old days. Adam's eyes moved lower, over her suede bomber jacket and brown wool trousers tucked into fawn suede boots, and she moved restively under the hard, dissecting scrutiny. At last he released her hand, and Lowri stiffened as she caught sight of the dashboard clock.

'I must get back this minute,' she said urgently. 'I'll leave the shopping. Could you please drive me back to— to the place where I work? I've got a colleague waiting for me before she can go.'

'If you insist.'

It was only a short distance to the elegant little side street of shops, most of them converted from houses built when the town had been a fashionable spa in Regency days. Lowri directed Adam past the antique dealer and the jeweller and the shop selling expensive shoes and leather goods, and asked him to pull up outside a double-fronted shop where one window held cleverly arranged baby clothes, the other a beautiful antique cradle, overflowing with lace and ribbons.

'Little Darlings,' said Adam, eyeing the name above the shop. 'Is this where you work?'

'That's right.' Lowri unfastened the seatbelt swiftly and gave him a polite smile. 'Thanks for the lift, Adam. Must dash. I'm sorry we had to meet again in such unfortunate circumstances—'

'Don't think you're getting off as easily as that,' he broke in. 'We need to talk. I'm at the Chesterton, where I'll expect you at eight for dinner.'

'Out of the question!'

He shrugged. 'If you don't, I'll come round here tomorrow—and stay until you consent to a meeting.'

Lowri stared at him, biting her lip.

Adam smiled coolly. 'Tell your husband, or lover, or whatever, that I'm an old friend who simply wants an hour or so of your time, nothing more. Which is the truth, lord knows.'

Lowri caught sight of Jenny peering through the blinds on the door and capitulated suddenly. 'Oh, very well. But I'll be late.'

'No problem. I can wait,' he promised her, in a tone so obviously a threat it raised the hairs on her spine. Lowri dived out of the car and across the broad pavement, shivering as the shop door opened at her approach. She slid inside and banged it shut behind her, ramming the bolts home, then held out her arms for the little girl in Jenny's arms.

'Sorry I was so long, Jenny. Hello, my lovely. Have you been good?'

Rhosyn Morgan beamed, displaying all six teeth as she said 'Mum-mum,' and struggled to get down. Lowri set her down in a playpen filled with toys, as she related her adventure to Jenny, who was the Montessori-trained assistant in charge of the crèche in the basement.

'Gosh, Lowri, what rotten luck,' said Jenny with sympathy as she shrugged into her coat. 'Rosie's been perfectly happy, only she's getting hungry. Where's your shopping, by the way?'

'Never managed it, one way and another.' Lowri blew out her cheeks. 'Never mind, Rosie can have something out of a jar tonight.'

'What about you?'

'I've got to go out, worse luck, if I can sort out a babysitter—anyone free on our list?'

'I'll do it,' offered Jenny. 'I've got nothing on tonight. I might as well look at your telly as mine.'

Thanking her warmly, Lowri locked the door behind Jenny, then picked up her daughter and let her crawl upstairs to the flat on the upper floor of the building. Once there they had a romp together, then Rosie ate her supper with gusto, had a walk round the sitting-room, pulling herself along from chair to chair. Lowri sat on the edge of the sofa, watching her little daughter's every move, raging against the fate which had sent Adam Hawkridge into her life again. The thought of the coming encounter scared her rigid. Yet if she didn't turn up he'd probably carry out his threat and come to the shop next day—the very last thing she wanted.

Rhosyn was hers, Lowri thought fiercely. Adam must never know the false alarm had been a lie. She didn't want his intrusion into the new life she'd made for herself. Bringing up a child single-handed was no bed of roses, but with help from her family she'd managed to achieve control of life both as a mother and as co-owner of the shop downstairs. She had no intention of letting Adam Hawkridge upset her hard-won little apple-cart.

Rosie launched herself away from the nearest chair and

toddled across the room to Lowri, holding up her arms in confident appeal.

Lowri swept her up, hugging the little body as she gave her daughter a smacking kiss and took her off to a protracted playtime in the bath. After much splashing and delighted squealing, there were the usual roars of protest as Rosie was taken out and dried, and her dimpled, flailing limbs fastened into her sleeping suit. Then there was a hush as Lowri fed her daughter her bedtime bottle of milk, both of them cuddled close together to enjoy the part of the day Lowri treasured, when work was over and she was alone with her daughter as Rhosyn grew sleepy, and her little body heavy. Lowri put the empty bottle down and held her daughter close. Mine, she thought. All mine.

Lowri hung over the angelic sleeping face once Rhosyn was in her cot, riven by an insecurity which kept her there for longer than usual before she could tear herself away to make reluctant preparations for the evening. Pride, if nothing else, prompted care with her appearance, and when Jenny came back Lowri's hair was coiled up smoothly on top of her head, and she was ready in the raspberry-red dress recently acquired as a reward for her low-calorie diet and the merciless exercises she'd sweated over every night to get her figure back.

Her ears glowing with Jenny's morale-boosting compliments Lowri took a last look at her sleeping daughter, made sure Jenny knew where she was going, then went out into the December night to walk the short distance to the Chesterton, a hotel so far above her touch she'd never yet set foot in it. As she walked briskly she worried over what had brought Adam to the town in the first place, and prayed his stay was just overnight. The thought of him in the vicinity for several days gave her silent hysterics. As she passed through the pillared portico of the hotel Lowri pulled herself together. Now she was here she might as well enjoy the meal. Tonight, she promised herself, the diet could go hang. Her blood-sugars had taken a nose dive at the sight of Adam Hawkridge earlier on. She badly needed some sinful calories to make the evening easier to bear.

Adam was waiting for her in the hotel foyer, reading an evening paper in one of the comfortable leather chairs near the entrance. He sprang to his feet at the sight of her, and seeing him with suddenly objective eyes Lowri felt a pang of unwanted reaction to his physical presence. She stifled it at birth. All that, she reminded herself brusquely, was behind her. This evening was just a chore to be got through. The Adam she'd known no longer existed. The mature, arrogant man smiling at her was no longer a lover. He was a threat.

'Hello, Lowri.' He took her hand for a moment, his eyes gleaming as she withdrew it quickly. 'You look good— roses in your cheeks from the cold.'

'I only hope my nose doesn't try to compete,' she returned lightly. 'It's very warm in here.'

Adam relieved her of her navy overcoat and handed it to a passing waiter. 'Let's have a drink in the bar while we decide what to eat.'

The bar was a small, dimly lit place designed to foster an intimacy which made Lowri uneasy. To her regret most of its customers were quiet twosomes engrossed in each other. She would have preferred noise and laughter, some cheerful background music to alleviate the awkwardness of the situation, and for once would have liked a drink to calm jangled nerves. But in a conscious effort to keep her wits about her Lowri refused anything stronger than a glass of mineral water, ignoring her companion's raised eyebrows.

'Right. Fire away,' said Adam, once their drinks had arrived. 'Why Pennington?'

Lowri settled back in her chair, glad to be spared any preliminary skirmish. 'I've got relatives only a few miles from here. That's where I went when I left London. I liked the area, so I stayed on after…' She stopped, biting her lip.

'After what?' he pounced.

'After I recovered from breaking up with you,' said Lowri woodenly.

Adam drank some of his Scotch. 'Did that take long?'

'No,' she lied without hesitation.

There was a silence broken by the welcome appearance of a waiter with two enormous menus. By the time they'd studied the dishes on offer the atmosphere was less hostile.

'So now you sell baby clothes,' Adam commented, and smiled quizzically. 'Rather a contrast to sexy underwear.'

'Ah, but Little Darlings is a bit different from the usual run of baby shops.'

'In what way?' asked Adam, his business brain quickly interested.

'We sell nearly new baby clothes,' she explained, glad of a safer topic. 'People bring us their outgrown children's clothes—in good condition, of course, with a lot of designer things like Baby Dior, plus cast-off buggies, prams, furniture and so on. We sell everything at knockdown prices and take half for ourselves.'

'Surely you don't make much money at that?' asked Adam, frowning.

'The shop does surprisingly well, but we do offer other services, too. There's a créche in the basement where mothers can leave their children with trained staff for so much an hour. We stock new shoes with a proper fitting service, keep a list of vetted, approved baby-sitters—' She stopped, flushing. 'I tend to rattle on a bit about it, I'm afraid.'

'Nice to see such enthusiasm for your work.' Adam rose to his feet as the waiter came to say their meal was ready. 'Let's eat. Afterwards, be warned. I intend to learn everything that's happened to you from the day you left me at the altar—so to speak—right up to the moment when fate sent you crashing into me tonight.'

Lowri's appetite died a sudden death. Her salmon with avocado sauce could have been dust and ashes for all the pleasure she took in the meal. Such a pity, she thought with regret. Meals like this weren't part of her life these days. In fact, she realised suddenly, the last time she'd eaten in such an expensive restaurant had been with the same man who was eyeing her barely touched plate with disapproval.

'That's an odd look on your face,' commented Adam. 'You don't like the food?'

'I don't seem to be very hungry,' she confessed.

'Leave it then and have some pudding. You used to like sweet things. Can't I tempt you?' He smiled, the gleam in his eyes all too familiar.

'No, thank you.' She smiled cheerfully. 'Some coffee would be nice, but nothing else.'

'Then let's go back to the bar to drink it.'

The bar was crowded by this time. But like magic, as always happened for Adam, some people got up to leave as they arrived, and he swiftly installed her in the vacated corner and suggested brandy, or a liqueur.

'No, really.' She shook her head. 'My day starts early. I daren't risk a hangover.'

'I don't think half a glass of wine can have done you much harm.'

'Exactly. That was my intention.'

Lowri poured coffee, and without thinking added one sugar lump to Adam's cup and passed it to him, then could have kicked herself at the smug look on his face.

'Your memory's good, Lowri.'

'Only for trivia.' She smiled sweetly.

'Like promises of marriage?' His eyes bored into hers, all trace of warmth vanished.

Lowri shrugged, oddly calm now the gloves were off. 'I

never actually promised to marry you, Adam. You just took my acquiescence for granted.'

His eyes narrowed ominously. 'You mean that you never had the least intention of turning up that day?'

'That's right.' She drained her cup, then refilled it, gesturing politely at his. 'More?'

'No. I need some cognac.' Adam signalled to the waiter, then turned back to Lowri. 'Why?'

'Why what?'

'You know damn well,' he snapped, his wide mouth tightening. 'Why did you string me along like that? What had I done? I asked you to marry me, remember.'

'True. But with such undisguised reluctance that I felt like some tawdry little schemer who'd set out to trap you into it.' Lowri shrugged. 'I was all too obviously some encumbrance you couldn't shake off. Whereas to me you were the only man I'd ever fallen in love with—up to then, at least.'

Adam paused to allow the waiter to serve him the brandy, then drank half of it in one swallow and set down the glass to stab Lowri with a cold, accusing look. 'I rang Rupert that day, afraid you'd had an accident when you didn't turn up. I couldn't take it in at first when he said you'd gone away. Then when I went round to collect the letter my reception from Sarah froze the blood in my veins.' He smiled grimly. 'I've not set eyes on either of them since. They made it bloody plain I was *persona non grata* in their home. I find it hard to forgive you that. I like them both. I was very fond of young Dominic and Emily too, but I doubt Sarah will ever let me near them again.'

Lowri shrugged. 'Sarah's family, remember. The Morgans tend to be a clannish tribe.'

Adam stared at her. 'Talking of which, no doubt you heard about my abortive trip to Wales to look for you?'

'Oh, yes. My father rang me the moment you left.'

'My reception was a damn sight worse there.'

'What did you expect?'

'Hell, Lowri, I was trying to find out where you'd gone. At the time my life was so fraught, one way and another, the last thing I needed was a chase about the countryside looking for you.'

'I didn't ask you to look for me,' she pointed out, unmoved. 'And one trip to Cwmderwen hardly counts as chasing about the countryside.'

Adam controlled himself with effort. 'It was a sheer waste of time, anyway. Your father flatly refused to tell me where you were, and all but threw me out. I never even met your stepmother. There wasn't a damned thing I could do, so I went back to London and did my best to forget you'd ever existed.'

'Very sensible.'

He eyed her morosely. 'You obviously forgot me easily enough if you're with someone else these days.'

'I'm sure you did the same.'

There was a pause while Adam finished his brandy.

'Strangely enough I didn't,' he said expressionlessly. 'No time for women these days. Work fills my life.'

Lowri gave him a sceptical smile. 'That's hard to believe.'

'The truth often is.' His answering smile lacked mirth. 'My mother's quite worried. At one time she complained about my endless string of girlfriends—her words, not mine. Now she complains because there aren't any at all.'

'None?'

'Not even one. She keeps telling me I need to settle down and produce a family.' His mouth twisted. 'Fortunately she'll never know how near I once came to granting her wish.'

Lowri gathered up her bag and scarf. 'Right. Well now you've discovered what you wanted to know—'

'Not so fast.' Adam's hand shot across the table to stay her. 'I don't know anything like enough, Lowri. I want to know where you went, why you wouldn't let anyone tell me where you were.'

'I told you where, Adam. I went to stay with relatives and swore everyone to secrecy because I didn't want to see you again. Simple, really.' She got up, a determined set to her mouth. 'Now I must go.'

Adam jumped to his feet. 'I'd drive you home, but the brandy was one drink too many. If you'll wait here for a moment I'll get someone to call you a cab.'

Lowri opened her mouth to say it was only a short walk to the flat then changed her mind. If she did that Adam would promptly volunteer to walk with her.

As they waited in the foyer Lowri searched for something neutral to say to ease the tension between them.

'Thank you for a delicious meal,' she came up with finally.

Adam eyed her sardonically. 'You ate very little of it.'

Another pause.

'Are you travelling back tomorrow?' she asked politely, wishing the taxi would turn up.

'I'm not sure yet.' He shrugged. 'It depends on the success of my mission.'

To Lowri's relief her ordeal ended with the arrival of the taxi, and with a bright smile she held out her hand to Adam.

'Goodbye, then. My apologies again about the car.'

'A small price to pay for the privilege of meeting you again.' Adam's smile mocked her as instead of shaking her hand he raised it to his lips then to her surprise let her go, making no move to follow her as she walked out of the hotel. Lowri's eyebrows rose. She'd fully expected Adam to see her into the taxi, if only to learn where she lived.

After an evening of unrelenting strain followed by a restless night Lowri was desperately tired next morning when the usual imperious demand came through the intercom to wake her up. But in an instant she was out of bed, yawning, and into her dressing-gown to collect her daughter, who was standing up in the cot in her little room, banging the rails with her rattle.

'Ba-ba, ba-ba,' Rhosyn chanted, then dropped the rattle to stretch out her hand to Lowri. 'Mum-mum!' She greeted her mother with her irresistible toothy grin, and Lowri picked her up and gave her a smacking kiss, then began changing her into the clothes put ready the night before. When her daughter was arrayed in a red sweater and tights, denim dungarees printed with huge red and yellow dots, the tiny feet in red checked sneakers, Lowri took Rhosyn through to the kitchen, installed her in her high chair and put a bottle of formula in the bottle warmer and filled the kettle. She made tea and toast, tied a bib round the little neck, put cereal in a bowl, added milk from the bottle to it, then sat down to feed her child, thankful the routine was so automatic after her wakeful night. Rhosyn ate her cereal hungrily, drank the rest of the milk in the bottle, then munched some toast soldiers while Lowri ate her own meagre breakfast.

Afterwards she set Rhosyn on the floor in the sitting-room with her sack of toys, made sure all the child locks were on the cupboards and the safety covers on the electricity sockets, put the gate in place in the open doorway between the two rooms and tidied the kitchen hurriedly. She put some laundry in the washing machine, sterilised Rhosyn's bottles and washed the dishes, one eye in constant surveillance on her daughter as the busy little girl took toys from the sack, toddled across the room with them to pile them against the gate, then trotted back again to fetch more.

Later Lowri took the child into the bedroom while she dressed and got ready for her day in the shop below. Rhosyn took the pile of magazines from the bedside table, as she always did, and sat on the floor looking at them, tearing the odd page as she tried to open them, while Lowri pulled on black jersey trousers and turtle-necked sweater and added a yellow corduroy overshirt cinched in at the waist with a wide black belt. She tied back her hair with a yellow scarf, made up her face with the swift efficiency she'd learned in the past few months, then changed Rhosyn's nappy again. Afterwards Lowri took her back to the sitting-room and spent some time reading and playing with her, and, in the end, sat cuddling the child in her arms on the sofa while the little girl slept for the half-hour nap she consented to at this hour.

When Lowri arrived in the shop at ten, as usual, her partner, Fran Hobbs, had opened up, Jenny was in the basement crèche ready to receive Rhosyn and any other comers, and several Christmas shoppers were already bargain-hunting among the clothes and furniture. Little Darlings was in business.

By five-thirty that evening Lowri was ready to drop. Because Fran opened up and did the first hour in the morning she left early, leaving Lowri and Jenny to cope for the last hour of the day. With Christmas only two weeks away the shop had been gratifyingly busy, but after hours of helping mothers with their choices, fitting toddlers with shoes and helping Jenny out now and again down in the crèche with only a short break upstairs for Rhosyn's lunch and rest, Lowri felt tired. At this stage she always brought Rhosyn up to play in one of the playpens set out under a battery of mobiles hanging from the ceiling, and tonight her little daughter lay happily on her back, cuddling her fluffy rabbit and waving at the moving ducks and clowns and Disney characters suspended above her while Lowri and Jenny did some tidying up preparatory to shutting up shop.

'That's about it, I think,' yawned Jenny. 'Everything's shipshape down below. Shall I lock up?'

'Yes, please!' said Lowri fervently. 'My feet are killing me—' She groaned inwardly as the bell went to admit a last-minute shopper, managed a smile, then stood very still, suddenly tense as a tigress with her cub. Her customer was Adam Hawkridge, tall and formidable in a dark city greatcoat, with flakes of snow melting in his thick brown hair.

CHAPTER NINE

'GOOD evening, sir,' said Jenny politely. 'How can I help you?'

He gave her a smile. 'I'm afraid I'm not a customer. I've come to see Miss Morgan.'

Jenny shot Lowri a questioning glance.

'It's all right.' Lowri nodded reassuringly. 'You go off. I'll lock up behind you and let Mr Hawkridge out later.' She turned politely to Adam. 'I imagine you've come to discuss the accident yesterday. Was the damage to your car worse than you thought?'

Behind his back Jenny, enlightened, pulled a sympathetic face, collected her coat then said goodnight and went out into the snowy December night, leaving an atmosphere hardly less arctic behind her.

Praying Rhosyn would stay quiet, Lowri thrust a strand of hair behind her ear and looked up at Adam in cold enquiry. 'I thought you'd have left by now. Was your mission unsuccessful after all?'

'The business part was very satisfactory,' he assured her, looking round the shop with interest. 'On the personal side I need to put some work in. You left a lot of questions unanswered last night, Lowri, so before I leave tomorrow I thought I'd call round and have a little chat.' Suddenly his eyes narrowed as he caught sight of the sleeping child. 'Good lord—has one of your customers left her baby behind?'

'No,' said Lowri, resigned. 'If you must know, she's mine.'

Adam gazed down at the child, stunned, then back at Lowri. '*Yours*? What's her name?'

'Rhosyn.'

'Unusual.'

'Welsh for rose. I'm afraid she gets Rosie from most people.'

'Including her father?'

Lowri stared at him impassively, saying nothing.

Adam returned to contemplation of the child, who looked very small and defenceless clutching a pink bunny almost as big as herself. Feathery strands of hair curled on the still visible crown of her head, one shoe had been kicked off, exposing a minute red foot. And suddenly, as though aware of his scrutiny, Rhosyn opened big dark eyes like her mother's and gave him a sleepy smile.

'Hello,' he said softly, and smiled back. He stared down at the child, fascinated, making Lowri very uneasy. 'She's the image of you.'

'So I'm told,' she said shortly.

'How old is she?'

'Nine months.'

Adam shot a hostile look at her. 'You got to know her father pretty bloody quickly!'

'Yes.' Lowri smiled sweetly. 'Love at first sight.' Noting signs of restlessness from her daughter, she bent quickly to pick her up. 'I'm afraid it's bathtime. I'll have to ask you to go now.'

'I was hoping for an introduction to the man in your life,' said Adam, his eyes bright with challenge. 'Tact forbade me to ask about his reaction to your night out with me, by the way. I take it you're not actually married to him?'

'No.'

'You're still allergic to marriage, then!'

'Not at all,' she returned. 'I'll get round to it one day,

no doubt. But if I don't it's not really any business of yours, Adam.'

'It was once,' he reminded her cuttingly.

'All that seems a long time ago.' Lowri struggled with her fidgeting daughter, who was demanding to get down. 'Look, I've got to take her upstairs.'

'Her father's not home yet?'

'That's right, he's not.' Lowri smiled politely. 'Goodnight, Adam.'

Adam's lips tightened. 'All right, Lowri, you win. Or rather this young lady does. Goodnight.' He put out a finger and touched Rhosyn's flushed cheek. 'Bye.'

'Bye-bye,' said Rhosyn and flapped her hand at him, beaming.

Lowri held her breath as Adam stared at the child in amazement.

'My word, young lady, you're pretty forward for your age!' He looked at Lowri quizzically. 'Do babies usually talk at nine months?'

'She doesn't talk, she just says "Mum-mum" and "bye-bye",' said Lowri, then wished she hadn't as Adam raised a sardonic eyebrow.

'I thought the first word was usually "Daddy",' he drawled, and went to the door. 'I may call in again before I leave,' he added, and gave her a deeply disturbing smile before he went out into the snowy night.

Lowri dumped Rhosyn into the playpen and hurried to lock up. Once the shop was dark apart from the lights trained on the window arrangements she scooped up her daughter and hurried up the stairs to the safety of the flat, feeling as if she'd escaped danger by the skin of her teeth.

A couple of action-packed hours later, when Rhosyn was finally asleep, Lowri made herself one of the low-calorie rice dishes on her diet. She sat down on the sofa with a book and a cup of coffee to eat it, still desperately worried about Adam. Which was silly, she informed herself trench-antly. Even if Adam did learn the truth about Rhosyn it wouldn't matter. The baby was hers, and hers alone. He'd forfeited all right to Rhosyn the day he'd accused her mother of getting pregnant to blackmail him into marriage.

Lowri had just emerged from the bath, her wet hair swathed in a towel, when the doorbell rang. She lifted the receiver cautiously.

'Yes?'

'It's Adam. Let me in, Lowri.'

'Certainly not.' She slammed down the instrument, but Adam replaced his finger on the buzzer and kept it there until she answered it.

'Go away,' she said furiously.

'Not until I've seen you.'

'It's not convenient—I'm not alone.'

'The only one up there with you is Rhosyn. So let me in, Lowri.'

She hesitated, in an agony of indecision.

'I won't go away,' said Adam, with a finality which won him the day.

'Oh very well,' she said angrily. 'But only for a minute or two. I'm tired.'

She released the catch on the outer door, then raced to check on Rhosyn. She turned the baby on her side and covered her up securely, then braced herself and went to open the door to Adam's knock.

He stood outside on the landing, dressed in the same dark overcoat, a smile playing at the corners of his mouth as he eyed her towel-swathed head and all-enveloping scarlet wool dressing-gown.

Lowri went ahead of him into the sitting-room. 'Come in here, please.'

Adam followed her into the small room, looking round him at the functional furniture and unornamented walls, the only splash of colour the crimson silk curtains, which added a touch of luxury to an otherwise stringently practical décor.

'So this is where you live,' he commented. 'May I take off my coat?'

'Are you staying long enough to make that necessary? I'm expecting my—my boyfriend back soon.'

Adam shook his head decisively. 'I don't believe you. After I left you tonight I made some enquiries. You live alone, Lowri. Except for the baby.'

Lowri stared at him malevolently, then shrugged. 'I see. In that case you'd better sit down and wait for a moment. My hair's dripping down my neck. I need to dry it a little. There's an evening paper somewhere.'

She hurried to her bedroom, her mind in a ferment as she rubbed furiously at her hair, then brushed it back from her face and secured it with a ribbon, hoping she wouldn't catch pneumonia by leaving it so wet. She eyed the dressing gown for a moment, then shrugged. That could stay. If Adam got a glimpse of striped pyjama it served him right for barging his way in like this.

Adam got up from the sofa when she rejoined him, a strangely bleak look on his face. 'Why did you pretend someone shared this place with you, Lowri?'

'I didn't. You asked me if anyone would object if I brought a strange man home and I said yes,' she said coldly. 'Rhosyn likes all my attention, I'm afraid.'

'So where's Rhosyn's father?'

'He and I are no longer in a relationship.' Lowri forced a smile. 'I'm afraid I don't keep anything to drink in the flat—alcoholic, I mean. Would you like some coffee?'

'No, I would not! Thanks,' he added belatedly. He leaned back on the sofa, eyeing her narrowly as she sat down in a nearby armchair. 'I went round to the garage this evening.'

'Garage?'

'The one who towed away your car. They said it would be ready next week.' Adam raised a sardonic eyebrow. 'The owner's a friendly sort of chap. Said he'd do his best for you. Promised he wouldn't do you over unnecessary parts, and so on, just because you're a woman on your own.'

Lowri stared at him, incensed. 'I never realised Mr Booker was such a chauvinist.'

'He told me you're a very plucky little thing, single parent and so on and making such a success of the business. He told me you lived over the shop, too.' Adam's smile was wry. 'You didn't tell me you owned it.'

'I don't. I'm in partnership with someone else. Fran lives with her husband and family not far from here.'

'I didn't realise you were a lady of substance.'

'I came into a very modest sum of money on my twenty-first birthday. My mother left it in trust for me.' Lowri smiled coldly. 'It came in very handy, one way and another.'

Adam's answering smile was ominous. 'This chap Booker said something else very interesting, by the way.'

'Oh?'

'Apparently you had the car serviced recently—wanted it in good time for your daughter's birthday. Which,' he added very deliberately, 'he told me was last week. Rhosyn's older than you made out.'

Lowri sat very still, her eyes on his.

'You lied to me,' he said harshly. 'Not once but twice. Rhosyn is not nine months old, neither was she a false alarm. She's mine! Why the hell did you lie to me? Why didn't you go through with the marriage, you—?'

'Stupid woman?' she finished for him. Her chin lifted. 'Let's get something straight, Adam. The accident of conception does not make Rhosyn yours in any way other than purely biological. You didn't want her, so she's mine—

mine alone. And I didn't marry you because I couldn't face the thought of life with a man who was taking me on sufferance. It would be nice to say I stopped caring for you the moment you accused me of engineering the whole situation—but I didn't, more fool me. I hoped right up to the last minute that you'd come round, revert to the lover I'd once had. When it was obvious that wasn't going to happen I made other plans. If it soothes your ego a little I freely admit I was in love with you, Adam. Otherwise I couldn't have let you make love to me. But to you I was just a surprisingly sexy little playmate to take to bed. You cooled off so completely once you knew I was pregnant that it painted a very vivid picture of what our life together would be. I couldn't bear the thought of it. So I lied. And I've never regretted it,' she added, then smiled sardonically. 'It was hard work keeping my father—not to mention Rupert—from telling you the truth. But in the end I had my own way.'

'No wonder your father threw me out of his house,' said Adam bitterly. 'Surely you told him I was willing to marry you?'

Lowri glared at him. '*Willing*? How very good of you, to be sure! But I needed someone passionately eager to marry me, not just willing.'

Suddenly a wail through the intercom put an end to the argument. Lowri leapt to her feet and ran to find Rhosyn was standing up in her cot, tears streaming down her cheeks. She held up her arms and Lowri scooped her up to hug her close.

'Oh, darling, you're all soggy. Mummy can't have fastened your nappy properly.' Her heart still thumping angrily, Lowri put the baby down on a bathtowel on the floor and changed her swiftly, then handed over Rhosyn's bunny. 'There, *cariad*, cuddle Flopsy while I change your bed.'

But Rhosyn scrambled up, clinging to Lowri's knees, her eyes like saucers as Adam appeared in the doorway.

For a moment all three seemed frozen in tableau, than in a strained, constricted voice he asked, 'Can I help?'

'No!' Lowri sat her daughter down again. 'I'll just change her cot then she can go back to sleep.'

But Rhosyn wasn't having any. She pulled herself to her feet on the end of the cot and stood eyeing Adam with hostile dark eyes. He laughed involuntarily.

'You look just like your mother.' He held out his hand coaxingly. 'Won't you come and talk to me?'

'Leave her alone!' ordered Lowri. 'If she gets excited I'll never get her back to sleep.'

But Rhosyn's curiosity had overcome her caution. Dropping the rabbit she trotted across the room to Adam, who watched her progress with something so like pride that Lowri went cold.

'She can walk!' he exclaimed.

Lowri ignored him as she whipped off damp sheets and replaced them with dry ones, tucking them in with a speed and precision any ward sister would have approved.

'Can I pick her up?' he asked, never taking his eyes off the child.

'She won't let you. She doesn't see many men.' Lowri added a cellular blanket to the bed then turned round to see her daughter in the careful, unpractised embrace of her father, who was holding the child in such a precarious way that Lowri would have laughed if it had been anyone else.

Rhosyn stared curiously at the strange face so close to hers. She reached up a hand to tug on Adam's hair, then turned to look at her mother, as if asking what this strange, male person was doing in her bedroom.

'You can give her to me now,' said Lowri, wanting to tear her child from Adam's arms.

He surrendered the small warm body with a reluctance

which struck fear into Lowri's heart. She switched on the bottle-warmer then wrapped the baby in a blanket and went into the kitchen to get a bottle of milk from the fridge, Rhosyn held tightly in her arms.

'Lowri,' said Adam, when she returned. 'Don't look like that. I wouldn't harm a hair of her head. You must know that.'

Lowri put the bottle into the warmer and sat down in a rocking chair with Rhosyn cuddled close. 'If you'll go back into the other room I'll join you as soon as I've put her back to bed.'

'Can't I stay to watch her drink her milk?'

'No.' Lowri refused to look at him. 'She'll never settle if you do.'

Adam left with such obvious reluctance that Lowri had to force herself to relax, deliberately emptying her mind of all the fear and worry crowding it as she fed her child, then cuddled her to sleep. Gently she put Rhosyn in the cot, drew the blankets over her and tiptoed from the room.

Adam was prowling restlessly round the sitting-room when she rejoined him. 'Lowri, I'd appreciate that coffee now.'

'All right,' she said ungraciously. 'But while I'm in the kitchen don't even think of going into Rhosyn's room.'

His face hardened. 'What the hell do you think I'd do if I did?'

'Disturb her—wake her up.' Lowri eyed him levelly. 'My day starts early, Adam. I need my sleep. And I won't get it if Rhosyn decides she needs entertainment at two in the morning.'

His mouth twisted. 'I promise I shan't move from the spot.'

'I'm afraid you'll have to go back to the paper while you wait. I do own a television, but it's in my bedroom.'

'For lack of any other company?' he said swiftly.

'No. Because now Rosie's walking I keep all electrical gadgets well out of her way,' returned Lowri coldly. 'I'll make that coffee.'

When she got back with it, Adam was doing the crossword in the paper. Lowri handed him a mug and resumed her chair to drink her own coffee. 'No biscuits, I'm afraid, I'm on a diet.'

He frowned. 'Why? You're thinner than you used to be.'

'Only because I work at it.'

Adam drank some of his coffee in silence, his eyes brooding, then he set the mug down on the table beside him and leaned forward, looking at her commandingly. 'Lowri, what are we going to do about this?'

Her eyes narrowed. 'About what?'

'About Rhosyn. As you know perfectly well,' he added with barely controlled violence.

'Nothing, Adam.'

'What do you mean, nothing!' His eyes glittered coldly. 'She happens to be my daughter.'

'That's right, Adam,' snapped Lowri. 'You just "happen" to be her father. It was an accident. And you hated the very thought of being tied down with a baby, remember. So I solved the problem for you.'

'You had no right to take it on yourself to do so,' he said savagely.

'I had every right!' She glared at him. 'Rhosyn is mine, Adam. So go away and leave us alone. We don't need you! I won't have you upsetting our lives just because you've discovered some stray paternal fondness you never knew you had.'

'I might have discovered it a bloody sight sooner, given the chance,' he retorted, white with anger. 'It's your fault I don't know my daughter, nor she her father. Left to me, you and I would be married and I'd have been there at her birth—' He stopped suddenly, looking grim. 'Who *was* with you, Lowri?'

She smiled mockingly. 'I was probably the least lonely single parent in the entire world. Sarah and her sisters Rhia and Mari-Sian were actually with me in the room, but my father and Rupert were downstairs with Holly and young Huw Morgan, my new little brother.'

Adam breathed in deeply. 'So the absence of a father went entirely unnoticed—and unlamented.'

'I wasn't in a hospital,' she told him quietly. 'I gave birth to Rhosyn at Rhia's home. She was the relative I went to when I left London. She's Sir Charles Hadley's widow.'

'Hadley Pharmaceuticals?'

'That's the one.'

His mouth twisted. 'I didn't realise you had such influential connections.'

'Kindness, not influence, is the key word in this instance,' Lowri contradicted. 'Rhia has two teenage stepdaughters, but never gave Charles a child of her own, to her great sorrow. The girls were away at boarding school, Rhia was still grieving over Charles's death, so when I told Sarah about my little problem—'

'You swore *me* to secrecy,' he reminded her swiftly, his jaw set.

'She came on me by surprise when I was crying my eyes out a few days before I was supposed to be marrying you.'

'Supposed being the operative word!'

Lowri's eyes flashed dangerously. 'As I said, she found me in tears because I was in the process of facing up to the truth. That you were never going to revert to the lover I'd been so besotted with. Sarah got the truth out of me, and decided Rhia was the answer to my problem.'

'I assumed you'd go home to your father.'

'He wanted me to.' Lowri's mouth twisted. 'A few heated arguments sizzled along the wires between London and Cwmderwen on the subject, believe me. But Dad already had more than enough on his plate with Holly, who was very poorly before Huw's birth and worried everyone to death. Besides Dad's very fond of Rhia, and Mari-Sian, who's frighteningly clever and lectures in modern languages at Cambridge, convinced him that my company, even with all its attendant problems—or maybe because of them—was just the thing her sister needed. So he gave in.'

'Wasn't Lady Hadley afraid your sorry little tale would be a bad example to her stepdaughters?' said Adam cuttingly.

Lowri gave him a hostile glare. 'On the contrary. Rhia felt my predicament served as a graphic warning to them in their future dealings with your sex.'

There was a fraught silence in the room for an interval, while Lowri stared down at her tightly clasped hands, very much aware that Adam never took his eyes off her averted face.

'So,' he said at last, at the point where Lowri thought she'd scream if the silence lasted any longer. 'I'm refused anything to do with my daughter.'

Lowri raised implacable dark eyes to his face. 'That's right, Adam. I like our lives the way they are.'

'What about Rhosyn?' he said swiftly. 'Shouldn't her preferences come into it somewhere?'

'At the moment I am all the preference she possesses. And I intend to keep it that way.' Lowri looked pointedly at her watch.

'I'm not going yet, so you can stop that,' he said angrily.

'You won't change my mind, Adam, however long you stay. So you might as well go.'

He jumped to his feet and stood in front of the fireplace, glaring down at her. 'I'm not the first man to feel shock at being rushed into marriage, dammit! Are you going to make me pay for the rest of my life because I didn't embrace the idea with open arms?'

'You've missed the point,' she said, unmoved. 'I wasn't the one rushing the marriage. You were. And for all the wrong reasons. Saving face, at a guess. The right thing to do and all that—which I could have coped with. Just. But you accused me of getting pregnant deliberately to trap you into marriage, Adam. And that I just couldn't take.'

'So you agreed to a wedding just so you could punish me by not turning up,' he said heavily.

She nodded. 'More or less. It was deeply satisfying at the time.'

Adam picked up his coat and shrugged into it. 'So we've reached an impasse. You can't forgive me because I said something stupid in the heat of the moment. While I can't forgive you for keeping his only grandchild secret from my father before he died.'

Lowri stared at him, arrested. 'Your father's dead? I didn't know.'

'He knew he had only a short time to live when he agreed to the cruise. At least he hung on long enough to enjoy that. But his condition was the reason for rushing me into taking over the company before he went.'

'Did you know?'

'Yes. And my mother knew too, of course. They never kept secrets from each other.'

The words hung in the air for a moment.

'But they were different,' said Lowri very quietly. 'They loved each other.'

'You said just now that you loved me,' he reminded her.

'Oh, I did, Adam. Past tense,' she added, to remove all possible doubt.

He stared down at her in frustration, anger in every line of him. 'The last word on your part, I assume.'

'Yes.' Lowri went to the door and opened it. 'Goodbye, Adam.'

He gave her a searing look as he went out into the hall. 'I take it there's no possibility of a last look at my daughter?'

'None at all,' she said without emotion.

'You've developed a bloody good talent for cruelty since the old days, Lowri,' he said with bitterness.

She smiled disdainfully. 'It's not really surprising. To quote Henry James, Adam, I was taught by masters. Well, one master really. You.'

CHAPTER TEN

AFTER Adam had gone Lowri shivered with reaction for minutes on end, until at last the need to talk to someone was so overwhelming that she rang Sarah to tell her what had happened.

Sarah whistled after she'd heard Lowri out. 'How did Adam react to your punchline?'

Lowri sighed. 'He stood there like a statue and just looked at me. Then he turned away. Sort of in slow motion. And left without another word.'

Sarah paused. 'Do you still feel bitter towards him?'

'I don't know how I feel. I just wish I hadn't met him again.'

'How was he with Rhosyn?'

'Fascinated. Terrifyingly so.'

'Understandable, in the circumstances.'

'But she's not a son to train up for the business—she's a girl.'

'What difference does that make? Besides, she's not just any little girl, is she! She's his daughter, Lowri.'

'No, she's not, Sal—she's mine!'

'You know what I mean,' said Sarah soothingly. 'He could help, you know, *cariad*. Financially.'

'I don't need help—' Lowri bit her lip. 'Oh Sarah, I'm sorry. I'll always be grateful for the help you've all given me. But Adam's help I'd rather do without.'

The run-up to Christmas was so busy Lowri was thankful she had little time to think. She was due to drive to Cwmderwen once she'd closed the shop on Christmas Eve,

132

and for weeks she'd been looking forward to a break with her father and Holly, and little Huw. The shop looked festive with cut-out figures from nursery rhymes and flights of gilt cherubs, and a Christmas tree in the window in place of the crib. And in the flat upstairs Lowri decorated a tiny tree for Rhosyn, and hung paperchains and sprigs of holly in the sitting-room. Takings in the shop were good and the crèche was doing a roaring trade while busy mothers did their Christmas shopping. But underneath it all Lowri couldn't rid herself of the unease which hung over her like a cloud since her encounter with Adam.

Her reaction was fierce when she found his visit to her garage had been motivated by more than mere idle curiosity. Adam Hawkridge had not only settled the bill for the quite extensive repairs, but had paid for a set of new tyres for her car.

Lowri's thank-you letter was a chore she laboured over for hours before she was satisfied with the polite, impersonal little note she finally addressed to Hawk Electronics, since she had no idea if Adam still lived in the riverside flat. Her first instinct was to send a cheque to him immediately for the amount, but after giving it thought something stayed her hand. The look in Adam's eyes as he'd left her that night had haunted her ever since. To throw his money back in his face smacked of a cruelty no lesson could ever have taught her.

Three days before Christmas a mammoth present was delivered to the shop for Rhosyn.

'Good heavens,' said Fran Hobbs as a glorious rocking horse emerged from the carton. 'Who in the world sent Rosie that?'

'No card,' said Lowri, pink-cheeked. 'Must be from Rhia. She's spending Christmas in Gstaad with the girls. She obviously thought it would come in handy in the shop, or down in the play area—no room for it up in the flat, that's for sure.'

Next day more packages arrived, but Lowri took these upstairs to open later in private, unwilling to risk any more embarrassment in front of Fran and Jenny. Not that either of them was ever tactless enough to ask about Rhosyn's father—or lack of one.

Later, when Rhosyn was tucked up in her cot, Lowri forced herself to have a bath and eat her supper before she let herself open the parcels. She took the wrappings off slowly at last, then stared as she opened a box full of clothes for her daughter: diminutive dungarees and expensive sweaters, cute little training shoes, a towelling robe and a strawberry-pink ski-jacket. She raised an eyebrow at the designer labels, then took out the card which lay at the bottom of the box.

'To Rhosyn,' it said, in familiar bold handwriting, 'with love'.

Again Lowri wanted to stuff everything back in the box and send it straight to Hawk Electronics. But after a moment she calmed down, trying to be fair. There'd been no veto on presents. And Rhosyn was too young to know where the clothes came from. Lowri shrugged, hardening herself to a practical point of view. After Rosie'd grown out of them they'd fetch a good price down in the shop. The larger of the other two parcels contained a long-haired teddy-bear as big as Rhosyn, but the smaller one was addressed to Lowri. She eyed it malevolently, wondering if Adam had the gall to think he could win her round with presents.

When she removed the paper Lowri found a small jeweller's box. Her eyes narrowed dangerously, then opened wide when she discovered a small gold cricket bat with a tiny gold cricket ball attached to it. Adam Hawkridge was too clever by half, she thought mutinously, staring at the brooch through a veil of sudden, treacherous tears. Nostalgia was a sneaky, underhand way to undermine her defences.

Next day was sheer chaos in the shop. Jenny needed to get off early in the afternoon and had asked permission to bring in her young sister Kay, who was on Christmas leave from her nanny-training. The extra pair of hands in the crèche came in useful, especially when Lowri needed to take Rhosyn upstairs for her lunch and a short nap. But with Jenny off in the afternoon it was hectic, and Fran volunteered to stay until closing time. At one stage Lowri dashed out to buy more of the balloons they were handing out to all their little clients over the Christmas period, then when the final wave of mothers rushed in to collect their children she went down to the basement to give Kay a hand.

'Where's Rhosyn?' she said to the girl in an undertone as Kay zipped up a little boy's windcheater.

Kay looked blank. 'What do you mean, Miss Morgan? Haven't you got her?'

Lowri felt the blood drain away from her face. 'No!' she said, and raced up the stairs while Kay handed the child over to his mother.

'Have you seen Rhosyn?' panted Lowri, grabbing Fran.

'Dear heaven, no. Isn't she down—?' Fran shook her head. 'Obviously not or you wouldn't be asking me.' She turned on Kay, who'd come running upstairs, white-faced as Lowri. 'Now then, young lady. What's all this?'

Kay began to sob. 'A lady—came down—and said she was Rhosyn's grandmother, that Rosie's mummy wanted her upstairs. I didn't know—I thought—'

Lowri pulled herself together, forcing herself to be gentle. 'All right, Kay—calm down. Can you describe the woman?'

For a while Kay was too hysterical to say a word, but

eventually a sharp admonition from Fran dried her up sufficiently to try to remember. 'Grey hair—elderly—nice clothes.'

'How did she talk—any accent?' said Lowri, trying not to panic.

'Sort of posh—you know.' Kay stared at her in misery. 'Oh, Miss Morgan, I could kill myself. But she was so nice!'

'Nice women don't steal babies,' said Fran forcefully, and went to the telephone. 'I'm calling the police.'

'Hang on a minute,' said Lowri in a strange voice. 'You two get off home. I'd better do some checking before I involve the police.'

'You mean you know who might have taken her?'

'No. But I've suddenly got a very strong suspicion.'

Fran's eyebrows rose. 'Do I take it the description actually fits Rhosyn's grandmother?'

'I don't know. I've never met her.' Lowri breathed in deeply. 'Look, I can't explain now—your family will be waiting for you, Fran. If I need you I'll ring you.'

'You're taking this much too calmly, love—'

'Then I must be a bloody good actress!' said Lowri with sudden savagery, and Fran nodded briskly in comprehension, hugged her hard and shooed the distraught teenager out of the shop. 'Right. I'll see Kay home, feed my lot and come back later. Sooner if you need me,' she added as she closed the door.

Lowri flew upstairs, in case by some strange quirk of fate her adventurous baby had somehow made it up to the flat on her own. But the rooms were empty. As she'd known they'd be. She picked up the phone, her breath rasping in her chest as she punched the buttons for the number of Hawk Electronics. She was put through to Adam's assistant. He informed her that Mr Hawkridge had just left and he himself was not at liberty to divulge his employer's home telephone number. In an agony of frustration Lowri tried the number of the Wapping flat and got Adam's terse voice on his answering machine. At screaming point, she left a brief, urgent message for him to ring her immediately he got in, then rang Directory Enquiries and asked for the number of the family home in Sussex.

In her anguish Lowri punched out the third number twice before she got it right, then sagged against the wall as a friendly voice gave the number and then said,

'Alice Hawkridge speaking.'

For a moment Lowri couldn't say a word and the woman said 'Hello? Is someone there? Hello?'

'Mrs Hawkridge,' said Lowri hoarsely. 'You won't know me—'

'Who is this?'

'My name's Lowri Morgan—'

'Lowri? Oh my dear, how wonderful to hear from you. Adam wouldn't let me contact you but I did so hope—what is it? What's the matter?' asked Mrs Hawkridge sharply, as Lowri gave a groan like someone in mortal agony.

'My *baby*,' she got out. 'Someone's stolen Rhosyn.' She sobbed her story out, even admitting she'd suspected Mrs Hawkridge of taking Rhosyn away.

There was a gasp of horror down the line, then a resolute, 'And why shouldn't you? You don't know me, after all. But I didn't,' added Mrs Hawkridge unsteadily.

'I know, I know, I only wish you had!' cried Lowri. 'At least I'd know where she was.'

'My dear, ring the police. Adam's on his way to supper with me at this very moment. I'll contact him on his car phone. You ring the police now!'

The police were wonderfully prompt. While Lowri was answering Fran's phone call the outer doorbell rang, and within seconds the small sitting-room seemed crowded as a detective inspector, accompanied by his sergeant and a woman police constable arrived to hear the details. Lowri, tear-stained but more composed by this time, answered their questions as fully as she could and supplied them with a description of Rhosyn's clothes, and gave them photographs and every scrap of information she could piece together as relevant.

'Don't worry about relevance, Mrs Morgan,' said Inspector Cox, 'tell us anything at all. We'll decide whether it's important.' He nodded to the woman constable. 'Maggie will make you some coffee.'

'Thank you.' Lowri took a deep, unsteady breath. 'But first of all I'm not Mrs Morgan, I'm Miss.'

'I see. Does that mean you live here alone with your daughter?'

'Yes.'

The inspector's eyes narrowed. 'So the father could have taken your child.'

'Oh, no. A woman took her, remember. Someone posing as Rhosyn's grandmother.' Lowri rubbed her eyes in sudden pain. 'I was only out of the shop for ten minutes! All for the sake of a few balloons—'

'Now, now, Miss Morgan,' he said kindly, and told his sergeant to telephone what details they had to the station and to send someone round to question Kay Hooper. 'However,' he said, when they were alone. 'This doesn't rule out the father. The woman could have been working for him.'

Lowri shook her head firmly. 'No. That's out of the question.'

The inspector looked unconvinced. 'Give me his name and address, please.'

Before Lowri could supply it, the phone rang. She jumped to her feet but the sergeant forestalled her.

'We'll see to this,' said the inspector firmly.

'It's a Mr Hawkridge for Miss Morgan,' said the sergeant, Lowri ran to take the receiver from him.

'Lowri?' said Adam, his voice almost unrecognisable. 'For God's sake, what's happening? Any news? Who was that on the phone?'

'The police. Oh, Adam, someone's stolen Rhosyn,' said Lowri shakily.

'Mother told me. I'm in the car right now, on my way. I've tried to get you a couple of times but the line was engaged. Hold on, Lowri—I'll be there as soon as I can.'

Lowri put the receiver down, scrubbed at her face, then sat down again, accepting a cup of coffee gratefully. 'That was Rhosyn's father. I think you can cross him off the list, Inspector, but if you need to question him he'll be here soon.'

'I'd like a few details about him just the same, if you would.'

When Inspector Cox discovered Adam Hawkridge was the head of a successful electronics firm he exchanged a look with the policeman, who sat down by Lowri on the sofa.

'Miss Morgan,' he said gently, 'would Mr Hawkridge be very wealthy by any chance?'

Lowri frowned. 'I don't know.'

The two policemen exchanged looks. 'What do you mean, you don't know?' asked the inspector.

Lowri shrugged. 'He's comfortably off, I suppose. But you'd have to ask him that. Why?' she added suspiciously, then lost every last vestige of colour. 'Oh, I see. Ransom.'

'It's a possibility. Anyone knowing the child's father...'

Lowri shook her head, regaining some of her colour in a rush. 'Hardly anyone does. In fact, until a few days ago only my family knew who Rhosyn's father was.'

'And what happened a few days ago?' probed the inspector.

Lowri explained the accidental meeting, and subsequent

discovery by Adam that he possessed a daughter. 'I kept the baby a secret from him for—for reasons of my own.'

'If those reasons throw any light on her disappearance, we need to know them, Miss Morgan.'

'I had no wish to marry Mr Hawkridge,' said Lowri woodenly, 'and saw no reason to inform him of Rhosyn's birth.'

'By which I take it you are not on good terms with Mr Hawkridge,' commented the inspector.

'I wouldn't say that. I had dinner with him at the Chesterton only recently,' she said with perfect truth, then suddenly lost her temper. 'But why are we just sitting here chatting? Why aren't you out there *doing* something about getting my baby back? She'll be in a terrible state, crying for me—' She broke down, crying wildly, and the policewoman put an arm round Lowri, trying to comfort her while the inspector explained as succinctly as possible that a missing child was treated with top priority. The photographs were being copied and would be circulated, and an appeal broadcast on both radio and television later that night. Everything humanly possible would be done to reunite Rhosyn with her mother at top speed.

At the sound of the doorbell Lowri leapt to her feet expectantly, her eyes dulling as the sergeant came into the room to say a Mrs Frances Hobbs and Miss Jenny Hooper were asking to come up.

'Mrs Hobbs is my partner, Miss Hooper runs the crèche.' Lowri subsided, mopping her face. 'Please let them in.'

Jenny rushed in ahead of Fran, ignoring the police as she threw herself into Lowri's arms, begging her forgiveness. 'I should never have gone off and left Kay on her own today; I wouldn't have let Rhosyn out of my sight. Oh, Lowri, I'm so sorry!'

Given the task of calming Jenny down, Lowri pulled

herself together, assuring Jenny she wasn't to blame. 'How's Kay?'

'I've left her with my mother. She hasn't stopped crying—she's in a terrible state.'

'Did you contact Rhosyn's grandmother?' asked Fran.

'Yes.'

'What was that?' asked Inspector Cox.

'Since the woman who took Rhosyn pretended to be her grandmother I naturally contacted Mrs Alice Hawkridge first before ringing you,' explained Lowri. 'She lives in Sussex,' she added. 'It was she who contacted Adam to give him the news.'

'I see. And there's no possibility that it could have been *your* mother, Miss Morgan?'

'My mother died ten years ago.'

'I'm sorry.' The inspector moved to the door. 'I'll get back to the station with Sergeant Boyce. WPC Porter will stay here with you for the time being. Overnight if you'd prefer. Try not to worry too much. We'll do everything in our power to get your child back, Miss Morgan.'

When the men had gone, Maggie, as she asked to be called, volunteered to make coffee for everyone, including sandwiches if Lowri would give her run of the kitchen.

'Good idea,' said Fran firmly. 'You must eat something, Lowri.'

Finding it easier to give in than to argue, Lowri nodded listlessly, deeply grateful for her friends' company. Then she jumped up in alarm. 'What am I thinking of? I've got to ring my father and Sarah before they see the news on television.' She shuddered. 'It all seems so much worse when it's put into words. How could anybody *do* this?'

By the time both phone calls were made Lowri was white and shaking and causing her friends considerable concern.

'Come and eat a sandwich,' said Fran sternly. 'It won't

do Rosie any good to come home to a mother in a state of collapse.'

Oddly comforted by Fran's no-nonsense manner, Lowri nibbled at a sandwich, and even managed a smile for Maggie, who had cut crusts off and found a pretty plate for the sandwiches.

'Do you do a lot of this sort of thing?' Lowri asked, as she sipped her coffee.

'Only once before on this type of case, and that's twice too many. But don't worry,' she added staunchly. 'We'll get her back. Inspector Cox is a family man himself. He understands what you're going through. He won't rest until your baby's safe.'

Jenny and Fran assured Lowri that the following day, Christmas Eve or not, they could manage without her at the shop. 'You won't want to be down there tomorrow,' said Jenny.

'I'd rather keep busy,' said Lowri quickly.

'But you may get a lot of nosy parkers coming in just to look at you if you're on the news tonight,' Jenny pointed out unhappily.

When the doorbell rang all three of them waited, tense, as Maggie went out to see who it was. 'It's Mr Hawkridge,' she announced, coming back into the room. 'He's on his way up.'

But Lowri was already on her feet and running out into the hall to open the door at the head of the stairs as Adam came leaping up to meet her. She took one look at his drawn, ashen face, and all her hostility and resentment towards him vanished as though they'd never been. She threw herself into his arms and he crushed her close, rubbing his cheek against hers.

He put Lowri away from him at last, staring down into her tear-stained face. 'No news?'

She shook her head forlornly, and filled him in on what

the police were doing so far. 'They thought you might have had something to do with it,' she told him bluntly.

Adam shrugged out of his overcoat. 'Did you?'

'No.'

He breathed in deeply. 'Thank God for that, at least.' He put his arm round her and opened the sitting-room door, then stopped dead at the sight of so many women.

Lowri made the necessary introductions and Fran and Jenny, after a few moments' conversation, began putting coats on, begging Lowri to let them know the minute there was any news.

'Don't worry,' said Adam decisively. 'I'll do all that.' He turned to the policewoman. 'I shall stay here tonight, Constable, so if you need to get back to the station?'

Maggie Porter nodded. 'Right, sir. I'll inform Inspector Cox you're here. He wants to ask you some questions.'

Adam exchanged a glance with Lowri. 'I may as well get that over right away—perhaps your friends could hang on until I get back.'

Fran and Jenny were only too pleased to be of help. When Adam had gone off with Maggie they both turned to Lowri in awe.

'*That's* Rosie's father?' said Fran.

Lowri nodded. 'Yes.'

Jenny gave a low whistle. 'In that case we leave you in good hands, Lowri. He looks equal to anything. I'd hate to be the woman who stole Rosie when he catches up with her.'

Half an hour later Adam returned, and Fran and Jenny went home, promising to be in earlier than usual in the morning.

'Now do you feel?' asked Adam.

'The same as you look, I imagine,' she said bleakly. 'You missed supper with your mother. Shall I cook you bacon and eggs or something?'

'Don't bother.' Adam lifted the cover from the plate of sandwiches. 'I'll have some of these. But I must ring Mother first.'

'Of course.' Lowri tried to smile. 'Please apologise for my hysterics on the phone.'

Adam touched a hand to her pale cheek. 'Under the circumstances she'd have found it strange if you were calm!'

Later, when Adam had spoken to his mother, and Lowri had made yet another pot of coffee, he pulled her down beside him on the sofa.

'Come and sit here, Lowri; we both need human contact,' he said grimly, as he took her hand. 'I've only seen Rhosyn once and I'm berserk with worry. God knows how you must be feeling.'

'I just keep praying that woman's kind,' said Lowri unsteadily, and swallowed hard. 'Rhosyn gets a lot of cuddling—from Jenny and Fran as well as me, not to mention from all the Morgan clan. She's only known love and kindness.'

'Don't!' said Adam roughly, and put his arm round her. 'At least we know some woman's got her. It isn't as though she's lost, or....' He halted, and breathed in deeply as he held her close. 'Have you told your father?'

'Yes. And Sarah. Rhia's in Gstaad with the girls and Mari-Sian. Sarah will contact them when—when—'

'When Rhosyn's back with us,' he said emphatically.

Us? thought Lowri, then leapt to her feet in sudden hope as the telephone rang. Her disappointment was so intense that she felt sick as she listened to Sergeant Boyce informing her there would be an item on the news at nine, and later at ten. There would also be regular radio bulletins asking for information.

When Lowri asked Adam to fetch her television from the spartan little bedroom they sat close together in front of it, waiting tensely for the news.

'You realise what this will mean?' said Lowri dully. 'It's an end to the crèche. No one will ever leave a child with me again after this.'

'In which case you branch out in some other direction,' said Adam the businessman, but his eyes were tender as he turned her face up to his. 'The only thing that matters is to get Rhosyn back. After the newscast someone, somewhere is bound to remember seeing her.'

Lowri's teeth bit into her trembling lower lip. She let out a deep, despairing sigh. 'Oh, Adam, I pray you're right.'

CHAPTER ELEVEN

AFTER the television newscast there were calls from Lowri's father and Rupert, both of them deeply shaken after seeing Rhosyn's photograph. Adam answered them both, Rupert unsurprised to hear his voice, Geraint Morgan too worried over the plight of his granddaughter to question Adam Hawkridge's presence in his daughter's life again.

'Did Dad understand why I couldn't speak to him?' said Lowri, hoarse from weeping.

'I told him you were shattered after watching the news,' said Adam, and stood looking down at her as she huddled in misery on the sofa. 'Why don't you lie down for a bit—get some rest.'

She glared at him. 'Rest? Don't be stupid!' She bit her lip. 'Sorry—'

'Don't be.' He touched a hand to her untidy hair. 'If you won't go to bed, have a bath. Try to relax a little if you can, Lowri.'

She consented reluctantly. 'All right. I'd like to change my clothes, I'll admit.' She gazed up at him imploringly. 'Call me if…'

Adam pulled her to her feet and turned her towards the door. 'Go. I need to make a couple of phone calls, then I'll make you some tea.'

Lowri gave him a pallid little smile and went off to run a bath. While she lay in it for a few minutes she heard his voice, and wondered if he wanted her out of the way so he could talk to someone in private. Adam had said there were no women in his life these days, but she found that hard to believe. Men like Adam needed women like they needed

146

oxygen and food. Pain suddenly struck her like a shaft of lightning. All *she* needed was to have her baby back in her arms again.

Wearing warm grey trousers and a thick scarlet sweater, Lowri emerged to find Adam waiting for her in the sitting room, a tea-tray on the small table beside him.

'I rang the police, then Mother again, to keep her posted, then I got in touch with Jim Wallace to give him this number,' Adam told her at once. 'He's my PA,' he added in response to her questioning look.

So it hadn't been a woman.

'What did the police say?'

'After the news they had several calls from people who'd seen a well-dressed, elderly lady carrying a child into a car near your shop.'

'A car,' repeated Lowri, swallowing. 'So she could be anywhere.'

'If the child was Rhosyn, yes. Descriptions varied somewhat.'

'I told the police what she was wearing, but she was indoors all day up to then. She didn't have a coat, so the woman could have wrapped her in a blanket or something.'

Adam shook his head. 'That would have been noticeable. She probably had something ready for Rhosyn to wear.'

Lowri drew in a deep, shuddering breath. 'So you think it was all premeditated?'

'It sounds like it. Women snatch babies from prams on impulse, but this has all the hallmarks of a well-thought-out plan.'

Lowri poured tea with an unsteady hand. 'You don't think—?' She stopped, hating to put her thought into words.

Adam took the teapot from her shaking hand and put it back on the tray, then sat beside her. 'Think what, Lowri?'

'That the woman intends selling Rhosyn to some couple too desperate for a baby to ask questions?'

He took her hand in a cruel grip. 'We're not even going to think of that one. But even if it's true, we'll find her. I promise you. At least,' he added, 'there's been no ransom demand so far.'

Lowri stared at him blankly. 'How do you know?'

'That's why I rang Jim Wallace. Nothing's come in at the office, anyway. In the meantime he's going round to my flat to check my messages. He'll ring later.'

'Why is your PA a man?' asked Lowri curiously.

'When my father abdicated, his assistant resigned.'

'Didn't she want to work for you?'

'She was a married lady who left because she was pregnant,' said Adam without expression. 'At the time I was still licking the wounds you'd inflicted, and ill disposed towards women in general. So I hired a man. It works well. Jim's highly qualified, dependable, and never objects to working late.'

'Any of which could apply to a woman just as well,' snapped Lowri.

'Good girl!' Adam smiled. 'I'd rather you ripped at me than wept. Your tears cut me to pieces.'

In which case, thought Lowri morosely, it was a pity she hadn't turned them on him full force when she'd first found out she was pregnant.

'I just wish we could hear something,' she said miserably.

Adam hooked her close with a long arm. 'I know, I know.'

'I just keep picturing her crying for me, Adam. The woman won't know what she eats, or what milk I give her, or—or anything.' She burrowed her head into his shoulder, utterly oblivious of him as a man. For the moment he just represented comfort she needed so badly that she forgot that he'd ever been her lover.

Adam, however, shifted restlessly after a while, and she detached herself quickly and sat erect in the corner of the sofa.

'I could do with a drink,' he said tightly. 'A pity you keep a dry house, Lowri.'

'The Green Man down the road is probably still open, if you're desperate.'

'Not that desperate.' He gave her a hard look. 'Alcohol, at least, has never been a problem for me.'

'Unlike women.' She gave him a sidelong glance. 'At one time the problem was a glut; nowadays it's a dearth.'

'Both circumstances solely by choice,' he reminded her cuttingly, then raised his hand in apology. 'Sorry. I'm on edge.'

'We both are,' she agreed, sighing, then her eyes narrowed. 'Wait a minute.' She sprang up and went into her bedroom, and came back waving a miniature barrel of cognac. 'How about this?'

Adam looked amused. 'Where did that come from?'

'I put it in my father's Christmas stocking.' Lowri tried to smile. 'I can easily get something else if—when—'

'When!' said Adam promptly, and jumped to his feet to take the barrel from her. 'Right. We'll both have some.'

Normally Lowri loathed spirits, but tonight she was in sore need of any help she could get to ward off the panic and grief she was holding at bay only by supreme effort of will.

'Better?' asked Adam, as she sipped cautiously.

'The effect, yes. I hate the taste.'

He smiled, and topped up their glasses. 'Neither of us will get drunk on this amount. But it might make the waiting marginally more bearable.'

The night wore on at such a snail's pace that Lowri was

glad of the inner, transient warmth derived from the brandy. Jim Wallace rang to relay the messages on Adam's phone, but no demand for ransom had been among them. The only other phone call came from Inspector Cox just before midnight to say that, while they had several eye-witness reports of the child being driven off in a car, nothing more could be done until morning. More appeals would be broadcast on breakfast television, after which there might be more leads to go on. He told Adam to advise Miss Morgan to get some rest and promised to be in touch the moment they had any news.

'How does he expect me to rest in these circumstances?' said Lowri in despair.

'You might sleep if you went to bed.'

She shook her head positively. 'I just don't want to be on my own—' She flushed, and Adam smiled mockingly.

'Don't worry. I know that wasn't an invitation. We'll just sit here and talk all night, if you like.' His eyes met hers. 'Whatever you want, I'll do, Lowri.'

She inclined her head gravely. 'Thank you.'

They resumed their places on the sofa. And this time when Adam put his arm round her Lowri leaned against him gratefully, thankful for the warmth and rock-like security of his hold.

'I haven't thanked you for all the presents you sent,' she said in sudden remorse. 'I forgot.'

'Did Rhosyn like the rocking horse?'

'She certainly did. Much excitement! Very extravagant of you—or did you decide on something as big as that so I couldn't send it back?'

He laughed a little. 'Something like that.'

'She hasn't seen the teddy yet—' Lowri swallowed hard on a sudden gush of tears. She cleared her throat. 'The clothes are beautiful. Did you choose them?'

'No. I wouldn't have known where to start. My mother did that.'

Lowri stiffened. 'You—you told her about Rhosyn, then.'

'Yes.'

'Why?'

'Why not?'

Lowri would have drawn away, but Adam's arm tightened to prevent her.

'How did she react?' she asked after a while.

Adam rubbed his chin with his free hand. 'She couldn't believe it at first.'

'That Rhosyn was yours?'

'No, that she actually had a grandchild. She couldn't believe her luck.'

Lowri screwed her head round to look up at him narrowly. 'Luck? I trust you made it clear you've got no claim on Rhosyn?'

His face hardened. 'I did. But my mother still thinks of her as her granddaughter!'

Lowri subsided, deflated. 'Yes, of course. If—*when* I get Rhosyn back, your mother's welcome to come and visit her.'

'How about me?' he said swiftly.

There was silence for a moment.

'Let's get Rhosyn back first,' she said gruffly. 'Until then I can't think about—about anything else.'

Another silence.

After a while Adam said casually, 'Did you receive the other package?'

Lowri flushed with embarrassment. 'Oh—yes. Sorry! I should have thanked you for that, too.'

'I wasn't asking for thanks.' He stared at his shoes morosely. 'I was collecting a ring my mother'd sent to a jeweller for enlarging, and the brooch caught my eye. I bought it for you on impulse.'

'It's lovely. I don't have much jewellery. Thank you,' said Lowri, who up to that moment hadn't decided whether she'd keep the brooch or not. But to hand it back to Adam under the present circumstances seemed hardly the thing to do.

'I thought it would serve as a reminder of happier days,' said Adam very quietly.

Lowri nodded silently. 'I haven't bought anything for you,' she said after a while.

He gave a mirthless laugh. 'I didn't imagine you would. Every time you look at Rhosyn you must curse the day you ever laid eyes on me.'

'Good heavens, no!' She looked up at him in astonishment. 'You've seen Rhosyn. How could I possibly regret anything to do with her? Any animosity I feel towards you, Adam, is for a quite different reason.'

His eyes hardened. 'You don't have to spell it out, Lowri. It's obvious that marriage to me was such an unbearable prospect that you chose the life of a single parent in preference to it.'

This was by no means accurate, but Lowri was in no mood to explain. 'Let's not talk about it,' she said shortly.

He took her at her word. The silence between them lengthened to such an extent that to her guilty surprise Lowri found herself growing drowsy. Her eyelids drooped and she blinked them open, horrified that she could even think of sleeping when Rhosyn was somewhere out there in the cold night with strangers. As he felt her deep, shuddering sigh Adam's arm tightened, his free hand stroked her hair in wordless sympathy and Lowri's body relaxed against his even as her brain ordered her to keep alert. The tension and anguish of the past few hours took their toll, and as the endless night wore on towards morning sleep overwhelmed her and granted her the boon of an hour or two's oblivion.

When Lowri woke she was stiff and cold, and alone on the sofa. Adam was nowhere to be seen. Frowning, she staggered to the bathroom, then recoiled in horror at the sight of his naked body in the bath. She shot back out again, blushing scarlet at the amusement she saw—belatedly—in his eyes.

She went into the kitchen and leaned her head on her arms on a counter top, her embarrassment obliterated as the misery of Rhosyn's absence swept over her in a tide. After a while she pulled herself together, washed her face under the kitchen tap and filled the kettle. By the time Adam joined her, his hair damp and his jaw dark with stubble, she'd made tea and was slicing bread to put in the toaster.

'Good morning,' she said, not looking at him. 'Would you like some eggs?'

'Good morning—and I'd like some eggs very much.' He pulled a face. 'One's appetite functions separately from the mind, apparently. I thought I wouldn't be able to face food in the circumstances, but apart from those sandwiches I didn't eat anything yesterday—'

'Then you must be starving! Give me a minute to wash and I'll make you an omelette.' Lowri disappeared to wash and tidy herself up, eyeing her pallid face and dark-ringed eyes with distaste. She brushed her hair, tied it back and returned to the kitchen, where Adam was drinking coffee. 'Make one for me, please,' she said casually, and put an omelette pan on the cooker.

'Let's eat breakfast in the other room,' said Adam, handing over a mug. 'It's almost time for a television newscast.'

Lowri nodded silently, swallowed some coffee, then broke eggs into a bowl. She added some herbs and seasoning, poured the mixture into the sizzling pan, and within minutes they were side by side again on the sofa, the tray on a table in front of them. They had finished eating by the time Rhosyn's photograph appeared on the screen, something Lowri was thankful for. One look at her daughter's face tightened her throat so painfully that it was some time before she could drink her coffee.

'We didn't talk about her last night,' said Adam suddenly. 'Tell me about Rhosyn—everything about her.'

Lowri gave him a startled glance, then decided he was right. 'Where shall I start?'

'With her birth. Was it hard?'

Lowri shrugged. 'It wasn't fun, but it was normal enough. She took twelve hours to arrive, by which time I'd had quite enough of the whole process. But one look at her and all the pain and effort was worth it.'

'Was she big?'

'Eight and a half pounds.' Lowri grimaced. 'I wouldn't like to produce a bigger baby, believe me.'

'Do you intend to do that?' said Adam quickly.

Lowri gave him a baleful look. 'None of your business,' she snapped.

There was a hostile pause.

'Was she a good baby?' Adam asked eventually.

'Yes, she was. From about six weeks old she slept all night most nights, except when she was teething or had the sniffles.'

'So how old was she when you started on this place?'

'Three months. And at first I was so tired I thought I'd bitten off more than I could chew. But I coped.' Lowri smiled ruefully. 'My father was convinced I wasn't up to it, and I was determined to show him I could. And I have. It's the ideal business to run with a baby, remember. And I've had Fran's experience to lean on, and then we took on Jenny, which means I make a late start, take a long lunch hour with Rhosyn, and when she's two she'll go to nursery school—'

'As young as that?' he said, startled.

'Oh, yes. It's all fixed up. It's a bit expensive, but it's a Montessori-type school, where they have French lessons, and ballet, too, if you like, only it's extra…' Lowri trailed away, her eyes haunted.

Adam pushed the table away so he could take her in his arms. 'We'll get her back,' he said hoarsely into her hair. 'Only for God's sake don't look like that.'

They clung together convulsively then jumped apart as the phone rang, and kept on ringing at intervals all morning. First it was Geraint Morgan, then Sarah, then Alice Hawkridge, after which Inspector Cox reported that the police were doing house-to-house questioning in the area, showing Rhosyn's photograph.

Jenny and Fran arrived early, asking what help was necessary, apart from manning the shop.

'Stay up here while I go shopping,' said Adam, and smiled at the amazement on Lowri's face. 'I didn't bring any luggage, remember, I need some shirts and so on, and a razor.'

'Don't be long,' said Lowri involuntarily, and flushed as he squeezed her hand.

'Direct me to the nearest shop and I'll be half an hour at the most.'

After he left practical Fran saw to the dishes, while Jenny apologised on Kay's behalf yet again.

'She asked to come and help today, but I knew that's the last thing you'd want—'

'Why?' said Lowri. 'For one thing I doubt you'll get any customers for the crèche today after what's happened. But if Kay wants to come and give a hand in the shop I think it's a good idea. It's Christmas Eve, remember. Besides,' she added, pressing Jenny's hand, 'Kay will feel a lot better if she helps. It wasn't her fault. I really don't blame her— she wasn't to know.'

Jenny hugged Lowri's hand. 'It's so *good* of you. I'll give her a ring right now.'

By the time Adam returned the shop was open and Jenny and a pathetically grateful Kay were manning it while Fran stayed with Lowri, her sane, practical presence doing a lot to keep her partner on an even keel.

Fran got up to let him in, smiling wryly at his load of packages. 'Father Christmas, I presume! I'll go down, then. Chin up, Lowri.'

When they were alone Lowri eyed the bags askance. 'I thought you'd only gone to buy a shirt.'

'I bought more than one, also the necessary equipment to shave, since your bathroom was innocent of razors—'

'I've got a little electric thing you could have used if you'd asked.' Lowri peered into a large carrier bag. 'And this is full of food!' she said accusingly.

'There isn't much in your kitchen,' he pointed out.

'I know. I haven't done much shopping lately because we—we were going away tonight—' Lowri turned away, determined not to cry. 'I'll put this stuff away. You can use my bedroom to change.'

'Sorry I was so long, by the way,' he said as he picked up the bags. 'My favourite caterer's foodhall was like a rugby scrum. Good thing I was there as they opened. But at least I got most of my shopping done under one roof.'

Lowri managed a smile. 'Do you usually wear chainstore shirts?'

'All the time,' he lied shamelessly. 'How about some coffee?'

Business downstairs was brisk all morning; not in the crèche, as expected, but otherwise the shop was busy. There were a few curious people eager to see the bereft mother, Fran reported, but there were a lot of genuine customers hunting for last-minute bargains; also some of their regular customers had come in, eager to offer sympathy. Two of these had given valuable information about the elderly lady seen taking a young child into a car. One young woman remembered the make of the car, and the other described the yellow wind cheater the child was wearing, also the obvious difficulty the woman had in fastening the little girl into the car seat.

'At least she had Rhosyn safe in a proper seat,' said Lowri, determined to be positive.

Fran nodded. 'Which means she'll be taking care of Rosie properly. By the way,' she added as she went to the door, 'I've had a couple of offers for the rocking horse. I turned them down, of course.'

'I should hope so,' retorted Lowri, avoiding Adam's eye.

The morning seemed endless, though to the impartial on-looker the scene was oddly domesticated as Adam read the newspaper he'd brought and Lowri dealt with the large basket of ironing she was never without. They drank endless cups of coffee, but neither of them had any appetite for the cookies and buns Adam had bought earlier, though Fran and her cohorts were grateful for them as lunchtime approached, as none of the three would hear of leaving the shop for lunch or any other reason.

Phone calls kept coming in, some of them with sympathy from local business people, others from Sarah and Holly, both of them unable to wait in silence for news, and towards midday Alice Hawkridge rang again, and after a brief conversation with her son this time asked to speak to Lowri.

'I just wanted to say I'm praying for you—hard,' said Adam's mother firmly. 'And I've told Adam he's to try and get you to eat.'

Lowri managed a little laugh. 'He does that constantly. He's been quite overbearing about it.'

There was a pause. 'Try not to be too hard on him, my dear.'

'Mrs Hawkridge, if—no, *when* I get Rhosyn back I don't think I'll ever be hard on anyone again for the rest of my life!'

'Then I'll pray even harder. And now I'll ring off to keep your line free.'

Lunchtime came and went, by which time Adam had given up all attempt to make Lowri eat. As time passed she became more and more tense, finding it hard to make any attempt at conversation, and Adam, in no better state, gave up trying to lighten her mood. Suddenly, halfway through the afternoon, Lowri buried her head in her hands and gave way to bitter tears, and Adam seized her and rocked her in his arms. When she raised a swollen, tear-stained face to his at last, Adam kissed her quivering mouth gently and smoothed her hair back from her damp forehead.

'Don't give up, Lowri.'

She detached herself and sat up straight. 'Sorry. It just came over me in a wave all of a sudden. I must look a fright. I'll go and do something to myself.'

When she returned, with a touch of make up on her newly washed face, Adam eyed her in approval.

'That's my girl.' He bit his lip at her quizzical look. 'Purely a figure of speech, Lowri.'

'Of course.' She gave a determined little smile. 'No more tears, I promise. I don't usually cry much, you know.'

'No,' said Adam bluntly, 'I don't know. You never gave me the chance to find out.'

'True.' For some reason she felt in command of herself again. 'Now I think I could manage one of those buns you bought—' She broke off as the phone rang and raced out of the room to answer it.

'Miss Morgan? Cox here.'

'Inspector! Any news?'

'Don't get your hopes too high, but it's possible I might

have. If we come round now we can take you to an address we've been given.'

Lowri gasped. 'You've found Rhosyn? Where is she? Who's got her—?'

'Miss Morgan, calm down. We don't know anything concrete yet. But we need you with us to identify a child.'

Lowri went cold, sagging against Adam. '*Identify*? What are you saying?'

'Nothing sinister. This child we've heard about is alive and well, I promise you. But I must stress that there's no guarantee that it's your child.'

As Lowri put the phone down Adam grabbed her hands. 'Well?' he demanded, his eyes blazing in his haggard face.

'They're coming to collect me—'

'You're not going without me!'

She nodded impatiently. 'Of course not!' She repeated Inspector Cox's news. 'He sounded a bit cagey—doesn't want to commit himself. Will you tell the girls?'

Adam raced down to the shop, then came back up the stairs two at a time and grabbed Lowri to him. 'Don't build too much on this, darling!'

'How can I not?' she said wildly, then breathed in deeply and pulled herself together. 'You're right, of course. But it's so *hard*, Adam.'

'Bloody hard!' He held her coat for her. 'Put a scarf on, or something. It's cold out there.'

When Sergeant Boyce came to collect them Lowri and Adam were in the hall, waiting, Lowri still as a statue, Adam pacing up and down like a caged tiger.

'Not far to go,' Inspector Cox assured them as they joined him in the car. 'The message came from one of those pricey flats in Gloucester Place.'

'Do you think it's Rhosyn?' said Adam urgently, before Lowri could speak.

'The man who rang thinks it is. He sounded in a bit of

a state. Just asked me to come as quickly as possible. We'll soon see.'

When the car drew up outside a block of imposing luxury flats Adam helped Lowri out, keeping his arm about her as they went up in a lift with the inspector. In tense silence they went out into a hall where the inspector rang the bell of one of the four doors leading off it.

A haggard man opened the door to admit them, looking utterly distraught. Inspector Cox introduced himself and his companions.

'My name's Charles Blanchard,' the man said as he showed them into a comfortably furnished room overlooking well-tended gardens. 'Could I just explain a little before you see the baby? She's perfectly safe, I swear.' He looked from Lowri to Adam despairingly. 'I can't apologise enough for what's happened. I can hardly take it in—I arrived only a short time ago to fetch my mother to spend Christmas with us. I'd seen the photographs of the missing baby on television last night, so you can imagine my horror when my mother handed the very same child over to me, saying she'd found the perfect Christmas present for us.'

'Please, Mr Blanchard, don't keep me in suspense,' broke in Lowri, unable to bear it a moment longer. 'Where is my baby?'

'I'll take you to her now,' said Charles Blanchard in quick remorse. 'She fell asleep, so I asked a neighbour to sit with her while I made arrangements for my mother—who's in a state of mental collapse. She's been hospitalised. Her doctor went with her, and I'll follow on once everything's sorted out here. Forgive me, but it's been hell on wheels this last hour or two. Will you come this way?'

Adam's grasp was cruelly tight on Lowri's hand as they followed Charles Blanchard to a small room where an elderly woman rose quickly from beside the cot, the sudden movement disturbing the sleeping child. The little girl's swollen eyes opened, then lit up like stars at the sight of her mother.

'Mum-mum-mum-mum!' cried Rhosyn, stretching up her arms, and Lowri swept her up in a fierce embrace, rubbing her cheek over and over again against the small head, hardly able to believe she had her baby safe. Then Adam's arms closed round them both, confirming beyond all doubt that this was actually happening, that the nightmare was really over.

CHAPTER TWELVE

IT WAS late that night when Rhosyn was finally, happily asleep in her own cot again. All the jubilant, thankful phone calls had been made and interviews given to the local television news team as well as a perky young cub reporter from the *Pennington Weekly Chronicle*.

'Won't come out until next week,' said the young man cheerfully, 'but it'll still be good news. Just the stuff for the festive season.'

Fran, Jenny and Kay went home by taxi at last, all three of them jubilant, and intoxicated more by thankfulness and sheer fatigue than the champagne Adam bought to celebrate Rhosyn's return.

The feisty little girl recovered from her adventure with remarkable speed, other than a tendency to cling round her mother's neck now and again, and responded to Adam's subtle advances with a flirtatious enthusiasm he all too plainly found irresistible. By the time her baby daughter had played with all her familiar toys, and had been bathed and fed and cuddled to sleep, Lowri felt exhausted, the adrenaline deserting her in a rush once the flat was quiet and she was alone with Adam.

Adam looked at his watch. 'It's late. I'd better make a move—'

'You're not driving back to London at this time of night?' said Lowri in dismay. 'You haven't eaten, and there was the champagne—'

'Only one glass, Lowri,' he said brusquely, not looking at her. 'Besides, I don't have much alternative. It's

Christmas Eve, remember. There'll be no room at the inn locally at such short notice.'

'But you can sleep here! There's a single bed in Rhosyn's room. I'll take that and you can have mine.' Lowri put out a hand in entreaty, finding she hated the thought of being alone. 'Couldn't you drive back to London in the morning? Please? You can still be with your mother in good time for lunch.'

Adam looked at her long and hard. 'Why, Lowri? Is this a need for *my* company, or a simple dislike of solitude after all you've been through?'

'Some of both,' she said honestly, and smiled in entreaty. 'Now the holiday plans are changed I thought perhaps you'd like to see Rhosyn open her Christmas stocking in the morning before we set off—'

'In different directions,' said Adam expressionlessly and put out a hand to turn her face up to his. 'Does this mean you've had a change of heart, Lowri?'

'As far as you and Rhosyn are concerned, yes.'

'But nothing more than that.'

Lowri met his eyes squarely. 'No other change of heart, certainly.'

'You mean you still hate the sight of me,' he said bitterly.

'You know that's not true!'

'Do I?'

They looked at each other in silence, then Lowri pocketed her pride. 'Please stay, Adam. I can't bear the thought of being alone tonight. I badly need someone to talk to until this feeling of helplessness recedes a bit.'

He smiled mirthlessly. 'You're honest.'

'You bought a lot of food and we've hardly eaten any of it. And there's some champagne left. Let's have a meal and celebrate Rhosyn's return together.'

'Put like that, how can I refuse?'

Lowri smiled at him with radiant gratitude. 'You listen for Rhosyn,' she ordered. 'I'll throw something together in the kitchen.'

'Can I help?'

'I'll manage better on my own—' She caught herself up, flushing.

'As usual!'

Lowri retreated hurriedly, and shut herself in the kitchen, away from the searching eyes that had haunted her dreams so often during the long, lonely months of their estrangement.

Half an hour later she called him to the small table she'd set with a checked cloth and red candles in saucers wreathed with holly. She'd cooked rice, concocted a tomato sauce fragrant with herbs and garlic and added the king prawns Adam bought to it, defrosted a loaf of wholemeal bread and accompanied it with a slab of her favourite Caerphilly cheese to complete the line-up. Adam exclaimed in surprise as she showed him to his chair with a flourish. 'Impressive—and fast!'

'I aim to please,' she said demurely.

'Not always—' he began, then threw up a hand in apology. 'Sorry. Tonight let's just forget certain bits of the past and concentrate on the pleasanter aspects of our relationship.'

'Right,' said Lowri quickly, not sure this was too wise a move. For her some of the most memorable and blissful time had been spent in his bed, a thought which struck Adam simultaneously she suspected, as colour rose along his cheekbones.

'This is wonderful,' he said, mouth full, and smiled across the candle-flames at her. 'Until this minute I didn't know I was starving.'

'Me too,' she agreed, and for a while there was a companionable silence while they tucked into the meal. But a little later, once the first edge was off her appetite, Lowri gave a sigh. 'I can't help feeling sorry for that poor woman, you know.'

'Mrs Blanchard?' said Adam, and nodded gravely. 'I know. She's obviously mentally disturbed, and now Rhosyn's safe it's difficult to condemn her. In her own mind she was just giving her son the one Christmas present he and his wife wanted most.'

'Poor thing. I keep seeing that little room with the cot and those toys—it was heartbreaking.'

While Lowri was dressing Rhosyn Adam had been present when the police questioned Charles Blanchard, who said that his mother had suffered a nervous breakdown after the death of his father a few months previously. He'd genuinely believed she was fully recovered, and blamed himself bitterly for letting his mother know when his wife miscarried a few weeks earlier. Charles Blanchard was the father of two healthy sons, Lowri learned to her relief, but admitted that his mother had a fixation about a granddaughter, never dreaming she'd take matters into her own hands to provide one by such disastrous means.

'A pity the police had to be involved,' said Lowri with regret.

'If they hadn't been, Blanchard wouldn't have seen Rhosyn's photograph. But at least there's no question of his mother being charged, now Blanchard's committed her to proper professional care.'

'Poor woman,' Lowri sighed. 'And all this happened just because I went out for balloons. Fran says she must have been in the store-room getting out more shoes for the child she was fitting, which is why no one noticed when Rhosyn was spirited away. My daughter thought it was one big game, probably.'

'Perhaps it was fate,' commented Adam, pouring the last of the champagne into their glasses.

'Pretty cruel if it was!'

'Now Rhosyn's safe I can't feel it was total cruelty where I'm concerned, if I'm honest.' His eyes locked with hers, bright and unwavering over the candle flames. 'Nothing else would have compelled you to contact me, Lowri, would it?'

Her eyes fell. 'Possibly not.'

'Which brings me to something you said earlier. My mother, you promised, would be welcome to visit Rhosyn, but what about me?' Adam reached a hand across the table to capture hers. 'Like it or not, I am Rhosyn's father, Lowri.'

'If you'd shown more enthusiasm for the idea from the start I'd be more sympathetic,' she retorted. Her chin lifted. 'To be accused of trapping a man into marriage is a pretty difficult thing to forget. Or forgive.'

Adam released her hand and sat back, his face hidden in the shadow beyond the candlelight. 'It was said in the heat of the moment, at a time when life was throwing quite a lot at me, one way and another. Now I can't think why the thought ever crossed my mind, but if it makes you feel any better I've paid for it ever since, one way and another. Haven't *you* ever said anything you regret, Lowri?'

'I regret the thing I didn't say,' she said bitterly, and swallowed the rest of her champagne in one gulp. 'As I mentioned once before, a good old-fashioned no to you in the beginning would have saved us all a lot of trouble.'

'Then there'd be no Rhosyn,' he said swiftly, and Lowri calmed down somewhat as she digested this incontrovertible truth.

'That's one point in your favour, I suppose,' she muttered after a while, and got up. 'You go in the other room while I clear up.'

'No. We'll do it together,' he said decisively, in a tone Lowri didn't dare argue with.

In taut silence they dealt with the detritus of their meal, and afterwards Adam took a tray of coffee into the other room while Lowri went to look at Rhosyn, something she'd been doing at regular intervals all evening, almost unable to credit the miracle of having her child safe once more. Adam came to join her, and in silence they looked down at the flushed, angelic little face together, then without a word he turned away at last and left the room as quietly as he came.

Lowri stayed where she was, her eyes on Rhosyn, but her mind on Rhosyn's father. What did she do now? Allow Adam a visit now and then? But if she did, explanations could be difficult once Rhosyn was old enough to understand why Daddy lived somewhere else. And always had.

The telephone brought her from her reverie, but by the time she got to the hall Adam had answered it.

'It's your father,' he said, handing her the receiver, and went back into the sitting-room, closing the door behind him.

Lowri joined him after a while, and poured coffee for them both in a silence Adam broke after a while as though he could stand it no longer.

'Your father anxious about Rhosyn?' he asked abruptly.

'He was pleased she'd settled down to sleep happily, yes.' Lowri got up from her chair and sat on the sofa beside him. 'Adam, what are you doing tomorrow?'

He frowned. 'Tomorrow?'

Lowri nodded. 'Yes, tomorrow, the twenty-fifth of December, Christmas Day.'

His face set. 'I hadn't forgotten. I'm spending it with my mother, what else?'

Lowri thrust a hand through her hair, coughed, looked away, then in a rush said 'Dad thought—I mean Holly suggested—and if you don't want to they'll understand, so will I, of course, please feel free to refuse—'

'Refuse what, for crying out loud?' Adam said in exasperation.

Lowri took a deep breath. 'The weather forecast is good, and it's not all that far, so Dad thought you might like to drive your mother down to spend the day with us, in Cwmderwen, I mean—to celebrate getting Rhosyn back safely for Christmas.'

A light flared in Adam's eyes. 'Your father's inviting *me*?'

Lowri nodded. 'And your mother.'

Adam gazed at her in silence, a very strange look on his face. 'How about you?'

'Oh, I'll be there too,' she assured him flippantly.

He caught her hands in his. 'You know perfectly well what I'm asking,' he said with sudden violence. 'Do *you* want me there?'

She nodded wordlessly, and he caught her to him and kissed her, and it was so good to feel his mouth on hers with the old, potent hunger Lowri let him go on kissing her and kissed him back. But when she felt the urgency rise in a powerful tide in his body Lowri drew away, shaking her head.

Adam's face set into an expressionless mask. 'So you're still punishing me.'

'No. I'm not. But you can't walk back into my life and expect everything to be the same, Adam.' Lowri got to her feet. 'I don't feel any animosity towards you now—I suppose the past twenty-four hours were something of a lesson in priorities. But when I asked you to stay tonight I made it quite clear it wasn't in my bed.'

'Such an exalted privilege never occurred to me,' he said bitterly, and jumped to his feet. 'All I took—and received—was a kiss, Lowri.'

They stared at each other in a taut, hostile silence broken at last by the sound of church bells.

Adam made a jerky, uncharacteristic gesture. 'It's Christmas, Lowri. Goodwill towards men.'

'Then, since you're indisputedly a man,' she said with a faint, reluctant smile, 'and entitled to goodwill, let's call a truce. Merry Christmas, Adam.' She closed the gap between them and stood on tiptoe to kiss his cheek.

'Merry Christmas,' he responded, and returned the kiss very carefully in kind.

'Now,' said Lowri practically, 'will it frighten your mother to death if you ring her this late? I hope not, because after insisting she joins the Morgans for Christmas you've got to remind her to put the turkey in the freezer.'

Christmas Day was at once the strangest and the most wonderful Lowri had ever spent in her life—and the longest. After only a few hours' sleep she woke Adam very early so he could give Rhosyn the teddy and help her open her Christmas stocking. After a hasty breakfast Lowri sped him on his way to London then dressed her daughter in the dungarees and ski-jacket chosen by Mrs Hawkridge, pinned the cricket brooch to the collar of her new red shirt and set off on the two-hour journey to Cwmderwen.

When she arrived at the familiar house with the sentry-box porch and long, rambling garden, Geraint Morgan appeared in the doorway before Lowri came to a halt. He came sprinting down the path, with Holly following more slowly, holding Huw by the hand, their faces so bright with welcome and love that Lowri had a fight to keep back the tears as she freed Rhosyn from her car seat just in time to be caught in a communal embrace as they all hugged each other, and Geraint Morgan kissed his granddaughter over and over again before hefting her on one arm with his little son on the other, leaving Holly and Lowri to follow him up the path to the house.

Holly Morgan, who was tall and slender, with smudges

of fatigue under her dark eyes, kept her arm round Lowri as they stood in the hall watching Geraint help Huw show Rhosyn the tall, brightly lit Christmas tree.

'It's a miracle,' she sighed, her eyes wet. She gave Lowri a searching look. 'How are you—really, I mean? I can see the dark marks under your eyes. We've all got a matching set after that terrible night. But are you feeling all right underneath?'

'I feel wonderful!' said Lowri with truth, and grinned. 'Ready to peel sprouts or baste the turkey, or whatever you like, now you've got two extra visitors to cope with.'

Geraint Morgan, whose powerful build was the kind more associated with a rugby scrum than a solicitor's office, looked up with a smile. 'That was Holly's idea, by the way.'

'You mean you still have reservations about Adam,' countered Lowri.

'Have you?'

Lowri shrugged. 'I don't know what I feel towards Adam, except that whatever it is it's nothing to do with animosity.'

'Then I'll extend true Welsh hospitality to both Adam and Mrs Hawkridge,' said her father firmly. 'In the meantime let's have a medicinal glass of cheer and open the presents before these two do it for us.'

By the time Adam arrived with his mother the sitting-room was a sea of wrapping paper, with two small, excited people playing happily with each other's toys while their elders relaxed under the influence of good sherry and a blazing fire and the sheer joy of being together after the trauma of Rhosyn's disappearance.

Lowri answered the door to the new arrivals, feeling a little tense until she looked into a pair of eyes so like Adam's she felt she knew his mother already. Alice Hawkridge, who was tall, grey-haired and handsome, with a no-nonsense air about her, bridged the awkward moment of meeting by taking Lowri in her arms and giving her a hug.

'Happy Christmas, my dear.'

'Happy Christmas to you, too, Mrs Hawkridge. I'm so glad you could come.' Lowri gave her a radiant smile.

'Nothing would have kept me away once your father was kind enough to include us in your celebration. Now don't keep me in suspense—lead me to my granddaughter!'

Adam, who had changed from his dark city suit into a tweed jacket and cords at some stage in his travels, looked rather weary as he smiled at Lowri. 'As you can see, Mother's priorities are firmly in place.'

Lowri led the way into the sitting-room, which was in such a mess all constraint evaporated as the introductions were made. Geraint Morgan clasped Adam's hand, laughing as Alice Hawkridge, once she'd thanked her hosts, promptly sat down on the floor with a child either side and embarked on a detailed examination of every last toy Rhosyn and Huw presented for her inspection, so obviously delighted Holly had no compunction in leaving her to it as she went off with Lowri to see to the meal.

'Do you think Adam will be all right in there with Dad?' asked Lowri, as she made brandy sauce for the pudding.

'Best to let them get on with it. Besides, your Adam looks well able to take care of himself,' commented Holly as she decanted vegetables into dishes.

'He's not my Adam,' protested Lowri.

'Pull the other one,' snorted her stepmother.

The meal was a lively, convivial affair, with no formality possible when two boisterous, noisy little people in high-chairs were joining in the fun. Alice Hawkridge insisted on seating herself between Huw and Rhosyn, who ate up their turkey and vegetables like little angels, utterly enslaved by this new playmate.

The only sober moment came when Geraint Morgan said grace, giving thanks for the blessing of Rhosyn's return.

'Amen,' said Lowri huskily, and looked up to meet Adam's eyes. She smiled shakily, and began passing the plates as her father carved the turkey.

During the meal Lowri finally relaxed as she saw her father and Adam seemed able to talk together far more easily than she'd expected. And it would have been a very difficult guest indeed who couldn't have got on with Alice Hawkridge.

'More wine, Adam?' said Geraint, proffering a bottle.

'Thank you, no, I'm driving,' said Adam with regret.

Geraint exchanged a look with Holly, who immediately suggested their guests stay the night.

'It might be a bit of a squash,' she said smiling, 'but we can manage if we shift round a bit.'

Adam obviously welcomed the idea, but his mother shook her head.

'You've been wonderfully kind having us here today, and we appreciate it very much indeed, but I think we should go home this evening. You've all had a terrible shock and tonight you'll be tired. The last thing you need is two extra guests for the night.'

'Mother's right,' said Adam at once, and smiled warmly at Holly. 'It's very good of you, but later on you'll be glad of some peace.'

'You'd be very welcome,' said Geraint quietly, and Adam gave him a very direct look.

'Thank you. I appreciate that. Another time we'd be glad to.'

After the big meal the two children were taken off for a nap while the others drank coffee in front of the fire. The conversation turned inevitably to Rhosyn's terrifying adventure, and after a while Holly, sensing signs of restlessness in Adam, turned to Lowri.

'Why don't you take Adam for a walk? Some fresh air before his long drive home might be a good idea.'

Adam sprang to his feet with such alacrity that Lowri had no choice but to follow suit. Her father, misunderstanding her reluctance, smiled at her reassuringly.

'Don't worry, *cariad*—Rhosyn's safe here.'

Lowri smiled. 'I know. And if she wakes up and needs entertaining I'm sure her grandma will be only too happy to oblige.'

There was general laughter, and Mrs Hawkridge nodded briskly, blinking as she sniffed hard.

'Very happy!' she agreed.

Outside in the frosty afternoon Lowri strolled with Adam in rather tense silence along a footpath which took them through the fields to the church.

'Would you like to see inside?' she asked politely. 'My uncle—Sarah's father—was the vicar here.'

'Would you mind if we just walked?' said Adam. 'I need to talk to you, Lowri, and since talking to you invariably leads to argument, a church hardly seems the best place.'

They fell in step again, taking a lane which led through fields crisp with frost.

'You know what I want to talk about,' went on Adam, a determined jut to his chin.

Lowri nodded. 'I assume you want to discuss arrangements for seeing Rhosyn.'

Adam gave her a black look. 'You assume wrong. I already know you intend to let me see Rhosyn. Which makes me very happy. What I'm not so happy about is my standing with you. Am I just to be Rhosyn's father, or are you going to let me back in your life as—'

'As what?' asked Lowri crisply.

They paused by a stile.

'I wish,' said Adam harshly, 'that I could go back in time and start again at the moment you announced you were pregnant.'

'But, since you can't, we just have to deal with things the way they are.' Lowri looked up at him in appeal. 'Let's not spoil Christmas Day, Adam, I need time. Surely you can understand that?'

'I thought we'd wasted enough time already,' he said bitterly. 'I hoped that after what we've been through together these past few days you'd softened towards me. Obviously I was mistaken.'

Lowri put a hand on his arm. 'No, you weren't. But neither of us is functioning normally at the moment—'

'I am,' he broke in swiftly, and pulled her into his arms, kissing her hungrily, his hold quelling her instinctive bid for freedom. When he raised his head at last he smiled crookedly into her upturned, scarlet face. 'I deserved one kiss, Lowri.'

'And one kiss is all you'll get,' she retorted, thoroughly irritable because her heart was thumping and she badly wanted to throw herself back in his arms and let him kiss her silly.

Adam was a great deal more cheerful on the way back to the house, where they found Huw and Rhosyn up and dressed and eager to welcome this other large playmate, who proved only too happy to keep them entertained. Tired out at last, the two excited babies had finally been settled down for the night before Adam and his mother took their leave.

'I can't tell you what this has meant to both of us,' said Adam with sincerity as he thanked Geraint and Holly.

'Adam's right,' said Mrs Hawkridge as she kissed Lowri. 'I never expected to enjoy a Christmas so much again.'

'I'll be in touch,' promised Lowri. 'You must come and see my shop and spoil Rhosyn as much as you like.'

'I'll keep you to that, my dear!'

Tactfully Geraint and Holly walked with Mrs Hawkridge to the car, leaving Adam and Lowri to say their goodbyes in private.

'When shall I see you again?' demanded Adam.

'I don't know,' she said evasively. 'Call me. We'll talk about it.'

For answer Adam swept her into his arms and kissed her hard, then took her hand and ran with her to the car waiting at the gate. After he got in he put his head out of the window and thanked the Morgans again, then gave Lowri the smile which still made her heart turn over.

'Soon!' he said and drove his mother away.

CHAPTER THIRTEEN

'How did it go?' asked Sarah a couple of days later, when Lowri was back in Pennington.

'It was a bit awkward at first,' admitted Lowri. 'I mean, the last time Dad and Adam met wasn't exactly a friendly occasion, was it? But no one could bristle in Mrs Hawkridge's company for long—'

'I told you she was lovely!'

'You were right. It was a mutual love affair between Mrs H. and Rhosyn from the first—Huw adored her, too. Under any other circumstances I might have been quite jealous. And oddly enough, once they'd got over the first hurdle Dad and Adam got on surprisingly well. Holly liked him a lot, I could tell, though she tried hard to hide it from me in case I thought she was being disloyal. Anyway, enough of me. How was your Christmas?'

'Exhausting, but fun. Though not as much fun as yours, by the sound of it. I'd love to have been a fly on the wall in Cwmderwen for the first half-hour!'

Lowri chuckled. 'Oh, by the way, did you ring Rhia?'

'I certainly did. She was horrified, needless to say, and sends loads of love; so does Mari-Sian. They'll be round to see you the moment they get back.' Sarah paused. 'So what happens now, Lowri?'

'I get back to work and life goes on, I suppose.'

'I mean what happens with Adam?'

'I'm not sure,' said Lowri guardedly. 'I can't stop him seeing Rhosyn after what happened, of course, but there's been no talk of—of arrangements, and so on.'

'Surely you've thawed a bit towards him by now?'

'Not much.'

Sarah sighed. 'You always were an obstinate little mule. Anyway, I trust you're all organised for my New Year's Eve soirée?'

'Yes. Fran's going to lock up and so on at the shop, so I'll drive down after lunch, well in time to get Rosie to bed.'

'Emily can't wait! And I'm quite looking forward to seeing you myself,' added Sarah affectionately. 'Buy a new dress. You deserve it.'

Lowri was visited with a strong feeling of *déjà vu* as she went down the curving staircase in St John's Wood to join one of the Clares' celebrated parties. She paused halfway down, suffering a sudden attack of stage-fright at the sound of laughter and music from the drawing-room, and gave herself a stern lecture. Her only problem was lack of practice these days when it came to socialising. Since Rhosyn's advent she'd had no time or opportunity for it. Tonight would do her good. Besides, she reminded herself, she'd already met several of the guests invited tonight. And the new dress she'd bought for half-price in the expensive shop just up the street from Little Darlings looked good on her, she knew. But a flattering dress and the glittering crystal earrings Holly had given her for Christmas were neither of them remedies for the butterflies fluttering beneath her green velvet midriff.

Then a familiar figure crossed the hall and looked up and Tom Harvey let out a crow of delight.

'Lowri! What a sight to gladden these old eyes. Let me ply you with strong drink and tell you how gorgeous you look.'

Suddenly Lowri was brimming with party spirit, and went running down to let Tom sweep her into the drawing-room into the crush of people gathered there to celebrate the new year. There were exclamations of pleasure from people she'd known before her flight from London, and a welcome from others meeting her for the first time. Now that her hair had grown and her rigorous diet and exercise routine had pared down her figure Lowri's likeness to Sarah was much more marked, and commented on by several people who mistook her for another sister. Rupert seized her hand to introduce her to a tall, lanky young man with a laughing intelligent face, and told him to take care of his little cousin.

'Lowri here did the donkey work for *The Atonement*,' said Rupert grinning. 'So be careful how you tread. She's a tigress in defence of my matchless prose.'

'I'm directing the adaptation for television,' the man told Lowri, as Rupert went off to welcome new arrivals. 'My name's Jack Benedict. Why haven't I met you before?'

'Because I don't live in London, I suppose.'

Jack led her to a secluded corner and began firing a barrage of questions at her, as to what she did and where she did it, whether she was spoken for and if not could he see her again as soon as possible.

Lowri, laughing, made her answers deliberately vague and settled down to indulge in the type of flirtation she'd forgotten she enjoyed so much. It was fun to talk light-hearted nonsense with a man not only expert in the art, but flatteringly determined to keep her to himself.

But after a while Lowri excused herself.

'Where are you going?' said Jack in alarm. 'It's not midnight yet, so don't vanish on me like Cinderella.'

'I'm just going upstairs to check on my daughter,' she assured him, and grinned at the crestfallen look on his face.

'So you are married,' he said, sighing theatrically.

'No, I'm not.' She handed him her glass. 'Hold on to that for me. I shan't be long.'

Lowri ran up the stairs and went along the upper hall to

the guest-room she was sharing with her daughter. She opened the door very quietly, then stared, transfixed. Adam Hawkridge, looking spectacular in formal black and white, was gazing down at his sleeping daughter, with a look on his face which flipped Lowri's heart over under the dark green velvet. He turned silently as he sensed her presence, and the thick dark brows drew together in a scowl as he seized her arm in a bruising grip and hustled her from the room.

'What the hell do you mean by leaving Rhosyn up here on her own?' he whispered furiously. 'I saw you downstairs with some man, enjoying yourself far too much to give a thought to our daughter!'

Lowri shook off his hand, incensed. 'There's an intercom on the table alongside the cot. The other half's in the next room with Dominic, who'd be down to me in a second if she woke. Besides, it's only half an hour since I left her to go downstairs. Not,' she added, shaking with rage, 'that it's any business of yours!'

'The hell it isn't!' Adam seized her by the elbows and shook her until her earrings tinkled together like wind-chimes. 'She's mine, too, remember.'

'Do you think I ever forget?' she spat, and at once his hands fell away and the fury drained from his face.

'So you're going to make me pay for the rest of my life,' he said dully.

Her eyes flashed. 'Certainly not. I don't want any pay-ment from you. Ever.'

They stared at each other in silence, then Dominic shot out of his room and came to a full stop, his eyes lighting up at the sight of the tall, tense man.

'Adam—hi!' he said, 'Mum was afraid you wouldn't come.'

Adam's eyes softened as he shook Dominic's hand, then

cuffed him playfully. 'What's your mother feeding you on?
You're shooting up like a beanstalk.'

Dominic grinned, then frowned anxiously. 'I came out
to see Rosie. She was making a bit of a noise over the
intercom.'

Lowri thanked him affectionately and hurried back into
the bedroom to investigate, then smiled as she heard the
noise worrying Dominic. Her daughter was snoring.

The tall young teenager put a hand to his mouth to stifle
his laughter as he peered over Lowri's shoulder. He turned
to Adam, made a thumbs-up sign and went out, leaving the
others to follow him more slowly. Outside on the landing
Adam rubbed a hand over his face wearily, then looked at
Lowri.

'I'm sorry. I over-reacted. Rhosyn's adventure seems to
have knocked my equilibrium endwise.'

'I never neglect her,' said Lowri flatly.

'I know.' His mouth twisted. 'I was just being bloody-
minded. I saw you with that guy downstairs when I arrived
and I was jealous, so I lashed out in the way I knew would
hurt most.'

Lowri's eyes widened. 'You were jealous?'

'Is it surprising?' His eyes moved over her slowly. 'You
look so beautiful, Lowri. So poised and self-contained; I
hardly recognise the girl who blushed at me over the sexy
underwear.'

Lowri eyed the stairs pointedly. 'We should go down.'

'In a minute.' Adam caught her hand in his. 'Before I
go tonight, Lowri, I want some kind of concession about
Rhosyn. Make any reasonable rules you want and I'll stick
to them religiously, I swear. But don't let her grow up
thinking her father doesn't care for her.'

'No,' she said, detaching her hand. 'I won't do that. I'll
work something out, I promise. Now we really must go
down. I promised Sarah I'd help with supper.'

The next couple of hours went by in a blur, as Lowri laughed and flirted with Tom Harvey and the patiently waiting Jack Benedict, happy to talk about Rhosyn to Carey Savage, who was insistent she take her baby to see her before she left London. At supper Lowri helped Sarah make sure no guest lacked anything in the way of food and drink, an arrangement which allowed her a little private conversation with her cousin.

'You didn't say Adam was coming,' she accused in an undertone.

'Rupert said you'd be mad, but I think it's a good idea,' said Sarah unrepentantly. 'Time to bury the hatchet.'

'Where exactly shall I bury it?' hissed Lowri, and turned with a smile to offer strawberry *feuilleté* to Jack.

Adam spent most of the evening talking to Rupert with Patrick Savage, but every time Lowri looked up she found his eyes on her, and looked away, hoping he'd leave early so she could enjoy herself properly. Which, she told herself bitterly, was a whopping great lie. If Adam left the party would be well and truly over for her.

Just before twelve Sarah brought in a transistor radio while Rupert and Lowri handed out glasses of champagne to everyone as they gathered together for the countdown to midnight. When Lowri handed Adam his glass he seized her wrist and kept her close by his side as everyone chanted the last seconds until Big Ben struck the hour to usher in the new year. Adam thrust his glass to Lowri's lips, and she drank involuntarily, then he put the glass to his own lips and drained it and took her in his arms and kissed her.

'Happy New Year, Lowri,' he said huskily.

'Happy New Year, Adam,' she answered mechanically, her eyes locked with his, and ignoring the mêlée of jostling, kissing people about them he set down the glass and took her in his arms again, this time kissing her at such length that only applause and catcalls from an audience of laughing people brought them both back to earth.

Lowri, scarlet-faced, was seized by Rupert, then by Sarah, with much kissing and laughter, then Sarah nodded significantly at Adam.

'Go on. I've got my instructions.'

Lowri had a quick glimpse of Jack Benedict's rueful face as Adam rushed her through the hall, and then the kitchen, and out through the back door he slammed shut behind them before racing with her across the frost-crisp grass to the coachhouse, deaf to her protests.

'What do you think you're doing?' she gasped, stumbling in unaccustomed high heels.

'What I should have done a long time ago,' said Adam tersely, and dragged her unceremoniously up the familiar iron stairs to the flat and unlocked the door.

'But Rhosyn—'

'Dominic will tell Sarah if she wakes.' Adam switched on a lamp, and shut the door, jerking his head at the telephone on the desk. 'One ring from that and we can be back in the house in seconds. But for the moment—' He let out his breath slowly and released her hand. 'But for the moment I need to speak to you in peace, without any amorous editors and TV directors butting in.'

Lowri's heart began to slow down again. 'You've spoken to me several times lately,' she pointed out prosaically. 'What's so special about tonight?'

'Our previous encounters were too emotive to allow for practical discussion,' he said quietly. 'And my phone calls to enquire after Rhosyn the last couple of days were hardly productive. Your telephone manner is straight out of the deep freeze, Lowri.'

She shrugged. 'You could at least have told me you were coming here tonight.'

'I was pretty sure you wouldn't turn up if I did.'

'If I'd had any idea you intended that—that exhibition in there just now I'd have stayed at home!' she snapped, and folded her arms.

'I didn't intend anything,' he cut back. 'It just happened!' He sighed impatiently. 'Look, Lowri, I want ten minutes of your time. Then you're free. To get back to the party, or whatever else you want.'

Lowri sat down on the sofa. 'All right. Get it over with, then.'

Adam loomed over her, frowning. 'Why are you so hostile, for God's sake? After what happened to Rhosyn, and Christmas and so on, I thought you were softening towards me.'

'I was,' she retorted, 'until I found you with Rhosyn tonight, at which point your accusations sent my good intentions up in flames!'

'I've apologised for that,' he said stiffly.

'True. So what is it that's so important you have to drag me from the party to say it?'

Adam let himself down beside her warily, as if he expected her to jump up and run at any moment. 'First of all, there's something my mother thinks I should have told you from the first.'

Lowri's eyes narrowed. 'Go on.'

'During our brief but unforgettable relationship,' said Adam tonelessly, 'you may remember I was up to my ears in taking over the company from my father. And an unkind fate made you choose the worst possible day to explode your little bombshell in my ear. I'd just learned that my father had only a short time to live.'

Lowri gazed at him in horror. 'You didn't know before?'

Adam shook his head. 'No one did, except my mother. And she firmly refused to let it spoil what time they had left. Their long, lazy cruise together, Dad told me at the end, was the best preparation for heaven a man could ever wish for.'

There was silence for a moment, then he cleared his throat and went on.

'He also told me that marriage to the right woman was exactly what I needed. But by then, of course, it was too late. My one hope of that vanished the day you disappeared from my life.'

'Oh, come *on*,' said Lowri scornfully, 'If that's the case why were you so perfectly bloody to me when I told you I was pregnant?'

'At that particular moment in time it was the straw that broke the camel's back. I was dog-tired from overwork, and Dad had just let me in on a tragic secret I had to keep to myself. I was off my head with grief when you arrived that night.' Adam took her hand in a painful grip. 'I'm not proud of it, dammit, but when you told me you were pregnant I flipped. And by the time I realised what I'd done and tried to redeem myself with a proposal it was too late. You'd retreated into your little shell and I couldn't do a blind thing about it.'

'But you grew colder and more remote by the minute right up to the date we'd set for the wedding,' cried Lowri, twisting round to face him. 'Why?'

Adam stared blankly. 'What are you talking about? You were the cold, remote one, Lowri. You made me feel so bloody guilty I was afraid to touch you!'

She eyed him dubiously. 'Are you telling me the truth?'

His mouth twisted. 'Yes, Lowri, I am. And while we're on the subject there's another little detail my mother bawled me out for keeping to myself, too.'

Lowri thawed a little. 'What was that?'

Adam shrugged. 'From your point of view it might be a total irrelevance. But you may as well hear it all. When I finally realised my bride wasn't going to turn up that day something hit me right between the eyes. Not having come up against it before, it had never occurred to me—until that moment—why you were so different from the other girls I'd known.'

'You made no secret of the fact that my girlish enthusiasm for your bed appealed to you most,' she said tartly, trying to release her hand.

Adam's grip tightened. 'It was part of it,' he agreed. 'But the difference between you and all the rest was the simple fact that I loved you.'

Lowri stared at him in utter disbelief. 'Would you mind saying that again?'

'Certainly.' Adam's colour heightened slightly. 'I'll say it as many times as you like now I've started. I discovered I loved you, Lowri, and I still love you, and just to put the icing on the cake I'm pretty sure, heaven help me, that I always will love you.' He let go of her hand. 'Right. That's all I had to say. Now you can go back to the party.'

She shook her head thoughtfully. 'I don't think I will, thanks just the same.'

He moved nearer. 'Why?' he demanded. 'Is a slight change of heart possible on your part now I've come clean at last?'

She shook her head. 'No.'

His face darkened. 'None whatsoever?'

She smiled a little. 'Adam, I fell in love with you the moment I first saw you. I battled against it but it wasn't any use—no—' She warded him off. 'It's because I loved you so desperately that your reaction to my news hurt so badly.'

'And you stopped loving me from that moment on,' he said heavily, his colour receding. 'Which is why you left me waiting that day.'

'No. You're wrong,' she said matter-of-factly. 'I loved you so much, in fact, that I couldn't face the thought of marrying someone who was only doing it because he felt obliged to.'

'It was never like that,' said Adam morosely, looking away. 'I admit I suggested marriage as the only possible solution to our little problem. But I only discovered the real reason for my proposal when it dawned on me you weren't going to turn up. That day or any other.' He breathed in deeply. 'If revenge was your object, Lowri, you got it in spades. I hope it was sweet.'

'No, it wasn't,' said Lowri swiftly. 'It was you I wanted, not revenge. I never stopped wanting you or loving you, either, no matter how hard I tried. When I had Rhosyn it was you I wanted with me, not Sarah or Rhia or even Dad. Just you. That's why there's no change of heart, Adam. I've never stopped loving you—'

Adam seized her in his arms. 'Is that the truth?' His eyes glowed with a light so brilliant that Lowri's closed, dazzled. She nodded dumbly, and he bent his mouth to hers in an oddly passionless kiss.

But after a while the kiss changed, Adam's mouth asking questions which hers answered with fervour, and suddenly her fingers were undoing his bow tie and his were busy with her zip, then the phone rang.

'Sorry to interrupt,' said Sarah. 'But there's a young lady over here who needs her parents.'

'Is she crying?' demanded Lowri breathlessly, her face scarlet.

'No. She seems to want to play. And while I'd be happy to oblige I still have guests—'

'We'll be there right now!' Lowri put down the phone and grinned at Adam. 'Our daughter demands our presence.'

Adam caught her close and crushed the life out of her with his hug. 'I never thought I'd hear you say "our". Let's go.' He smiled ruefully as he smoothed back her hair. 'A pity she couldn't have waited just a little longer.'

Lowri chuckled as they clattered down the iron steps. 'Welcome to fatherhood, Adam Hawkridge. Are you sure it's what you want?'

'Positive,' he panted as they raced across the lawn. 'And I'm not really sorry we were interrupted. When I get you in my bed at last I want you there all night.'

'You'll be lucky,' whispered Lowri, as they stole up the stairs. 'Rhosyn wakes up sometimes, remember.'

Adam stopped just outside the guest-room door. 'In which case we take turns—no more single blessedness for you, Lowri Morgan. Soon,' he added sternly, 'to be Hawkridge, I'd remind you.'

'We've got a lot of sorting out to do before then—'

'Then come and do it in here with your daughter,' said Sarah, hurrying from the room. She grinned at them both and hurried off. 'Blessings, my children,' she said over her shoulder. 'Come and have some more champagne when Rosie's settled.'

Lowri and Adam found their daughter standing up in her cot, banging the rails with her new teddy.

'Mum-mum!' she said with a wide smile, then spotted Adam. She bridled a little flirtatiously, dropped the teddy and held up her arms. He scooped her up and held her close, his eyes meeting Lowri's over her head.

'She knows me,' he said incredulously.

'She knows you're a soft touch!' said Lowri, grinning, then raised an eyebrow at a look of panic on his face. 'What's up?'

'She's a bit damp round the edges!'

Lowri's lips twitched. 'Right. You may as well start as you go on. You can change her nappy.'

Laughing uproariously at Adam's look of horror, Lowri gave him step-by-step instructions on the process, which

Rhosyn proceeded to make as difficult as she possibly could, sensing an amateur. Lowri looked up with a smile as Dominic popped a tousled head round the door, brandishing the intercom speaker.

He smiled cheekily. 'I can hear every word on this, you know, so just in case you're going to get soppy I've brought it back.' He sauntered over to eye Adam's panting exertions with the wriggling baby. 'Gosh, you're not much good as a dad, are you?'

Adam looked up at Lowri with a smile of such triumph that her eyes filled. 'Not yet,' he agreed, 'and for this particular job I don't intend to be, frankly.' He picked up his daughter and tossed her in the air. 'But otherwise, all I need is practice!'

Modern Romance™
...seduction and
passion guaranteed

Tender Romance™
...love affairs that
last a lifetime

Sensual Romance™
...sassy, sexy and
seductive

Blaze
...sultry days and
steamy nights

Medical Romance™
...medical drama on
the pulse

Historical Romance™
...rich, vivid and
passionate

29 new titles every month.

*With all kinds of Romance for
every kind of mood...*

MILLS & BOON®

Makes any time special™

MAT4

MILLS & BOON®

NEW
Blaze™

TWO SEXY! *by Stephanie Bond*
HOT CITY NIGHTS
Chicago
Schoolteacher Meg Valentine was no sex goddess but
she'd been dying to put some excitement into her life.
So when gorgeous bodyguard Jarett Miller asked her to
stand in as a body double for a famous, sexy beach-
babe, she jumped at the chance. One makeover later,
Meg discovered in herself a sensuality she just loved
exploring with hunky Jarett!

THE PLEASURE PRINCIPLE *by Kimberly Raye*
Advertising executive Brady Weston thought he knew
what women wanted—until his ex-wife left him with a
bruised ego! Now, he was out to prove he could satisfy
a woman—and sultry bar owner Eden Hallsy was keen
to indulge all his erotic fantasies. One red-hot night
turns into many, until Brady realises he wants more
from Eden than just a good time…

On sale 2nd November